Two heroines—
one as determined ... as the
other ...

Two heroes—
cool and proud, brash and carefree—were
brothers ever more different?

Two stories—
both sparkling with wit, intrigue, and drama.

One book—
from one of Regency romance's most inspired
authors for the first time in one volume!

**Praise for Lynn Kerstan's
Enthralling Historical Romances**

Dangerous Deceptions

"An enigmatic heroine tormented by her past, a rak-
ish hero who is more honorable than he thinks, and
a splendidly sensual plot steeped in equal measure of
dark intrigue and delicious desire all come together
beautifully in the first installment in Kerstan's spell
binding new Regency trilogy."

—*Booklist* (starred review)

"Kerstan holds you spellbound with another utterly
enthralling exploration of the dark underbelly of
society." —*Romantic Times*, Top Pick

continued . . .

"Features complex characters who are anything but formulaic and a setting that's truly unique. Lynn Kerstan has a powerful voice." —All About Romance

"Riveting and romantic, sensual and suspenseful, passionate and poignant . . . and the first book in what is certain to be another spectacular trilogy."
—Romance Reviews Today

The Silver Lion

"With typical Kerstan flair, this riveting conclusion to the author's stunning trilogy combines electrifying sensuality with strong, passionate protagonists caught in a seemingly impossible situation."
—*Library Journal*

"An exquisite tale of revenge, honor, and redemption. This spellbinding story ensnares you witth passionate characters caught in a tangled web. Kerstan reaches new heights in sensuality and storytelling with this keeper, which enthralls straight to the dramatic climax." —*Romantic Times*

"If you can only read one book this fall, make it *The Silver Lion*." —*The Contra Costa Times*

Heart of the Tiger

"An unforgettable romantic adventure. Don't miss it!" —*USA Today* bestselling author Susan Wiggs

Celia's Grand Passion

AND

Lucy in Disguise

LYNN KERSTAN

A SIGNET BOOK

SIGNET
Published by New American Library, a division of
Penguin Group (USA) Inc., 375 Hudson Street,
New York, New York 10014, USA
Penguin Group (Canada), 10 Alcorn Avenue, Toronto,
Ontario M4V 3B2, Canada (a division of Pearson Penguin Canada Inc.)
Penguin Books Ltd., 80 Strand, London WC2R 0RL, England
Penguin Ireland, 25 St. Stephen's Green, Dublin 2,
Ireland (a division of Penguin Books Ltd.)
Penguin Group (Australia), 250 Camberwell Road, Camberwell, Victoria 3124,
Australia (a division of Pearson Australia Group Pty. Ltd.)
Penguin Books India Pvt. Ltd., 11 Community Centre, Panchsheel Park,
New Delhi - 110 017, India
Penguin Group (NZ), cnr Airborne and Rosedale Roads, Albany,
Auckland 1310, New Zealand (a division of Pearson New Zealand Ltd.)
Penguin Books (South Africa) (Pty.) Ltd., 24 Sturdee Avenue,
Rosebank, Johannesburg 2196, South Africa

Penguin Books Ltd., Registered Offices:
80 Strand, London WC2R 0RL, England

Published by Signet, an imprint of New American Library, a division of Penguin Group (USA) Inc. *Celia's Grand Passion* and *Lucy in Disguise* were previously published by the Ballantine Publishing Group, a division of Random House, Inc., New York.

First Signet Printing, April 2005
10   9   8   7   6   5   4   3   2   1

Celia's Grand Passion copyright © Lynn Kerstan Horobetz, 1998
Lucy in Disguise copyright © Lynn Kerstan Horobetz, 1998
All rights reserved

 REGISTERED TRADEMARK—MARCA REGISTRADA

Printed in the United States of America

Celia's Grand Passion

*For Joel Hoersch, one of the truly nice guys,
and Doris Bailey, always a terrific friend.
Thanks, good buddies!*

Chapter 1

Second only to marrying Lord Greer, this was beyond a doubt the most lunatic thing she'd ever done.

Celia knew, with blazing clarity, that she had slipped her own leash. Indeed, even while she had been preparing her makeshift costume, she'd repeatedly ordered herself to stop. But the rational part of her mind must have been closed for the evening, because here she was, risking everything she had set her heart on.

And all for the merest glimpse of a man.

He might not even be the *right* man.

All the same, how was she to know unless she got a closer look at him?

From her position by the door of the front parlor, she made certain the coast was clear. Then, lifting a tray laden with empty wineglasses, she stepped into the passageway and began to walk slowly toward the back of Lord Finlay's town house.

The double doors leading to the dining room stood open. She heard voices, laughter, and the clink of silverware against china. One voice, heavily accented, rose above the others. That must be the guest of honor, a Russian general come early to London for the victory celebrations.

He was on his feet, she noted as she dawdled past the door, his fringed epaulets and bejeweled medals glittering. Since the other guests had turned in his direction, she could see only the backs of their heads.

Rats! Celia sped to the servants' staircase, paused on the landing for a few moments, and then launched herself again in the direction of the parlor. This time her view of the dinner guests was blocked by a pair of footmen standing behind Lady Marjory, Lord Finlay's wife, who was ensconced at the end of the table closest to the door.

Celia made three more daring trips between stairs and parlor with equal lack of success. At this rate, she would likely wear a rut on the marble floor before catching a glimpse of her quarry. Arms aching, she set the heavy tray on a pier table in the parlor and reevaluated her plan. Obviously, it wasn't working. There were too many guests—thirty at least—and half as many servants in that dining room. On each of her passes, she had no more than three or four seconds to look inside.

Moreover, every time she ventured into the passageway, she faced the possibility of exposure. Her improvised maid's uniform, a black bombasine mourning dress with a lace-edged chemise pinned over it in lieu of an apron, would not stand close inspection, even though the house was swarming with temporary staff hired on for the evening.

Social ruin on her very first night in London? It did not bear thinking of. Worse, her conscience had begun to gnaw at her again. Only the most ungrateful of wretches would violate Lady Marjory's hospitality in such a fashion. She was monumentally ashamed of herself. Which did not prevent her from resolving to make one last trip past the dining room before calling it a night.

Taking up the tray, she charged into the passageway and all but collided with a startled footman. She jerked to a halt before running him down, but several glasses on the tray kept going without her. In dismay, she watched them shatter on the marble tiles.

"Mercy me," she murmured past the lump of horror in her throat.

In a swift motion, the footman seized the tray from her hands and swept her into the parlor, closing the door behind him. Then, to her astonishment, he bowed.

"Lady Greer," he said. "How may I be of service?"

Well and truly caught. "I suppose," she began haltingly, "you could clean up that mess in the hall."

"Yes, certainly." His neck and cheeks were an alarming shade of red. "But first, I'm afraid that Lord Finlay must be informed."

"That I broke a few glasses? Surely not." She took a deep breath. "I'll pay for them, of course. And he cannot wish to be disturbed while he is entertaining guests."

"It will be awkward, I agree. But the staff has strict instructions to report anything out of the ordinary. Immediately," he added, crossing to the bellpull. "Carver will know how to proceed."

She rushed after him, grappling his arm before he could summon the formidable butler. "Please don't. Truly, this is no more than an act of irresponsible foolishness on my part."

He stepped away and regarded her closely, uncertainty written on his round, pleasant face. "Lord Finlay is an important man, m'lady, and matters of state are conducted in this house."

Light dawned. "Good heavens, I'm not a *spy*! Well, not of the sort you are imagining," she added in strictest honesty. "How is it you know my name?"

"I held the horses when your carriage arrived this afternoon, and helped carry in your luggage. We were informed that Lady Greer would be staying for several weeks." He frowned. "But unless I am much mistaken, you were not expected until tomorrow."

Celia nodded. "It was insufferably rude of me to descend on Lord and Lady Finlay a day early, but the weather was fine and the road so good that we made excellent time. Perhaps I should have spent the night at a posting house outside the city, but it never occurred to me to do so. This is my first trip to London, you see, and I simply could not wait to arrive."

How absurd she sounded. How like the impulsive chit she had been when she married. She ought to have grown more wise, or at least more cautious, considering where her last major plunge into folly had landed her.

She dropped onto a chair. "Well, you may as well go ahead and turn me in. I deserve whatever happens, I suppose."

"It is none of my business," he said in a tentative voice, "but if you could possibly explain—"

"Oh, I can!" Did he mean to let her off the hook? Dear heavens, her fate was in the hands of a *footman*! She would have enjoyed the irony, were she not so furious with herself. "It is most embarrassing, though. I'm not altogether sure my tale will make the slightest sense to you."

A smile flickered across his lips. "Wait here if you will, m'lady, while I see to the disorder in the entrance hall."

Celia had only begun to regain her composure when he returned, a boar's-hair brush in one hand and a dustpan mounded with broken glass in the other.

"I was sent to tidy this room," he said, emptying the dustpan into a trash basket. "If someone enters, perhaps you will turn your back to the door and pretend to be helping."

She leapt to her feet and began gathering up sherry glasses. When he gave her an appalled look, she shrugged. "I've cleaned worse messes in my time, you know. Will you tell me your name?"

"Thomas, ma'am. Thomas Carver. My uncle is Lord Finlay's butler, and I mean one day to rise to that position myself." He gave her a conspiratorial smile. "As it happens, the first lesson he taught me was the importance of absolute discretion."

"You are a treasure, Thomas," she said sincerely. "Should I survive this misadventure with my reputation intact, I shall find a way to repay your kindness."

As they worked, gathering glasses and small plates, she made several stammering attempts to explain herself without revealing too much. But it was no use. Her skill at deception was, to put it mildly, nonexistent, and she generally resorted to the truth because no one ever believed her taradiddles.

"Lady Marjory was most apologetic, to be sure, but I could not be invited to the dinner party at such late notice. It would make the numbers uneven, you see, and spoil her seating arrangement. She kindly refrained from pointing out that my wardrobe is wholly unsuitable for such fine company. I didn't mind terribly much at first. I had a tray in my room, which overlooks the street, and contented myself with watching out the window as the guests arrived. The thing is, Thomas, I thought I saw someone I knew. Well, I never actually met him, but I have private reasons ... that is, I wish to make his acquaintance."

"Tonight?"

"Mercy, no." She held out her arms. "Looking like this? A demon must have possessed me, though, because I felt compelled to discover if he was really here, in this very house. If so, it would be an omen. A sign from heaven."

Thomas put down the plate he was holding and turned to her, confusion painted across his face.

He must think her demented, she realized. And perhaps she was. She was certainly behaving like the veriest bedlamite.

"I believe that I understand, m'lady," he said after a moment. "A matter of the heart."

Was it? she wondered. But how could it be? "Perhaps so, Thomas. In any case, I was determined to see his face in full light. It was shadowed by the brim of his hat when he left his coach and mounted the stairs, so I could not be positive of his identity. But something about him was uncannily familiar. The way he moved, perhaps."

She went still, a wineglass dangling from her fingers as she remembered the first time she had seen him. It was on his wedding day. . . .

Gently, Thomas plucked the glass from her hand. "You have convinced me, Lady Greer. Lord Finlay need hear nothing of this. But I expect you ought to return to your chamber now, for the ladies will soon retire to the first-floor salon. Indeed, the maids have doubtless begun to lay out the tea-and-coffee service. Perhaps I had better go ahead of you, to make certain no one is on the stairs."

With a sigh, still itching for one more look inside that dining room, she followed him to the door.

Hand on the latch, he turned again, his round cheeks apple red. "Not that this will be of interest to you, Lady Greer, but should *I* wish a closer look at the dinner guests, I would conceal myself in the maid's closet just down the passageway from the first-floor salon. With the door cracked open, one can enjoy an excellent view of anyone mounting the stairs. And later, to make my escape, I'd use the servants' stairs at the other end of the hall."

Celia burst out laughing. "Why, Thomas, I begin to suspect that *you* are a spy."

"I've a fondness for the young woman assigned to tend the rooms on the first floor," he confessed. "Sometimes we steal a kiss or two in that closet. So now you and I have exchanged confidences, ma'am. I trust both our secrets are safe."

He could not have found a better way to reassure her. Celia nearly planted a friendly kiss on his blazing cheek but recalled in time that she was Lady Greer. Already she had failed her first test, violating any number of civilized rules within hours of arriving in London to begin her new existence as a wealthy, titled widow.

"Thank you again, Thomas. I may just have a look at that closet. And I'll be very, very careful not to be discovered."

When Thomas gave her the sign that the passageways were clear, she scurried upstairs and into the closet. Sure enough, the view was excellent. But even with the door slightly ajar, the small room soon grew unbearably hot. She endured the stultifying atmosphere for half an hour, distracted by the sight of elegantly gowned ladies gracefully ascending the stairs and wafting into the salon.

After that, except for the occasional servant coming and going, nothing of interest occurred. The gentlemen, she understood, would converse over port and cigars in the dining room, possibly for hours, before joining the ladies.

Her attention was drawn to a closed door directly across the way. The view would be equally fine from that room, she thought. Even better, since the gentlemen would turn in that direction as they entered the salon, providing her a better look at their faces. From her current angle, she saw more backs than fronts.

When the passageway was temporarily deserted, she slipped across the hall and through the door.

She was in a study, she saw, a large one, with bookshelves along one side and an oversized oak desk filling half the opposite wall. Two wingback chairs were set before the hearth, and at the far end of the room, a bay window like the one in her bedchamber faced onto the street.

The room was too bright, though, lit by colsa lamps and several candlebraces. Fearing the light would draw attention to the slightly opened door, she snuffed the candles and all but one lamp before taking up her position. Gingerly, she cracked open the door.

Nothing happened for an exceedingly long time, if she discounted the movements of the servants. When her feet began to ache, she dropped to her knees for a bit, but still no gentlemen appeared. They must have taken root in the dining room, she thought when the mantelpiece clock chimed the passing of another hour.

She was sitting on the polished floor, half-asleep, her shoulder resting against the wall, when a loud, accented male voice shot her awake.

In groups of two and three, the men trooped up the staircase and turned into the parlor. Celia tried to stand, but her calves and feet were painfully cramped. She struggled onto her hands and knees, pressed her cheek against the door frame, and watched for him.

Suddenly there he was! Thank heavens she had stayed the course long enough to see him. Best of all, instead of turning directly into the salon, he paused at the top of the stairs to speak with Lord Finlay.

She looked her fill of him. And he was spectacular. No, that wasn't precisely true. Handsome, yes. Absolutely. But quietly so. His very stillness amid the bustle surrounding him impressed her enormously. Try as she might, she could *never* be still, let alone so poised and self-contained as the Earl of Kendal.

Item by item, she marked him top to bottom. Sleek, close-cropped hair, light brown. Well-shaped lips. Firm jaw. Wide shoulders, slim hips encased in formfitting black satin, hard calves under those white silk stockings—oh, mercy!

For seven years she had dreamed about him. Now he stood within a few yards, closer than he had ever been to her in real life, and her fantasies drifted away like smoke. In their place, a diamond-hard certainty took possession of her.

She must have him. She *would* have him.

But only for a short time, she amended hastily. In her experience, men should be taken in small doses. Never again would she permit a tyrannical male to control her life.

It occurred to her that this particular male was already directing her every move. Dear heavens, here she was before him on her hands and knees!

Her brain felt like egg custard and her body was heating up in the oddest places. She wished he'd proceed into the salon so that she could safely make her way to her bedchamber. Then Lord Finlay, his paunch bouncing as he made a wide gesture, turned in her direction and pointed to the door.

To her horror, both men started directly toward her.

There wasn't time to clamber to her feet. Celia scuttled to the only concealment within reach—the desk—and heard a loud tear as she inadvertently crawled up the inside of her skirt. She dove into the shelter of the desk's kneehole just as the study door swung open, sending a wide shaft of light into the dim room.

Chapter 2

James Randolph Elliott Valliant, Lord Kendal, was prodigiously bored.

It took precious little to bore him of late, he had reflected on his way to Lord Finlay's house in Curzon Street, and nothing had transpired during the interminable dinner party to change his mind. Even the mildly deranged guest of honor, a Russian general with an obsession for English poetry, could not hold his interest beyond the first few minutes.

Kendal had spent the evening making polite, tedious conversation with his dinner partners and wondering how soon he could take his leave. When the ladies withdrew, he tried to seize the opportunity to depart, but Lord Finlay was having none of his excuses. There were matters of importance to be discussed, he insisted, so Kendal was forced to endure the Russian's poetic ecstasies over port and cigars.

"Here's our chance," Finlay said nearly two hours later as they made their way upstairs to the salon. "Join me for a brandy in the study?"

"As you wish." Kendal glanced in the direction of the study door, which was slightly open. And unless he was very much mistaken, there was the tip of a nose silhouetted against the door frame.

It withdrew an instant later, but he caught a glimpse of white as whoever had been crouched behind that door moved away.

Interesting.

Placing his hand on Finlay's arm, Kendal turned to Lord Pace, who was passing through the hall, and spoke to him briefly about nothing of significance, deliberately allowing the intruder a few moments to conceal himself. A foolish caprice, he knew, born of ennui, and he'd not live to regret it should the man prove to be a hired assassin. In any case, he trusted what had always been a reliable instinct for danger, and for the proximity of an individual worth meeting.

In this particular case, he sensed trouble, although not of the lethal sort, and decided to handle it himself. First, however, Finlay must be permitted to conduct his business, after which he would be summarily shuffled out of the way. Kendal released his arm.

Slicing him a puzzled look, Finlay made his way to the study door and pushed it open. A single lamp glowed from a table at the far end of the room. "What the devil?" Grumbling, Finlay stomped around lighting candles while Kendal closed the door. "The servants know I expect this room in readiness at all times."

"Good help is hard to find," Kendal said, his gaze fixed on the curtains drawn over the bay window. The intruder could well be hiding behind them, although he would then be visible from the street.

Finlay aimed himself at a decanter of brandy on the sideboard. "If ever I doubted it, James, the past few hours in company with that Russian steppe hound have convinced me the war was easier than this peace is likely to be."

"Not for the soldiers," Kendal observed mildly.

"Yes, yes. I'm always forgetting you had a brother in the army."

"I still do, or so I believe." Kendal accepted a glass of brandy. "Mind you, I was sure he'd sell out when the Forty-fourth was dispatched to America, but he sailed with the regiment after all."

"Damnable business. Damnable. I've been too preoccupied with the French to protest this absurd quarrel with the Americans, but someone should have put a stop to it long ago. Instead, they're sending good English soldiers to quash a minor rebellion by a ragtag band of farmers and a poorly armed militia. At least *this* war, such as it is, will soon be over."

Less convinced that the Americans would be so easily

routed, Kendal made a slow, careful circuit of the room. There were few places to hide once he'd eliminated the bay window, and he quickly narrowed his search to the cubbyhole under Finlay's massive, paper-strewn desk.

"Do stop prowling, James. It is most annoying."

"Then tell me why you brought me here. It wasn't merely to elude Chirikov, I am persuaded."

Sure enough, he saw as he came around the desk, a dark shape was making itself small in the deep kneehole. Well, it was time to give him something to worry about. Lowering himself onto the leather-padded chair, Kendal leaned back and crossed his ankles atop the desk.

From underneath came a tiny squeak of dismay.

It was, he was reasonably certain, a female squeak. Or that of a young boy, but the faint scent of perfumed soap, redolent of honeysuckle, confirmed his first impression. He wondered if she knew he was onto her.

She would find out soon enough, but first there was the tiresome matter of ejecting Finlay from his own study. "You may as well spit it out," he said, lacing his fingers behind his neck. "Bad news has been stuck in your craw all evening. But I advise you to be discreet, William. With so many strangers crawling about the house, the very desks have ears."

There was a barely detectable gasp from the female.

"Oh, this is nothing to do with matters of security." Finlay pulled out his handkerchief. "Fact is, Castlereagh wants you to return to France. Tomorrow, if you can manage it."

"Unthinkable. I've been home precisely one day, and you're the one who recalled me from Paris."

"I wanted you here. But the foreign secretary overruled me this morning, and there we have it. He says you are needed in Boulogne, so to Boulogne you must go. As usual, you will have no official duties, but I expect you understand the situation well enough. Do whatever needs to be done, and try not to be too obvious about it."

Kendal did understand. The ruling princes, generals, and ministers of the allied powers gathering for the lavish victory celebration had already begun to assemble in the port town.

Within the week they would make the channel crossing aboard the *Impregnable*, captained by the Duke of Clarence. Apparently Clarence was finding the clash of egos and temperaments a bit more than he could handle.

Finlay mopped his forehead with his handkerchief. "Can't say I envy you. They'll all be posturing and jockeying for precedence, taking offense at perceived slights, and generally behaving like spoiled brats. I'd almost rather an invasion by Napoleon than Prinny's notion of a victory party, especially if General Chirikov is any sample of what we may expect."

"He is irritating, certainly. Why did he arrive in advance of the Russian delegation?"

"I daresay they had their fill of his blather and sent him on ahead. He wants to meet some English poets, by the way. Know any?"

"Not a one, blessedly."

"In that case, you are of little use to me until the circus arrives. Go to Boulogne, James. Soothe tempers, smooth waters, and keep our honored allies from going to war with one another. It will be good practice for the Vienna Congress." Finlay set down his glass. "I expect we should join the others before Marjory—"

"You must excuse me, William. If I'm to travel tomorrow, arrangements must be got under way. May I make use of your desk and writing materials for a few minutes?"

"Yes indeed. Ring for Carver if you require anything." He paused at the door. "Naturally you will send frequent reports from Boulogne, James."

When Finlay was gone, Kendal stood and went to lean against the closed door, in case Madame Spy decided to make a break for it. "You may come out now," he said, a pleasurable sense of anticipation vibrating under his skin.

There was a rustling sound, and the rap of bone against wood. Finally, a soft but distinct, *"Rats!"*

"Oh, I think not. For one thing, Lady Marjory would not permit them in her house. And for another, rodents cannot speak."

"Who said they could?" More rustling and thumping from

12

under the desk. "I'm trying to get out of here, but my hair has caught on something. A nail, I th—ouch!"

"Ah." He went to crouch by the kneehole and peered in. Little light reached to where she had curled herself, but he could make out the gleam of golden curls and a pair of enormous dark eyes.

Like a small animal cornered in a cave, she gazed nervously back at him. "It's too narrow in here, sir. I cannot reach whatever is gripping my hair."

"Then permit me." Dropping to one knee, he slid his arms alongside her head, his palms brushing her smooth cheeks as they went by. His forearms rested lightly on her shoulders as he felt for the tangled curl. Sure enough, it was knotted around a protruding nail.

This close to her, the fragrance of honeysuckle was distinctive. Also seductive, which struck him as prodigiously odd under the circumstances. Even odder was his surprising reluctance to move away from her.

"I am afraid," he said, his voice raspy, "that scissors will be required and a lock of your hair sacrificed if you are to be extricated."

"Fine. But do hurry. Both my legs have gone to sleep."

He could find no scissors in the desk drawers, but the small knife used for sharpening pens would do as well. Again on his knees, he slid his fingers through her hair and carefully sawed through the strands twisted around the nail. When she was free, he stood and moved away from the desk.

She emerged slowly, rose with a slight groan, and clung for support to the edge of the desk while she shook the cramps from her legs. Since she was careful not to look in his direction, Kendal was free to observe her closely.

Her uniform, if that's what it was meant to be, concealed most of her body. Still, the black dress fit her closely, outlining perfectly shaped breasts, a willowy waist, and the gentle, feminine slope of her hips. A connoisseur of the female form, he had rarely seen another so perfectly proportioned, or quite so suited to his particular taste. The top of her head would reach his chin, were they to embrace—

"I suppose you want to know what I was doing under the desk," she said, sounding more than a little put out at having to explain herself.

"Dusting?" he supplied helpfully.

She sighed. "That's a far better excuse than the one I was considering. But I don't suppose you'd credit any story I managed to devise on such short notice."

"In fact, I'd have expected you to come prepared with one."

"Well, I didn't. Had I been thinking in any coherent fashion, I would not be here at all. Could I persuade you to go away and forget I ever was?"

"Possibly."

She turned to face him, hope flaring in her eyes. They were the color of rich molasses, large and expressive, with dark lashes and brows. He wondered briefly if her hair had been dyed golden, but decided not. It shone naturally, and quite gloriously, in the candlelight. All in all, despite the swatch of torn lace dangling over her left ear and the wisp of a cobweb on her cheek, she was a remarkably beautiful young woman.

His gaze dropped to a spot just beneath her bosom, where her skirt had pulled from the bodice. Through a tear the size of his palm, he saw the filmy material of her chemise and, through that, a tantalizing glimpse of creamy skin.

The room had gone alarmingly hot of a sudden. Kendal wrenched his thoughts to the matter at hand. "Before permitting you to leave, I would first need to know who you are and precisely what you were doing."

"But those are the very things I don't wish to tell you, sir. If it helps, though, you may be sure that I am not a spy."

"Exactly *how* am I to be sure? You are most certainly not a housemaid." Stepping closer, he fingered a strap of muslin and lace pinned to the shoulder of her dress. "Unless I am much mistaken, this is a female undergarment masquerading as an apron."

A flush crept up her neck. "I never said I was a housemaid. Perhaps I merely have no sense of fashion. But if you must know, I am a house*guest*."

He had to give her credit for sheer nerve. Although clearly

embarrassed, she gave him back eye for eye, defying him to refute that declaration.

He realized that he was still clutching the filmy lace, his thumb a bare inch from the soft flesh at the side of her neck. Mouth dry, he let go and moved beyond the dangerous reach of her fragrance.

"Well?" Her chin went up a notch. "I am speaking the truth."

"Oh, I believe you," he said, unaccountably disoriented. "I'm also certain that Lord and Lady Finlay have no idea how you are spending the evening."

Alarm flashed across her expressive face. "Do you mean to tell them?"

"Is there some reason I should not?"

"Yes, indeed. I would find it exceedingly m-mortifying," she said earnestly. "And betraying me would thrust Lord and Lady Finlay into an awkward situation, which they do not deserve."

"On that count, I heartily agree. Perhaps we need not draw them into this affair, but only if you can satisfy me that they have no reason to hear about it."

He wondered where his diplomatic skills had fled. He sounded like a bloody Grand Inquisitor.

She was clutching at her skirts with both hands.

Deliberately, he gentled his voice. "I have no wish to betray you, my dear. Simply tell me the truth."

She gazed at a point over his shoulder. "This is my very first day in London, sir, and I am, not to put too fine a point on it, the veriest country yokel. So there I was, alone in my bedchamber and missing all the excitement, which as you can imagine was not to be borne. At length, I contrived this amateurish disguise and crept downstairs, hoping for a glimpse of the fashionable dinner guests. And most particularly, what they were wearing," she added in a rush.

"I see." Her account was not unreasonable, but he knew that she was lying. Although quick-witted, she lacked the ability to mask her emotions.

She shot him a swift glance from the corners of her eyes,

15

seeking reassurance that she had bamboozled him. But as ever, his facial expression revealed nothing of his thoughts.

He had decided immediately that she posed no threat to the Finlay household, save the likelihood that she would one day prove an embarrassment to her hostess. It was his own curiosity about her that continued to hold him in the room. She wasn't of an age to be engaged in schoolgirl follies, but for the life of him he could not imagine what the devil she'd been up to. And he'd bet a pony she wasn't going to tell him.

His silence must have unnerved her. She spun on her heels and flounced to the door.

"I wouldn't do that if I were you," he advised softly.

"*You* wouldn't be here in the first place, sir. *You* are wise enough to keep yourself out of trouble, which I am not." With a resigned exhalation, she turned and held out her wrists. "Go ahead, Lord Kendal. Clamp on the manacles and haul me before the magistrate. I have nothing more to say to you."

He tapped his forefinger on his chin. "How is it you know my name?"

"I—" She nibbled at her lower lip. "Lord Finlay must have spoken it while I was under the desk."

When they were in private together, Finlay invariably called him James. Kendal reviewed their conversation. Admittedly, he had been distracted by the figure under the desk, so perhaps his title *had* been mentioned. But he doubted it.

The wonder of it was that he could not be sure. One of his chief skills was the ability to remember in vivid detail every word of a discussion, as well as the subtle gestures and the facial expressions that indicated what was *not* being said. He resented her for vaporizing his legendary presence of mind.

Would she, if he made her an offer, consent to be his mistress?

Her hand was on the door latch when he regathered his wits. "Tell me your name," he said.

He watched her draw in a slow breath. Then she gave him a graceful, rather old-fashioned curtsy. "Celia Greer, my lord. *Lady* Greer."

The name meant nothing to him. And she wasn't accustomed to using the title, he could tell.

"I do wish you would make up your mind," she said plaintively. "What are you going to do with me?"

Not what he wanted to do, he thought, his imagination taking flight. Not just yet. "Run along, Lady Greer. Your secrets, those few you have chosen to reveal, are perfectly safe."

Her radiant smile all but knocked him to his knees.

"Oh, thank you!" she exclaimed, practically bouncing with relief. "You are exceedingly kind, sir. Is it too much to ask that you wipe every trace of this encounter from your memory?"

"That would be impossible, I'm afraid. But I shall pretend I have forgot. Will that do?"

"I suppose it must." She dipped another curtsy, but her smile no longer reached her eyes.

He could barely make out her words as she turned again to the door.

"After tonight," she murmured, "it cannot matter."

Bemused, he watched her crack open the door, check the passageway in both directions, and dart away.

For a long time he stood in place, staring blankly at the door. She seemed to have taken all the air in the room with her. He had difficulty drawing a breath, and his lungs were not the only sectors of his anatomy mounting a rebellion. He hoped to hell she hadn't noticed.

Who the devil *was* she?

With effort, he took himself to the desk and collapsed onto the chair. He was tired, that was all. The long trip from Paris had worn him to flinders, and then he'd drunk too much wine at dinner and endured too many poetic rhapsodies from that absurd Russian.

Besides, he was not free to pursue the singularly enticing Lady Greer. For one thing, he would be on a boat to Boulogne by tomorrow afternoon. And for another, he could scarcely seduce a lady, one who might well have a husband salted away, while she was under the protection of the Finlays.

Nor did he wish to, he told himself firmly, pleased that his brain had begun to function again. Only once before had he experienced such an instant, overwhelming attraction to a

17

woman, with the same bewildering loss of self-control. On that occasion, though, he had followed his benighted impulses and stumbled headlong into disaster.

He had learned his lesson in a hard school. Now he chose his brief liaisons cautiously, with sophisticated women experienced in the sort of dalliance he had come to prefer. For that matter, he was rarely in one place long enough for matters to become complicated. *Good-bye* was implicit from the first kiss, and passion inevitably burned out about the time his duties called him elsewhere.

As they did tonight.

Finlay would understand if he took his leave without ceremony. Kendal made his way to the entrance hall and ordered his carriage brought around. As he drew on his gloves and accepted his hat and walking stick from the butler, he deliberately refused to spare another thought for Lady Greer.

By the time he returned to London, she would be no more than a distant memory.

Chapter 3

Mired in a long line of carriages slowly advancing in the direction of Berkeley Square, Celia and Lady Marjory plied their fans against the sultry June air.

"We have scarcely moved this last fifteen minutes," Lady Marjory complained, wrinkling her nose. "And whatever is that horrible stench?"

"Horse droppings, I believe." Celia stuck her head out the open window and quickly pulled it back again. "Definitely horse droppings. Shall I lower the window glass?"

"It's far too warm for that, I'm afraid. We should have come earlier or later, to avoid the worst of the traffic, but I never expected such a tremendous crush. Sally must be in alt."

"I imagine she was horrified to learn that the Regent planned to carry the foreign dignitaries off to Oxford tonight."

" 'Twas rather the other way 'round, my dear. Long before sending out her invitations, Lady Jersey knew perfectly well what Prinny was up to. As to why she chose the very same evening for her midsummer ball, who can say?"

"Must you spy a conspiracy around every corner?" Celia asked with a laugh. "I wager you think this has something to do with the czar, but I assure you there is no truth whatever to the rumor. Czar Alexander may be an outrageous flirt, but he is not the least bit in love with Lady Jersey."

"Is that what your Russian general tells you?" Marjory shook her head. "You are sadly naive, my dear. Of course there can be no question of love between them, although I'd not rule out the possibility they are more than acquaintances. But I am persuaded they would enjoy tweaking Prinny's nose, and that may well be the purpose of this ball, although I cannot imagine how they mean to accomplish it. Nor can Finlay, who was sufficiently concerned to send me here as an observer instead of taking me along to Oxford."

"I am relieved to hear that," Celia said. "Not the part about Lord Finlay being worried, certainly, but I feared you had chosen to remain in town on my account."

"Not at all. Indeed, you scarcely require my escort any longer, now that cards have begun to arrive for you quite separate from those addressed to Lord and Lady Finlay." Lady Marjory smiled. "You are no longer 'and guest' on the invitation lists, my dear."

It was true, Celia realized with a shiver of pleasure. She had not considered it before, but the beau monde had definitely begun to regard her as something more than the Finlays' houseguest. Well, perhaps a few of them, anyway. In the great crush of the victory celebrations, most people never noticed her at all.

Certainly Lord Kendal did not, although she had spotted him at four routs, two balls, and one musicale since his return to London.

True, he could not be expected to single her out. They were supposed to be perfect strangers, after all, and she was pleased that he continued to honor their agreement with such exactitude. Apparently that required him to move away whenever she came anywhere near him, so in return, she ignored him with equal deliberation.

All the same, she invariably knew his precise location whenever they were in the same room. And she had an alarming tendency to drift in his direction, although he always managed to elude her when she drew close enough for a purely accidental meeting.

Just as well, she thought as the carriage lurched forward and jerked to a halt almost immediately, throwing her back against the padded leather squabs. At this rate, they would reach Lady Jersey's town house sometime next February.

Not that she minded. Since Kendal was surely in Oxford with the Regent and his guests, Lady Jersey's midsummer ball had lost its flavor before she even arrived. Despite the humiliation of their meeting two weeks earlier, she continued to moon over him like a flea-wit, never mind that she would probably melt into the carpet if he actually spoke to her.

How, she wondered fifty times a day, does a woman stop herself from longing for a particular man? Especially when getting her wish would be a sure prescription for disaster?

"Your Russian will be here tonight," Lady Marjory said. "Did he tell you?"

Celia snapped to attention. She was so accustomed to being alone that she often went sliding off into her private dreamworld, as Lady Marjory had more than once pointed out to her. "General Chirikov reserved two dances with me," she said, trying not to wince. What with his great size and rollicking ebullience, dancing with Chirikov was akin to wrestling with a bear. "And he is not *my* Russian, thank heavens. The general has a wife and five children. They are practically all he ever talks about."

"When he isn't reciting poetry," Lady Marjory noted dryly.

"I greatly wish he'd stop doing that. But otherwise, he is exceedingly considerate. And gallant, and sweet. I'm very fond of him."

"So am I, actually. Most men are amazingly transparent, but now and again comes along a man who is not what he seems. Half of London assumes Chirikov to be no more than a boorish clown, you think him sweet, and Finlay tells me he is the very devil on a battlefield. The czar consults with him on matters of state. In short, he is that rare creature who cannot be accurately judged on first impressions, which in my experience are generally reliable."

Celia knew Lady Marjory was trying to tell her something in the roundabout way of a practiced diplomat, and it had nothing to do with Chirikov.

Nor could she be speaking of Lord Kendal, because she had no idea Celia Greer had ever met the earl. Nevertheless, like Chirikov, he was assuredly a complex man. All but impenetrable, in her opinion. Even so, she suspected—purely on her untried instincts—that Kendal was not altogether the distant, self-contained gentleman he appeared to be.

Or perhaps she only wanted him to be otherwise. Seething, for example, with a desperate passion for Celia Greer.

Oh mercy! What if—?

She hid her face behind her fan as the unwelcome notion sprang into her head. Had Kendal told Lady Marjory and Lord Finlay about that night in Finlay's study? Possibly he felt obligated to advise them that they harbored a viper in their nest. Well, not precisely a viper, but a houseguest who disguised herself as a servant and hid out in closets and under desks with no credible explanation for her behavior.

"Have I misbehaved in some fashion?" she asked Lady Marjory, preferring to air her dirty laundry if the cat was already out of the bag. Or something of the sort. Heart racing, she could barely order her whirling thoughts, let alone her metaphors.

"Misbehaved?" Lady Marjory looked surprised. "Not to my knowledge. I admit you are something out of the usual, and perhaps a trifle enthusiastic when it is the fashion to appear bored, even should a Congreve rocket happen to whiz by your head. But your natural exuberance has made you exceptionally popular at a time when most fairly ordinary young widows would be overlooked. What with all these princes and ministers and czars swarming about, I mean to say. During a regular Season, you would be ranked as an Incomparable."

Only until she made a goose of herself, Celia thought, which sooner or later she was bound to do.

As for her unfashionable enthusiasm, she could not help herself. To think that the Haut Ton considered ennui a desirable state of mind. How little they knew! Had those jaded aristocrats spent so much as a week at Greer's farm, they'd have quickly learned to appreciate the pleasures of London.

"But since you brought up the subject of behavior," Lady Marjory said with uncharacteristic hesitation, "and while your deportment has been unexceptionable, there is a matter I have wished to address concerning a particular gentleman."

A cannonball thudded into Celia's stomach. Kendal *had* told on her, the lizard! "Please do," she said politely.

"The thing is, my dear, I was wondering if your intentions had altered. 'Tis none of my business, of course, but I was certain you told me that you would never, under any circumstances, consider marrying again."

A wave of relief swept down Celia's rigid spine. Kendal was not a lizard after all. Lady Marjory must be referring to someone else, for there could be no question of Celia Greer wedding the Earl of Kendal.

Nor any other man, for that matter, so what on earth was Lady Marjory talking about?

"My determination is fixed," she said brightly. "One marriage was quite sufficient, thank you. I'll not risk another. Why do you ask?"

"Well, my dear, Lord Henley's mother, who possesses all the tact of an avalanche, has been quizzing me regarding your lineage and fortune. I am certain the viscount means to make you an offer."

"Basil Henley? But he's the veriest puppy."

"He is seven-and-twenty," Lady Marjory corrected. "Precisely your own age, never mind that he trails at your heels like a besotted spaniel. Only one of a large pack of spaniels, to be sure, which is probably why you have paid him little notice. It's as well you have not developed a *tendre* for him, because his unfortunate wife, whoever she may be, will join him under his mama's thumb."

Celia shuddered. "Apparently I have misinterpreted Henley's intentions. He has invited me to join a house party at his estate when the victory celebrations are done with, but I shall most certainly refuse."

"That would be best, my dear. And while we are on the subject, there are others among your admirers apt to mistake your natural friendliness for something more particular. I cannot believe you wish to leave a scatter of broken hearts in your wake."

"Emphatically not." Celia was vividly aware that she

understood next to nothing about masculine intentions, beyond the obvious ones. "I have been thoughtless."

"No, indeed. Go on just as you are, but take care not to single out any gentleman who shows the slightest inclination to snap at dangled bait. I refer to those who are hanging out for a wife, of course. Lovers are a different sort of fish altogether."

The carriage made a turn, entering Berkeley Square precisely as the conversation was becoming exceptionally interesting. But if anything, the coach made less progress than ever, practically inching its way along on the rare occasions that it moved at all.

A lover. Celia had come to London fully intending to take a lover, of course. That had been her plan from the first. A vague plan, since she had no idea how to go about it, but she always figured something would turn up. *Someone.*

But then she saw Kendal from her bedchamber window and knew instantly that she had always been looking for him. No other lover could measure up to the one she had dreamed of for all those dreary years.

Whereupon she proceeded to make an absolute buffoon of herself, demolishing any frail chance she might have had to impress him favorably.

"So long as we are discussing unpleasant matters," Lady Marjory said, waving her fan with uncommon energy, "you may as well know that you have become the object of several wagers. At his club, Finlay spotted more than a few references to Lady G in the Betting Book."

"Whatever is *that*? And there must be a hundred Lady G's in London." Celia frowned. "Precisely what are they betting about?"

"The usual sort of thing. Who will offer for you and be refused. Who will offer less than marriage and be accepted. Do not concern yourself, my dear. A lovely young widow of sizable fortune cannot escape White's Betting Book. I simply wished you to be aware of the situation, lest a tidbit of gossip take you by surprise."

Clearly, certain gentlemen had far too much time on their hands, Celia thought in amazement. Wagering about *her*, of all people. As if she had done a single interesting thing in her entire life!

"How very absurd," she said. "And none of them can possibly win. I'm done with marrying, as you know, and have no intention of taking a lover."

"Indeed?" Lady Marjory raised an artfully plucked eyebrow. "It would be perfectly acceptable for you to do so, in case you have wondered. Virtually expected, as a matter of fact."

"I rather expected it, too," Celia confessed in a low voice. "Not an ordinary liaison, though, and certainly not a back-corner affair. Was a time I dreamed of a grand passion, but it was purely fantasy. I daresay that for all my wild imaginings, I shall dwindle to a pattern card of widowly propriety."

Marjory regarded her speculatively. "Is there something you wish to tell me, Celia?"

For a tempting moment Celia yearned to confide the truth. Not merely her overwhelming attraction to a man she could never have, but her deepest, most hopeless, desire. A child. Many children, with a father who loved them nearly as much as he loved her.

Of all her dreams, that was the one she herself would not permit to come true. Down to the marrow in her bones, she was terrified of passing control of her life to another man. Her independence had been hard won, and she intended to preserve it. Not even a proposal of marriage from Lord Kendal could change her mind on that subject.

A slip on the shoulder from Lord Kendal would be another matter altogether, but she wouldn't bet tuppence on the chances of that happening now. On a single night, in an act of singular stupidity, she had met . . . and lost forever . . . the man of her dreams.

Still, this wasn't the first time she'd scraped herself together after a foolish decision or a crippling disappointment. After crying buckets of tears and mentally kicking herself on the backside a few hundred times, she always accepted the inevitable and soldiered on.

Of course, in the past she'd had her improbable fantasies to sustain her. It hurt to bid them farewell, but she would have to make do with something other than a grand passion.

Perhaps she'd take up gardening.

At long last the carriage arrived in front of Lady Jersey's town house. Laughter and music spilled from the open windows as liveried servants, torches in hand, let down the steps and assisted the ladies to the pavement.

Celia took the arm of a freckle-faced young servant, firmly resolved to enjoy herself at the ball. After all, until a year ago her summer evenings were spent holding her nose with one hand and scouring chicken poop from wooden cages with the other.

No question about it, Celia Greer had come up in the world.

Chapter 4

His shoulder propped against a marble pillar in the ballroom, Kendal watched her move gracefully through the line of the cotillion, greeting each new partner with a delighted smile as if she'd been waiting all evening to dance with him. And when the figure separated them, the men invariably cast lingering looks at where she'd gone.

He was as transfixed as all the others. Supple, graceful, and incalculably lovely in a gown of emerald satin, she had captured his attention the moment she entered the room. As she always did.

He thought back to when first he saw her, clad in that crumpled black dress, a coil of lace from her faux housemaid's cap dangling over her ear.

And to the look of recognition in her eyes.

That continued to puzzle him. By her account, she had arrived in London that very day. She could not have seen him before, nor had he ever seen her. He'd an excellent memory for faces, and hers was unforgettable.

With considerable self-restraint, he had contrived to avoid her since his return from Boulogne, reckoning that he would eventually shed this almost pathological fascination with her. But if anything, it had grown to the point of obsession.

The time had come, he decided, for a formal introduction.

Wrenching his gaze to the crowd milling at the edges of the dance floor, he located Lady Marjory and set out in her direction.

"There you are, Kendal!" she said, when he approached her

and bowed. "Finlay told me you were assigned here for the evening, to put out fires. Will there be any, do you suppose?"

"I sincerely hope not. But there is little doubt that everyone else in the room wishes otherwise."

"Not I. Indeed, I shall be all too happy when our foreign guests have returned whence they came. A great lot of temperamental whiners they have turned out to be, insufferably tedious when they aren't creating a nuisance for their hosts."

"This from a diplomat's wife, Marjory? You shock me."

"Fustian. Do you know, I should very much enjoy seeing you genuinely shocked, or at the mercy of at least one sincere human emotion. But alas, I'm more likely to hear a pig sing a Mozart aria."

"Far better entertainment than I would provide, to be sure."

"Ah, I believe that was a set-down. And richly deserved. Will you forgive my impertinence if I introduce you to a beautiful woman?"

"There is nothing to forgive," he assured her, although she had scratched too close to home. But Marjory had not known him when an excess of very human passion had tumbled him into hell.

Before risking another such disaster, he'd sing a duet with that pig.

"Ah, there she is." Marjory pointed her fan at a knot of gentlemen clustered near the terrace doors. "Celia, Lady Greer, our houseguest for the last several weeks. I was at school with her mother, although we lost touch many years ago. It was something of a surprise to receive a letter from Celia, but naturally I invited her to stay with us. Has Finlay not spoken of her?"

"In passing. She is a widow, I understand, with a considerable fortune."

"Yes. And as such, she has drawn considerable attention, not all of it from desirable sources. I worried for her at first, but she is quick to learn." Marjory took his arm. "Come. I shall be interested to see what you make of her."

Even more interested to know what had already passed between them, he thought as she led him toward the circle of men. He was surprised to feel his pulse begin to race. Lord

Mumblethorpe, always gracious, moved aside to make room for them, and Kendal found himself standing directly behind Lady Greer.

Standing for a considerable time, as it developed, since her attention was focused on that damnable Russian. Aglitter in medals and shimmering epaulets, Vasily Chirikov was expounding yet another poem in a voice that threatened to shatter every chandelier in the ballroom.

" 'When all at whonce I saw a crowd, a host, off golden daffodeels.' "

Someone ought to stuff a wad of daffodils down his throat, Kendal thought irritably.

Lady Greer had turned slightly, and he saw from her profile that she was enjoying the recital. That dropped her several notches in his estimation. He was invariably polite to the general, but it was his duty to cater to politically important idiots. With no such obligation, she bloody well ought to find some way to be rid of Chirikov.

Especially while the Earl of Kendal stood waiting—with unaccustomed impatience—to be introduced. He looked forward to the expression on her face when she recognized him.

Would she be flustered? Defiant?

And why the devil was he putting her to the test? He could have arranged to meet her privately, after all. Or avoided her altogether, which would certainly have been the wisest course.

" 'And then my heart wiss pleasure feels, And dances wiss ze daffodeels.' "

Chirikov bowed with a flourish, and the small audience applauded politely.

"How very lovely," Lady Greer exclaimed. "To think you know all of Mr. Wordsworth's poems by heart."

"Ah, not all. I haff not time to learn them because of war. And the poems iss not so beautiful as you." Chirikov took her gloved hand and planted a lingering kiss on her wrist.

Kendal felt his own hands curl into fists. With effort, he straightened his fingers and relaxed his posture, which had unaccountably gone rigid. And just in time, because Marjory tapped Lady Greer on the shoulder with her fan.

She spun around, a bright smile on her face.

It stayed in place when she saw him, but he could not mistake the alarm that flickered briefly in her eyes and the slight squaring of her shoulders. She had set herself for a blow.

Maintaining an expression of polite curiosity, he gave her full marks for poise as Marjory made the introduction. When he bowed, she made a graceful curtsy.

And then, for what felt like a month, they simply gazed at each other.

Kendal knew only a few seconds had passed before he rallied his wits and devised a pleasant greeting, but she was a beat ahead of him.

"I am honored to make your acquaintance, sir. Lord Finlay has sung your praises so often that I came to imagine we had met long since."

The gauntlet hit the parquet floor with a clang only he could hear.

Did she imagine he meant to betray her? Insulted, he let the challenge lie where it fell. "It is my loss that we have not," he said smoothly. "If you are not otherwise engaged, shall we repair the omission during the next dance?"

A young officer of the Horse Guards stepped forward, flushing hotly. "Lady Greer has promised this waltz to me, sir."

Good manners required him to cede the field graciously, but Lady Greer's look of gratitude at her rescuer changed his mind. With a meaningful lift of one brow, Kendal dispatched a silent order to the would-be waltzer.

"B-by all means," the youngster stammered, resigned to his fate. "It would be my honor to do you a service, my lord. Perhaps another time, Lady Greer?"

"At the first opportunity," she promised with a smile, reserving her scowl for Kendal as he led her to the circle of dancers. Hand in hand, they began the formal promenade.

"That was bad of me," he admitted into the stiff silence between them. "But you needn't advertise it to all the world."

"I was expecting worse," she replied candidly, adjusting her face. "Shall I look for an ax to drop at the moment of your choosing?"

"Ax?" He turned her gracefully under his lifted arm. "Whatever can you mean, Lady Greer?"

"Oh, do cut line, sir. We both know I am at your mercy. You can ruin me with a single word."

"As if I would do such a thing. Or have I mistaken the situation? Was I not supposed to forget that we ever met?"

"Yes. But in my experience, people rarely do what they are supposed to do. Can you mean to prove an exception?"

"I mean to keep my word, certainly. Did I give it? Our first encounter is somewhat blurred in my memory."

"Because it can be of no significance to Your Loftiness," she fired back with an open grin. "But thank you, sir. You have restored my faith in gentlemanly honor."

At right about the time he was mightily tempted to abandon it, he thought, desire for her flaring as the dance figure drew them into a more intimate embrace. Her hand settled gingerly on his shoulder as he wrapped his fingers around her slender waist and twirled her in dizzying circles.

On the Continent, the waltz had already escaped these formal patterns, freeing couples to dip and turn free of the other dancers. But this was England, always behind the fashion, and far too soon he was forced to let go of all but her hand for another promenade.

"I'll not speak of our first meeting to anyone else," he said. "But shall we two abandon the pretense it never happened?"

"I believe we already have. But where does that leave me in your estimation, sir? Have I sunk below disgrace? Do put me out of my misery before I make futile attempts to redeem myself."

"The last thing I wish," he said honestly, "is to make you miserable. Quite the contrary. Would you prefer that I keep my distance in the future?"

She stumbled, and he tightened his grasp on her hand.

"No, my lord," she murmured. "I do not wish you to keep your distance."

The words put wings on his feet when they came together again in the close embrace of the waltz figure. For a few measures they both seemed to be dancing on air.

"Mercy me," Lady Greer said with a gasp.

Kendal failed to realize that the music had come to a faltering stop until his partner became a deadweight in his arms. She let go of his shoulder then and pointed to the ballroom door. Resplendent in a bottle-green uniform with a high gold collar and gilded epaulets, Czar Alexander was making a grand entrance. Lady Jersey, a cattish smile of triumph on her face, swept over to welcome him.

Everyone in the ballroom understood the significance of this startling event, Kendal better than most. The czar must have left Prinny's party in the early going and traveled neck or nothing from Oxford in time to make his appearance here. It was without question a deliberate, public snub, designed to humiliate the Regent.

This was precisely the fire Finlay had sent Kendal to extinguish, in the unlikely event it flared up. Now it was a conflagration.

And a bloody damned nuisance, in Kendal's opinion. Short of physically removing Lady Jersey from her own ballroom or the Czar of Russia from a London town house, what the devil could he do about it? Like all scandals, this one would soon be replaced with another. Perhaps, in the not too distant future, London would be gabbling about his affair with Lady Greer.

Did he mean there to be one?

Certainly not when he was thinking with his brains. She was undeniably beautiful, and he was most definitely attracted, but an affair with Celia Greer was certain to become unpleasantly complicated.

The czar, with an imperious gesture, signaled the orchestra to resume playing and waved everyone else from the ballroom floor. Then, with the grace of a couple who had practiced together for just this moment, Czar Alexander and Lady Jersey began dancing the waltz as it was meant to be danced.

Kendal glanced over at Lady Greer, who was gazing with horrified fascination at the spectacle. "Oh, how I should love to dance like that," she said in an awed whisper. "Have you ever done so?"

"Many times. And I expect you will have the opportunity

very soon, now that Sally has so flamboyantly launched it into fashion." Seized by an impulse he was certain he'd later regret, he offered her his arm. "Shall we steal a breath of fresh air, Lady Greer? While this carnival is playing in the ballroom, I daresay we'll have the garden to ourselves."

With barely perceptible hesitation, she placed her hand on his arm.

He led her through the French doors onto the terrace, a wide semicircle of polished marble edged with a railing of wrought iron. Just beyond was a parterre with a small formal garden, and beyond that, a scatter of trees and winding gravel paths.

They stood for a few moments by the railing and gazed in silence at the Japanese lanterns hanging from the tree branches, swaying in the soft June breeze and scattering colored light over the walkways. The scent of roses wafted from the garden, and he thought vaguely that he much preferred Celia Greer's sweet honeysuckle fragrance. Somewhere, a fountain played, the music of the water mingling with the waltz that floated from the ballroom.

He felt an odd sensation, as though he were standing on the edge of a high cliff, knowing that one false step would dash him to the jagged rocks below.

Perfect nonsense. It was only two steps down into the rose-bush garden, where the only danger was the possibility of catching his sleeve on a thorn.

Most females of his acquaintance would be chattering away by now, but Lady Greer seemed content to stand quietly, enjoying the music and the view.

Or perhaps she, too, could think of nothing to say.

What would she do if he led her into the far reaches of the garden, into the shadows of that leafy oak, and kissed her?

No, he told himself firmly. *Not yet*, a restless demon inside him amended. *But soon.*

What he needed, and quickly, was a change of subject before his unruly flesh betrayed him. "Forgive me for chewing on an old bone, Lady Greer, but one matter continues to perplex me. When we met in Finlay's study, you used my name. And I am certain he never mentioned it."

She sighed. "Is that why you brought me out here? To quiz me about that deplorable night?"

"Not at all, I assure you. Please forget I mentioned it."

"You may as well know, I suppose." She placed her palms on the railing, lifting her gaze to the sky. "As it happens, I had seen you on two previous occasions. That was many years ago, and from a distance, but I recognized you immediately."

"Well, that is a perfectly harmless explanation. Why did you not say so when first I asked?"

Her fingers curled around the railing. "Because at the time, sir, I was suffering the death throes of terminal mortification. My sole thought was to escape that room before expiring at your feet."

"Then I must thank you for clinging to life, Lady Greer. It would have been an awkward business, explaining your corpse to the constable."

She gave him a dimpled grin. "I live only to serve, my lord."

Laughing, he unpried her fingers from the railing and turned her to face him, still holding her hands. "Where did you see me before?"

"Well, the first time was in the town of Kendal, where the Earl of Kendal quite naturally draws one's attention. On the second occasion, you were riding in the countryside near the village of Sedgwick. My husband's farm is not far from there."

"Indeed?" He frowned. "I recall no one by the name of Greer. If you resided so close by to my estate, how is it we never met?"

A shadow passed over her face. "Oh, we rarely went out in Society. Greer preferred a quiet life, you see. For the most part, he was content to remain on the farm with his books and his . . . hobbies."

You were not content, Kendal thought, wondering why this vivacious young woman had married such a stick-in-the-mud. But he could scarcely ask so personal a question, nor was her marriage any of his concern. He damn well wouldn't appreciate questions about his own.

Or perhaps she knew all about it. The scandal was common gossip in Westmoreland, or had been at the time. For a few painful months he'd even imagined that the sheep were baaing the latest *on dits* behind his back when he rode by.

"Is something wrong, my lord?"

He wrenched his thoughts from a past that was better left where it generally resided, somewhere near the pit of his stomach. "Was I frowning? Pardon me. I was searching my memory for Lord Greer, but failed to locate him. Were you married long?"

"Nine years, two months, and three days. His death was unexpected. A heart attack, the doctor said later, and mercifully quick. I was gathering eggs when it happened, and by the time I heard the servants' cries and ran to the house, it was over."

Her hands had tensed as she spoke. He began to rub them between his fingers. In the silence, the slight scratch of his gloves against hers sounded in his ears like distant thunder.

"I'm sorry," he said gently.

She withdrew her hands and brushed them against her skirt. "Mercy. How came we to such a morbid subject? This is a party, after all, and there is never any point to wallowing in the past. Will you be present at the treaty conference in Vienna?"

The lady certainly knew how to slam a door. And just as well, because he had intruded into territory he did not care to visit. Wanting her was not the same as wishing to become personally involved with her, and he felt distinct relief that she shared his distaste for emotional entanglements. Perhaps an affair with Lady Greer was not out of the question, if she, too, meant to keep her distance outside the bedchamber.

Now he need only discover if she shared his interest in joining him *inside* a bedchamber. After he answered her last question, of course. What was it? Something about Vienna.

"I expect so," he said, wrestling to control a few galloping primal urges. "Mind you, I'm not looking forward to yet another trek across the Continent, although this time I'll not be forced to make long detours around Bonaparte's army."

The orchestra had struck up a country dance, and the sounds of laughter and conversation streamed across the terrace. The party was in full swing again, and Kendal knew they wouldn't be alone under the stars for very much longer.

In unspoken, mutual agreement, they descended the stairs and began to walk side by side in the garden.

Should he test the waters now? Make an approach? Draw her into his arms?

They came near the oak tree. If he led her to the other side, where no one could see them from the ballroom or the terrace, and if he kissed her—damn it all. He felt like a fumbling adolescent, suddenly unsure of himself, shy of a rejection that might not even come.

What the devil was the matter with him? He could hear his voice making polite conversation, which meant a part of his brain was still functioning. And he sensed, bone-deep, the subtle feminine invitation in her sideways glances and the feminine tilt of her head in his direction as they walked.

But he kept moving, past the oak tree and all the other trees where they might have shelter, back onto the curving path that led again to the terrace.

If she was disappointed, she gave no sign of it. Pausing at the top of the steps, she turned to him with a smile. "I suppose you wish to discover what the czar is up to now. Lord Finlay will expect a complete report."

"Lady Marjory will tell him what occurred," he said from a dry throat. "But I have meetings at the Foreign Office early tomorrow morning, so I'd best take my leave now. And I'd as soon not run into any of the Russian contingent, most especially General Chirikov, on my way out. Will you mind if I don't return with you to the ballroom?"

"Not in the least," she assured him. "Vasily Chirikov is a lovely gentleman, but he persists in treating me to rather lengthy poetry recitals. You do well to make a stealthy exit, for he is likely to leap at me the moment I step inside."

"Now I feel guilty for leaving you unprotected," he replied. "Shall we face him down together?"

"Make your escape while you can, sir. And thank you for our walk in the garden. It was quite the nicest part of the evening."

"Yes. I daresay we'll meet again, at some party or another. Have I managed to convince you that you have nothing to fear from me?"

She studied him for a moment. "If you refer to our mutual secret, yes. I am most grateful."

He recognized evasion in her reply. Did she fear him on some other count? Seduction, for example?

Before he could summon a response, she curtsied and turned for the ballroom.

As he watched her, appreciating the fluid sway of her hips, he thought to go after her. But the moment she stepped through the doors, men swarmed over her like bees on a bright flower, Chirikov among them.

He was beginning to hate that damnable Russian.

Couples began to wander onto the terrace, so he slipped back into the garden, meaning to make his exit through the rear gate and to the mews, where his carriage had been ordered to wait.

Alarms were clamoring in his head. No doubt about it, Lady Greer was trouble on two long, shapely legs. And should the pressure of his work ease long enough for him to consider a mistress, there were any number of straightforward females ready and willing to warm his bed.

Why complicate his already complicated life with a woman who confused the hell out of him? He didn't understand her at all, and resented the way she had of thumping his otherwise logical mind into mush. Yes, he would do well to keep a distance between them in the future.

How soon, he wondered, could he contrive to see her again?

Chapter 5

Celia was alone in the breakfast room, nibbling toast and reading the newspaper, when Lord Kendal appeared at the door.

Startled, she dropped a wedge of toast onto her lap.

He bowed. "Pardon me for intruding, Lady Greer. I was hoping to speak with Lord Finlay, but the butler informs me that he is not at home. Do you know where he can be found?"

Remembering her manners, Celia rose. "I'm afraid he cannot. Last night, Lady Marjory received word that her sister has been taken ill. They set out immediately for Maidstone. I have their direction, if you require it."

"Not at all." He went to the sideboard and lifted the coffee pot. "May I?"

"To be sure. It is probably tepid by now, though. Shall I ring for—"

"This will do, thank you." He filled a cup, added a large chunk of sugar, and pulled out a chair across the table from her. "Please, finish your breakfast. Is the illness serious?"

"I believe not. But as Lady Esther's husband is from home, Lady Marjory means to stay with her until he returns. I understand that unless he is needed there, Lord Finlay will come directly back to London. We've no idea when to expect him, though."

Stop babbling, Celia! She seized her teacup and took a deep swallow, unable to mistake the glint of amusement in his eyes. Did he *enjoy* making her nervous?

Not that he had done anything remotely nerve-racking or improper, save to appear in the breakfast room at seven o'clock in the morning, for pity's sake, looking just as elegant in a dark blue coat and fawn pantaloons as he always did in formal evening dress.

While she, anticipating a quiet, solitary morning, had slipped on her plainest muslin gown and barely run a brush through her hair.

The silence grew agonizing, at least to her. Lord Kendal, perfectly at ease, seemed content to sip his coffee and gaze at her from a pair of disconcerting blue eyes.

What *did* a man and woman talk about over the breakfast table?

He certainly knew better than she. And he was a diplomat as well. Wasn't it his duty to make conversation? She bit into a square of toast, regretting it instantly as the crunch crackled like thunder in the small room.

Demonically, in her opinion, he waited until her mouth was full before speaking. "You are up and about exceptionally early for a lady of fashion, Lady Greer."

Now certain he was deliberately baiting her, Celia chewed slowly and rallied her delinquent wits. Some of them were firmly fixed on his broad shoulders and the elegant, long-fingered hand curled around his coffee cup. He had propped his elbows on the table, obviously waiting for her to take his hook.

She let him wait another few moments. Then she shrugged. "I am used to rising with the chickens, sir. And for that matter, it is my understanding that gentlemen of fashion rarely crack open their eyes before noon."

His lips curved in an appreciative smile. "Just so. We appear to share a sordid fondness for mornings, although mine are usually given over to tedious meetings with even more tedious bureaucrats. What do you do with your mornings, Lady Greer?"

Feed the chickens, she thought immediately. They were gone now, of course, along with Greer, but most days she still awoke with the same sense of dread.

"Mostly I laze about," she said blithely. "Lord Finlay has

usually joined me by this time, and we discuss the latest *on dits*. More accurately, I discuss. He only grumbles until well through his third cup of coffee."

Kendal laughed. "I know that grumble well. But it appears I'll not be forced to decipher his instructions this particular morning. Even better, I seem to have been granted a brief, unexpected holiday. Shall I use it to laze about, Lady Greer?"

"I highly recommend lazing, sir. Although I cannot quite imagine you doing so."

"Nor can I. It has certainly been a long time since I had the opportunity. But after a conference this morning at Whitehall, and before my departure for Bath tomorrow with Marshal Blücher, there is nothing that requires my immediate attention."

He set his cup carefully on the saucer. "Except, perhaps, the pair of bays I've been neglecting to exercise. Have you plans for the day, or might I coax you to join me for an afternoon excursion?"

Heat lightning flashed through the breakfast room. She felt the charge pass through her body. And through the electrified haze, she saw the source in his eyes.

He meant seduction. She knew it. In his casually voiced question was the promise of everything she had wanted since the first time she saw him.

No. Not everything. Not nearly so much. One afternoon was all he promised, a few hours only. Already he had given warning that he would be off to Bath the very next day.

She respected his honesty and hated him for it. Which did not stop her wanting him, not the least little bit.

Mercifully, or perhaps with deliberate cunning, he gave her time to consider by returning to the sideboard and refilling his coffee cup. She regarded his back, wondering if he felt even a spark of the fire raging inside her.

There was no sign of it. Save for a slight miscalculation as he cut off an oversized chunk from the sugar cone, he appeared perfectly at ease. She, on the other hand, was splintering into a thousand pieces of female desire, all of them barely held together by sheer power of will.

He wasn't any ordinarily attractive male. She had met a few since coming to London, but none had roused her interest in the slightest. Kendal was . . . compelling. She assumed that he obsessed her because she had dreamed about him for so many years, but in her fantasies he was generally wearing armor, with a recently dispatched dragon lying in a heap at his feet.

Seduction at the breakfast table, over the remains of a soft-boiled egg and cold toast, was not what she had pictured. Not at all.

She had aimed herself higher than this. She aspired to a grand passion. Although, to be painfully honest, that was more than she could realistically have expected from a man such as this one. The flesh-and-blood Lord Kendal offered much less than the Lord Kendal of her dreams.

Was it enough?

He glanced at her over his shoulder, not quite meeting her eyes. "Well, Lady Greer? Will you join me for a drive in the country and a picnic lunch alongside the Thames? I promise to have you home in time for your evening engagements."

With a shot of awareness, she understood that the flesh-and-blood Lord Kendal offered far more than her chaste, fantastical dreams. Surely one afternoon of passion was better than none. And he was the one more likely to be disappointed when it was over. What had she to offer him, when it came right down to it?

"I would be delighted," she said from a constricted throat, surprised to see his shoulders relax. Only fractionally, and solely to a degree that anyone not concentrating so intently on him would have missed, but she was sure of it.

He had wanted her to say yes.

That was all the incentive she required to dive headlong into her very first, and probably only, affair.

She examined her fingernails. Celia Greer was not the stuff of which notorious widows were made, she knew. Cutting a dash in Society was fun, and she meant to do so for years to come. But this once, her heart held firmly in check, she would take a lover.

When she looked up again, he was standing at the door.

"I shall be occupied at Whitehall for an hour or two," he said. "Can you be ready to depart at, say, ten o'clock?"

"Certainly." Once again, unspoken understanding hovered between them. Without words, they had agreed to far more than a picnic luncheon.

She ought to have followed him to the main door, she realized after he was gone, and bade him a formal farewell. Instead, she waited until certain he had left the house before charging upstairs to ring for her maid.

The next several hours spun by in a frenzy. Although she had bathed before going to bed, she bathed again and washed her hair. She ordered a fire built so she could dry it, never mind the warm June morning. Then she tried on every gown in her closet suitable for a drive in the country, taking into account what would surely happen afterward.

Modest or enticing? Buttons in the back, or should she provide easier access to her person? Spencer or no spencer? Which reticule? Which fan? Which bonnet?

At precisely three minutes before ten, she studied herself in the mirror and told herself she looked as well as possible, if she discounted the stunned glaze in her eyes.

The jonquil muslin dress, with a cream-colored sash tied in a bow at the back of her waist, was nicely balanced between seductive and innocent. It left her arms bare under skimpy puffed sleeves, but the bodice was cut high enough to require a bit of effort on a lover's part to reach what lay underneath.

Accessible, but not flagrant. *Yes,* with a hint of *no.*

They could both change their minds well up to the point of no return, after all. But would she know when they had reached that point? Or had it already passed?

When she heard the door knocker, a surge of panic knifed through her veins. Mercy me, she thought. Can I do this?

In a last-minute rush to protect herself, she wrapped a Norwich shawl around her goose-bumpy arms and descended the stairs with what she hoped was impressive poise.

Lord Kendal, now wearing a russet driving coat and buff-colored trousers, greeted her with a smile and led her out to the curricle. Two enormous and apparently ill-tempered horses wrestled with the street urchin clinging tenaciously to their reins.

Celia eyed them doubtfully. "They look a trifle . . . impatient, my lord."

"I'll let them run it off when we reach the countryside." He handed her onto the bench. "Or would you prefer otherwise?"

"Indeed no," she replied at once. "I should like it above all things."

"Well, perhaps not *all*," he said, climbing up beside her and taking the reins.

Oh my. Did he mean what she thought he meant?

A sophisticated woman would have trilled a clever riposte, Celia supposed, but she couldn't think of a single one. Heat burning in her cheeks, she watched him guide the restive bays onto the busy street with impressive ease.

She had never before ridden in a curricle, and was surprised how little room there was for driver and passenger on the narrow padded bench. He wasn't touching her, not quite, but her wind-ruffled skirt had begun to dally with his thigh.

He slid her a glance. "Do you ride, Lady Greer?"

Thank heavens, an innocuous topic of conversation! "Not since coming to London," she replied, "and precious little before that. When I have located a suitable town house to lease, I will straightaway buy a horse of my own. I have always wanted one."

"Your husband kept no stable?" He deftly steered around a lumbering coal wagon. "Wherever I am sent, for however brief a time, I immediately secure a good riding horse and a pair like this one for driving. Mind you, I have sometimes bought and sold nags without ever having the opportunity to put them to use."

He spoke of horses for a while, and then of several eccentric characters he'd met on his travels, surprising her with his sly sense of humor. And allowing her time to relax in his company, she was certain, grateful that she had no more to do than enjoy his anecdotes.

And look at him.

Surreptitiously, to be sure, for she had no wish to be caught gaping like a hayseed. She began with his hands, strong and graceful in their tan kidskin gloves as he gently wielded the reins. He was going to touch her with those hands, touch her in places that began to burn just from imagining it.

Her gaze wandered to the well-shaped thigh beside hers, so close she felt it press warmly against her whenever the curricle made a turn. His breeches fit so snugly they might as well have been painted on.

Not yet out of London, and already she was tumbling in a maelstrom of decidedly erotic fantasies!

She wondered if he knew, and reckoned that he did.

He gave no obvious sign of it, though, continuing to speak lightly of his experiences with only the occasional glance in her direction.

But what did she expect, after all? For Lord Kendal, this assignation was one of many, not in the least earth-shattering. Perhaps not even of much interest to him, beyond the masculine pleasure he would enjoy for a few hours. Or minutes. She had no idea how long it would take, once he got started.

Ignorance was most assuredly *not* bliss, she decided. Sometimes, and especially now, ignorance was purely disconcerting. At the least, she ought to muster up a little intelligible conversation instead of sitting beside him like a lump.

But in fact, she realized of a sudden, he, too, had gone mute. They had left the city behind without her noticing it and were traveling along a narrow road lined with hedgerows. To her right, she caught an occasional glimpse of sunlight flashing off water whenever the road curled near the Thames.

Away from the smells and noise of London, she became acutely aware of subtle odors and sounds. The clopping of hooves on the hard-packed dirt road. Birdsong. The rustle of her skirts in the breeze. The faint scent of a citrony cologne, clean and masculine, and the heavier odor of rich leather from his boots and gloves.

She stole a glance at his face, half-shadowed by the brim of

44

his hat under the bright noonday sun. He looked, she thought, remarkably at peace.

Perhaps a quiet afternoon in the country was a treat for him. While she longed for excitement and adventure, Lord Kendal probably relished his rare opportunities to escape them.

She wished he were not quite so tranquil while she was practically smoldering a bare half inch away. Even her inventive imagination could not picture the elegant Lord Kendal smoldering, but he might at least stir up a dollop of enthusiasm.

They came around a sweeping curve and the road straightened for as far as she could see.

Lord Kendal looked over at her. "Shall I let them out?"

One of the bays whinnied, as if in approval.

Laughing, Celia took hold of the panel next to her hip. "Tallyho!"

And then, with the barest flick of Kendal's wrist, they were off.

Eight hooves dug into the ground until the bays found their stride and began to run in perfect unison. The curricle seemed airborne, wheels turning without the slightest bounce. Hedgerows whizzed past in a blur of green.

Exhilarated, she lifted her head to the wind. The horses could not go fast enough for her. Never before had she felt so truly alive. The thrill of speed and danger. Abandon. Freedom!

Her bonnet flew off, catching the wind like a sail a few inches behind her head. The ribbons tied under her chin began to choke her, and she clawed at them with both fingers, lurching from side to side now that she'd let go her grip on the panel.

Noticing her distress, Kendal reined in the bays.

Celia's bonnet settled against her back like a deflated balloon, but the ribbons had got tangled in the fringe of her shawl.

"Permit me," he said, gently pushing her fingers away. His leather gloves grazed her neck and chin as he unknotted the ribbon and detached the fringe. "There."

He set the bonnet on her lap, his gaze never leaving her face. "How lovely you are, Celia Greer." One finger brushed slowly, intimately, down her cheek. "I tried to resist you, you know. It would have been best."

"Not for me," she whispered, spellbound by his sapphire-blue eyes. Who *are* you? she wondered at the edges of her besotted mind. She wanted to *know* him, heaven help her. She wanted him to know her, too, and not turn away when he did.

Then she forgot all the things she wanted, because he lifted her chin with the back of a gentle hand and kissed her.

It was the barest kiss, light and tantalizing and far too brief, but it promised everything she dared to expect. She leaned into him, shamelessly begging for another, starved for affection and beyond pretending otherwise. Her hands curled around his neck.

"Sweet heavens," he murmured, drawing her closer. This time he lingered, touching her eyelids and cheekbones with his lips, licking the corner of her mouth, sliding his tongue across her lips and back again.

She mumbled a protest as he deliberately set her away. When his hands left her shoulders, she felt startlingly naked without the feel of him.

"I think we should go on," he said, chucking the bays into a trot. "More slowly, perhaps. The side road leading to the inn where we'll have . . . luncheon"—his voice cracked—"is easy to miss."

They arrived on the narrow track minutes later, long silent minutes, and he steered the curricle into the turn like a man who had made this same turn many times before.

Had he brought other women here? she wondered, a knife of jealousy digging between her ribs as the inn came into view.

It was a large half-timbered building two stories high, set in a wide field ringed with oaks and willows. She saw a graystone stable to one side and a vegetable garden at the other. Flowers bloomed around the whitewashed inn walls, hyacinths and tea roses and snapdragons. Three brown-and-white-spotted cows grazed placidly in a paddock beside the stable.

Just beyond the buildings and gardens, a sweep of lush green grass led down to the bank of the Thames, flowing narrow and gentle though this fairyland.

Or so it seemed to her. Surely magic had created this beautiful place. The inn must be centuries old, the trees older than that, and the river timeless.

Here, in this place, she would make love with the man who had haunted her empty nights and brightened her days with hope.

Chapter 6

Kendal wondered if she had been expecting him to sweep her directly into a bedchamber.

He certainly wanted to.

But it was not in his nature to behave impulsively, or had not been until he met Lady Greer. It had been nothing short of reckless to bring her to the White Swan, and he could scarcely credit that he'd done so. Before taking any further missteps, he needed to cool down. Considerably.

While Lady Greer waited by the door, he greeted Mrs. Belcher and ordered a light meal to be served alfresco. He also reserved, only for the afternoon, a bedchamber. *The* bedchamber.

Mrs. Belcher blinked.

Her husband popped out of the taproom just then, with the jovial welcome accorded all his customers and more than one curious glance at the young woman silhouetted in the doorway.

Kendal felt a shot of acute regret. Of all the places he might have taken her, why choose an inn where he had been a frequent guest? It was all of a piece, he supposed, with his perplexing behavior of that morning, when Carver informed him that the Finlays were not at home. The natural thing, the expected thing, would have been to leave his card and move on to his next errand. But he could not resist a falsely casual inquiry after Lady Greer, and when informed she was alone in the breakfast room, he heard himself announce that he would pay his regards in person.

So now, willy-nilly, here they were. Ostensibly for a picnic lunch, and perhaps only that. It wasn't too late for either to have a change of mind about unspoken intentions.

He was reasonably certain she had resolved to have him, though. Either that, or she was the most unconsciously seductive female he had ever met. It was his own decision hanging in the balance, his reluctance to take so intoxicating a drink as Lady Greer warring against his undeniable inclination to drink his fill.

Ignoring Mrs. Belcher's pursed lips and disapproving glare, he instructed John Belcher to ice his best bottle of champagne and see to the horses. Then, with unaccustomed impatience racing up and down his spine, he returned to Lady Greer.

She appeared remarkably poised, as though an afternoon tryst was nothing at all out of the ordinary. And perhaps it was not, he thought with an unpleasant jolt. Yes, she was newly come to London, but who could say what she'd been up to in the country? Every male instinct in his overheated body assured him that she was a woman of extraordinary passion.

Men flocked to her in droves, that was certain. He knew, because he had spent far too much time watching her at balls and routs and musicales when he was supposed to be attending to foreign dignitaries.

"My lord?" she said softly.

He realized that he had been standing in front of her like a fencepost for several minutes. Lady Greer had a way of sending his wits and most of his practiced charm to the far side of the moon.

"Mrs. Belcher will escort you upstairs and provide whatever you need," he said in a strained voice. "I expect you'll wish to refresh yourself before lunch."

"L-lunch?"

"We'll take it alongside the river, unless you prefer to remain indoors. And we are in luck, because this morning she baked her famous almond-custard tarts." He smiled. "Join me outside when you are ready."

Looking a bit stunned, she curtsied and followed Mrs. Belcher up the stairs.

Yes, she had definitely expected *him* to be leading her up those stairs. Rarely had he met a woman so transparently eager for a toss between the sheets. He thought for a moment of granting her wish immediately, but reminded himself that he meant to retain absolute control of whatever happened, or did not happen, between them.

Her urgency was both flattering and unsettling. Also powerfully arousing, which is why he made his way outside instead of following her to the bedchamber. Lady Greer had much to learn about the delights of anticipation, and it would be his pleasure to teach her.

Two geese honked a greeting as he crossed the sweeping lawn and made an arc around a sprawl of snoozing ducks, their bills neatly tucked under iridescent wings. When he stopped at river's edge, a trio of hopeful swans cruised by, eyeing his fingers for a possible handout.

Nothing had changed since his last visit more than three years before. He supposed little had changed here since the sixteenth century, when the White Swan was built as a summer residence for a duke's mistress. Her large, elegantly furnished chamber had been Kendal's haven whenever he contrived to escape the city and his duties.

At this moment and in that very room, the lady he meant to bed this afternoon, a lady who might well become his own mistress for so long as he remained in London, was splashing water on her face or brushing her wind-tangled curls. He wondered what she thought of the enormous bed atop its pedestal, and the colorfully explicit frescoes on the ceiling and walls.

The ducks jumped up, squawking as two freckled young Belchers tramped by with a small wooden table and a pair of chairs. Kendal directed them to the shade of a nearby sycamore tree, and a maid soon arrived to lay out the table with linens, silverware, glasses of cool water, and champagne flutes. She was followed by servants carrying platters of sliced ham and roast beef, a salmon pie, potato pudding, a tureen of lobster bisque, fresh-baked saffron rolls, cucumber salad, almond tarts, and a bowl of ripe peaches.

He had just snatched one of Mrs. Belcher's irresistible tarts when Celia Greer materialized at his side.

"What's this, my lord?" she demanded cheekily. "Dessert before grace?"

He returned the tart to its platter and settled her on a chair. "As you observed, I've a lamentable fondness for sweets. Were the Valliants prone to gaining weight, which by sheer good fortune we are not, I'd be round as an ascent balloon by now."

"The Prince Regent should be as fortunate," she said, unfolding her napkin. "Is it treasonous to remark that he looks nothing whatever like any prince I ever imagined?"

"In my experience, few princes measure up to expectations. Royal blood pumps through perfectly ordinary bodies, I'm afraid, a great many of them equipped with bulbous noses, sagging bellies, and warts."

He sat across from her, dismissing the servants with a wave of his hand. "Shall we forget the czars and archdukes and princes who have been cluttering England and making a nuisance of themselves? I wish to hear about Celia, Lady Greer, who is of far more interest than any royal I ever met."

"To the contrary, sir. The story of my life would bore you senseless."

"Nevertheless, I wish to hear it. And since I am paying for lunch, you are obliged to indulge me."

"Am I?" She raised a brow. "But as I didn't think to bring any money, I suppose you must have your way. No doubt you are accustomed to getting it."

"I have that reputation," he acknowledged.

"Very well then, but I'll take no responsibility if you fall asleep with your chin in the soup bowl. Until a month ago, you see, I had never ventured beyond the backwaters of Lancashire, where nothing of interest ever happens. Or if it does, it never happened to me."

She went quiet then, requiring a bit of encouragement to continue, but he knew better than to provide it. The best way to draw information from those reluctant to give it was to create a silence that ached to be filled. Soon enough, she would tell him what he wanted to know.

He applied himself to his soup and waited.

She put down her spoon only a minute or so after he had expected her to. "Very clever, my lord. What means do you use to extricate information should the silent treatment fail? Thumbscrews? The rack?"

He choked on a sprig of parsley. Lady Greer was not to be underestimated. And how many times since meeting her had he told himself that very thing? "I cannot think what you mean," he said after taking a long drink of water.

"Rubbish! I won't pretend to be up on all your tricks, sir, but I do wish you will stop trying to play them on me. Had I any secrets to withhold, you may be assured I've sufficient wit to keep them to myself."

"Thumbscrews notwithstanding."

"Precisely."

Laughing, he leaned back on his chair. "Very well, Lady Greer. Tell me as much or as little as you wish. But I admit to inordinate curiosity about the doings of a Lancashire lass. Keep me entertained, and I promise not to trot out any more of my devious ploys."

"Oh, you will," she replied sagely. "I suspect you cannot help yourself. Nevertheless, I shall provide you a brief sketch of my decidedly uninteresting life, urging you to stop me when you've heard enough."

"Agreed. Now, do cease these absurd protests and tell me your story."

Annoyance flaring in her eyes, she defiantly finished her soup.

He regarded her with admiration. The strong-willed bays that brought them here could take a lesson in obstinacy from Celia Greer.

When she'd let him wait a minute longer than he had forced her to wait, back when he had foolishly thought to manipulate her, she flashed him a grin of satisfaction. Take that, she might as well have said aloud.

He absorbed the blow with a grin of his own. "Touché," he acknowledged, relishing the surprising battle of wits with an opponent more than capable of matching him. This afternoon was not turning out as he had expected, but so far he was glad of it. When the time came, however, he would take up her reins and bring her into check.

"Well then," she said as if delivering a report on the wheat harvest, "I am an only child. My father was grievously disappointed to be saddled with a daughter instead of an heir, but Mama died of a fever before she could repair her mistake. When I was ten and seven, I married Lord Greer and moved to his farm."

She forked a slice of ham onto her plate.

"Did you love him?"

She looked astonished at the question, nearly as astonished as he felt for having asked it. He had never meant to say such a thing, and for a tense moment he was sure she would tell him to go to the devil.

But she only shrugged. "It was an arranged marriage, with my willing consent. Greer was a good deal older, of course, in his late fifties when we wed and rather set in his ways. I adapted to them, sometimes with ill grace, and we rubbed along as well as could be expected."

In those stark words, he sensed years of heartbreak. But why the devil had she given *willing consent* to a man old enough to be her grandfather?

She cast him a shrewd smile. "You are wondering, of course, why I agreed to the marriage. But the reasons were more or less the usual ones in such cases. Father had accumulated a great many debts and planned to escape his creditors by emigrating to Canada. I didn't want to go with him. But there were few alternatives for a young woman with only a patched-together education and no money at all. Then Greer stepped in, providing funds for Father's voyage and a bit extra to help him make a new start. He also gave me a home. It was a good bargain for everyone concerned."

Sickened, Kendal dished cucumber slices onto his plate and pushed them around with his fork. For the cost of passage across the Atlantic, her father had sold her like a cord of firewood.

But perhaps he mistook the situation. After all, Lord Featherstoke had wed a young bride under similar circumstances, and from all accounts, they remained a devoted couple until his death. Lady Featherstoke still mourned her spouse, and was in no hurry to replace him with another.

Besides, he knew very well that marrying for love was no guarantee of happiness.

"So there you have it," she said with impressive nonchalance. "Greer's heart failed him a little more than a year ago, and I was left with a tidy fortune and the right to call myself a lady, although by birth I merely border on respectable. Mama was the daughter of an obscure baronet and father the third son of a country squire. You needn't spread that information around, by the way. I am trying to cut a dash in Society."

"So you have," he assured her, more fascinated by Celia Greer with every word she spoke. He sensed courage in this slender, sometimes naive young woman. A will of iron.

Also an aching vulnerability, which he was by no means willing to address. Restrained admiration was one thing, concern for her personal feelings quite another. Caring about her meant . . . well, caring. Never a good idea, that.

Happily, John Belcher loped across the lawn just then, carrying a silver bucket filled with ice chips and a bottle of champagne. "Not properly chilled yet, m'lord, but I thought you might be wantin' a sip of the bubbly."

"Thank you, John. Put another on ice, if you will, for later."

After uncorking the bottle, his gaze fixed all the while on Lady Greer, Belcher slowly took himself off.

She gazed after him with a wistful expression. "He disapproves of me. Although that is, I suppose, to be expected."

Kendal made haste to reassure her. "Like most men, John Belcher enjoys looking at beautiful women. You must accustom yourself to admiring glances, Lady Greer, for they will follow you wherever you go."

"They have never done so before. But then, I've hardly ever gone anywhere." She split a crusty roll and dipped her knife into the pot of butter. "London has been my target, though, since I was in leading strings. When Greer died, it was all I could do to keep from jumping on the first mailcoach south. But there was the year of mourning to observe, and I was by no means ready to launch myself into Society. Well, I was certainly *ready*, but I'd have sunk like a stone."

"Unimaginable."

Her brows arched. "Have you forgot detaching me from the underside of Lord Finlay's desk? And that, sir, was after two extremely proper ladies had spent a grueling year polishing me up."

"Ah, but diamonds are generally to be found in dark places," he reminded her, pleased to see her small frown vanish after so slight a compliment. For a woman of such extraordinary beauty, she was remarkably unaware of her charms. "Tell me about the grueling year."

"You are a glutton for tedium, it seems. But very well. When Greer was in the ground, I took myself off to Giggleswick. Do you know it?"

He would certainly have remembered such an unusual name, but it rang no bells. "Should I?"

"Well, it's not so very distant from your estate, perhaps thirty or forty miles. But it's true that little Giggleswick is quite overshadowed by Settle, which lies directly across the River Ribble. I grew up in Settle, and was acquainted from an early age with Miss Wigglesworth and her sister—"

"Wigglesworth?"

"A common name in that area, actually. There are several Wigglesworths in Giggleswick, although none are held in such high esteem as my mentors." Her lips curved. "Wilberta and Wilfreda."

He spilled the champagne he had been pouring into her glass. "Wilberta and Wilfreda Wigglesworth of Giggleswick? You are humbugging me, Lady Greer."

"I assure you, sir, that the Wigglesworth ladies are quite real. They are, as a matter of fact, my closest friends, and have always set the style in Giggleswick society. They had a London Season, you see."

"Indeed? I do not recollect meeting them. But perhaps I was out of the country at the time."

"Perhaps. It was half a century ago."

Kendal found himself laughing again—he who so rarely laughed aloud that he scarcely recognized the unfamiliar sound.

"You may well find this amusing, my lord, but they were the

most fashionable ladies of my acquaintance. And since I had made up my mind to learn how to go on in the beau monde, I applied to them for instruction."

"Aside from your penchant for skulking under desks, Lady Greer, I am persuaded you did not learn your manners from a pair of elderly Giggleswick spinsters."

"Not altogether, it's true. I read a great many books about proper deportment, most of them woefully out of date. You'll be impressed to hear that I can, if necessary, glide smoothly through narrow doors wearing wide panniers, and enter a sedan chair without knocking a speck of powder from my towering hair arrangement."

"Remarkable. I should like to see it."

"Perhaps one day, at a costume ball, I shall have the opportunity to demonstrate. Wilfreda's specialties were somewhat obscure, I admit, but Wilberta provided a good deal of practical advice." She took a sip of champagne. "Indeed, by the time I set out for London, I thought myself a paragon of savoir faire. But then I met Lady Finlay and came smack up against the distinction between a veneer of sophistication and the real thing. It was a considerable comedown, I can tell you."

"If it matters, I find your manners enchanting. Far more charming than the languid world-weariness in fashion these days."

Color washed over her cheeks. "Thank you, sir, even if you said so only to be kind. I know it is a flaw I must overcome, but compliments never fail to turn me to pudding."

They had wandered into personal territory again, he understood by the alarms sounding in his head. How was it he wanted to know everything about her, and not know at the same time? "I am curious to hear more about the redoubtable Wigglesworth ladies," he said, steering the conversation to safer ground.

For some minutes, with unfailing good humor, she described their valiant efforts to transform a country bumpkin into a woman of the world. Now and again he interjected a question, or ventured a comment when she paused for a drink of champagne or a bite of almond tart, which she pronounced delectable. But for the most part, he simply watched her, vibrating like a tuning fork in response to her guileless femininity. She was pure music, he thought, graceful and airy, each line and curve of her body playing on his senses like a Mozart sonata.

The curl of her fingers around the stem of her glass mesmerized him. The dance of her lips and the flash of small white teeth as she spoke sent him spinning in circles. And her eyes, gleaming like polished mahogany in the sunlight, held all the mysteries of the universe.

Not in any London ballroom, not in the glittering courts of Europe, had he ever encountered such a woman as this. The spell she cast stole every shred of reason from his carefully disciplined mind. She disordered him. She took him apart, with no promise he'd ever be whole again.

And, he was certain, she had absolutely no idea the effect she had on men. On him. Artless and genuine in a world of artifice and fakery, the world where he felt comfortable, she was altogether terrifying.

Especially when she smiled at him the way she was smiling now, one brow lifted inquiringly.

Had she asked him a question?

He didn't care.

With trembling fingers, he selected a ripe peach from the fruit bowl, removed the fuzzy peel with a small, sharp knife, and cut the fruit into wedges. He was aware of her watching his hands, and of the shuddering silence that had fallen between them.

Lifting a slice of peach between his thumb and forefinger, he brought it to her lips.

After a moment, eyes wide, she nibbled delicately. When she was done he fed her another, and then a third, their gazes locked in a fevered embrace. A bead of juice hovered at the corner of her mouth. He dabbed it with his finger and slowly stroked it across her lips. Her tongue, small and pink, followed his finger.

Never losing his gaze, she found a wedge of peach and offered it to him. He bit deeply, savoring the squirt of rich juice in his mouth, the feel of soft, yielding flesh between his teeth.

She discovered a drop of liquid that had fallen to his chin, sluiced it onto her fingertip, and brought it to her mouth.

Oh dear God. He felt himself dissolving into the grass. At the same time, on fire for her, the need to make love with her searing through his body, he erupted from his chair.

His elbow hit a platter, knocking it to the ground. Rounds of saffron bread tumbled across the lawn.

And then all hell broke loose.

Chapter 7

Ducks, geese, and swans charged up the hill, webbed feet at a gallop, feathers flying. In a clamor of honks and squawks, they fell on the scattered bread like maurauding Huns. And when the rolls were demolished, the more brazen among them swept onto the chairs and table, bills clacking as they fought over morsels of ham and custard tarts.

Stunned, Kendal looked around for Celia and saw her fleeing in the direction of a copse of oaks, three belligerent swans at her heels. She screamed and dove into the trees, disappearing from his sight.

Caught up in the feeding frenzy, geese and ducks nibbled at his boots and trousers for crumbs. Surrounded, he could scarcely move without tromping on a wild-eyed bird.

"Shoo!" he shouted to no effect. "Dammit, *shoo!*"

Fighting his way to the table, he grabbed the bowl of fruit from under the bills of two rapacious geese and heaved it across the lawn. Some of the birds went chasing after the peaches, clearing his path. He broke free and ran in the direction Celia had gone, following the sound of her shrieks.

When he caught up with her, she was perched on a branch about six feet above the ground, flapping her skirts at the swans to hold them at bay.

"Get them *away* from me," she cried. "Oh please!"

He wrenched a clump of gorse from a thick bush and flailed at the swans, sending them off in regal high dudgeon.

Celia sank onto the branch in a heap, arms wrapped around the tree trunk, tears streaming down her cheeks. "Oh, thank heavens."

Kendal approached her gingerly. "It's safe now, my sweet. I promise."

Scared brown eyes searched the undergrowth for lurking swans. "Are you sure they're gone?"

"Absolutely. I'll wring the neck of the next bird that comes within a hundred yards." He held out his arms. "Can you jump down if I swear to catch you?"

"Y-yes." Slowly, she loosed her death grip on the tree and sat upright. Then, with a small sigh, she slid into his embrace.

He held her closely, feeling her heart pound against his chest as she clung to him. "They were only looking for food," he murmured. "They wouldn't have hurt you."

"Little *you* know," she said with a return of spirit, letting go of him and backing away. "I'd sooner take on Napoleon's army than any one of those monstrous beasts. They are too stupid to know the difference between food and people. And when they are hungry, they are *mean*."

"But now they are gone, Celia." He smiled. "Since we have battled an army of fowl together, may I be permitted to call you that? Feel free to smack me for the impertinence, if you are of a mind to strike out at someone. Or some*thing*."

"When you address me as Lady Greer," she replied with an answering smile, "I always hear 'Celia.' So yes, please let us not stand on ceremony. Mercy me. After my disgraceful cowardice, I wonder you have not flown off with the birds." Her smile sloped into a self-mocking grin. "I behaved like the veriest goose."

Lord, what a woman! he thought, laughing appreciatively. Were it possible for him to fall in love again, he would surely be head over heels for her.

As it was, he wondered if it would be the better for the both of them if he eased her politely back to London and left her alone to find her own wings. An empty-hearted man, a man such as he, would only anchor her to ground.

But as she gazed up at him from those hungry, heart-wrenching eyes, he lost all will to resist her. She wanted him, in an unfathomable way that was part lust and in larger part something beyond his comprehension.

"Let me show you something," he said, offering her his arm.

She took it immediately, leaning into his body as he led her onto the narrow path beside the river.

His private hideaway, where he used to spend long afternoons with a book and his own thoughts, lay only a few hundred yards from the White Swan. There was nothing special about it, he thought as they came into the clearing. Just a gnarled outcropping of roots against an ancient oak tree where he liked to sit in the shade, and yellow irises springing up in small bouquets, and the soft sound of water rippling over smooth pebbles. Dragonflies hovered in the air, as always. Bees swept past his ears. Small purple flowers huddled among the mosses.

This was as close to home as he ever came, this place of silence and quiet reflection. He glanced over at Celia, expecting to see disappointment on her face.

Her lips slightly open, she looked around her with a dazed expression. "How unutterably lovely," she whispered, letting go his arm to roam to river's edge, and to the boulder where he had sometimes stood to cast a line for trout, and then to the great oak tree. With a swish of muslin skirts, she sank onto the exact spot he had always favored.

Sunlight dappled her face through the leaves as she lifted her chin to the sky. "I could stay here forever," she said. "It sings of peace."

She had found words for what he felt every time he came here. What little peace he had ever found, he found in this place. But the very fact that she recognized that he was bringing her *here* sent shivers down his spine. The intimacy of their shared joy frightened him even more than the unwelcome emotions battering at his heart.

He knelt across from her, sitting back on his heels, determined to quash the maelstrom raging inside him. "Not to rouse unpleasant memories," he said, meaning to do exactly that, "but how is it a few impetuous birds sent you, quite literally, into the boughs?"

She took a deep breath and let it out again. "If you must

know," she said, flushing hotly, "I have a profound aversion to large p-poultry."

He bit back a laugh. "I had noticed. My youngest brother was once attacked by an ill-tempered stray he tried to befriend, and after that he could never abide dogs. Had you a similar experience when you were a child?"

"Much later. Greer kept chickens, you see. Hundreds of them, for scientific research. The farm and nearly all his time were given over to experiments with crossbreeding, and he produced scores of articles and pamphlets on the subject. It was his dream to be admitted to the Royal Society of London for Improving Natural Knowledge."

"Was he?"

"I'm afraid not, although he was highly regarded by those who shared his preoccupation. You may be certain that I was not among them." Her head tipped to one side. "I can tell you this much about chickens, sir. They are stupid, they stink, and they peck."

When she held out her hands, palms down, he leaned forward to see. A scatter of tiny white scars, nearly imperceptible, stretched from the tips of her fingers to several inches above her wrists. "Good God," he swore softly. How could Greer have permitted his wife anywhere near those brutally sharp beaks?

She must have been reading his mind. "Sometimes I was called on to feed them," she said, folding her hands in her lap. "Greer didn't trust the servants to provide adequate care, and he was so besotted with his pets that he never minded when they pecked him, which, of course, they did with enthusiasm. But it did not do for anyone to criticize their natural chickenly behavior, so I dared not protest when they took after me. You may be sure I kept as clear of them as possible, although it wasn't always. Possible, that is."

Her voice faded at the end, but she managed a gallant shrug.

He profoundly wished it weren't too late to grind Lord Greer into bite-sized morsels for his damnable chickens. "I well understand why you detest them," he said.

"And all their relations," she affirmed. "With the exception of songbirds, so long as they mind their manners and stay in their trees."

He silently applauded her attempt to lighten the conversation, but he wasn't quite ready to dismiss the subject. "Speaking of trees, however did you make the leap up to that branch where I found you?"

"I've no idea. Propelled there by sheer panic, I suppose. I wasn't even aware of where I was until you charged to my rescue." She smiled. "Did I ever thank you?"

"Since it was my fault the swans attacked in the first place, I can only be grateful you suffered no harm. But tell me, what became of Lord Greer's chickens after his death?"

"I didn't slaughter them, if that's what you are implying. But neither did I feel an obligation to honor his memory by providing them a home. Letters went out to his friends, announcing that the chickens would be given to anyone willing to carry them off."

She chuckled. "That, I can tell you, was a mistake of the first order. But I never expected such a response. Scores of gentlemen swooped in like locusts on the appointed day and promptly began to squabble over the prize specimens. Fistfights broke out in the barns, the chickens were squawking up a storm, and for once I was almost in sympathy with them. It was quite a scene, I promise you. But by nightfall every last one was gone, and good riddance to the lot!"

He stood. "You never fail to astonish me," he said, holding out his hands. She took hold of them and let him draw her to her feet. Then, gently, he brushed his lips across her scarred wrists, one by one. "I admire your courage, Celia Greer. It is unparalleled among the females of my acquaintance. And most of the men, for that matter, excepting those who fought on the Peninsula."

"You *admire* me?" she said with a gulp. "Truly? I thought you would be revolted to learn I had been living in a barnyard. Well, practically. And I'd never have told you, I vow, if not for those dratted swans."

"Then I must remember to thank them for loosing your tongue. You should not be ashamed of what you could not help, Celia."

"Oh, I'm not," she assured him. "But that doesn't mean I wish everyone and his brother to know of it."

"We diplomats are proficient at keeping secrets, my dear. Yours are perfectly safe with me."

She nodded, and as she did, her eyes went round as dinner plates. "Mercy me!" Snatching her hands away, she began to brush them frantically at her skirts.

Had she only just noticed the dirt and bits of tree bark? he wondered. Clambering up that oak had soiled her pretty yellow gown from bodice to ruffled hem, not to mention the jagged tear along her right hip.

"Oh, no," she wailed. "What have I done?"

"It's of no importance," he said dismissively. "Dresses are easily replaced."

"But I look like I've been dragged backward through a hedgerow!"

Her feminine outrage at not looking her best had been amusing, until he saw a tear gathering at the corner of her eye. It began to dawn on him that she was genuinely distressed. And since he had already decided that she was not in the least vain on her own account, it must be because she had wished to make a favorable impression on him.

She had certainly done so, in more ways than he was ready to admit. Scooping a handful of dirt from the ground, he smeared it over his driving coat and doeskin breeches as she watched in wide-eyed horror. "There. Now we are a matched set."

"I cannot believe you did that," she said in an awed voice. "Whatever were you thinking?"

"Very much what I've been thinking since the first time I saw you," he confessed. "And if you haven't guessed what that is, will you let me show you?"

When he opened his arms, she immediately flung herself into his embrace, welcoming his kiss with blazing fervor. Her small hands clutched at his waist, as if uncertain where to put themselves, and with a tiny gasp of surprise she opened her lips at his whispered instruction.

Had she not been married so many years, he thought at the edges of his disorderd mind, he might have taken her for an innocent. But no innocent would crave, as she so clearly did, everything he was ready to give her. None would kiss him back with such unbridled sensuality. Greer must have been a poor bedmate indeed for his enthusiastic young wife, so little had he taught her.

And then he forgot Greer, and everything else, captivated by the feel of her lithe body pressed against his. She tasted of peaches and champagne. Her earnest passion ignited him like dry tinder, and it was all he could do to stop himself from carrying her to the ground and making love to her on the riverbank.

But she deserved better than a wild tumble on the hard dirt, and he wanted more than the explosive culmination of his own urgent need to have her. Satin sheets and a long, slow afternoon of pleasure, he resolved, gently setting her at arm's distance.

A dazed look on her face, she regarded him uncertainly. "Have I done something wrong?" she asked. "Was I too f-forward?"

"Never that. You are perfect. Beyond perfect. It was I who nearly spoiled everything." He was breathing so heavily he could hardly speak. "Shall we go where we can be more comfortable, sweetness? Or am I rushing my fences with you?"

She scuffed the toe of her half boot in the dirt. "I'm not certain what you mean. That is, I have no experience in these matters. None whatever. Tell me what I am supposed to do."

"Tell me what you want to do, Celia. Tell me what you want."

"S-surely you know. I want *you*."

Alone in the bedchamber, Celia hurriedly scrubbed her face and hands and used a tortoiseshell brush she found on the dressing table to untangle her hair. Then, dampening the ends

65

of a towel, she tried to blot the worst of the grime from her dress. Since there was nothing to be done about the long tear in the skirt, she resolved to forget it was there.

It occurred to her that she might be expected to remove the dress altogether.

Had Kendal left her alone to strip off her clothes? Was she supposed to be waiting for him naked? On the bed? *In* the bed? Oh mercy.

She wandered over to the formidable Elizabethan tester bed atop its high pedestal, the posts and headboard ornately carved from dark mahogany, the crimson velvet canopy and counterpane fringed with gold. Lascivious, she thought. And downright intimidating.

How many other women had he brought to this room, made love to in this bed?

Well, that did not bear thinking of.

She wished he would hurry up. In his company, thinking was impossible. But as the minutes passed there was nothing else to do. And the more she thought, the more nervous she became.

She would disappoint him, of course. But perhaps he wouldn't mind too much. She'd already warned him what to expect, after all.

Ought she to close the curtains? Sunlight flooded the room, and she had the impression lovemaking was generally done in the dark. One by one, she pulled the heavy velvet curtains over the windows until the room was in total blackness. Not good. How would they even find each other? Selecting the window farthest from the bed, she adjusted the curtains until a wide shaft of light fell across the lush carpet. That was better.

Her clothes, she had decided, would stay where they were for now. Possibly he wished to remove them himself. Was she expected to perform that service for him, too?

This was all so mysterious. So *complicated*!

So very delicious.

Her toes curled inside her half boots. Today, her dream of a grand passion was coming true. She could scarcely believe her good fortune. The very man she had longed for all these years would soon take her in his arms and teach her what it was to be a woman.

Hugging herself, she whirled around in a little dance of joy.

And heard applause coming from the direction of the door.

Stumbling to a halt, she saw Kendal framed in the light from the passageway, watching her. He was smiling.

Mortified, Celia swept him a profound curtsy.

He had removed his coat, she saw, and untied his neckcloth. It hung in two swaths of white linen over his tan waistcoat. There were damp spots on his breeches where he had scoured the mud away. She thought he must surely be the handsomest man God ever created.

Still smiling, he stepped inside and closed the door. "You prefer the room to be dark, I take it."

"N-no. I thought perhaps it was supposed to be. Shall I open the curtains again?"

"I've a better idea." Draping his coat over the back of a chair, he went to the hearth and used the tinderbox to ignite a taper. There were a great many candles in the room, set in ornate silver braces on the side tables, and he lit them one by one until the room was bathed in a warm, honeyed light. Finally he crossed to the window and shut out the last bit of sunshine.

The bedchamber felt smaller now, Celia thought. More . . . intimate. Candlelight flickered over his face, highlighting his cheekbones and the strong line of his jaw. He looked overwhelmingly masculine. Infinitely desirable. Heat pooled in her breasts and at the base of her stomach.

He held out his arms, his hands open. "Come, Celia."

Oh, *yes*. Ceiling and walls and floor vanished. She floated into his embrace and anchored herself there, his confidence wrapping securely around her, banishing the last of her fears.

"You have bewitched me," he said softly, grazing the pad of his thumb down her cheek. "Will you cast a spell for both of us now, Celia? Will you give me all your magic?"

"I will give you all I am," she whispered. "Please kiss me."

Gently at first, and then with deep, demanding passion, he promised with his kisses everything that was to follow. She felt his hand at her waist, and felt it move down, sliding over her hip, drawing her closer. Mindless, boneless, she melted into his body, glad of his strength. Needing it. Needing *him*.

She heard him groan low in his throat when her hands began to skate over his back, up to his wide shoulders, along the hard muscles of his arms, shaping him as he shaped her.

Then he swept her into his arms and carried her to the bed. Lowering her onto the soft velvet, he lifted himself over her, his legs pressed to the sides of her legs, his weight resting on one elbow as he buried his face against her throat. She slipped her fingers through his hair, loving its softness.

Whatever she had imagined and hoped for from the lovers in her fantasies, he was so much more. Warm and powerfully male, he transformed illusion into hard flesh and warm blood.

His hands were at her back, undoing the buttons of her dress. And suddenly, vagrant misgivings skittered around in her head like gnats. She found herself wondering about his boots. And hers, although they would be more easily removed. She became two people, one lost in his kisses and murmured words, the other worrying about boots and chemises and breeches.

About bleeding all over this expensive red velvet counterpane.

There would be bleeding, she was reasonably sure. She'd read about it in a book.

His fingers tickling over her breasts scattered her capricious thoughts, but when he knelt to unbutton his waistcoat, they came rushing back again.

How long did this take? She wished it to last forever, which was impossible, and although it had scarcely begun, she began to dread the moment when it would be over. And would it hurt? She didn't care, but she wanted to know.

He must have sensed the questions turning somersaults in her head. Bending down, he brushed light, reassuring kisses on her cheek. "What's wrong, sweetness? Where have you gone?"

"I'm here," she said as he nibbled at her earlobe. "But . . . no. Never mind. I just—"

"Just what? Tell me, Celia. How can I please you?"

"Oh, you do. Wonderfully. But I was wanting to ask you the same question, you see." Once she began to speak, the floodgates opened. "And what about our boots? I'm afraid I'll ruin this bedspread. And I was wondering what is to happen next, and what after that."

He gazed at her in astonishment. "But there is nothing whatever to worry about. The boots will come off when we are ready. We are in no hurry, my sweet. And if it concerns you, I'll take care not to . . . that is, you need not fear any . . . consequences. As for the rest, you know what happens next."

"No," she said. "Not exactly."

His eyes clouded. "I don't understand."

"But I told you. I've never done this before."

Smiling, he flicked a tendril of hair from her forehead. "Yes, I remember. It's all right, you know. Indeed, you honor me. And dear heavens, how I want you. It's not too late, if you have changed your mind, but please tell me you haven't."

She raised a fingertip to his lips. "I want you so much I am dying for wanting you. But do you really hear what I am saying? *I have never done this before.* None of it. Not ever."

He froze, staring at her blankly.

She saw the moment when comprehension dawned. And then, with an oath, he flung himself off the bed.

"You're a virgin?" He jabbed a finger in her direction. "A bloody damned *virgin*?"

Sitting up, she wrapped her arms around her waist. "I thought you understood."

"How could I? It's unthinkable. Impossible! You were *married*!"

"Even s-so, it's the truth. I couldn't help it, I promise you." His fury washed over her in hot waves. "All I had to give you was myself. You said you wanted me. Why does this matter?"

"It . . . I . . . of *course* it matters. Do you think I'd have brought you here if I had the slightest clue what you were about? What you *are*?"

Before she could summon a reply, he had stormed to the door and slammed it behind him.

Chapter 8

Kendal, relieved to find the passageway empty, looked around for somewhere to be inconspicuous until his body and his temper calmed. But there were no cubbyholes where he could take refuge, and he dared not open any of the other bedchamber doors. Someone might be inside, doing what he had meant to do with Celia.

Retreating to the far end of the passageway, he stared at the nubby plaster and forced himself to breathe in a steady rhythm.

Anger. He'd not felt it like this—gut-wrenching and hot— since . . . no! He would not, he *must* not dredge up what he'd long since put behind him. What happened then had nothing to do with what was happening now.

He pressed his palms against the cool stone of the wall, pushing hard, expending the tension in his taut muscles.

How had he given Celia Greer the power to do this to him? From the first he'd sensed that she was trouble, but he had refused to heed the alarms that sounded each time he saw her. Or she had a way of silencing them, with her enticing smile and the purely female way she moved, graceful and seductive, altogether irresistible to any man with blood in his veins.

Worse, she was interesting. Unusual. She intrigued him. She slid inside him, into his thoughts, and he'd let her stay. He had enjoyed thinking about her, imagining how she would feel against his body. How she would taste and—

Hellfire! Whatever she was, she was not for him. His only problem now was how to return her to London, because damned if he'd drive her there himself. Another two hours pressed against her on the narrow bench of his curricle would undo him past recall.

Gradually, the raging anger and steaming lust seeped from his body, leaving him cold. Weary, too, and disillusioned, as if he'd run a long hard race only to lose at the wire.

Giving free rein to emotions did that to a man. He knew that from experience. The mystery was that he'd allowed it to happen to him again. Indeed, he had walked willingly into the trap, not to put too fine a point on it, because he thought himself impervious to the wiles of any scheming female. He had fancied himself a man rigidly in control of his passions, always measuring out his natural desires in careful doses.

Apparently not.

Already he was wildly tempted to go back and finish what he had started, even though he was the one who had put a stop to it. Rightly so, he told himself. Necessarily so. But for safety's sake, he had better take himself away from here—from *her*—with all possible speed.

He did not glance at the door to the bedchamber where he'd left Celia as he walked swiftly past it to the staircase. No doubt she wanted to see him as little as he wished to see her, although he could not leave the inn altogether until he'd made sure she was safely on her way back to London.

After a few words to John Belcher, who quickly dispatched his son to the nearest posthouse for a carriage, Kendal took a bottle of brandy and an empty glass to a table in the corner of the taproom.

The innkeeper, of course, knew very well that something had gone wrong. Even the scullery maid had heard the news by now. One by one, servants popped in and out of the taproom, manufacturing errands in order to steal a look at Lord Kendal in his shirtsleeves. He felt like the featured attraction at a raree show.

What was Celia doing now? he wondered before mentally kicking the thought away. But it bounced back again, and brought with it the knifing awareness that he could not leave her alone in that erotically charged bedchamber for the next hour.

At the least, he should send a maid to explain the arrangements he had made for her return to the city. And while she was in the room, the maid could retrieve his coat. Then he could be on his way without risk of a chance encounter with Celia. The idea was remarkably appealing.

But of course he would do no such thing.

Kendal drained the brandy glass and left the taproom, striding purposefully up the stairs.

There was unfinished business between them. He had stormed away like a tantrumish schoolboy without demanding the truth from her. She owed him an explanation, dammit, for what she had done.

A quick review of his own behavior confirmed that he had been perfectly straightforward, a man of the world doing what men of the world did when lovely widows signaled blatant interest in an affair. His conscience was clear. He had promised nothing, and when it came right down to it, he had never deliberately tried to seduce her. Without question, Celia Greer had been the aggressor. She had pursued him quite shamelessly.

His only fault was succumbing to the surprisingly intense pleasure he felt when she gazed at him with flagrant, flattering desire. And, too, he had sought her out in defiance of his long-standing rule against taking a personal interest in any female, especially one who showed signs of taking a personal interest in him.

Once he began listing his own mistakes, they mounted in alarming increments. But always, he was reasonably certain, he had only himself to answer to for what he'd said and done, and for what he had allowed himself to feel. At no point had he given Celia the slightest indication that he wanted more from her than a tumble between the sheets. One only, come to think of it. He'd made it perfectly clear that his duties would take him to Bath on the morrow, and to Vienna within a few weeks.

He realized that he had been standing in front of the bedchamber door for a considerable time, his land lifted to knock. Exhaling a harsh breath, he rapped lightly.

No response.

He tried again, and thought he heard a faint "Come in."

73

Dear God, what if she was curled up in a knot of feminine misery, weeping her heart out?

Well, what of it? That had been Belinda's favorite trick, until he finally realized she could cry at will. Once she understood that her bouts of weeping would avail her nothing, they stopped cold. Female tears were a weapon, no more than that.

But his hand was shaking as he opened the door, and he dreaded what he would see when he entered the room.

Whatever he had expected went up in smoke.

Celia, wearing her bonnet and gloves, was sitting on the window bench directly across from him. She had opened the heavy curtains, and sunlight poured over her still body through the leaded panes. She gazed at him from unreadable dark eyes, her usually vibrant face expressionless.

She might as well have been carved from ivory, he thought, instinctively watching for the subtle, telltale indications of mood and intention he had learned to recognize. Even the most experienced politician unconsciously revealed, with the set of his muscles or the throbbing of a vein, something of what he was thinking.

Not Celia. She remained, under his intense scrutiny, as remote and indecipherable as he was reputed to be.

He envied her. It was all he could do to keep his knees from buckling.

He resented her, too, for rendering him defensive. Unsure of himself. She didn't appear to notice that he was practically crumbling before her eyes. For a hundred other nameless reasons, he longed to cross the room and seize her by the shoulders and shake her until she raged at him, freeing him to vent his own surging rage on her.

Perversely, she simply looked at him with that steady, unnerving calm, as if nothing of consequence had passed between them. As if he were an insect that just crawled out from the woodwork.

"I have sent for a carriage to convey you to London," he said, hating the sound of his voice as each word clipped out.

"Thank you," she replied with unruffled politesse. "You will

74

wish to be on your way immediately, of course. There is no need to wait here on my account."

"Nevertheless, I shall remain until you are safely on your way."

"As you wish, sir."

The silence that followed her cool pronouncement roared in his ears.

"Have you nothing more to say to me?" he demanded, hands clenched behind his back.

Her head tilted slightly as she considered. "No. I can think of nothing. Except, thank you for paying for our lunch."

"Bloody hell, Celia! You know what I mean."

"Not really. I thought I did, until half an hour ago, but I was wrong." Her eyes clouded. "If you don't mind, I'd rather not try to guess what I am supposed to say or do to please you now. I'd only get it wrong."

"*Wrong* is pretending this is over until you explain why you lied to me."

One delicate brow lifted slightly. "Lied, sir? About what?"

"Not telling the whole truth is a lie," he shot back, knowing he sounded like a self-righteous prig.

She knew it, too, he could tell from the sardonic curl of her lips. "Oh. You are annoyed because I failed to draw you a map that even a blind man could follow. Forgive me. But I was always so conscious of my own inadequacies that it never occurred to me a man of experience would fail to recognize them. When did I give you any indication that I'd the least claim to sexual proficiency?"

"When you told me you had been married for nine years. When I saw you flirting with every randy young buck in London."

"That," she said with a dismissive gesture, "is an exaggeration. Surely I missed one or two young bucks, if only because there were so many of them hovering about."

Teeth gritted, he stomped across the room and wrenched his coat from the chair back where he'd draped it. With a clatter of wood on wood, the chair toppled to the floor.

"Make up your mind, Lord Kendal," she said too sweetly.

"Are you enraged because I am a wanton flirt, or because I have never been bedded?"

"In your case, the one does not rule out the other. Assuming you are the innocent you claim to be. I have no proof of that."

"You would have got ample proof, had you stayed the course. Or so I believe." Her voice quavered on the last few words. "I'm not altogether certain how a man knows, but Wilberta Wigglesworth assured me it is perfectly obvious."

He drove his arms into the sleeves of his coat. "You should have told me from the start."

"Were you not listening when I did? More than once I told you that I lacked experience. I cannot recall my exact words, but I promise you that it mortified me to say them."

"I—that is, you gave me the distinct impression you had been faithful to your husband, and that I was the first lover you had taken after his death. That much was clear, I agree."

"Never mind the randy London bucks, then?" she inquired equably.

Although he was standing in the middle of the room, he felt as if she had him pinned against the wall. It didn't help that the enormous pedestaled bed loomed as a stark reminder of the passion that had flared between them. Even now, loathing her and loathing himself even more, he wanted to fling her down on that bed and quench the fire blazing inside him.

"Let us come to the point," he said. "You prevaricated. Lack of experience does not equal absolute—" Unable to say the word, he waved a hand.

"Absolute what? *Virginity?* Pardon me, Lord Kendal, but at what moment during the little time we have spent together should I have addressed the subject? When we waltzed at Lady Jersey's ball? Over breakfast this morning? In your curricle this afternoon? While you sliced a peach and fed it to me beside the river?"

She stood, clutching her torn skirt with both hands. "Enlighten me, sir. Exactly when should I have announced, out of the blue, that I was a virgin? Perhaps when I was up in the tree. 'Oh, by the way, sir, I happen to be a virgin.' Or, better yet, when you were crouching in front of Lord Finlay's desk, loosing my hair from that nail. 'Thank you, sir, and did you know that you have just had the honor of rescuing a virgin?' "

"Enough!" He slapped his hand against his forehead. "Blast it, I had every right to presume you to be . . . what I thought you were. How could any man wed to you for nine years keep his hands off you, for pity's sake? Can you blame me for finding it unimaginable? And if it were true—"

"Oh, it is."

"Then why the devil did you stay with him?"

"What choice did I have? We took vows in a church, before God and witnesses." She came directly up to him, color hectic in her cheeks. "Little you know of it, damn your eyes. Greer understood that I wanted children. He promised to give them to me. And to his credit, he tried. Only after I persisted, it's true, but eventually he came to my bed every Saturday night and made an effort to do his duty. But he could not."

She poked him in the chest with a hard finger. "I don't know why, and all I can bear to remember of those horrid gropings is *nothing*. After a few months we both gave it up with profound relief."

Shame nosed up his spine. He should have deduced the truth, or suspected it when he learned that she had been sold off to an old man. And yet he could not let go the idea she was somehow at fault. "Impotence is clear grounds for annulment," he said. "You could have been rid of Greer with ease."

She looked startled for a moment. Then her eyes went hard. "In the first place, I didn't know that. In the second, however does one prove such a claim? And in the third, I had no money to hire a solicitor. Do not judge me by your lordly standards, sir. When you want something—justice, for instance, or the freedom to go where you will—you have the means to acquire it."

"You were not a prisoner, surely. And I cannot credit that a woman of your intelligence and spirit endured an intolerable marriage for nearly a decade without contriving some means of escape. Or was it the legacy, madam? He was an elderly man when you married him. Did you stay for the money, resolved to hold out until Greer cocked up his toes?"

She regarded him with immeasurable contempt. "You know nothing, sir. *Nothing!*"

"Then tell me what I am failing to understand. I have asked for no more than the truth."

"On the contrary. You have been too busy inventing falsehoods about me to heed a word I have said. I'll not try to defend my actions or my honor to the likes of you, Lord Kendal. But if you genuinely wish to understand what happened here today, the truth is amazingly transparent. You simply failed to get what you wanted. And in my experience, men cannot bear to be thwarted. They invariably lose their tempers and cast about for someone to blame, or to punish. It's all one and the same."

Not invariably, he thought, clenching his fists. He could not recall a single time in his thirty-four years that he had lost his temper in such a fashion, however great the provocation. He could not accept that he had done so today, with her, never mind that it was patently obvious he'd abandoned every shred of hard-won control in the last few minutes. But why? He had to know *why*.

She wasn't finished raking him through the coals. "You expected what you always expect from an affair—a pleasant interlude to be enjoyed at your convenience. Above all things, it must be played by your rules. No surprises. No entanglements. No *complications*. Believe it or not, sir, I accepted those terms unconditionally."

"So you say. But you did *not* play by any rules of fairness. You must have known that I would never bed an innocent without accepting—in advance—the inevitable consequences."

"And what are those, pray tell? Do virgins expect you to marry them when the deed is done? Well, rubbish. You were simply afraid that your afternoon of inconsequential pleasure might become—oh, the horror of it!—*personal*. But you'd nothing whatever to worry about. You may be sure that the last thing on earth I want for myself is another marriage to a self-absorbed despot who wouldn't recognize a genuine human feeling if it bashed him on the skull. I wonder now that I ever wanted you, for even the few hours we had agreed to share.

Please do me one kindness, sir. Go away, now, before either of us says anything else we might regret."

Although she was standing within arm's reach, he felt as if he were gazing at her across an enormous chasm, separated by her secrets, and his, and the aftermath of disaster. Unfamiliar emotions hammered at him like a storm in the desert—fascination, respect, desire, anger, an inexplicable longing to begin again with her, an absolute terror of spending one more minute with her—oh damn! He could not absorb it all. Not now.

When the storm had passed, he knew, all this would be consigned to oblivion. He was, if nothing else, a master at forgetting what he could not bear to remember.

"As you wish, Lady Greer." He bowed and turned for the door. But when he reached it, he could not help but look back at her.

Like a long-stemmed rose, straight and proud and impossibly beautiful, she waited with awful dignity for him to be gone.

I'm sorry, he wanted to say. There were a thousand things he wanted to say. But without a word, he raised the latch and left the room.

Chapter 9

It was barely seven of the morning, already promising to be a sunny day, when Thomas Carver arrived with the hired carriage. He nearly overran Celia as he steered the horses into the inn courtyard. Face red, he tossed the reins to a stable boy and jumped to the ground.

"Clumsy of me," he apologized with a bow. "And the landau has seen better times, I'm afraid. It was the best of the lot, though, and the nags have some spirit to them."

"They will do very well indeed," she assured him. "Was there no driver to be had?"

"I didn't like the looks of him, ma'am. A drinker, I warrant from the stink of his breath. I'm no whipster, but better me than a woozy sot."

Smiling, she stepped into the carriage. "I know we've a long journey, Thomas, but I wish to make a stop along the way. We'll be turning off about a mile past Sedgwick."

"Yes, ma'am." He jumped to the driver's bench and steered the pair of roans from the courtyard at a brisk trot.

It was pleasantly cool for late July. Celia had all but suffocated in the postchaise during the long trip north, and wasn't looking forward to another seventy miles round-trip in any vehicle, even an open one like the landau. Removing her bonnet, she sat back on the cracked leather padding and let the dew-damp breeze sift through her hair.

Thank heavens for Thomas, she thought. What would she have done without him these last few days? She might almost feel guilty about stealing him away from the Finlays, except that they could easily replace a footman and she badly needed him. Indeed, Lord Finlay had insisted she take a reliable servant with her, although he'd doubtless expected that servant to come back again.

But when Thomas saw the Lake Country, it was love at first sight. Or so he maintained, although Celia suspected he was merely reluctant to leave her there on her own. And it was only fitting, she supposed, that he be present at the conclusion of her ill-fated adventure, since he had stood her friend at the beginning of it. When she set up her new household, assuming he chose to remain in her service and despite the fact that he was only three-and-twenty, she meant to appoint him butler.

The trouble with long carriage rides, she decided within a few minutes, was that they gave one too much time to think. In the postchaise, her last encounter with Lord Kendal had replayed in her mind again and again, so vividly she might as well have been reliving it.

For the first two days, encased in a protective mantle of icy calm, she analyzed with remarkable detachment everything he had said and done, and dissected her own behavior with equally sharp scrutiny. At the end, with faults and mistakes abounding on both sides, she acknowledged that she'd only herself to blame.

Lord Kendal had always been leagues beyond her reach. It was she who risked a flight to the sun, and like Icarus, she had been tossed unceremoniously back to earth. All the same, heart-bruised, humiliated and scorned, she could not regret having seized her one forlorn chance to have him.

For Kendal, of course, she had been no more than a pleasant diversion. He never pretended otherwise, and could not have known that she'd fixed on him as the center of all her hopes and dreams. Her sole consolation was that he would never know.

She had fled London the very next morning. Fortunately, Lady Marjory was in Maidstone with her sister, and Lord Finlay too preoccupied with matters of state to question the hasty departure of a houseguest. He had accepted her story about a sick friend with distracted sympathy, helped her arrange for a coach and driver, and sent her on her way.

It was bitter irony that she knew no place to go except where she had lived before, even though it lay within a few miles of Kendal's estate and close by a town that bore the same name as his title. But while she was returning with her tail between her legs, she had no intention of hiding out forever. She had enjoyed her few weeks in London and meant to go back, perhaps as early as the next Season. She would lease a house, launch herself into fashion, and host an extravagant ball. If he were very lucky, Lord Kendal might receive a coveted invitation.

With such thoughts, she endured the first part of her journey home.

And then, on the morning of the third day, the shell of ice that had held her together broke apart and she began to weep. Great racking sobs they were, leading Thomas to descend from his place beside the postchaise driver and hesitantly inquire if she was ill. She sent him back again, pleading a summer cold, and faked coughing and sneezing to cover the sounds of her distress and explain her swollen eyes.

She had cried all the way from Warwick to Manchester, where they stopped for the night, and she cried all the next day, too.

The death of a dream must surely be mourned.

But when they drew up at a comfortable inn not far from the town of Kendal, the tears abruptly ceased. Exhausted, she had welcomed the kind attentions of the proprietor and his wife, who settled her in a spacious room overlooking the River Kent and fed her hot soup and mulled wine. For the first time since leaving London, she slept dreamlessly and awoke the next morning with a trace of optimism bubbling in her veins.

She would make a new life for herself, she resolved over a substantial breakfast. She had done it before, and she could do it again. No more schoolgirl fantasies about grand passions and unattainable men, thank you. It was past time she came to terms with the real world.

In company with Thomas, she had made plans for her

immediate future, arranging to stay in residence at the Merry Goosegirl while they were put into action. The previous day she'd employed an agent to find a suitable house for her in the area of Windemere Lake. And today, she was on her way to lay one ghost to rest and seek advice about the other spirit that continued to hover, despite her every effort to banish him, in the vicinity of her heart.

Celia snapped open her parasol and forced herself to concentrate on the road. They were near the turnoff to Greer's farm, a narrow byway on the left side marked only by a weathered plank nailed to a tree.

When she spotted it, she poked Thomas on the shoulder. He drew up immediately.

"I'll walk from here," she said. "Chances are the track is overgrown by now, but follow me as far as you can and find a place in the shade to wait. I won't be gone more than an hour."

Thomas frowned, clearly disliking her plan. He reminded her to don her bonnet against the morning sun and helped her alight, muttering under his breath. She felt his gaze against her back until the rutty road took a sharp curve.

Celia followed its twists and turns for half a mile. Then she veered off, clambering over a stile that led to a hilly pasture spotted with grazing sheep. At the far end, she knew, was a promontory overlooking the farm.

When she reached it, somewhat breathless, she could barely force herself to look down at the prison where she had been all but enslaved for nine years. Since the day after giving Greer's chickens away, when she left to take up residence with the Wigglesworth sisters, she had not set foot there. Two of the servants agreed to stay on as caretakers in exchange for an exorbitant bribe, which she was happy to pay. At the time even the effort of disposing of the property had been too much to bear. She'd wanted nothing more to do with it, not ever.

Dropping cross-legged onto the thick grass, she gazed at the lovely valley nestled in a fold of hills. Directly below her, the farm spread out in a careless disarray of Lakeland-stone buildings. The house itself was squat and ugly, redeemed only by a flourishing vegetable garden at the back. Wisps of smoke wafted from the kitchen chimney, indicating—to her surprise—that the caretakers were still in residence. She had rather expected them to take the money and flee.

Spreading out from the house like spokes on a wagon wheel were the low buildings that had housed Greer's chickens. Simply looking at them conjured up the sound of their interminable clucking and their pervasive, stomach-turning stench.

She wrapped her arms around her knees, staring with intense loathing at the farm. Kendal could not begin to understand what it had been like. She had scarcely believed it herself, once she discovered what a ghastly mistake she had made.

But when she accepted Greer's offer, she could not imagine a more intolerable existence than the one in her father's house. She despised the ill-tempered brute who had driven her shadowy mother to an early grave, and he despised her in equal measure because she refused to cower under his fist. Any fate, she had thought when he proposed an arranged marriage, would be better than the misery of living with him.

Even her first meeting with Greer, shocking as it had been, failed to deter her. Three times her age, skinny, spindle-legged, and sparse of hair, he was the antithesis of all her girlish dreams. But unlike her father, who always shouted, Lord Greer was soft-spoken. And when she rallied the courage to ask what she might expect from their marriage, he did not slap her for being impertinent. Instead, she had the altogether novel experience of being asked about her own wishes.

That was probably the moment she put aside her revulsion at his appearance and resolved to accept him.

Yes, she would have the running of his household, he had replied. She would, in fact, be wholly responsible for seeing to it that his daily instructions were carried out. And yes, she would be Lady Greer. It sounded so glamorous to her then. *Lady Greer,* not raggedy Celia Stoke, the town bully's daughter.

When she asked about children, though, his lips compressed into a narrow slash of white. His first two wives had been barren, she knew from her father's report, and she had assumed

Greer was sniffing after a young bride in order to get an heir on her. Why else would he marry again?

And dear God, she had wanted children. A lifetime of love was stored near to bursting inside her, waiting to be poured out on them.

With startling reluctance, he professed himself willing to oblige her in the matter of children—so long as she kept them well away from his scientific experiments. At first mention of his vocation, Greer's eyes came alight. He sat straighter on the chair as he boasted of the papers he had published and the remarkable new hybrids he had engineered.

Caught up in his excitement, she imagined herself working side by side with him, engineering hybrids. Whatever they were. She had no idea.

Finally, he pulled a folded sheet of paper from his pocket and read the litany of his own expectations. She was hardly listening by then, lost in a fantasy wherein the fashionable Lady Greer wafted from the nursery, where her precious babes lay sleeping, to her husband's laboratory, where she instantly found the key to his knottiest scientific problem, and on to play hostess to the local gentry at an elegant ball.

She was far too young and inexperienced to sense the rod of iron in that stooped back, or understand the significance of his long list of wifely duties, or recognize his maniacal zeal to be celebrated for his scientific achievements.

He had been a way out, and she had leapt at it. How bad could it be, after all, a marriage of convenience to a kindly old gentleman?

Very bad indeed, she quickly discovered.

Greer didn't, in fact, want a wife at all. He had set out to purchase a household drudge, one who could not up and quit like all the others. Figuring a marriage settlement would be cheaper in the long run, and legally binding on his unfortunate spouse, he struck what was for him a very good deal.

For Celia, it had amounted to indentured servitude.

Leaving the farm without permission was expressly forbidden, and permission was rarely granted. Nor had she time, what with the schedule of duties Greer handed her every morning over breakfast. Her days were spent preparing meals and cleaning up after them, scrubbing floors and laundering sheets. The few servants willing to settle for Greer's cheese-paring wages were lazy and insolent. She soon learned that any attempt on her part to prod them to actual work sent them packing, and a little begrudging help was better than no help at all.

When he put her to feeding the chickens and cleaning cages, she was at the point of despair. By then, knowing her hope of bearing children would never be fulfilled, she had nothing whatever to look forward to. She had wished him dead. She had wished *herself* dead.

A dragonfly hovered near her cheek, the faint whir of its transparent wings recalling her to the present moment.

How long had she been here? Her watch was in her reticule, which she had left in the landau. But no matter. Thomas Carver would simply have to wait for her. She could not leave until every last demon had been exorcised.

She needed to move, though. Rising, she shook out her cramped muscles and began to walk along the top of the hill. Sheep trundled out of her way as she passed, placidly turning their attention to a new patch of grass.

If nothing else, she thought, Greer had taught her the meaning of endurance. However much she longed to pack her few belongings and steal away one moonless night, to do so would have been to cast her integrity in the dust. Better to live with Greer than be unable to live with herself.

On the first anniversary of her disastrous marriage, which went unmarked except in her memory, she made up her mind to stay the course. She'd elected to shackle herself to this awful man, and somehow she must learn to deal with the horrifying consequences.

To begin with, her own attitude required mending. Her constant mood of sullen resentment only fueled her misery, and it was past time she stopped wallowing in self-pity.

In a hundred ways, she could be smarter than she had been.

Now that she had become familiar with Greer's peculiarities, it would not be all that difficult to winkle a few pleasures for herself.

Above all things, she longed for books. Not the ponderous scientific tomes in Greer's library, which he would not permit her to touch in any case, but stories of unfailing heroism and undying love. The next day, she began to scrimp on the meager funds allowed for running the household. Fortunately, Greer never cared what he ate, nor did he take notice of threadbare linens, or tallow candles instead of wax in the rooms he rarely visited.

Within two months she was able to purchase a tattered volume of Shakespeare's plays at a stall in the Kendal market, where she was occasionally permitted to shop for "female items." He even gave her a quarterly allowance—two shillings—although it clearly pained him to part with so vast a sum.

Over the years, book by book, she scraped together a tidy little collection. She also won permission to ride one of the sluggish carriage horses every afternoon for half an hour, and when Greer was particularly pleased with the results of one of his experiments, he could be persuaded to frank her letters. With no one to talk to, she had sought friends by correspondence, writing to people she read about in the newspaper. A handful, Dorothy Wordsworth among them, actually responded.

Always, she performed the tasks Greer assigned her without complaint, giving him no cause to withhold the few privileges she had been granted after she learned when and how to approach him with her requests. So long as it cost him no money or effort, he liked making a show of generosity.

For the most part, though, she lived in a world of her own creation, built from the stories she read voraciously in her tiny bedchamber at night. Come dawn, she transformed herself into Helen of Troy, or Isolde, or Guinevere. While the real Celia cooked and cleaned, Roland defended her honor in mortal combat. Lancelot stole into her bed.

And then, on a sunny Saturday morning in Kendal, she saw

a man emerge from the parish church and cast a radiant smile upon his gloriously beautiful bride.

Something inexplicable struck her to the heart at that moment. Standing there with her basket of turnips, she felt the earth begin to spin wildly under her feet. She'd had to grab hold of a lamp-post to keep from flying off the planet, and was still clinging to it long minutes after the wedding party drove off.

From that day nothing was the same. Once seen, he was unforgettable. And while she never consciously intended to draw his image into her fantasies, every one of her heroes began to wear his face.

Worse, she found herself burning for one real experience to make her feel alive. She had gone from child to wife without knowing what it was to be a woman, and was to continue in ignorance for many more long years. But now she had a goal. If ever given the chance, she meant to have for herself a soul-stirring love affair to match the ones she lived in her imagination.

Celia realized that she had come to a stop near an outcropping of limestone. Her Crying Rock. Mercy, this was the last place she had meant to come today.

When even her imagination failed her, when her spirits were at their lowest ebb, she used to climb up here in the middle of the night and sit for hours, tears streaming down her face, trying to pray. She had always believed in a loving God, but sometimes thought He had forgot all about creating her. And when she gazed up at the stars, she could scarcely blame Him. What was she, after all, in the vastness of His universe?

At dawn, feeling more alone than ever, she had stumbled back to the farm and raked the coals of the kitchen fire. Another day, just like the one that preceded it and the one to follow, must be got through as best she could.

But at long last, she reminded herself, a few of her desperate prayers had been answered. A lowly speck of creation ought not be too greedy. She had even been granted a fleeting rendezvous with the man of her dreams, although she suspected that was only because the Lord understood she could not let him go until Kendal had firmly rejected her, in person and without a backward glance. When she could manage it, she would be grateful.

Meantime, she was here to reject Greer and put him behind her once and for all. She had honored every one of her vows, save the one about loving her husband, and had surely earned the right to be free of him.

But he'd not let her go. Even what he had *not* done came back to hurt her. She was still a virgin, and it seemed likely she would always be.

Perhaps, if she'd not seen Lord Kendal her very first night in London, she would have found another man to slake her urgent, unnameable longings. But she did see him. Her brief taste of him had spoiled her for anyone else. And she might have had him, too, if not for her husband's inadequacies.

"Damn you, Greer," she swore aloud. "You have done your worst. From this day forward, I refuse to give you power to hurt me."

A ewe nudged at her skirt, as if concerned for her. She stroked its woolly head, a smile curving her lips. Sheep had little appreciation for melodrama. "I'm all done now," she said, receiving a calm baa in reply as the ewe wandered off.

Celia made her way back to the road where Thomas was waiting, feeling a heavy burden lifting from her shoulders. She would sell the farm as soon as possible, severing the last ties with her former life.

Onward to the future, she told herself. Well, after one last visit to her past, because Lord Kendal was not so easily dispatched as her late, unlamented husband.

But she'd rid herself of him, too, perhaps within a few hours.

Thomas looked distinctly unhappy when she hove into view, skirts stained with grass and her bonnet askew. "I thought you'd gone lost," he said, assisting her into the landau.

"On my own farm? I was merely looking the place over, deciding what repairs to make before putting it up for sale." She located her watch and gasped to see the time. "Mercy me,

Thomas. I never meant to be gone so long. Can you get us all the way to Giggleswick in time for luncheon? The Wigglesworth sisters are expecting me."

Chapter 10

Nestled in the shade of two great chestnut trees, the lovely old graystone house conjured memories of the happiest year of her life. A lump in her throat, Celia took Thomas's hand and stepped from the landau, her gaze roaming from Wilfreda's hand-laced curtains billowing at the open windows to Wilberta's beloved flower garden. The heady scent of roses perfumed the air.

Her foot had scarcely touched ground when the door flew open and Bertie charged out, arms open in welcome. A few paces behind her, leaning heavily on her cane, Freda made her slow way along the gravel path, her wrinkled face wreathed in a smile.

"About time you got here," Bertie scolded, drawing Celia into a breathtaking hug. "We had just decided that we had got our days mixed up, and that you were meant to come tomorrow."

"Your letter said Friday," Freda put in, looking a bit confused. "This *is* Friday, isn't it?"

"Yes indeed," Celia assured her, turning to plant a kiss on her papery cheek. "I am very late, and it's all my fault. Bertie, will you direct Thomas to an establishment where he can see to the horses and have himself a good meal?"

"The Ribble Inn will be best, I think. Do you like salmon, young man?"

While Bertie spoke with Thomas, Celia took Freda's frail arm and assisted her into the house. Other memories flooded back as she stepped into the small foyer. There was the polished staircase she had ascended and descended with a book atop her head until Bertie pronounced her posture satisfactory. *A javelin in your spine, my girl, a javelin!* And there, the long passageway where she had practiced her gliding. *Smoothly. Smoothly. Ladies do not tromp about like common field hands.*

A plump ginger-colored cat ambled from the drawing room and twined around her ankles, purring huskily. She bent to scratch him behind the ears. "Hullo, Mincemeat. Have you missed me?"

"We all have, my dear," Freda said as a pair of identical white cats joined them, tails swishing languidly. "Pudding and Syllabub have been watching out the window all morning for you."

Watching for birds, more like, Celia thought, although they greeted her prettily enough. Stone-deaf and exceedingly spoiled, they wandered off in search of better entertainment the moment she stopped petting them.

Celia placed her reticule on a pier table and untied the ribbons of her bonnet. "I hope you haven't gone to a great deal of trouble, Freda. It was rude of me to descend on such short notice, but I was so longing to see you."

"None of that!" Bertie swept through the door and took the bonnet from her hand. "This is your home. I expect you'll want to freshen up, so take yourself upstairs while I help Mrs. Twill put the finishing touches on our luncheon. She has prepared all your favorites."

A few minutes later Celia joined Freda and Bertie in the small dining room. They had brought out their best china, and the elaborately ornamental silverware was polished to a blinding sheen. One of Freda's embroidered cloths, neatly ironed, graced the small cherrywood table, and the napkins had been folded into the shape of a peacock's tail.

Mrs. Twill bustled in from the kitchen with a tureen of beef barley soup, lingering until Celia had tasted it and rewarded her with a smile. Acknowledged as the finest cook in Giggleswick for the past several decades, Mrs. Twill disdained compliments, considering them redundant.

The visit to Greer's farm had dampened Celia's appetite. She sampled every dish, and there were a great many of them, but was relieved when Mrs. Twill finally retired to her kitchen and she need no longer pretend to eat. Moreover, although they were far too polite to say so, Bertie and Freda were eagerly awaiting an account of her London debut.

Celia put down her fork and began to dish up every snippet of gossip she could recall. Eyes gleaming, the ladies leaned forward in their chairs as she described Marshal Blücher galloping through a mazurka, the wall-eyed Prussian king weighed down with all his medals, and the thousands of common citizens who milled around the Pulteney Hotel day and night in hopes of catching the merest glimpse of Czar Alexander.

She told them about the Ascot races, and the Sunday-afternoon procession in Hyde Park, and the *bal masqué* at Burlington House where she had gone costumed as a shepherdess, only to find scores of shepherdesses in attendance. Fortunately, only one of them had brought an actual sheep, which was soon hustled off to the mews.

She spoke of banquets and balls, routs and musicales, and the scandalous new waltz. Bertie and Freda listened avidly, nodding and smiling, their own forks long since set aside. But as one story followed another, Celia was put in mind of Lord Kendal entertaining her in similar fashion as they drove together to the White Swan. Mercy, would not the man leave her in peace!

"Did you meet the king?" Freda asked in a trembling voice when Celia paused to sip from her water glass.

Bertie shot Celia a meaningful look, and she remembered that Freda had not been informed of the king's madness. It would have overset her to learn of it.

"I believe he remained in residence at Windsor during the victory celebrations," Celia replied. "After all, *someone* had to see to the running of the country, and His Majesty has ever been a dutiful sovereign."

"So he has," Freda affirmed. "So he has. I do wish you had been presented to him, though. He spoke very kindly to me when I made my curtsy not so long ago."

Celia and Bertie exchanged smiles. Freda's recollections of her London Season were gilded by time, wishful thinking, and her own uncertain memory.

After lunch, the ladies withdrew to the parlor for another round of stories. With Mincemeat curled on her lap, purring blissfully, Celia gave a highly censored version of her own minor successes among the beau monde. Above all things, the Wigglesworth sisters longed for assurance that their protégée had made a great splash in society, so she told them what they wanted to hear.

She had become rather adept at skating around the truth, Celia realized with some degree of pride. Not once had she mentioned Lord Kendal, although he had been at the center of every significant moment of her London adventure.

It was not long before Freda's eyes drifted shut and her chin sank onto her lace-edged fichu. Soon a gentle snore vibrated in chorus with Mincemeat's rumbling purr.

Bertie rose. "I have promised the vicar to send a bouquet of roses over to the rectory," she whispered. "Let us continue our visit in the garden."

Freda popped awake with a loud snort. "Visit? But whom are we to visit, Wilberta? I am not properly dressed to pay a call."

"Never mind, my love," Bertie soothed. "It's not until tomorrow. We'll have plenty of time to select our gowns."

Within seconds Freda had dozed off again.

"My sister is not in good health," Bertie confided as they emerged from the garden shed, where they had stopped to procure clippers and a large open-weave basket. "Dr. Ramp has warned me to prepare for a sad day within the year. Poor, gentle Freda. How I shall go on without her, I cannot imagine."

"Surely something can be done," Celia protested. "Another doctor, perhaps, or a change of air . . . ?"

"It is her heart, Celia. And her constitution has always been weak, you know. Our one season all but brought her down, and I never dared permit another. It is a credit to her indomitable spirit that she has gone on so well these many years. She'll wish to die in this house, where she was born, and I shall hold her when she breathes her last. But let us turn the subject before I become weepy."

"Yes, in a moment, but first I must know about your own health."

Bertie selected a lush white rose and snipped the stem. "I'm hale as a draft horse, glory be, and mean to see more of the world before I stick my spoon in the wall. At the very least, I shall bid farewell to Giggleswick when Freda has passed into heaven. Too many memories, you understand. A surfeit of memories never fails to clog one's mind."

How very true, Celia reflected. "Perhaps you'll move into my new house, which would delight me enormously. Mind you, I've not yet decided where to put down roots. What think you of Bowness?"

"You don't mean to return to London?" Bertie frowned. "But you have had your heart set on London since you were a child. Was it such a trying experience, my dear?"

"Mercy me, quite the contrary. I enjoyed myself immensely. Were you not listening for the past two hours?"

"Oh, indeed. But what you failed to say spoke even more pointedly." With a sigh, Bertie placed a rose in the basket. "Forgive me, Celia. I'm an old busybody. One whiff of a secret and I cannot help but snoop it out like a pig nosing for truffles."

Celia brushed her finger over the furry petals of the rose. "You are right, of course. Something did happen, and I wish to tell you about it. But I fear you will be terribly shocked."

"I very much doubt it. Freda is the one pulls out her hartshorn at the slightest hint of scandalbroth. Did you embroil yourself in a scandal, Celia?"

"Not precisely." She dug the toe of her half boot into the gravel. "I threw myself at a gentleman, and he threw me back. It seems I was too small a fish for his supper."

"Mmm."

When Bertie moved to the next rosebush without further comment, Celia stomped after her. This was Kendal's trick, leaving a silence to be filled. "Is that all you have to say? *Mmm?* It was probably the most devastating experience of my entire life."

"More so than accepting Greer?" Bertie lifted a brow. "That *does* shock me. In any event, I cannot help but dislike a man who fails to recognize a diamond when it drops into his hands. Or flings itself there, as you say that you did."

"Oh, it's quite true. Sometimes foolishly, more often shamelessly, I did everything possible to secure his attention. But it was not simply because he is remarkably handsome and uncommonly charming. As it happens, I had seen him before, many years ago. And when I did, something extraordinary happened."

She nibbled at the inside of her lower lip, casting about for words to describe the experience. "It was as if the ground dropped from under my feet, Bertie. Or perhaps I went airborne. And all the while I felt . . . well, as if my whole body, hair to toenails, had gone on fire. The sensation was quite overwhelming."

"Mmm."

Easy for *her* to say, Celia thought dourly. "In any case, by the time I came back to earth, he was gone. And later I realized that my odd flight of fancy was propelled by an explosion of envy. It put me forcibly in mind of my own woeful marriage to Greer, the sight of so splendid a gentleman gazing with unconcealed love at his new bride."

Bertie dropped the clippers and spun around. "Never tell me you have been speaking all this time of a married man! Oh, my. I am severely disappointed in you, Celia. An affair between two individuals free to indulge their passions is one thing, but adultery quite another."

Celia took a step backward, nearly falling over a low hedge. "Mercy, no! The gentleman is a widower now. Some three or four years after the wedding, his wife died of a fever. I read a notice of it in the newspaper."

With a stricken look, Bertie held out her hands. "Oh, my dear, I beg your pardon. It was inexcusable of me to leap to so absurd a conclusion."

Smiling, Celia picked up the clippers. "Clearly I have been a bad influence on you, Wilberta Wigglesworth. Impulsive leaps have always been *my* specialty. And the misunderstanding is purely my fault, for giving you this tale in so disordered a fashion."

When the light had returned to Bertie's eyes, Celia handed her the clippers. "I am terribly confused, you see. I had hoped that speaking of what happened would help me regain some bit of perspective. Not that I ever had the least particle of it before, to be sure. But since this is my day for banishing ghosts, I should like to tell you the rest."

Some of it, anyway, Celia reflected as Bertie nodded and moved on to the next rosebush. She would take to her grave the secret of her romantic fantasies about Lord Kendal, which would only sound ridiculous if spoken aloud.

She watched Mincemeat pad to the shade of a chestnut tree, belly rounded with the leftovers from lunch Mrs. Twill must have served him, and settle down to groom himself. Life was so simple for a lazy house cat—eat, sleep, and be made much of. Mincemeat probably wouldn't recognize a mouse if it bit him on the nose.

"Go on, child," Bertie urged softly.

"I was trying to remember where I'd left off. But no matter. Onward to London, where by sheerest chance, I encountered the gentleman in question the very first day I arrived. It was, I imagined at the time, a sign from heaven." Aware that her cheeks were flaming, Celia was glad that Bertie had gone back to clipping roses. "Pray don't ask me to explain what happened next, but it was the second most mortifying experience of my life. Suffice it to say I made a cake of myself."

"Well, I daresay you did not permit one setback to deter you."

"I'm afraid not. On any number of occasions I spotted him at a social event, but he was careful to keep his distance. And when I pursued him, he always managed to evade me."

Bertie turned to place a handful of roses in the basket. "You finally chased him down, I presume?"

"Not exactly. You recall that Lady Marjory had invited me to stay with her if ever I visited London? Poor thing. I doubt she even remembered knowing my mother at school, and greatly hoped I would never show up. In any event, unaware that the gentleman and I had already met under somewhat unusual circumstances, she presented me to him. Lord Ke— the gentleman, that is, must have felt obliged to ask me to

97

dance. And a few days later he invited me to join him for a drive in the country."

"I see."

"Do you? It came as a great surprise to me. Naturally I leapt at the chance to be with him, and—oh, mercy. How can I explain the rest?" Celia glanced over at Mincemeat, now snoozing blissfully on his back with all four paws in the air. "I w-wanted him," she confessed. "To be precise, I wished—"

"To have him in your bed," Bertie said succinctly. "You needn't be ashamed to say so, at least to me. It is perfectly natural, my dear, and in my opinion, very wise of you. What better way to purge your revolting memories of Lord Greer?"

"Is that what I was trying to do?" Celia's fingers tightened on the straw basket. Bertie knew of Greer's inability to consummate the marriage, of course. Celia had blurted the tale one evening after too many helpings of elderberry wine. "Well, perhaps you are right," she said. "Whatever the reason, I assuredly went to London in search of a glorious love affair. And for a few hours, Bertie, I thought I'd found it. But when he discovered I was not the worldly woman I pretended to be, he threw me off in a flash."

Bertie turned, a militant glint in her eyes. "After making love to you? The cad! Was he resentful to find that he had broached a virgin?"

"He was not to blame, you know. And besides, things had not progressed to the point of . . . broaching when I told him precisely what to expect. Well, I might as well have told him I was a leper. Next I knew, he had charged out of the room.

"I'd no idea what to do, so I sat down and waited for something to happen. It was probably no more than half an hour before he came back again, but it felt like years. And he was frightfully angry. Cold at first, and excessively proper, which is how he tries to present himself, but very soon he was raging at me."

"I trust you raged right back!"

Bertie's shrill cry must have roused Mincemeat, because he trotted up with an expression of catly concern on his pudgy face. Grateful for a warm body to cuddle, Celia set down the basket and lifted him into her arms. "For my sins, Bertie, yes. I was the veriest shrew. And that should have been an end to it. He arranged for a carriage to take me back to London, and I've not seen him since. But I cannot seem to put him from my mind. Had all this happened with any other man, I daresay this would score up as only one more example of folly on my part. But you see, it was *him*."

"The gentleman who pulled the ground from beneath your feet. Yes, I do understand. Are you in love with him, Celia?"

Love? Mercy! It did not bear thinking of.

"How would I know?" she asked reasonably. "I am seven-and-twenty, and the only love I experienced in all those years came from you and Freda. Well, and Mincemeat, but he loves anyone who will pet him."

"Don't be missish, child. You understand the question."

"Yes. I just can't think how to answer it. Is it possible to love a man after only a few hours in his company?"

"One can fall in love in the space between heartbeats, my dear."

"Oh."

"I once did, you know." Bertie laughed. "You needn't look so surprised. I was not always a shriveled old prune, and during my London Season, more than one gentleman professed himself head over ears in love with me. They were nothing of the sort, you may be sure, but in those days flirtation was a high art and we all played at it with far more skill than sensibility. There was one gentleman, though, a quiet young man who caught my eye. And at that very moment, I knew I was in love with him."

Enthralled, Celia regarded her closest friend with awe. Bertie Wigglesworth in love! It must have come to nothing, since she had returned home to live as a spinster all these years, but Celia heard no bitterness in her voice. Quite the contrary. Whatever happened between them had left a treasured memory. "May I ask how you could be so certain it was love, Bertie?"

"One simply knows. Mind you, I speak only of love at first sight, which is exceedingly rare. Most poor souls are not so favored, and they must wrestle with their confused emotions until the truth becomes clear to them. But Henry and I knew before a word had passed between us that our hearts were one."

Bertie selected a rose from the basket and brushed the petals against her crinkled cheek. "I am sorry to say that love stories do not invariably draw to a happy conclusion. His family refused to approve the match, and he was never a strong-willed man. It was a difficult time for everyone. I might have persuaded him to settle for love in a cottage, had I persisted, but Lord Henry was accustomed to wealth and privilege. At the end of the day, he would have regretted leaving it all behind."

"He should have done!" Celia declared. Startled at the sudden outburst, Mincemeat sprang from her arms. "You said he *loved* you."

"I am certain that he did. But we do not always love wisely, Celia. And some cannot bring themselves to make great sacrifices, even for what they most want in the world. You must not be sorry on my account. I willingly let him go, after all. And it had become apparent that Freda required me to tend to her, which would have been yet another burden for Henry to accept. He eventually wed the young woman chosen by his parents, and died some ten years ago."

Celia was amazed at how breezily Bertie was able to dismiss her one grand passion. No, more than that. The love of her life. Of course, she'd had fifty years to come to terms with her loss, but still . . .

"Forgive an old woman her reminiscences, my dear. It was not my intention to lower your spirits. Indeed, I cannot think why I began this story, unless it was to demonstrate that love often takes us by surprise, and sometimes requires more of us than we can give. I have never pined for Henry, and while it may appear to have been remarkably dull, I count my life a happy one."

She smiled. "And there, Celia, is the point. However difficult the course, it is always a good thing to love. And should you never complete the race, it remains a good thing to have loved, even for the briefest moment."

With a strangled sound, Celia wrapped her arms around the old woman, crushing the rose between their bodies. A thorn dug into her shoulder, but she scarcely felt it. "Thank you," she murmured. "I will think on what you have said. It will help me understand what is troubling me, I believe, once I have untangled the knots in my head."

Bertie wriggled free, brushing at her skirts. "Is understanding all you are after, child? I would not have expected you to give up on your gentleman so easily. Or have I mistaken the matter? Was he only trifling with your affections?"

Celia took a moment to sort out the questions. "Yes, at this point, understanding is the most I can hope for. He was always beyond my reach, Bertie. I knew that from the start. For all my foolish imaginings and reckless behavior, not once did I mistake his attentions for more than they were. His affections were never involved, nor did he pretend otherwise."

"Mmm."

"Oh, do stop *mmming* at me," Celia said, laughing as she picked up the basket of roses. "There is not the remotest chance that love played any part in the decidedly bizarre little drama we played out together on a summer afternoon."

"And if you are wrong about that?"

"Then you have heard the beginning of yet another love story that cannot possibly come to a happy ending. Be sure I do not mean to go into a decline, Bertie. And be even surer that I will never again go in pursuit of a man who does not want me. Especially *that* one."

"We'll see," Bertie said, taking her arm. "For now, can I persuade you to stay the night? After such a long journey, it would be a pity to leave us so soon."

"Really, I must go back today. At the market tomorrow in Kendal, I plan to buy myself a horse. Thomas is doing his best, of course, but he was not cut out to be a coachman and I require some other means of getting around. What's more, if I am to keep him in my service, I must locate a house and hire on a staff as soon as possible."

"I understand, my dear. Promise that you will visit us again as soon as may be."

"You know that I will, Bertie. And I shall write you every

day with word of my progress. Shall we wake Freda so that I can say good-bye, or is it better to let her sleep?"

"Of course you must make your farewell, wretched girl! Then I shall walk you to the Ribble Inn and give strict instructions to that nice young man regarding his duty to look after you. I cannot like the notion of you riding about on your own like a hoyden."

"Widows do not require chaperons these days, you know. Allow me a bit of freedom, Bertie. Surely I have earned it."

"Yes indeed. But you have not proven yourself able to control your wilder impulses, Celia. I greatly fear you will soon dive into trouble again."

"Not I!" Celia protested with a laugh. So long as she steered clear of Lord Kendal, what sort of trouble could she possibly find?

Chapter 11

Celia took another carrot from the bucket and offered it to the mare, laughing as the horse's lips tickled her palm. "Well, Thomas, what think you? Shall I buy her?"

He set down the bucket and passed her a clean white handkerchief. "Seems to like you well enough, she does. But more than that I cannot say, not knowing much about the beasties."

"Nor do I," she said, remembering the sad creatures she had ridden on Greer's farm. Wanting a good horse and knowing how to choose one were quite different matters. Mr. Rollins had practically sung an oratorio in praise of the mare, but since he'd come to the Kendal market to find a buyer, he could not be considered a disinterested party.

Love at first sight led only to folly, she reminded herself. And the white mare's show of affection was more for the carrots than for the strange female who fed them to her. Was Celia Greer so desperate for a friend, even a four-legged one, that she'd overlook any flaw so long as the creature *liked* her?

Mr. Rollins, who had left her alone to make her decision, waddled back across the paddock with an apologetic smile. "Pardon me, milady. I don't mean to rush you. But it happens a gentleman is taken with the mare and wishes to examine her. I told him you had the prior claim, but he is most insistent."

"Don't believe him," said a voice at her ear. "It's a humbug."

Startled, Celia looked up at a handsome, smiling face. A pair of amused sky-blue eyes gazed back at her with open admiration.

"There is no anxious buyer competing for the horse, I

promise you. Only a shill, paid to diddle you into reaching a hasty verdict."

"Oh." She glanced at Mr. Rollins, whose face had gone beet red.

"No insult intended, ma'am. Just business, you understand. I'll take meself off while you decide about the mare."

Celia smiled at the blond gentleman. "Thank you, I think. I had really meant to buy her. Is there some reason I should not?"

"She appears sound enough," he said. "But I'll take a closer look."

To Celia's astonishment, he vaulted gracefully over the fence and began to run his hands over the mare, an intent expression on his mobile face. Seeming to enjoy the attention, the horse made no fuss when he examined her hooves, ears, and mouth.

The man was about her own age, Celia decided, tall and rangy, with a pair of broad shoulders under his white shirt and brown leather waistcoat. She straightaway imagined him standing on the prow of a ship, but of course, she invariably cast every handsome man she saw into one of her absurd fantasies. This one would make an exceptionally fine pirate, she decided. Or perhaps a highwayman.

"You're a seductive wench," he said, "and a bit of a tease."

For the briefest moment Celia thought he was talking to her. But he scratched the mare affectionately behind the ears and moved to the fence, folding his arms across the top rail.

"Were she up to my weight, I'd buy her myself. How much is Rollins asking?"

When Celia told him, he whistled. "Extortion. Offer him half and stand firm."

"But what if he says no?" Now certain the horse was a prime goer, she could not bear to lose her.

"Oh, he'll take the deal. Tell you what. I'll handle the negotiation if you'll watch the brat for a few minutes."

At his gesture, Celia turned and saw a boy standing a few feet away, so immobile that it was no wonder she had failed to notice him. His enormous dark eyes were fixed on the mare with unmistakable adoration.

Knowing little about children, she could not guess his age. Six or seven, perhaps? A cap of black hair was neatly clipped, and he was dressed as formally as any aristocrat she had ever met outside a ballroom. His dark blue jacket was flawlessly tailored, his thin legs were encased in nankeen trousers, and starched shirt points reached nearly to his ears. All this finery for a country market? Poor child. Her heart went out to him.

"Charley, come make your bow to the lady," said the pirate. "I need to see a man about a horse."

Celia heard him leave, his boot heels crunching on the packed dirt in the paddock, but could not wrench her attention from the solemn little boy. He approached her slowly, his posture straight, his arms and small hands rigid as fence posts.

He bowed. "Lord Paxton, ma'am. At your service."

Oh dear. Unsure how to deal with this exceedingly proper young lordling, Celia curtsied. "I am pleased to make your acquaintance, my lord. My name is Cel . . . er, Lady Greer."

"Honored." His face was expressionless, shaped in marble, but his gaze had strayed again to the mare.

Celia studied his coffee-brown eyes, flaming with barely restrained longing under their long, sooty lashes. She had met him before, she thought suddenly. Not this boy, but someone so like him that the marrow in her bones tingled with recognition.

Or perhaps she saw only a reflection of herself, churning with a passion for life that clamored for release.

In any case, she knew this child. Soul-deep, she felt kin to him.

Meantime he was feeling kinship with the horse. "There is one last carrot in this bucket," she said, plucking it from the small pail Mr. Rollins had given her. "Would you care to feed it to the mare?"

His eyes widened. "Oh, yes," he said eagerly. "Will she bite me, do you think?"

The adventure of being chomped by a horse rather appealed to him, she thought. "Well, it's a dangerous business, to be sure. All depends on whether or not she likes the smell of you. Come closer and give her a whiff."

Haltingly at first, and then in a rush, he came directly up to the mare. She obliged by poking at his narrow shoulder with her muzzle.

"I think she likes you," Celia said, giving him the carrot. "Lay this on the palm of your hand and hold it out where she can reach it."

She might as well have offered him the moon. Trembling slightly, he followed her instructions. She could sense him pleading silently with the horse to take the carrot from his hand.

He needn't have worried. After a graceful toss of her head, the mare nibbled at the carrot for a moment and then gobbled it up.

"She did it," the boy cried, jumping with glee. "Did you see?"

"My, yes. And you gave her the carrot in just the right way. Well done."

He beamed with pride. "I never fed a horse before. It was fun."

Celia had to clasp her hands behind her back to keep from hugging him. At this moment she'd have spent half her fortune to buy the horse and the other half to stock up on carrots, merely to see that heartbreaking smile again.

She suspected that young Lord Paxton did not smile very often.

"You, madam, have just bought yourself a horse."

Celia looked up to see the blond gentleman approaching her with an athletic stride. "Did you save me any money?" she asked, grinning. He looked very full of himself.

"A mere four hundred pounds." With careless agility, he leapt over the fence and swept her a theatrical bow. "I begin to think I am in the wrong business. Clearly I have a native talent for horse trading."

"You have certainly convinced *me*," she replied. Until recently, four hundred pounds had been as far beyond her reach as the Milky Way. The fact that such a sum now made scarcely a ripple in her fortune did not alter her appreciation in the slightest. She had spent most of her life scrimping and saving, and had hesitated that very morning to buy herself a three-penny packet of spicy gingerbread. It had seemed too great a luxury, spending such a vast sum for a few moments of self-indulgence. She bought it anyway, gave half to Thomas, and felt guilty as she ate her share.

She realized that the gentleman was regarding her curiously. Or perhaps expectantly. Ought she to offer him a reward? Although his son was rigged out in fine broadcloth and impeccable linens, his own shirt had seen a few too many washings and his boots were scuffed and well-worn. Most odd. Perhaps she had mistaken the situation. For all she knew, he was a servant, or possibly the boy's tutor.

"Most assuredly I owe you a commission, sir, for striking such a bargain. Tell me what is fair in these circumstances."

He rubbed his forehead in a dramatic fashion. "Ah, I have it! Glasses of lemonade all around, and you pay the shot. Agreed?"

"Certainly. What more?"

He cast her a rueful smile. "Fact is, you could meet me ninety-nine times of a hundred and I'd jump at the chance to fill my pockets. But this is definitely your lucky day all 'round, because I happen to be solvent, with a bit to spare."

"He's going to buy me a pony," Lord Paxton piped up.

The man ruffled the child's hair affectionately. "I haven't forgot, brat. But we won't settle for just any pony. You want a real goer. Now, do you recall where we saw that booth with the lemonade?"

Remembering his manners, Lord Paxton bowed. "It's near to where we saw the puppies."

"Lead the way, then. And don't run off."

As if he would, Celia thought, watching the boy steer a path through the crowded marketplace with frightening dignity.

"Scary, isn't it?" the man said, as if reading her mind. He held out his arm. "My name is Kit, by the way."

It was impossible to stand on ceremony with him. "Celia," she said, resting her hand on his forearm. "And yes, he is astonishingly poised."

"Poor chap. Between his tutor, who was spawned in the Middle Ages, and the Nanny from Hades, he doesn't have a chance. Well, you can see for yourself. They are turning him into a machine."

"If you disapprove, why don't you dismiss them both?"

"Would that I could. It's all I can do to keep from strangling them." He inclined his head. "I have nothing to say in the matter, you know. And I'm the last one anyone would listen to. The steward admits me to the house because he must, but with very ill grace. As my lofty brother would put it, I am persona non grata."

"Forgive me." Heat rose to her cheeks. "I didn't mean to pry. I had assumed you were Lord Paxton's father."

"Only his uncle, I'm afraid. Widely known as the Black Sheep. Usually worse, truth be told, but some words are not fit for a lady's ears."

There was nothing remotely sheeplike about him. But her first instincts must have been on target, for he was most assuredly a rogue and wholly unrepentant about it. She liked him enormously.

He led her through the tangled crowd, following Lord Paxton's stiff back. "I am about to let him down, and cannot think how to break the news. There are no ponies to be had. Well, only a pair of demoralized nags hired out to give rides to the children at a penny a pop. The mare you bought is the only decent piece of horseflesh at the market."

"That is surely not your fault."

"Oh, but it is. I raised his hopes, you see, and now I cannot fulfill them. Thing is, I should have known better. The Kendal market is no place to look for horses, and I don't expect I can interest him in a sheep."

Despite his light tone, Celia could tell he was truly distressed. "If you explain the circumstances, I'm certain he'll understand."

"Oh, aye. He's well trained to swallow misfortune without choking, poor lad. If disappointments were golden guineas, Charley would be rich as Croesus."

The boy had come to a stop in front of a stall selling lemonade and cheese pies. He waited like a sentry, arms straight at his sides, regarding their approach with stern indifference.

"Lady Greer? Did you wish me to see to the horse?"

"Mercy!" Letting go of Kit's arm, she spun around. "Thomas, I'd forgot all about you. And I expect Mr. Rollins wishes me to make an accounting. I'll need to acquire a bank draft, and—"

"I told Rollins you would settle with him next week," Kit interjected. "It wouldn't do to pay up before you've put the mare through her paces. You can take her with you today, of course."

"He'll let me take the horse without paying? But he's never seen me before. How does he know I won't simply make off with her?"

"I've given my word," Kit said gently. "Not that it carries much weight, to be sure, but Rollins knows he can dun my brother if you fail to honor your debt. The family has a bit of influence in these parts, my own reputation notwithstanding."

Flustered, Celia introduced Thomas Carver and realized too late that servants were not supposed to be presented to gentlemen, even gentlemen of the black-sheep persuasion. But Kit, smiling broadly, shook Thomas's hand as though they were meeting on level ground.

Thomas, his face a startling shade of purple, stepped back and bowed. "I am Lady Greer's footman, sir."

"My butler," she corrected immediately. "Not that I have a house yet, but when I do, he will be in charge of it."

Since that news came as a complete surprise to Thomas, his mouth dropped open.

"Unless you decide to return to London," she added quickly, "but I hope you will not."

"N no, my lady. I'll be proud to serve you in whatever position you choose to place me."

"Well then, that's settled," Kit said briskly. "What say we toast your promotion with some lemonade? And after that, I suggest you claim the horse from Mr. Rollins and transfer her to—" He turned to Celia. "Since you have no house, where are you staying?"

Thomas had regathered his poise. "Thank you, sir. I'll see to the horse now, and wait for her ladyship where we left the carriage." With a bow, he took himself off.

"An impressive young man," Kit observed. "And probably the youngest butler in England."

"He's been a godsend," Celia said simply. "Without him, I don't know what I'd have done these last few days."

Kit wagged a finger at her. "You've been holding out on me, *Lady* Celia Greer. And that name is familiar, for some reason. Have you family in Westmoreland?"

"My late husband had a farm not far from here. But he was somewhat reclusive, so we rarely went into Society." To deflect any more questions about her identity, she waggled her own finger at Kit. "Speaking of holding out, I expect you are actually Lord Something-or-Other."

"Dear me no!" he protested. "Merely a younger son, of no distinction whatever. But had we been formally introduced, not that I ever go where formalities are observed, you would have met the Honorable—and I use the term loosely—Christopher Valliant."

Celia's knees turned to butter. Oh mercy!

"I gather you have heard something of my sorry reputation," he said, his face drained of color. "That is unfortunate. I had hoped we could be friends."

"Y-yes. Certainly." She waved her hands. "I mean, of course we can be friends. I should like that above all things. And I've heard nothing about you at all. Well, nothing to the point. You may have been mentioned to me in passing."

His head tilted. "Then what has overset you, Lady Greer?"

"Oh, do call me Celia. And I'm not in the least overset." A bouncer of the first order, she thought, struggling to reclaim her wits. "You simply took me by surprise. The thing is, I believe I am acquainted with your brother."

"Indeed? I presume you mean James—Lord Kendal—since Alex has not been in England for several years. Actually, neither has James, come to think of it. Last I heard, he was in Prussia."

"He returned to London for the victory celebrations, or so I believe. In all that crush, there was little opportunity to speak with anyone for more than a few minutes, but I recall meeting him on one or two occasions. He was exceedingly . . . polite."

"He would be," Kit said dryly.

Realizing that she was wringing her hands, Celia lowered them to her sides. Lord Paxton—Charley—was Kendal's son! She had not known he had a child. Heaven knew he had never spoken of the boy. And while she used to scour the newspapers for any mention of Lord Kendal, Greer generally took the papers off to line his chicken cages before she got her hands on them.

That sweet, starched, highly proper young boy was Kendal's son. Oh my. She turned back to the lemonade stand, heart in her throat, to look at him.

He wasn't there.

Kit realized he was gone at about the same moment. "Lucifer," he swore under his breath. "Where's the brat got off to?"

Celia clutched at his sleeve. "He said something about puppies—"

"Right! Good girl. They were—damn. I can't remember." Taking her hand, Kit led her around the lemonade stall, past a cart filled with turnips and cabbages, and by a small tent spangled with moons and stars. "Fortune-teller," he said. "We came in from this direction." He turned, orienting himself, and tugged her back to where they started.

Just beyond the lemonade seller and a flower booth, Celia saw a high-wheeled wagon heaped with hay. Underneath, on a mound of straw, Lord Paxton sat cross-legged inside a small makeshift pen with a dozen black-and-white puppies swarming over him, yipping for attention.

"Thank God," Kit murmured, squeezing her hand.

When he started to move closer, Celia held him back. Together, they watched Charley giggle happily as puppies clambered over his small body and lapped at his face.

"Kit," she said softly, "a puppy isn't exactly a pony, but—"

"Ah. A supremely good idea, and bless you for thinking of it. Truth be told, I'm not exactly partial to dogs, not even little ones. There haven't been any at Candale since I was a boy." He winced. "It seems that is about to change."

Celia remembered that Kendal had mentioned a younger brother being spooked by a dog. "Shall I help him select one to take home? Are you certain the puppy will be welcome there?"

"Nanny Yallop will have a fit, and Tommy the Tutor will draft letters of protest to Kendal, which will never be read, if I know my brother. Other than that, no problems to speak of."

"I was referring to *you*, Kit. If you hate dogs—"

"Don't hate 'em! They just scare me senseless. But I'll get over it. Besides, I'm rarely in residence at Candale. The mutt will have to find something else to chew on. Do me a favor, though, and extricate Charley from the herd. Tell him he may choose one, and one only, for his special pet. And while you're at it, mention that the pup will require his full attention for a week or two. That will give me time to chase down a pony."

The Valliant men, Celia thought with some amusement, were expert at shifting responsibility when it suited them. Nodding, she went to join Charley inside the puppy pen.

A rotund woman sat on a three-legged stool in the shade of the hay wagon, Mama Dog sprawled at her feet, both observing the scene with mild interest. "You want a puppy, ma'am? Only half a crown. They be weaned and healthy."

"Thank you," Celia replied, sinking next to Charley on the straw. Immediately, five or six puppies swarmed into her lap. "What think you, Lord Paxton? Kit says you can choose a pup to take home with you, but only if you really, really want one."

His eyes shone. "Oh, I do. Really, *really*. Cross my heart."

It took him a long time to make his decision. While they waited Kit brought lemonade for everyone, including the woman who owned the dogs, and stood at a careful distance with his shoulder propped against the wagon as Charley fell in love with one puppy after another.

"Them's sheep collies," the woman said. "Got any sheep?"

"A few thousand," Kit replied, tossing her a coin. "If you have any dogs left at next Saturday's market, the estate manager may want to have a look at them."

"This one!" Charley finally proclaimed, lifting a wriggling

ball of fur in his hands. Scrambling from the pen, he held the pup to Kit. "Is it a boy or a girl?"

Kit examined the dog's backside. "Boy. He'll need a name, so start thinking about it while I speak with Lady Greer."

Brushing straw from her skirts, Celia emerged from under the wagon. "You may wish to keep your distance, Kit. Charley and I will be smelling of more than hay and fur until we have our baths. But wasn't it wonderful to see him so happy?"

"More than I can find words for," he said. "The puppy was only part of it, you know. Half the time he was looking at you. Will you come visit him at Candale, Celia? It's all I can do to pry him from his tutor's clutches, and a guest will give me an excuse to take him from the schoolroom." He gave her a pleading, slightly lopsided smile. "Please?"

Suspecting that Kit Valliant generally got what he wanted sooner or later, Celia swallowed her objections. Lord Kendal would not be pleased to know she was running tame on his estate, but then, he had not even bothered to tell his family that he was back in England. More than likely he would never know she had become acquainted with his brother and his son.

"I would love to pay a call on Lord Paxton," she said. "For the time being, I am in residence at the Merry Goosegirl. Send word there when it is convenient for me to come."

"You'll not escape so easily, Celia. Charley and I will walk you to where your butler is waiting, and on the way we'll settle on a time for your visit tomorrow afternoon. Unless you care to join us for church services in the morning? We could have breakfast after and plan a day in the country. Even Charley is not expected to ply his books on Sunday."

Deeper and deeper, Celia thought. Ever deeper into trouble. "What hour are services?"

Kit planted a kiss on her cheek. "I adore you! Ten o'clock, St. Peter's, and we'll meet you in the vestibule."

The very church where she had first seen Lord Kendal. Oh mercy! But while she was there, perhaps she could persuade the Lord, the true Lord, to extricate her gently from her latest folly.

She absolutely must not become entangled with the Valliant

family. Above all things, she could not let this sweet little boy get caught up in a disaster of her making. Tomorrow she would pray for help in detaching herself from her new friends without causing pain. And until it was accomplished, she hoped Lord Kendal would keep himself far, far away.

Chapter 12

Three days in Bath playing nursemaid to Marshall Blücher, bluffly charming as he was, had done nothing to improve Kendal's dark mood. He arrived at his town house in St. James's Square well after dark, looking forward to a few hours with a brandy bottle, only to find an urgent message from Lord Finlay.

Matters of importance, were they? Kendal scribbled a reply and dispatched it with a footman. If Finlay wanted to speak with him, he could damn well come here to do it.

Kendal had been traveling half the day. He refused to climb into another coach, even for the short trip to Curzon Street, and his reasons had absolutely nothing to do with Lady Greer.

True, he'd been glad of the Bath assignment, which allowed him to escape London—and her—for a few days. But now that he was back, they were bound to meet sooner or later. Not tonight, though, at Finlay's house. She might be out for the evening, but then again, she might not.

Reminding himself not to think about her, which was proving surprisingly difficult for a man accustomed to ordering his thoughts, he washed up, changed into shirt, trousers, and a brocade robe, and waited for Finlay in the library. The sooner this was done with, the sooner he could find out if an excess of brandy would permit him to sleep. Nothing else seemed to work.

When the butler showed him in, Finlay went straight to the sideboard and poured himself a hefty drink. "I'm in a foul mood, James. You'd better have a devilish good excuse for dragging me here."

"None to speak of." Kendal held out his own glass for a refill. "And if you recall, it was you who called this midnight meeting. I merely changed the location."

"Well, no matter. Marjory wasn't sorry to get me out of the house, I can tell you. I've been snapping at everybody today."

"She is returned from Maidstone, then? I trust her sister has recovered."

"Yes, yes. Dicey for a time, and Marjory is worn to a nub, but that particular crisis has passed." Finlay dropped onto a wingback chair with a groan. "Needless to say, there are any number of others queued up to take its place. Heard anything about the Gaverton affair?"

"Gaverton? Good Lord, what's he to do with the Foreign Office?"

"Not a thing. You've met the man. A mushroom with more money than wits, but that can be a dangerous combination. Last night, he hosted a supper party at the Clarendon. Called it a 'salute to the generals,' can you believe! No one of any importance turned up, but Gaverton managed to assemble a few second-rate peacocks, mostly Austrian and Prussian. Every last one of them thinks he won the war single-handedly, of course."

"Let them squabble," Kendal said indifferently. "They've been doing so since the crossing from Boulogne. What of it?"

"This is secondhand information, mind you, but it comes from several reliable sources. There was the usual drinking and boasting, with everyone mad at everyone else. Safe enough, what with the hostility spread around fairly evenly. Then Chirikov jumped on the table, demanded they put peace in their hearts or some such thing, and started spouting poetry."

"Idiot."

"I rather like the man, actually. Good-hearted, if a trifle obsessed. In any case, he centered the fire. They all started insulting him instead of each other. Except for the other two Russian generals, who felt obligated to defend their countryman."

"Brawling schoolboys and a few bloody noses." Kendal sipped his brandy. "This is scarcely an international crisis, William."

"Not yet. But I hear rumblings. At least one Austrian and two Prussians are threatening to call Chirikov out, and I don't need to tell you the consequences if an allied general is shot down on Hounslow Heath. You will see to it that doesn't happen."

"Am I to throw myself in front of the bullet?"

"Almost as bad," Finlay said with a weary smile. "Obviously, Chirikov has to be got out of London. But he refuses to go, because it would appear he was running away."

"So it would. If you expect me to convince him otherwise—"

"I've already tried. Even Wellington tried. York offered to draw him off to Oatlands Park, but still he refused to budge. There was only one man in England worth leaving the city for, said he."

"Some damnable poet, right? I already told you, I don't know any poets."

"Nevertheless, the one he wants to meet lives in your neighborhood. Some chap named Wordsworth. I mean for you to escort Chirikov to the Lakes, nose out his pet poet, and introduce the pair of them."

"The devil I will!" Kendal set down his glass with a thump.

"You leave day after next," Finlay said, brushing a spray of brandy from his sleeve. "I'd rather it were immediately, but Chirikov is going to a mill in Crawley tomorrow. At least he'll be out of London."

Kendal retrieved his glass and turned it in his hand, watching the amber liquid swirl around. There hadn't been a guest at Candale since he could remember. For that matter, he hadn't set foot on his own estate for nearly two years. Nor did he want to go there now, not since old sins and black-shadowed memories began chasing one another through his sleepless nights. Perhaps after the Vienna Congress he would make one of his obligatory visits, but not now.

"No," he said flatly. "It's out of the question."

"I sympathize, James. Really I do. But I've already told Chirikov that you'll be happy to oblige. On the bright side, he's agreed to settle for Coleridge or Southey if you can't unearth that Wordsworth fellow. From what Chirikov says, the Lakes are practically swarming with poets."

"Not that I ever noticed. Shall I put an advertisement in the local newsrags? 'Poets seeking idolators should apply at Candale'?"

"Frankly, I don't give a rat's arse if Chirikov meets up with a rhyming scribbler. I just mean you to herd him north and keep him there for at least a week. Preston will take him off your hands after that. He's organizing a shooting party in Scotland."

He can start by shooting me, Kendal thought. After a week in company with Chirikov, any previously sane man would welcome a bullet in the head. "You will owe me, Finlay," he said in a dark voice. "And don't think I'll fail to collect."

"Fine. Whatever you say. Just get that damnable Russian out of my hair. I'll make arrangements for the journey, of course, and send word of the departure place and time. All you have to do is show up."

"On no account will I spend four days in a carriage with Chirikov. Tell him I've gone on ahead to sniff him out a poet. Tell him what you will. I leave tomorrow, traveling alone."

"I figured you'd say that," Finlay said with a cat-in-the-creampot smile. "He's bringing along a few of his cronies, and I expect they'll drink their way from one pub house to the next. You'll have plenty of time to prepare the house and devise a week of entertainment. One word of advice, James. Provide some women, or know where they can be found."

Kendal erupted to his feet. "I'm not a bloody procurer, Finlay, and damned if I'll turn Candale into a brothel."

"Nobody expects you to. Forget the women. I daresay one of your servants will be able to direct them to the local establishments. Just be prepared for trouble. Some of these chaps are not quite civilized, if you know what I mean." Finlay emptied his glass and stood. "I'll send over a packet of reports regarding the Congress for you to study on the journey. Any questions?"

Is Lady Greer in good spirits? Kendal nearly asked. But of course, he could not inquire about a houseguest with whom he supposedly had only the merest acquaintance. "None that I can think of at the moment," he said, reaching for the bellpull. "Pardon me if I don't show you out."

From the door, Finlay looked back at him. "Whatever is troubling you, James, put it aside for now. Until the treaty is negotiated and signed, none of us can afford to be distracted by matters of a personal nature."

"Go to the devil," Kendal advised him with a chilling smile.

Four days later, on a sunny afternoon, Kendal's coach drew up at the Candale gatehouse.

Wiping his hands on a towel, Angus Macafee hurried out to lift the bar, a look of apology on his face. "Welcome home, m'lord. But we wasn't expectin' you. Should I send word ahead to the house?"

"That won't be necessary, Angus. Your wife and family are well, I presume?"

"Got another bairn since last time we saw you," he said proudly. "A sweet lassie."

"My congratulations." Kendal smiled. "I suppose that means I'll have to adjust your wages again."

"Mr. Spence already did that, and I thank ye heartily. He's in Keswick, by the way. Due back tomorrow, I think. Mr. Christopher is to home, though. Been here nearly a month this time."

Nodding, Kendal signaled the driver to proceed down the tree-lined road to the main house.

So his scapegrace brother was at Candale. He was glad of it, although he'd intended to spend the rest of the day closeted with his estate manager. Apparently business would have to wait until tomorrow, and just as well. Sleep continued to elude him, and after the long trip he was in no mood to arrange a house party for a horde of raging Cossacks.

When the coach drew up at the stable, Kendal found it an effort to wrench himself from the squabs and step outside. It seemed he'd been traveling for a lifetime. Now he had to rouse himself to greet the unfailingly energetic Kit and the household staff, which would be at sixes and sevens to make him welcome when all he longed for was a good night's rest.

And there was Paxton, of course. A knotted rope twisted around his throat. No way to escape an awkward, stilted meeting with the boy, although he might be able to put it off until the morning.

Ostlers rushed to unhitch the horses, and he saw a stable boy scurry toward the house to alert the other servants that Lord Kendal had arrived. Stamping his boots on the ground to loose his taut muscles, he noticed a fine-boned white mare tethered just inside the stable, nibbling oats from a trough. She wore a sidesaddle.

Kit must have invited one of his female friends for a visit, Kendal thought, displeased. Kit was rarely without a woman, if he could possibly help it. He had all the charm in the family, and no sense of responsibility whatever. Really, he ought not bring his ladybirds to Candale with Paxton in residence. Kendal knew he would have to speak to him on the subject.

But that could wait, too. Everything could wait.

He aimed himself toward the house, hoping to enter without ceremony, but was distracted by shouts of laughter coming from behind the stable. What the devil? He took a few more steps before turning back, certain Kit was up to something disreputable. As usual. He might as well find out what all the commotion was about and let his brother know he had come home.

The last word tasted bitter on his tongue, even though he had not said it aloud. Candale had not been *home* to him for a great many years.

The sun was directly in his eyes as he rounded the corner of the stable. Lifting his hand to his forehead, he could barely make out what was going on inside the grassy paddock. He saw Kit first of all, leaning against the railing with his arms folded over his chest, his overlong blond hair gleaming in the sunlight.

A surge of affection swept over him at the sight of his handsome, loose-limbed youngest brother, dressed carelessly as always in leather breeches and a full-sleeved white shirt, his collar open and his waistcoat unbuttoned. Kit the Rogue. Kendal despaired of him. And rather too often he envied him. Kit was the only Valliant brother who knew how to be happy.

There were at least a dozen children in the paddock, dashing about and shrieking like banshees. He recognized two of Angus Macafee's brood, and reckoned from the filthy home-spun clothing worn by the others that they were all offspring of servants or tenant farmers.

All but one.

Paxton must have spent the last hour rolling around in the mud. His pants were torn, his shirt filthy, and his dark hair wildly tousled. Kendal hardly recognized him. This was Kit's doing, he thought angrily. At this time of day Paxton ought to be at his studies. And under no circumstances should he be romping in a horse paddock with a pack of commoners.

Shading his eyes with both hands, Kendal looked closer. A figure, a slender female figure if he was not mistaken, was at the center of their game. A wide blindfold concealed most of her face, and a floppy straw bonnet hid her hair. Nevertheless, she was strikingly familiar. One of the housemaids, he supposed, or perhaps the girl Kit was currently favoring with his attentions. The one who belonged to that elegant mare.

She wore an apple-green dress, smudged with dirt, and her supple body made it impossible to look away from her. Arms waving in the air, she wove circles in the paddock, apparently trying to catch hold of the children who darted in and out, making sure to keep just beyond her reach.

"The ogre nearly got you, Betty," Paxton yelled.

"Did not!"

"Did, too!"

The would-be ogre, fingers curled, stomped in the direction of the voices. "I'm hungry!" she growled. "Where is my supper? *Grrrrrr!*"

"You can't eat *me!*" cried a curly-headed boy, flexing his stringy muscles. "I'm too tough."

"Me tough, too," Betty chimed.

Amid a chorus of "me-toos," the ogre stalked the paddock, snarling dramatically. "I fancy tough meat," she warned. "And the first one of you I seize will be swallowed down whole. Feed me. *Feeeeed* me!"

Paxton tiptoed up behind her, silently daring her to catch him. *Wanting* her to catch him, Kendal realized.

And then she did, swooping around and grappling the boy under his arms. "Supper!" she proclaimed, pretending to chomp his neck. Paxton squealed in delight.

"I get to be the ogre now," he declared, when she finally set him down.

"So you do," she said, crouching with her back to the child. "But first you must untie this blindfold."

Paxton fumbled with the knot for a long time, but eventually got it loose. And when the cloth dropped from her face, every muscle in Kendal's body went rigid with shock.

She spotted him at the same moment and went equally still.

For an eternity, or so it seemed to him, they gazed at each other. The children went quiet, too, as if sensing the onset of a storm.

Kit's voice broke the tense silence. "Game's over, ducklings. Take yourselves off now."

Marginally aware of children and onlookers scampering away, Kendal struggled to order his wits. Celia. Here! It was the last thing he expected. The last thing he wanted. Standing now, staring back at him with icy calm, she all but brought him to his knees.

"I take it the two of you are acquainted," Kit said lightly, crossing to Celia and draping an arm over her shoulder. "Hullo, Jimmie. Fancy *you* showing up unannounced. Not your usual style. Shall I take it England has decided it can dispense with your services?"

Kendal restrained himself from vaulting over the fence and decking his brother with a hard right to the jaw. How *dare* he touch her like that? Wrap his arm around her, damn him, as if staking a claim.

Suddenly a madly barking collie pup streaked through the paddock, ducked under the lowest bar of the fence, and attacked his boots with sharp teeth and claws.

"Stop that!" Kendal ordered to no effect. It was impossible to tell if the puppy was assaulting a supposed enemy or merely

playing, but there was no doubt about his tenacity. Kendal could have kicked him away, of course, but Celia would think him lower than a snake for it. Not that she didn't think so already.

It hadn't taken her long to replace one Valliant brother with another, he thought venomously. Had she set out deliberately to snare Kit in some obscure female plot of retribution? It could not be sheer coincidence that she was here, now, four hundred miles from London, smiling at Kit. . . .

Very well, she wasn't smiling at Kit. She was openly laughing at what the black-and-white mutt was doing to his own beleaguered boots. Having abandoned his efforts to rip the leather to shreds, the pup, one small leg lifted in the air, was pungently marking his territory.

A red haze of fury obscured his vision. And out of it swam a small boy with tangled black hair and dark, scared eyes.

Paxton. Kendal had forgot all about him.

The boy came directly up to him and seized the puppy, raising it protectively to his narrow chest. Immediately the pup began squirming with pleasure and lapping its wet red tongue over the boy's face.

"He's mine, sir," Paxton said in a trembling voice. "His name is Wellington."

"Indeed? Have you taught him no manners, then?"

"Here we go," Kit said with a groan. Uncoiling his arm from Celia's shoulder, he mounted the fence and sauntered over to Kendal. "You sound exactly like Nanny Yallop, Jimmie. And I can think of no worse insult than that. Charley, I suggest you go and clean yourself up. I'll see to Wellington."

Astonished, Kendal saw his dog-loathing brother take the pup from the boy's arms and plant it on his shoulder. Immediately, the dog began chomping on his hair.

After a worried glance at his rag-mannered pet, Paxton sped away.

Celia was walking toward the paddock gate, the blindfold dangling from her hand, never looking in his direction.

Let her go, then, Kendal thought, watching her drape the

blindfold over the fence before raising the latch. If he spoke to her now, there was no telling what he would say.

"Go make your bow to Lady Greer," Kit said, an unholy gleam in his eyes. "I'd introduce you, but I'm informed that you have already met. Besides, this spawn of Satan is ripping my hair out. I'll go have him amputated from my scalp and order up some tea while you escort the lady inside."

He was gone before Kendal could stop him. And for that matter, so was Celia. But he caught a glimpse of her skirt as she turned the corner of the stable, and of their own accord, his feet began moving in the same direction.

He followed her to the courtyard, arriving just as a stable boy led the mare outside. Celia's back was to him, and if she was aware he had followed her, she gave no sign of it. He watched her take the reins and stroke the horse's neck.

Go and be damned, he told her silently.

She looked down at the stable boy. "Thank you for taking such excellent care of Aphra, Timothy. I've rarely seen her mane brushed to such advantage. May I beg another service of you? It seems I've left my reticule in the house, which was exceedingly thoughtless, and now I am embarrassed to go in search of it. Will you mind asking one of the house servants to locate it for me?"

"Yes, m'lady. I mean, no, m'lady." Cheeks scarlet, the boy loped off toward the servants' entrance.

Kendal gave quick thought to following him, but before he could move, it was too late.

"Good afternoon, my lord," Celia said, without turning. "Is there some reason you are lurking about?"

Teeth clenched, he aimed himself to a spot about ten feet from where she stood, determined to keep a healthy distance between them. "I had thought to ask you the same question, Lady Greer. Why are you not in London?"

"It occurs to me that my whereabouts are none of your business, sir. But if you must know, I came north to settle my late husband's affairs, primarily the sale of his farm."

"A sudden decision, I apprehend."

"Apprehend what you will. But while you are fabricating unlikely scenarios—a habit of yours, as I recall—you might consider that Lady Marjory had also left London to attend to her sister. In consequence, I had little choice but to remove myself from Lord Finlay's home."

"Never tell me you were concerned about *propriety*."

She came around to face him, her brows arched disdainfully. "The Finlays were preoccupied with family matters. I was more concerned about being a nuisance."

"Understandable. But how is it you have come to be a nuisance at Candale?"

She clicked her tongue. "Are we to have another row, Lord Kendal? Did we not say more than enough when last we met? Really, I see no point to this inquisition."

"Do you not? I arrived home only to find a gaggle of brats racketing about my paddock, with you, of all people, egging them on. It's only natural that I wonder what in blazes you are doing here!"

"On this occasion," she said after a moment's consideration, "playing blindman's buff."

"That is no answer, madam. And I do not welcome your impertinence."

"No more than you welcome *me*, I collect. We are of like mind in one regard, sir. Had I the slightest notion you were on your way home, you may be sure that Candale is the last place on earth I would have been found."

"But here you are," he said incontrovertibly. "In company with my brother, with whom you appear to have struck up a close relationship in a remarkably short time."

Her lips curved. "Yes. We were drawn to each other the moment we met."

She was leading him on, Kendal knew. Deliberately provoking him. And he, saphead that he was, kept rising to the bait. "You must have known I would not approve contact between you and any member of my family after what passed between us."

"Oh, aye. But then I recollected that so very *little* had passed between us. Surely not enough to prohibit friendship with quite the nicest young gentleman I have encountered in recent memory. But lest you imagine otherwise, our meeting was purely coincidental. He came upon me at the Kendal market while I was trying to decide whether or not to buy this mare, and helped me to negotiate with the horse trader."

"A likely story. But you have ever been remarkably inventive."

She gave him a look of mock horror. "Mercy me! Did you fancy I deliberately sought him out because he was your brother? How peculiar. Why would I do such a thing?"

He could think of a score of reasons. To punish the man who had walked out on her, for example. To prove she could seduce at least one of the Valliant brothers. Or just because she was a hot-blooded female in search of a lover, which Kit would have recognized immediately. Kendal could hardly blame him for jumping at what she so freely offered. Lord knew that *he* had jumped.

But none of the reasons that shot to his mind made the least bit of sense. Celia Greer was a complete mystery to him, but there was no mistaking the bright core of integrity at her center. He gazed directly into her eyes and saw it burning there. Burning into him, daring him to go on making an ass of himself.

All the same, knowing he was wholly in the wrong did nothing to quench his unaccountable rage. The rage only *she* was able to stir up in him. That alone was reason enough to want her gone.

She had seemingly lost interest in him. Turning back to her horse, she scratched behind the mare's ears and received a whicker of pleasure in return.

Kendal cast about for something to say. Perversely, he was loath to end this encounter, however unpleasant it had been thus far. He could not bring himself to walk away, nor think of a way to prolong their time together. And for all her disclaimers about the coincidental meeting with Kit, she had said nothing that ruled out an affair between them.

Was his brother the man who finally claimed her virginity?

A knife twisted in his gut. If they were lovers, he would—

What? There was nothing he *could* do.

"Lady Greer," piped the stable boy, darting across the courtyard with a delicate knit reticule in his hand. He presented it to her with a beaming smile.

"Bless you, Timothy," she said, drawing the strings and pulling out a coin. "I am most grateful."

" 'Twaren't nothin', ma'am. Betsy found it under a chair."

"Then she must have a reward, too." Celia extricated another coin. "Give her this, will you, with my thanks."

Unused to being ignored, Kendal was amazed that his own stable boy had failed to take note of his presence. Or perhaps the child had not been in his employment when last he made an appearance on the estate. Most likely there were any number of servants at Candale who had never clapped eyes on the man who paid their wages.

Young Timothy scampered back in the direction of the house, coins clutched tightly in his hand. Clearly he was looking forward to presenting Betsy with her vail.

"He's a lovely boy," Celia said. "His father died last year, leaving seven children and a sickly wife. Timothy was sent out to work to help support the family. Betsy is his sister."

"I see," Kendal said, a lump of guilt rising to his throat. In so short a time Celia Greer knew more about his household than he did. But what matter the woes of a few families when the fate of Europe had been at stake, he told himself. It wasn't as if he had been doing nothing of value all these years.

And why would she so admire Kit, whose sole concerns were wine, women, and adventure?

"If you mean to order me off your property and advise me never to darken the doors of Candale," she said mildly, "pray go on about it. I hope you will not forbid me to see Charley again, although I expect you will. And I shall do as you say, of course. Only, please make yourself clear this time. I so easily misunderstand your intentions, as well you know. What exactly do you want of me, Lord Kendal?"

Infernally, *come to bed with me* was his first thought. His body raised a cheer of approval.

Hoping desperately she wouldn't see what was painfully

obvious to him, he came directly up to her, seized her around the waist, and lifted her onto the saddle. The reins had got tangled in the process, so he helped sort them out, grateful for the slight distraction.

When she was settled, he stepped back, more in control of himself now, although his hands felt on fire from touching her. "You must do as you like," he said tightly. "I trust you will not disrupt Paxton's studies or interfere with the schedule mapped out by his governess and tutor. Otherwise, you are free to come and go at Candale."

For the first time he had startled her. It gave him a perverse delight to see the look of surprise on her face, especially since he had not meant to say what he had just said. It had been his firm intention to tell her it would be better if she stayed away, at least while he was in residence.

Once he was gone again, a week or two from now, it made no difference what she did. Surely in Vienna, where sophisticated and uncomplicated females would be trolling for the sort of casual liaisons he favored, he would be able to exorcise Celia Greer from his thoughts.

"I'll not come here until you have left," she said quietly. "To do so would be difficult for me, if not for you. But likely Kit and I will arrange a few excursions with Charley, if you've no objection. It's summer, after all, and young boys cannot spend all their time with books."

Kendal nodded. "As it happens, I expect guests within a few days, and I'm not altogether certain they will conduct themselves in proper fashion." Lord, how pompous he sounded! He tried again, more simply this time. "If you take Paxton off of an afternoon, I'll be glad of it."

She closed her eyes for a moment, and he saw her hands clutch at the reins. Why had permission to spend time with the child affected her so greatly? She must have wanted it very much, in spite of her apparent indifference to whatever decision he made.

"Thank you, my lord," she said. "Be assured I'll not take undue advantage of your kindness."

He bowed, fairly pleased with himself for having regained the poise that generally went missing whenever he was in her presence.

She nudged the mare into a turn and rode away in no great hurry as he stood frozen, gazing after her with terrible, unthinkable desire. *Look back,* he begged silently. *Look back and tell me you are not so indifferent to me as you seem.*

But she did not.

Chapter 13

His headache had grown worse, but Kendal persisted, determined to make a start at catching up with estate business. He meant to be ready for an accounting when Spence returned from wherever the devil he'd gone. Keswick, was it?

Not that he'd made a sliver of progress since settling at his desk four hours ago. He had given strict instructions that he wasn't to be disturbed, but the butler had brought a supper tray to the study anyway. To his credit, Geeson only placed it on a side table and withdrew as silently as he'd come.

It was still there, the tray. Kendal had no appetite. Nor very much interest in tracing profits and losses from the several enterprises that kept Candale and the Valliant family in funds, although there had been a time when he'd enjoyed managing the estate and expanding the family businesses.

So far, he could tell that his steward oversaw Candale with the parsimony of a born accountant. But it was equally clear that Spence lacked the imagination to increase production and develop new markets. In the final analysis, that meant that the tenant farmers and shepherds had little opportunity to improve their own lots.

Most of their families had been at Candale since before he was born, and few were better off than they'd been when he left to take up his duties with the Foreign Office. He had not precisely neglected them, he told himself. But neither had he done anything of value on their behalf.

On the other hand, what did they expect of him? Until a few months ago England had been at war. Everyone was called on to make sacrifices during the war years, and his own services were required elsewhere. He refused to feel guilty for what could not be helped.

There was more than enough guilt heaped on his head already. He couldn't remember the last time he had gone to bed without a score of unaccomplished tasks weighing on him. A diplomat, even a good one—and he fancied he had some claim to that distinction—never actually completed anything. Nothing of significance, at any rate. He had spent five years catering to swollen egos and smoothing the path for men with the authority to make decisions. When it came right down to it, he'd done little more than chat up important people and winkle information from them.

He was heartily sick of the whole business, but the alternatives were even less appealing. Candale was poisonous to him now, he had no taste for soldiering, and what else was there for him to do? Sometimes he could almost envy Kit, who did whatever he liked with no thought of the consequences.

As if summoned, his brother sauntered into the study without knocking.

"Go away," Kendal grumbled. "I'll deal with you in the morning."

"And I'm glad to see you, too," Kit replied cheerfully. "Have a drink. Looks like you need one. Hell, I'll even pour it for you."

Kendal accepted a glass of claret with murmured thanks and set it on the desk. "Did you come to beg another loan? I promise you, there will be nary a farthing until you provide me a coherent plan for spending it to some useful purpose."

"Shall I tell you I mean to buy a plot of land and a flock of sheep? Will that open your pockets?"

Kendal swallowed a laugh. "You will have to tell me something credible, although I cannot imagine what that could be."

"No more can I. But relax, Jimmie. I've no intention of dunning you, at least this one time. In fact, I wasn't expecting to see you at all. What brought you home of a sudden?"

"Nothing good." Kendal put down the pen he'd been holding and steepled his hands. "My superiors have ordered me to entertain a contingent of Russians who came over for the victory celebrations. There are reasons to spirit General Chirikov out of London, and for my sins, I was elected to do it. How many friends he'll bring along with him and how long they will stay, I've no idea. I set out ahead to alert the staff and arrange for suitable pastimes. Hunting, shooting, that sort of thing."

"Hmm. I may stick around, then. Is it too much to hope these particular Russians are flush in the fob and partial to gaming?"

Kendal released a small sigh. "I will be very glad if you stay, Kit. And no, you may not pick their pockets at cards and dice. But I might be convinced to pay you—straight out, not a loan—for helping me keep them occupied. I don't suppose you happen to know any poets?"

"Good God no!" Kit shuddered. "Exactly what sort of house party is this to be? If you mean to stage amateur theatricals and poetry readings, you can't pay enough to keep me here."

"Understood. But I expect—devil it, Kit, I don't know *what* to expect. Something closer to chaos than musicales, most like." He stood, picked up the glass of wine, and walked over to the open window, welcoming the cool evening breeze against his face. "I won't blame you for fleeing in advance of the Cossack hordes."

"Hordes I can live with. It's opera singers that terrify me. You can count on me, Jimmie, no salary required. Not that I won't remind you of my devoted service at some later time, when my finances are at low tide."

"I never doubted it," Kendal replied easily. "Tomorrow afternoon, if you have no other plans, let's go for a ride and try to figure out what we are to do with a troop of Russian soldiers."

"Agreed. In the meantime, despite the fact that you officially barred the study door even to family, I have come here to talk about Charley."

Damn. Kendal swung around and gave his brother a stern look of dismissal. "Can this not wait, Kit? I presume he is well enough for now."

"He is healthy, if that is what you mean. But I saw Pruneface

Yallop galloping out of here shortly before supper. You must have quizzed her with your usual lack of mercy."

"Rather the other way around," Kendal said with a harsh laugh. "From her report, Lord Paxton is generally well behaved until his Uncle Christopher pays a call, at which point he runs wild as a baboon. You are regarded as an unwholesome influence, I'm afraid."

"God forbid the poor kid be allowed to enjoy himself for a week or two. She's turning him into a mole, James. He's allowed a short walk in the morning and another in the evening, but only if the weather is fine. It's bloody unnatural."

"He should be permitted more exercise, I suppose. When our Russian guests depart, Miss Yallop and I shall discuss a reordering of the boy's daily schedule."

"Bully for you. Will that include five minutes of your own time, or do you mean to avoid him altogether while you are home?"

"Certainly not. But I shall be kept busy with Chirikov and his entourage, and must return to London when they have gone. On this trip, there will be little time to spare for personal matters."

"As opposed to which of your previous trips?"

"Do you mean to read me a lecture, Kit?"

He laughed. "That *would* be a change, considering how many times you have drawn and quartered me for the most trivial of offenses. Actually, I quite like the notion of changing places with you. Best do it right, though." He went to the desk and settled in Kendal's chair, propping his elbows on the desk and steepling his hands.

Kendal could not fail to recognize his own habitual posture whenever there was unpleasant business to be dealt with. "Cut line, infant."

"Don't be impertinent, young man," Kit said, mocking his brother's cool voice. Then he frowned. "You are supposed to be standing before me with your head bowed, Jimmie, looking suitably penitent."

"Ah. I beg your pardon. But am I not playing Mr. Christopher in this farce?" Slouching to the chair in front of the desk, he slumped down, crossed one ankle over his knee, and lounged back, wineglass dangling from his hand. "What *now*?" he drawled sullenly.

Kit shouted with laughter. "Very good, for a stiff-necked diplomat. But if you are going to play me, you require a touch more insouciance, not to mention a devilish gleam in your eyes. Can you be devilish, Jimmie?"

"Not for any sustained period of time." It was true, Kendal noted with some surprise. Already his posture had begun to straighten, his body re-forming itself to its natural shape without instructions from his mind. "If I must hear a litany of my flaws," he said, losing interest in the game, "please get on with it. I have work to do."

"Right. And that's flaw number one. Here am I, the brother you have not seen for what, eighteen months? But you can scarcely wait to shovel me out of the room. Are you not the least bit curious what I've been up to?"

"I'm rather sure I don't want to know," Kendal said dryly.

"Good, because I'm damn well not going to tell you. Not anything you wouldn't like hearing, at any rate. Suffice it to say I have been a model of rectitude."

Kendal felt guilt nibbling at his conscience. "You know I'll always make time for you, Kit. Forgive me. I'm tired from the trip and out of sorts."

"Because of Celia?"

The question took him by surprise. But then, Kit always did know how to set an ambush. "What has Lady Greer to do with anything?" he asked with false disinterest.

"You tell me. Lightning bolts were flying between the pair of you, Jimmie. I expected the grass to go on fire."

"That was your imagination. If I seemed . . . annoyed, it was only because I arrived to see Paxton rolling about in the dirt and chumming with the servants."

Kit's eyes flashed with anger. "You weren't used to be so high in the instep, my lord earl. Pray tell, who *is* the boy to play with if not the servants' children?"

"I have no idea. But overfamiliarity with the staff is not an option. I shall make that clear to everyone concerned, and trust that you will not countermand my orders once I am gone."

"No promises on that score," Kit advised him in a mild voice. "If you wish Charley raised by your own inflexible standards, then you must remain at Candale and see to it yourself."

Kendal took a drink of wine. "I suggest we change the subject now," he said, his voice tinged with warning.

"Fine." Kit waved a long-fingered hand. "I was wanting to get back to Celia anyway. She told me the two of you met in London."

Not to *that* subject, Kendal thought, sweat breaking out on his nape. "And—?"

"Little more, I'm sorry to say. By her account, you were introduced at a ball and met in passing a time or two after that, purely by chance. But as you doubtless know, the lovely Lady Greer gives much away with her expressions and her eyes. She was attempting to conceal a fascinating tale, I am persuaded." Kit waggled his brows. "Perhaps a *scandalous* tale?"

Kendal made sure his own expression revealed nothing at all. "Do you accuse the lady of lying?" he inquired gently.

"Only of being tiresomely discreet. And really, I thought little of it until you clapped eyes on her in the paddock and went whiter than salt. What's more, I doubt you followed her to the stable to inquire about her health."

"I *escorted* Lady Greer to her mount, as any gentleman would do. You, as I recall, preferred to accompany a yapping puppy."

"Damn stupid choice on my part, I agree. Celia—"

"Lady Greer."

"To you, perhaps."

"And what precisely is she to *you*?" The question snapped out of its own accord, carrying in its wake a thunder of regret. Kendal stilled his breath, not wanting to have asked, not wanting an answer.

"Oh. I see," Kit said softly. "You're bloody jealous."

"Spare me!" Kendal erupted from the chair, the glass he'd forgot he was holding dropping from his hand. It rolled to a halt near the desk, leaving a pool of claret on the carpet.

For several moments he stood there watching it soak in, his thoughts a red blur.

"It's not so unlikely, the two of us," Kit said diabolically. "I'm only a younger son, but she could do worse."

Kendal roused himself for a wintry reply. "I fail to see how. Unless she has a taste for carrying food and a change of linens to whatever gaol you happen to be favoring with your presence."

"Oh, I don't know as how that would be necessary. For a woman like Celia, I might even consider reforming." Kit stretched broadly. "She is looking for a house to buy, you know. Wants to be on the lake. I mean to teach her to sail."

Kendal began to pace the room, if only to keep himself from throttling his brother. There was no telling if Kit was serious about paying his attentions to Lady Greer, although it seemed unlikely. He'd always been a hell-raiser, sent down from school a score of times and often disappearing for months on one of his unsavory adventures. It was unimaginable, Kit settling into parson's mousetrap.

Or was it? He'd a weak spot for children and might well trade his independence for a passel of brats, so long as he managed to snag a wife with sufficient fortune to support the family. Kit could not be an especially successful smuggler, for he never seemed to have any money.

On the other hand, he never had the least bit of trouble getting any woman he wanted. If he had set his sights on Celia Greer, she might decide to take another husband after all.

Kendal realized that he had come to a stop in front of the hearth, and wondered how long he had stood gazing blankly at the empty fireplace. Kit was ominously silent, which generally indicated that trouble was brewing, but Kendal refused absolutely to address the subject of Lady Greer again tonight. Or any other night.

He turned, forcing an impassive expression to his face. "Do me the kindness, Kit, to take yourself out of my chair."

Ignoring that, Kit fixed him with a cold stare. "Do you know what Charley is doing at this moment?"

Kendal glanced over his shoulder at the mantelpiece clock.

"It's nine o'clock. I expect he is at his studies, or readying himself for bed."

"Which shows how little you know. I doubt he's even had his supper. Right now, and for the past several hours, he has been sitting in his room on pins and needles awaiting your summons."

"Did he expect me to ring a peal over him for that display in the paddock? I assure you, I had no such intention."

"Old Yallop assumes that you will. She has been threatening him with your wrath ever since hauling him upstairs and into a bathtub. What's more, she made sure the footman scrubbed him with a horse brush, lest the smell of grass or dirt from an afternoon of play offend your aristocratic nostrils."

Kendal banished the picture that shot into his mind at hearing those words. Miss Yallop's notion of discipline was unacceptable, but what was done, was done. He would see that nothing of the sort happened again. "I've no intention of speaking with Paxton tonight," he said. "Perhaps you should inform Miss Yallop that he is to be put to bed now."

"The hell I will!" Kit bore down on him like a bull on the charge. "Charley would only lie awake for hours with the sword of Demosthenes hanging over him."

"Damocles. Sword of *Damocles*."

Kit slammed his hand against his own forehead. "You cold-hearted, uncompromising jackass! That's precisely what is needed here—a literary emendation! Meantime a little boy is shivering in his boots, and you won't spare a few minutes to put him out of his misery. Who the devil *are* you, James?"

Damned if he knew. Nobody his own brother wanted to know, that was clear enough.

And what use was he to Paxton? However miserable the boy might be now, he would only feel worse after a few minutes in the company of a man who could scarcely bear to look at him. "I have no idea what you mean, Christopher. Lord Paxton need have no fear of a raking down. You are the one can convince him of that. Tell him that I shall speak with him tomorrow after breakfast and hear an accounting of his studies."

Kit raised his chin and his fists. "You'll see him *now*, dammit."

"Are you giving me orders, Kit?"

"I'm trying to help a seven-year-old boy who is terrified of his own father."

"You know better than that, on every count."

Kit stalked to the wall and rammed a fist into the plaster. "Next time it will be your face," he swore in a raw voice. "Was a time I idolized you, James. Almost as much as Charley does. What became of the brother I grew up with?"

"I thought you knew," Kendal replied glacially.

"Yes. But the child is not to blame. Stop punishing him."

"I have never done so. You don't know what you're talking about. Duty keeps me away. And besides, what have I to offer a boy of his age?"

"Nothing, apparently." Kit turned, rubbing at his injured hand. "Not any longer. Was a time you took me on your lap and read me stories, and played at marbles with Alex, and did all you could to hold what remained of our family together. You were little more than a child yourself, James, but I begin to think you were a better man then than you are now."

Kendal had a sudden, vivid memory of Kit a score of years ago, hair pale as flax, thin and bony, although his long legs and wide shoulders promised the height and strength he'd grown into. And Alex, who began small and dark—rather like Paxton, come to think of it—only to develop into the tallest of the Valliant brothers and the most striking in appearance.

It had been left to him, about the time his voice began to change, to see to their welfare. He remembered getting through the days as best he could and then sitting alone in his room at night, shivering at the thought that he was doing it all wrong. The responsibility had very nearly overwhelmed him, and he would have run from it if he could.

He wanted to run now, from Paxton. Kit would say he had been doing just that.

Crossing to his desk, he sat and buried his face in his hands. Distantly, he was aware of Kit at the door speaking to the butler, and knew what he had in mind.

Well, let it be. Might as well get it over with, but Lord, what a hellish day. Raising his head, he sifted through the file of reports he'd been examining, unable to remember why he'd brought them out in the first place.

A few minutes later, hearing a light rap on the door, he planted his elbows on the desk and steepled his hands.

Kit snorted.

Blast it, a man had to do *something* with his hands. With a sharp look at his brother, Kendal left them where they were.

Paxton, impeccably dressed, his newly washed hair shining, took two steps into the room. "You wished to see me, sir?"

"Yes." Kendal made an effort to gentle his voice. "You needn't keep such a distance. Move closer, where I can see you."

The boy took a few more steps, his gaze fixed on the carpet, only to come to an abrupt halt. He looked up at Kendal with wide, pleading eyes. "I didn't do it, sir. Cross my heart."

"Do wha—? Oh. The wine stain. No, I did that." He cleared his throat. "How are you getting on, Paxton?"

"Very well, sir." He glanced once more at the carpet, as if unable to credit that Lord Kendal had made such a mess.

"Your lessons are progressing on schedule?" Kendal persisted when the boy failed to say anything more.

His face brightened. "Mr. Symington says I will likely take honors at Harrow, sir." The light dimmed. "He says I am to be sent away at Michaelmas."

"Do you not wish to go?"

"Mr. Symington says there will be lots of other boys there. I expect I shall like that."

Kendal doubted it. In his experience, the heirs of wealthy peers were invariably singled out by the senior boys for special torments. "Well, perhaps you needn't be enrolled until the spring. I'll discuss the matter with your tutor. In the meantime Miss Yallop has brought a few matters to my attention. Most can be taken up at a later date, but she insists that the dog be dealt with immediately. Is it true he spends the night in your bedchamber?"

"No, sir. Well, not *all* night." He slid a glance at Kit, who

139

was leaning against the mantelpiece with his arms folded over his chest. "He is there when I go to sleep, but he is gone when Nanny Yallop comes to wake me up."

"And how does that come about, do you suppose?"

Paxton flushed. "I cannot say, sir."

"There is also the problem of where he chooses to do his business. Your dressing-room floor, I believe."

"Only a few times," Paxton said quickly. "Sir. And I always clean it up right away."

"Even so, Miss Yallop objects most strenuously to what she describes as a 'lingering stench.' Until the puppy has learned to control himself, he will do better in the barn. Don't you agree?"

Paxton shot another look at Kit, who nodded encouragement. "But, sir, I'm the one who lives in my room, and I don't mind the lingering stench. Besides, how can Wellington be trained to control himself if he's always in the barn?"

Good question. Kendal rubbed the bridge of his nose, thinking an international treaty would be easier to negotiate than this absurd civil war between nanny and mutt. "I take it that your uncle has a hand in all this, most particularly the mystery of how the dog disappears into the night?"

Lips white, Paxton shook his head. "Wellington is my responsibility, sir."

"I see." Kendal had fully meant to banish the dog from the house, but that no longer seemed a good idea. There was no real harm done, except to Miss Yallop's sensibilities, and she had far too many sensibilities. Besides, he was not of a mood to play the villain tonight. And a villain is what he would be, should he snatch Paxton's puppy away within hours of arriving home. "Kit, ring for the butler again, will you?"

Paxton stood like a condemned felon waiting for the noose to drop around his neck.

Kendal wanted to reassure him, but had no idea how to speak with a child. Especially this one. "Young man," he said in a severe voice, "I expect you to make every effort to instill a bit of discipline into your puppy, and to keep him out of Miss Yallop's sight whenever possible. Do you understand?"

"N-no, sir." His eyes lit with hope. "Does that mean I can keep him in my room at bedtime?"

"For the time being. We'll have to see how well he adjusts, but I'll not evict him until he has been given a chance to prove himself. Tomorrow, I shall inform Miss Yallop that the dog is permitted to remain in the house, subject to your own discretion, and that you will not abuse the privilege."

"Oh, I won't, sir. Except, I don't know exactly what my discreption is."

"Just use your head, child. None of us wants Miss Yallop plaguing us, right? Give her no reason to do so."

"I'll try, sir. But sometimes," he added candidly, "I think she doesn't need a reason for plaguing."

Kit barked a laugh.

"Your lordship?" the butler said from the door.

Relieved to put this awkward encounter to an end, Kendal stood. "Geeson, please inform Miss Yallop that she may retire for the night, and ask her to attend me here at nine o'clock tomorrow morning. I'll expect Mr. Symington at nine-thirty. Also, send one of the maids to help Lord Paxton ready himself for bed. Have you had your supper, Paxton?"

"Yes, sir."

"The tray was returned to the kitchen untouched," Geeson informed him blandly.

"Indeed?" Kendal almost laughed. The butler, who had known him since he was in short pants, was always properly deferential when he spoke out of turn. "In that case, instruct the maid to bring up a glass of milk and a plate of biscuits. And a bone, if one is to be had."

"Very good, your lordship."

When he was gone, Kendal turned back to Lord Paxton, who was regarding him with openmouthed astonishment.

Why was that? he wondered. He had never been unkind to the boy. True, he had seen him no more than a handful of times in the last several years, but the household staff had been ordered to treat Paxton with all the respect due to the Kendal heir. He would reaffirm that order before returning to London, in case a few of the servants had become lax in their duties.

141

He reminded himself to have Geeson arrange for the floor of Paxton's dressing room to be scoured every morning. That should mollify Miss Yallop, who would be seeking new employment once Paxton was dispatched to Harrow. He would make sure to bring up the subject of references when he spoke with her tomorrow, if only to keep her quiet about the dog.

What else? He was too tired to order his thoughts. "Kit, why don't you take Paxton upstairs, in case Miss Yallop has misunderstood Geeson's instructions."

"Oh, she's skulking around, I have no doubt." Pulling himself from the wall, Kit held out his hand. "Come along, Charley. We'll face her down together."

Instead of hurrying over to his uncle, as Kendal had expected, Paxton took the last few steps to the edge of the desk and bowed. "Thank you, sir," he said. "I promise that Wellington will behave himself. And I'll use my discretion, too. Cross my heart."

"Very well, Paxton. We'll speak again tomorrow at ten o'clock. Good night."

"Good night, sir." With another bow, he crossed to where Kit was standing and took his hand.

Kendal didn't dare to look at his brother again. He'd had enough disapproval for one day, thank you very much. "Don't come back, Kit," he said. "I've work to do."

Kit closed the door behind him without a word, which spoke louder than anything he'd said all evening. Settling back on the chair with a groan, Kendal mauled his hair with a shaking hand. Damn! In this house, he never seemed to put a foot right, or say what he ought, or do what was best. Was a time he had loved Candale, but now he could scarcely abide a single hour here, let alone the ten or more days he'd be forced to play host to a Russian maniac.

And there was Paxton, who deserved better than he could give him. And Kit, who seemed to have appointed himself unofficial conscience to his brother, which was rather a stretch for a man generally one step ahead of the constables.

And Celia Greer. The very last person he ever wanted to see again right here on his doorstep, and nothing he could do about it. Not since she gave him the opportunity to forbid her to set foot on the estate, which he ought to have done, but didn't. He could hardly withdraw permission now.

Still, she had appeared no more pleased to see him than he was to see her. With any luck, she'd keep well out of his way.

He was counting on it.

But devil take it, how could he purge her forever from his thoughts? She haunted his days. She drifted through his dreams, on the rare occasions he had been able to sleep since—

No! He would *not* gnaw on old wounds tonight. With deliberation, he reached for the ledger of household accounts and set to work.

Chapter 14

Three days later General Vasily Chirikov charged onto the Candale estate with four junior officers in tow. He seemed to have been expecting that Mr. Wordsworth would be there to greet him, but allowed that there was no way the time of his own arrival could have been anticipated. Tomorrow would do well enough.

It was going to be, Kendal reflected dismally, a very long week.

He had traced the poet's direction and sent a letter, but his courteous request met with a firm no. Mr. Wordsworth could not spare the time for a meeting, not even with a gentleman come all the way from Russia to see him. He conveyed his good wishes to Lord Kendal and General Chirikov.

Kendal tried again, this time by sending his agent to deliver a note. But the birdlike woman who answered the door refused to admit him, promising to give the letter to her brother. There was no reply.

So much for Wordsworth, and Kendal had yet to scratch up a substitute. He'd been informed that writers were thick on the Lake Country ground, but they all seemed to have scarpered— Southey to London, De Quincey to Scotland, and Coleridge to the devil knew where.

Only Mr. Tittleton, who claimed to be the true author of *Paradise Lost*, was available to grant an audience. Kendal rather thought Tittleton and Chirikov deserved each other, but reluctantly declined the offer.

Poetless, he set himself to distract Chirikov and entertain his pack of hard-drinking subordinates with hunting parties and fishing parties and dinner parties. But there was nothing of interest to shoot, they complained. No tigers. No bears. As for fishing—*pah!* A sport for little boys.

The dinner parties were disasters of the first order. The young officers, who spoke no English, drank deep and chewed with their mouths open, occasionally bursting into raucous song. The neighborhood gentry, shocked to their toes, sat petrified until the last cover was removed. Then, with mumbled excuses, they fled.

Meanwhile Chirikov moped.

The men took target practice on the sheep, trying to lop off their ears. Kendal put a stop to it, so they turned to shooting at the chimney pots.

Chirikov sulked.

A lieutenant tried to force himself on a kitchen maid, who clobbered him with a rolling pin. Kit plucked a terrified tweeny from the grip of a sodden major and gave him a bloody nose.

After four days Kendal had had enough. Ruthlessly, he offered the ambitious Lord Lonsdale a chance to be the envy of his cronies. Would he care to host a contigent of the Russian delegation for a week of shooting on his estate? Beginning the very next day?

Lonsdale, heaven bless him, accepted immediately.

Next, Kendal convinced the officers that there was better hunting farther north, where Lonsdale resided. Perhaps even a bear or two.

Chirikov was roused from his brown study long enough to wave agreement to Kendal's plan, although he himself refused to budge from Candale. He meant to stay until he shook hands with William Wordsworth or the arrival of Judgment Day, whichever came first.

On this particular morning, Kendal was tramping up Crosby Fell in the company of his brother, trailing Chirikov at a considerable distance. For all his size, the man could climb like a goat. Earlier, the Russian general had set out on a pilgrimage in search of daffodils. A *host* of daffodils, to be precise, just like the one in Mr. Wordsworth's poem.

Kendal hadn't the heart to tell him there wasn't a daffodil to be found in late July, any more than he'd been able to confess that Wordsworth had twice refused invitations to meet his most devoted acolyte.

"You know, I quite like the fellow," Kit said as he clambered over an outcropping of stone. "He's a trifle queer in the attic, of course, but a great gun when he forgets all that rhyming twaddle."

"Don't mention guns to me," Kendal said, following his brother over the rocks. "And when does he *ever* forget?"

"Oh, I've managed to pry him from the house for a few neck-or-nothing rides while you were doing whatever it is you do. He takes Charley up with him and they race across the countryside, shrieking like Mongols."

Paxton *shrieking*, for pity's sake? Riding out with that great Russian bear when he should be at his lessons? Kendal suspected that Lady Greer made up a fourth during those riding expeditions, although she doubtless arranged to meet with the others somewhere beyond the boundaries of Candale.

They had not, he noted with a sting of resentment, invited *him* to come along.

Naturally, he would have refused. Nevertheless . . .

He dug his whitethorn walking stick into the ground. Kit was taking unholy pleasure from watching him twist in the wind, but the scoundrel had also been damnably useful of late. Yesterday he removed Chirikov from Kendal's hair for an entire afternoon of fishing at Derwent Water.

And they hadn't fished alone.

Lady Greer had found the best worms and baited her own hooks, Paxton informed him when the small party—all but Lady Greer, of course—returned to Candale with their catch. The boy had snagged a tiny, paper-thin fish all by himself, and shyly presented it to his father.

Standing there, fish held by its tiny tail fin between his thumb and forefinger, Paxton looked so earnest that Kendal could not help but accept it with feigned delight, promising to have it cooked up for his supper.

For once, Kit had shot him a look of approval.

Kendal wondered what had become of that fishlet. It made

one bite for a kitchen cat, he supposed, wrenching his thoughts to more urgent matters. "I've run out of poets, Kit. What makes Chirikov imagine the countryside is littered with them?"

"You only need the one," Kit pointed out. "He wants that Wordsworth chap."

"Who has already turned me down. Twice."

"Indeed? Did you offer to pay him? Writers are notoriously poor, you know. Or perhaps you ought to haul your aristocrat arse to Rydal and ask him in person. Your letters can be more than a little off-putting, Jimmie. The handful you've sent me these last five years certainly were."

"I daresay. But considering that half were addressed to whatever prison you were currently patronizing, with a bank draft enclosed to secure your bail, I can scarcely be blamed for—"

"Right." Kit lifted his arms in surrender. "I forgot that part. But even your Christmas letters—and I was always at Candale for Christmas—sounded like a cross between a sermon and a government dispatch. When I read them to Charley, I had to make up the words. God knows I couldn't use the ones you actually wrote. 'Convey my regards to Paxton,' of all things. 'Buy him something and charge it to the estate.' "

"I take your point, Christopher. Thank you."

"Oh, you're welcome, Lord Kendal. Always happy to oblige. And you needn't glower. Indeed, were I you, I'd be flattering a younger brother who happens to be in a position to do me—meaning you, that is—an enormous favor." He grinned. "But then, what do I know? You're the diplomat in the family."

"What favor?" There was only one service he required at the moment, as Kit very well knew. "Never tell me *you* can produce Wordsworth?"

"Hardly. I haven't read a poxy poem since school days. But I know someone who can serve him up on a platter, should that someone rouse herself. She won't do it on your behalf, I am convinced, but it's just possible that I can persuade her."

Her was Celia Greer, naturally. Kendal dropped onto a convenient boulder, swearing under his breath.

"Are we stopping?" Kit sank cross-legged to the ground.

"Past time. These new boots are rubbing blisters. What say we wait here until Chirikov comes back down?"

"Fine. And you can explain to me why Lady Greer has failed to come forward before now. Why the devil didn't she tell me she was acquainted with Wordsworth?"

"The fact that you have not seen her since the day you came home might have something to do with it," Kit observed mildly.

"Yes. Very well. But she's seen Chirikov, and she knows he is enamored of that bloody poet. Has she refused to introduce them merely to spite me?"

"My, my, *someone* has a lofty opinion of his own significance. In fact, Jimmie, when our little group sets out on an expedition, poetry is a forbidden subject of conversation. That's supposedly for Charley's sake, but primarily for my own. Yesterday, though, and I don't remember how it came up, Celia happened to mention the Wordsworth connection to me."

"And you can persuade her to use that connection?"

"I believe so. Your problem is convincing me to exert myself. Bribing me, to be more accurate, and this is one favor that won't come cheap. How often do I get you in my power, Jimmie? This once? Can't blame a fellow for taking advantage."

"No. But I can fling you off this mountain, and I bloody well will if you don't stop gloating. Name your price and be done with it."

"That impertinence will cost you an extra fifty pounds," Kit advised him. "But here's the primary deal. Saturday is Charley's birthday, which I expect you had wholly forgot. He wants to go fishing again, so we've planned a picnic on Windemere Lake just across from Belle Isle. You know the place. We used to go there when we were lads. You will be on hand for the picnic and on good behavior, which means pretending you are delighted to be there and going along with the fun." Kit's face hardened. "What's more, Charley wants a pony. But I've been unable to find one fine enough for him, so you will make sure he has the best pony to be had north of Birmingham. Agreed?"

Kendal turned his back and folded his arms, gazing out over

the fells. "If you couldn't do it, how the devil do you expect *me* to locate a plaguey pony?"

"The Foreign Office lets you negotiate the future of England, Jimmie. Surely you can unearth one small horse for a little boy."

It always came back to Paxton. Hellfire! Why wouldn't Kit leave this alone? It was none of his damn business, for one thing. And he, more than anyone else, ought to understand why—

"I'll try to rustle up a pony," he said tightly. "But will Lady Greer keep her end of the bargain, once you inform her what that is?" He never questioned that Kit could convince her to try. From the time he learned to babble his first words, Kit could talk the birds out of trees.

"Fact is," Kit admitted with a shrug, "she doesn't even know Wordsworth. But she's been writing back and forth with his sister, and I'm counting on her to convince said sister that her brother ought to meet my brother. Who will bring his resident Russian along to tea, naturally. It's not such a long shot as you are thinking, by the by."

"At the moment it sounds as if I'd have a better chance of flying to the moon."

"Well, that's because you've always underestimated me, Jimmie. And I expect you have no idea what Celia is capable of. Miracles, I'm hoping, and I'm not referring to recruiting the poetry fellow. But never mind that. Have we a deal?"

"Just deliver the poet, Kit. I don't care how you do it. I'll be at the picnic, and I'll find a damned pony. Good enough?"

"Not nearly," Kit replied. "But it's a start."

Chapter 15

From the parlor window, Celia watched the Earl of Kendal's crested carriage pull into the courtyard of the Merry Goosegirl. It had barely come to a halt when the door flew open and Vasily Chirikov sprang out.

Despite her jittery nerves, Celia could not help but laugh. The general meant to greet his idol in style, and he looked splendid indeed in a dark green coat edged in red and trimmed with yellow buttons, braid, and epaulets. His sash was white, striped with gold and tied with fringed knots. The entire left side of his chest dripped with medals, and an enormous sword was slung from his belt in a brass-studded scabbard.

She hoped the Wordsworth household was prepared for an invasion.

Lord Kendal waited for the steps to be lowered before alighting with his customary grace, looking austerely elegant in dove-gray pantaloons, a charcoal-gray coat, and pristine white linen. The silver knob atop his black walking stick shone under the bright noonday sun.

Celia adjusted her bonnet, pulled on her gloves, and went outside to meet them.

"Lady Greer!" Chirikov boomed, sweeping his black cocked hat from his head and thundering in her direction.

Next she knew, Celia was enveloped in a pair of tree-trunk arms, with her nose buried in medals and a sword hilt plowing into her stomach.

"You haff saved me!" he proclaimed. "I vill build a church in St. Petersburg to honor you."

"Unless you also mean to bury the lady there," Kendal said pointedly, "it might be well to permit her to breathe."

Chirikov let go so abruptly that Celia was thrown off balance, and she might have toppled had not Kendal steadied her with a firm hand on her elbow. The touch of his soft kidskin glove against her bare flesh sent lightning zigzagging up and down her arm.

"Thank you," she said, stepping free of his dangerous grasp.

Chirikov was gazing at her with the woebegone expression of an oversized puppy that had committed an indiscretion. "Forgiff me. I am haffing many nerffs today."

She smiled brightly. "Miss Wordsworth assures me that her brother is most eager to make your acquaintance, sir. But I do believe that she will be a trifle taken aback if you greet her wearing such an impressive weapon."

"Hah! Kendal tells me same think. I must leaf it in coach, yes?"

"Decidedly," said the earl, gesturing to the carriage. "Shall we be on our way?"

Chirikov and the stack of books he'd brought along for Wordsworth to sign filled all of one bench, so Celia was forced to sit beside Lord Kendal on the other for the journey to Rydal. She was forcibly reminded of the last time they had traveled side by side, and where they were going, and what had happened there.

If he remembered that day, he gave no sign of it. He was wearing what she thought of as his "diplomat face," ineffably calm, gravely polite. She'd wager *his* heart wasn't jumping about in his chest like a mad March hare.

He inclined his head. "If I may inquire, Lady Greer, how was it you succeeded in bringing about this meeting so expeditiously? Your message this morning was unexpected, though certainly welcome."

She tried to match his cool tone. "I have long intended to pay a call on Miss Wordsworth, and Kit's . . . er, Mr. Valliant's request merely coincided with my own wishes. I am only sorry that she insisted you make one of the party. The afternoon will prove tedious for you, I'm afraid."

"Not at all." He looked over at her, his eyes wintry. "But I regret that you find yourself *sorry* on my account. Does my company offend you, madam?"

Stunned at the question, she shot an embarrassed glance at Chirikov. Fortunately, he was paying them no attention, wholly preoccupied with the volume of poetry spread open on his lap.

"How can you ask such a thing?" she hissed under her breath. "I had thought the situation quite the reverse. And in my message, I told you that I meant to travel on horseback and meet you at Rydal Mount. It was you who insisted on picking me up at the Merry Goosegirl."

"The morning was overcast, and I feared you would be caught in a downpour. But let us not squabble, Lady Greer. Why is it Miss Wordsworth requires my presence at tea, do you suppose?"

He was deliberately setting her on edge, she decided, and then making it her fault when she tumbled over the side. It was a diplomat's trick to gain the upper hand, but she was having none of it.

"I expect it was your purse she invited to tea, my lord. Poets are ever in search of wealthy patrons, and you happen to be the local potentate. Likely she hopes you will commission her brother's next epic, or at the very least, fund a ballad or two."

"God forbid," he said with a grimace. "I'd sooner sponsor a band of pestilential Morris dancers. But tell me, why have you taken rooms at the woefully named Merry Goosegirl? Would not your own home be more comfortable than a country inn?"

She'd sooner sleep under a hedgerow than spend another night at Greer's farm. "The property will be put up for sale when repairs are completed," she explained. "At the moment workers are tearing down most of the outbuildings and reroofing the house, which is naturally creating a great deal of noise and dust. An agent is trying to locate a suitable house for me in Ambleside or Bowness, but meantime I shall remain where I am."

He cast her a sideways glance. "Alone?"

What in blazes was he implying? "For the most part," she said between her teeth. "If you discount the queue of lovers waiting in the passageway outside my bedchamber. I don't admit just anyone, you know."

She was pleased to see his head snap back against the leather squabs as if she'd slapped him.

A tense silence enveloped the compartment for nearly an hour as the coach wound its way through Applethwaite and Ambleside, finally slowing as Rydal came into view.

Up a steep lane from the road, Rydal Mount was set amid several acres of gardens, with a lovely view of Rydal Water and the northern reaches of Lake Windemere. A perfect setting for a poet enamored with the beauties of nature, Celia thought, calmer now.

She had spent most of the last hour devising clever, sophisticated replies to Lord Kendal's provocative questions—far too late, of course. It was a wonder the carriage hadn't ignited from the invisible sparks shooting between them. At one point she had wrenched her gaze from the window long enough to see his hand clutching the knob of his walking stick with enough force to melt the silver.

But he had donned his diplomat face again by the time a footman opened the carriage door, and he handed her onto the gravel walkway with distant courtesy.

She longed to kick him where it would hurt.

Chirikov jumped down, mustache twitching and arms full of books, his sword still swinging from its scabbard. He had forgot to remove it, and Celia hadn't the heart to remind him.

What a dear man, so excited at the prospect of meeting his idol. With blistering willpower, she consigned Lord Kendal to the devil. This was Vasily Chirikov's day, and nothing must be allowed to spoil it.

A short, thin woman with gypsy-brown skin scurried out to greet them, hands fluttering in agitation. "Lady Greer? But of course it is. Who else could it be? I am so delighted to meet you."

"Thank you for inviting us on such short notice," Celia

replied, torn between a polite curtsy and a warm hug. She had exchanged only a few letters with Dorothy Wordsworth, but their correspondence had been precious to her. Most of the people she wrote to during her bleak years with Greer never wrote back, but Dorothy had faithfully replied each time, perhaps as hungry for pen-friends as Celia had been. She'd have written more often to Dorothy, but Greer was never convinced that franking a letter didn't cost him anything. He had even begrudged the price of paper and ink.

Reminding herself yet again that her husband's parsimony had made her a rich widow, Celia introduced Lord Kendal and the crimson-faced General Chirikov. Several books toppled from his arms onto the gravel when he bowed, but Dorothy quickly scooped them up, brightening when she saw her brother's name on the spines.

"You admire William's poetry?" she inquired dubiously, eyes fixed on his sword.

"With all my heart," Chirikov swore. "Bless you, luffly lady, for permitting me come into your beautiful home."

Celia caught Kendal's amused glance and could not help smiling back when he took her arm and led her behind Dorothy and Chirikov into the house.

The poet waited for them beside the mantelpiece in a large drawing room, one wall lined with bookshelves and the others covered with framed portraits. A sofa and a few wooden chairs were set around the fireplace, and a thick Turkey carpet covered the floor.

As for William Wordsworth himself, Celia could not be impressed. Although he stood taller than average, Kendal topped him by a hand and Chirikov, of course, dwarfed everyone. Wordsworth's narrow, slightly droopy shoulders and a Brutus cut designed to conceal his receding hairline, not to mention legs somehow out of proportion to his body, did not help his cause.

But there was clear intelligence in his sharp eyes as he greeted his guests with old-fashioned formality.

Chirikov, suddenly shy, held back, and Celia regarded his

blanched face with concern. He looked, impossibly, on the point of swooning.

Then Kendal, with practiced ease, got them all settled—Wordsworth and Chirikov together on the sofa, Celia perched on a hard chair next to the one holding Dorothy's skinny body, and himself with one arm relaxed on the mantelpiece as he stood, overseeing the lot of them.

Well done, my lord, Celia thought, resenting his aloof appraisal of the scene he had orchestrated. He needn't look as if he'd gone slumming by coming to Rydal Mount. This wasn't exactly Versailles, to be sure, but the general and the poet seemed to be hitting it off well. They were totally absorbed with each other, although Wordsworth seemed to be doing all the talking. His words were indistinguishable from where she sat, and he appeared to have forgot anyone else was in the room.

She looked over at Dorothy, who was squirming on her chair and watching her brother with rapt attention. Celia had hoped to become better acquainted with her pen-friend, but her attempts to begin a conversation met with so little encouragement that she soon abandoned the effort. For half an hour she sat quietly, watching the hands of the ormulu clock on the mantelpiece.

Kendal had grown sufficiently bored to leave his perch and explore the bookcases, which put him from her sight unless she swiveled on her chair to look at him. She refused to give him so much satisfaction. Not that he was likely to notice, of course. She wished she had thought to wander over to the bookcases before he did. When, she wondered, would Dorothy rouse herself to serve tea?

Finally, unable to sit still a moment longer, she reached over and plucked at Dorothy's sleeve. "Will you show me the gardens, please? We had the barest glimpse of them from the carriage."

Dorothy started as if jolted from a trance. "Oh, yes indeed. I have been so very rude. Do forgive me, Lady Greer. William was unsettled all morning, you understand, what with an earl and a general of the Russian Imperial Guard coming to call. But he seems quite comfortable now, so I believe it is safe to go."

As they left the parlor Celia glanced over her shoulder at Lord Kendal. He held open a large, leather-bound book, to all appearances thoroughly absorbed with its contents. Had he looked up, she might have beckoned him to join them in the garden. Or perhaps not. In any event, he did not give her the chance.

Kendal saw her go, her pale lavender skirts clinging deliciously to her rounded hips and long, graceful legs. He might have followed her, had she given him the slightest indication his company would be welcome. But what did he expect? After his inexplicable, stunningly cruel attack in the carriage, she could only be wishing him at Jericho.

What had possessed him to speak in such a way to her? Had Chirikov been paying the least bit of attention to his caustic remarks, the general would have called him out on the spot.

Not that Lady Greer required a champion to defend her. She had rendered him to sausage with chilling ease, leaving him to stew in his own fury while she blithely turned away and proceeded to enjoy the lakeland scenery.

The blame was entirely his, which infuriated him all the more. Each time they met, his reprehensible conduct astounded him. Celia Greer had demolished a lifetime of rigid self-discipline simply by existing, but he could scarcely expect her to disappear from the face of the earth merely to preserve his sanity.

What remained of it. Quite irrationally, he resented her for being what she was. With so small a thing as a toss of her golden curls or the flash of a dimple when she smiled, she snatched away his reason like a cat making off with a mackerel.

Above all, he resented her for wielding such power over him. Naturally, the solution was to avoid her company at any cost. But the cost, he had already discovered, was exceedingly dear. Ever since that afternoon at the White Swan, he had been paying with sleepless nights, aching loins, and suicidal notions of leaping again into the fire.

He had done precisely that by insisting they travel together to Rydal. Oh, he'd justified his folly with the assumption that Chirikov's presence would keep his temper in check, but he suspected the entire Russian army could not do that. Not with Celia Greer in the vicinity.

After today's debacle, he knew better than to tempt fate or his own flagging self-control ever again. He would, he resolved, put miles between them. Whole countries. He would be the first to arrive in Austria for the Congress of Vienna and the last to depart when it was concluded, perhaps on a ship bound for China.

But now, he accepted after several minutes trying to convince himself otherwise, he had no choice but to make his apology to Lady Greer.

Returning the book he'd been holding to the shelf, he glanced over at Wordsworth and Chirikov. The poet was still nattering about some topic of monumental unimportance while his audience of one regarded him with unabashed adulation. They wouldn't notice a herd of woolly mammoths charging through the drawing-room doors, let alone his quiet departure.

Kendal stepped outside, blinking against the bright sunshine, and heard laughter coming from the rear of the house. He followed the sound, pausing in the shadow of an ivy-covered pergola when he saw her.

She was swinging from a tree.

Her skirts flew up, revealing shapely ankles and a generous portion of stockinged legs as she soared, laughing with delight. Beside her on another swing, a young boy was straining to match her dizzying height.

"Harder!" he shrieked to the girl who was pushing him.

"I'm *trying*!" she shouted in reply. "When is it my turn?"

Immediately Lady Greer scraped her half boots on the packed dirt to slow herself and jumped off the wooden bench. "Mercy me!" she exclaimed, staggering in circles as the two children laughed uproariously. "I am quite colly-walloped. You had best take my place, Dora."

"Will you push me, ma'am?" the girl asked, settling in the swing.

"Just to get you started." She glanced in his direction, and Kendal suspected she had been aware of his presence the moment he arrived. "Then you must excuse me while I find my balance again. I am too ancient a creature for such exertion."

When Dora had been propelled to a satisfying height, Lady Greer spoke briefly with Dorothy Wordsworth and another woman seated beside her on the grass. Kendal had not even noticed them. Then she moved in his direction, brushing down her ruffled skirts, a look of polite inquiry on her face.

"Is it time to depart, my lord?"

"Not unless you can figure a way to detach General Chirikov from his poet. They are growing together like vines. Will you walk with me for a few minutes, Lady Greer?" He held out his arm, rather afraid she would refuse to take it.

With transparent reluctance, she placed her hand on his wrist and permitted him to lead her across the lawn, away from the children and the avid eyes of the ladies, who had been watching curiously.

Suddenly unwilling to launch himself directly into troubled waters, he cast about for an innocuous remark. "What exactly does it mean, Lady Greer? To be colly-walloped?"

"What?" She frowned. "Oh, *that*! I have no idea, sir. I just invented the word. How shall we define it?"

The way he was feeling defined colly-walloped fairly well, he would guess. Scatty. Fuzzy-headed. Poleaxed. "Perhaps we should leave it as is, meaning whatever anyone wishes it to mean."

She smiled approval. "Dorothy was wondering if she ought to serve refreshments, but she dislikes interrupting her brother when he is in full cry. He rarely has occasion to discuss poetic theory since Mr. Coleridge took himself off to wherever he's gone, and he seems to be enjoying himself with General Chirikov."

"The salivating worship of an acolyte has its appeal, I suppose."

"And sarcasm does not become you, sir." She removed her hand from his arm. "The general is, to be sure, somewhat extravagant in his devotion to Mr. Wordsworth, but he is by nature a man of excessive emotions. Has he told you how he came to love the poems with such ferocious zeal?"

Chastened, Kendal shook his head.

"Perhaps you won't think him such a fool if I explain. A winter campaign in Russia is all but unendurable, by his account, and in the long, cold nights, his undernourished men froze to death by the score. But Bonaparte was advancing, and Chirikov had been ordered to hold position whatever the hardships. Requiring a distraction to preserve his clarity of mind, he elected to improve his command of English."

She took a deep breath. "Really, you should ask the general to tell you about his experiences in the war. It quite broke my heart to hear of such unimaginable horrors."

"I am astonished that he spoke of them to a lady," Kendal said stiffly.

"You *would* be," she said with a sigh. "But I do not wish to be sheltered from life, even at its worst. In any case, Chirikov's physician offered to tutor him, using the only book written in English that could be found. It was *Lyrical Ballads*, containing poems by Mr. Wordsworth, and the general memorized every one of them. I'll not try to explain how they affected him during those hellish months, or why he found peace of heart by reading them again and again."

She made a graceful gesture. "Indeed, I scarcely understand it myself, being unacquainted with his circumstances or Mr. Wordsworth's verses. But they resonated in his soul, and he promised himself that should he survive the war, he would make a pilgrimage to England and pay honor to the poet who gave him the will to endure."

A wood warbler chirruped overhead, and Kendal realized they had come to a stop under the branches of a silver birch. Celia—he could not think of her as Lady Greer, however hard he tried—gazed up at him with eyes that dared him to ridicule Chirikov.

All he wanted to do was kiss her senseless.

Which only proved that he, not the Russian, was the real fool. He took a backward step, and then another, putting distance between them. Putting her beyond arm's reach, truth be told, because he could not trust his arms to behave themselves. They remembered all too well how it felt to be wrapped around that slender, vibrant body.

Damn his arms, and every other part of him that had gone to battle with his thoroughly honorable intentions. He had set out to clear his conscience with an apology, escort her back to the Green Goose, or whatever that stupid inn was called, and wash his hands of Celia, once and for all.

And he could do it, too. Serenely. With practiced ease. What use were his years of diplomatic service, after all, if he could not rid himself of one troublesome young woman without giving offense?

It helped not to look at her, though. He fixed his gaze at a point beyond her shoulder and shaped his lips into a thin smile. "I have misjudged General Chirikov," he acknowledged graciously. Conceding the obvious was the usual strategy in these situations. "Thank you for clarifying what I failed to recognize."

"Oh, you are most welcome," she said, mocking his stilted tone. "Should you require enlightenment on any other subject, I would be most happy to provide it."

"Thank you yet again. But what I *require* . . . that is, what I wish—" He seized a deep breath. "In point of fact, Lady Greer, I owe you a most profound apology for my disgraceful behavior in the carriage."

Silence.

A minute—or was it an eternity?—went by, and still she failed to respond. It was nothing, she should be saying. Or, better, I was at fault for overreacting to a few perfectly innocuous remarks.

But she only looked at him, head tilted expectantly, her stillness drawing his gaze to her face despite his every effort to hold it away.

"*What?*" he asked from sheer frustration.

"You said that you owed me an apology, sir, and I quite agree. I was waiting to hear it."

When pigs take flight! was his first, admittedly childish thought. No one of his acquaintance actually apologized in so many words. They acknowledged the need to do so and that was the end of it. Groveling was not expected from gentlemen of his class, and it was certainly not in his nature.

"But never mind," she said airily. "I've heard worse from you than I did today, although your lamentable manners never fail to astonish me. Were it not years too late, Lord Kendal, I would certainly advise you to reconsider a career in the diplomatic corps."

The thin slice of his brain that still functioned ordered him to bow and walk away, but he felt his heels dig in. "And I would advise *you*, Lady Greer, to remove your lovely nose from any and all matters concerning my family."

If he thought that his open declaration of war, which he immediately wanted to call back, would deter her, he was dead wrong.

"At last we come to it," she said. "I'm only surprised you waited this long."

"Surely it is obvious that this situation is intolerable for everyone concerned."

Her brows arched. "Not for me, sir. Not for Kit. And certainly not for Charley, who needs all the friends he can get. No, Lord Kendal, *you* are the one thinks it intolerable, which I find incomprehensible given that you are no part of anything we do. Can you explain it to me? Why does it so disturb you that I have spent a few hours in company with the boy?"

"Nearly every day," he gritted. "His lessons are disturbed. His governess complains. Household discipline has suffered."

"Good heavens, just listen to yourself!" She speared him with a look of disdain. "The child cannot be locked up with his books all summer for the convenience of your *servants*. He should be outside, like Tom and Dora Wordsworth, laughing and playing as ordinary children do."

"Lord Paxton," Kendal said icily, "will have responsibilities beyond those of a rustic poet's offspring. As heir to the title, he must prepare himself. And I assure you, one day he will be grateful for the education, self-discipline, and sense of duty his teachers instill in him now."

"I see, my lord. You wish him to become a facsimile of yourself."

"That is highly unlikely, madam. What I do *not* wish is your continued meddling. It disrupts order. And have you considered the effect on Paxton when you lose interest in him and wander off to find yourself a new toy?"

"As you have done?" she fired back, her small hands clenching at her skirts.

"That will be quite enough, young woman." His voice was a file grating on metal. "I'll take no lessons from a presumptuous female, especially one whose own standards of conduct and morality have been deplorable, to say the least."

The blood drained from her face. "You would know," she said softly.

"Indeed." The devil was driving him now. "Are we clear on this matter? Candale is closed to you. That applies from this moment, and continues when I am gone back to London. You will not set foot on the estate."

She nodded.

Fight me, damn you! But she only gazed at him, pale and still, her thoughts unreadable. She had been just so when he returned to the bedchamber at the White Swan after—no. He must not think on that again, not ever again.

He meant to read her a list of instructions, but could no longer remember what they were. He knew only that he must, *must* escape her now. Sketching her a bow, he walked away, ordering his legs not to break into a run.

Her voice floated to him from a vast distance, although he'd gone no more than a few yards. "What of Charley, my lord? I understand that you despise me, but am I forbidden to see him altogether, simply because he is your son?"

He stopped. Turned. Rage and pain distilled inside him,

coming together in a searing knot before erupting in a blast of white heat.

"But that's the thing, you see. He is *not* my son."

Chapter 16

"He *told* you?" Kit's gaze shot up from his sketchbook to fix on her in disbelief.

Celia gazed back helplessly. She had not meant to repeat Kendal's words to anyone, let alone to his brother, and had made it through most of the day with her determination intact. But out the words had come, and she could not call them back.

Nor did she want to. Adult secrets and adult strategies for concealing them were hurting Charley, and *something* must be done to change that. What that something could be, she'd no idea, but surely the place to begin was with the truth. It had not occurred to her that Kit might be hearing it for the first time, and she was relieved to learn that he already knew.

"I'm certain he never meant to say what he did," Celia replied at last. "But I provoked him, and he spoke before he could stop to think."

"Kendal spoke without thinking?" Kit folded his arms across his bent knee. "Now you really do amaze me."

"I seem to have that effect on him, likely because I am forever blurting out the most prodigiously awful things when we are together. This time we were quarreling about Charley, and I said something particularly unconscionable. He fired back, and I cannot say which of us was the most stunned to hear his words. He went white as paper, while I just stood there with my mouth open. Then he turned on his heel and walked away. Chirikov and I waited with the carriage for an hour before giving up on him. I've no idea how he got home again."

"On a job horse," Kit said, his voice bemused. "After midnight, come to think of it. He went directly to his study and locked the door, but that's not so unusual these days. Not since Chirikov moved in, at any rate. And he was gone this morning before I came downstairs. Walking on the fells, according to his valet."

Celia looked down the long sloping hill to a nearly dry riverbed, where Charley and Vasily Chirikov were gathering pebbles to build a fort. Kendal would be furious to know she was here with them. With Charley. But his anger no longer had the power to hurt her, and there was too much at stake to fear his displeasure. She already had *that* in abundance.

Kit had resumed his sketching, his pencil moving swiftly over the large sheet of paper. He sat with his back against a tree trunk, one knee propped to hold the sketchbook and the other leg stretched in front of him. "Hold still," he ordered when she tried to ease a cramp in her leg. "And don't lose that expression."

She froze, annoyed that he could be drawing a stupid picture at this particular moment. Did he fail to understand *why* she had addressed the subject of Kendal and Charley? They should be making plans. Devising solutions. "What expression?" she muttered between clenched teeth.

"You'll see in a minute. And I need to concentrate, so be quiet."

The Valliant men just loved ordering people about, she thought with considerable ire. Even Kit, usually sweet-natured, expected to be obeyed without question.

"There!" he said after what seemed to her like an hour. "Come have a look."

Unwrapping her stiff, crossed legs, she crawled the few yards to where Kit sat and leaned over to see the picture.

"Oh mercy!" It was her face, she supposed, although surely that murderous grimace belonged to someone else. So did the breastplate and the leather lacings crossing over otherwise bare legs, not to mention the notched spear raised for a strike. "Is this how you see me?"

"On occasion, such as now. Beneath the surface of the exceedingly proper Lady Greer, there lurks the fierce spirit of an Amazon warrior."

She whooped with laughter. "The Amazon analogy is dubious at best, but *proper*?"

"My exquisite tact is famous throughout Westmoreland," he said with a grin. "Have a peek at the rest and tell me what you think."

She took the sketchbook and studied the drawings he had made of her. There were seven in all, some only a few telling lines, others shaded with delicate precision. He had caught her laughing, and in a pensive mood, and once looking positively angelic.

"I believe you flatter me," she said. "For the most part, anyway. But this?" She pointed to a sketch of herself reclining on a Grecian couch, one knee lifted in a decidedly wanton pose. "This is not the creature I see in the mirror."

"You don't know how to look. But it's true that you will never see yourself as a man does, and I expect a man in love with you would draw you quite differently. He would keep pictures like this one in his heart."

She'd no idea what to make of that astonishing statement. "I know nothing about art, but you appear to be extremely talented. Have you considered a career as a painter?"

"Actually, I don't paint, not even with watercolors. Sketching is an occasional hobby, no more, and what you imagine to be talent is primarily a gift for observation. James would not credit it, but I am an excellent judge of character, most particularly that which lies beneath the surface."

"I can well believe it." She slanted him an assessing look. "For example, you probably know what I am thinking at this very moment."

"Far too easy," he said, taking back the sketchbook. "You are itching to know if James spoke the truth about Charley."

"Well," she demanded. "Did he?"

Kit leafed through his sketches until he located a page with five small, detailed renderings of Charley's face from different angles.

She studied them and saw, or thought she saw, a clear resemblance to Kendal in the line of the boy's jaw, the lift of his cheekbones, the narrow, aristocratic nose. "To judge by these—"

"Ah, but you mustn't. That's how *I* see Charley, and naturally I seek any possible resemblance to my brother. Or perhaps I put it there, unconsciously. If Charley were standing here now, you'd notice that his face is softer and more round, like that of most boys his age. The face I drew is the one he will grow into. Perhaps. Only perhaps."

"Have you shown these to Lord Kendal?"

"Perish the thought. He already considers me idle and useless, and I'd not have him know that I laze about drawing pictures. Besides, it would not help the situation. When James looks at Charley, he sees only Belinda."

"Her loss must grieve him terribly," Celia murmured, never having considered that possibility. It made cruel sense, she supposed, to avoid a child who brought the pain of losing his wife to mind simply by existing. "I once saw them together, you know. On their wedding day."

"Yes? I don't recall meeting you."

"Mercy, I wasn't an invited guest. But I happened to be in Kendal for the Saturday market, and when the bells began to peal, I dashed to the church along with everyone else. The bride and groom had just emerged from the vestibule, and I remember a flower seller rushing up the steps to shower them with daisies. Lord Kendal plucked one midair and presented it to his new wife. Then she kissed him, and the crowd cheered."

"Did you applaud as well?" he asked wryly.

"Oh, indeed. He was elegant and handsome, and she was the most beautiful creature imaginable, and they looked so happy they could fly."

"I expect they were happy, that particular morning." He leaned back against the tree, folding his arms behind his head. "And I fear you have a romantic heart, Lady Greer."

"I did. At the time." She picked up a fallen leaf and began to tear it into small pieces. "Well, perhaps I understand the situation a bit better now, although I cannot approve. Thank you for explaining."

Kit's brows shot up. "I've explained nothing. You have leapt to conclusions, is all, and shot past the target by leagues. Kendal neither misses his wife nor mourns her, except in the way civilized people mourn any untimely death. If he lost anything, it was only the romantic dream you thought you were witness to outside that church. Nothing could have been further from the truth, I assure you."

"Oh." Her heart began to turn somersaults in her chest. She wasn't at all sure she wanted to hear the explanation, but wild horses could not have dragged her away now.

He had closed his eyes. The warm July breeze ruffled his hair, burnished to gold by the sunlight streaming through the leaves and branches overhead.

"James would cut out my liver with a spoon if he knew I had spoken to you of these matters," he said after what seemed an eternity. "Tell me why I should give you the rest of it."

"There is no reason. Unless you think my knowing will somehow be of help to Charley."

"Precisely." He opened one eye. "I can't imagine how it could, but at this point there is nothing I wouldn't try. When I'm gone again on my travels, he will need a friend."

"He has that already, for all the use I can be. Lord Kendal has forbidden me to come onto his estate, but he neglected to specify that I was never to spend time with Charley outside of Candale. I'm sure that's what he meant, though."

"Do you always do what you are told, Celia?"

"I'm here, aren't I?"

His lips curved. "Well, so you are. And I believe we are of one mind where Charley is concerned. But where to begin? The thing is, these roots grow deep. What has James told you of himself?"

"Nothing to the point. Certainly nothing remotely personal. We are the barest of acquaintances, Kit."

"If you say so. And I suppose he wouldn't confide this particular story, even to a lover."

Celia's cheeks went on fire, but she managed a careless gesture. "In my case that cannot apply. And if you have ever thought so, think again."

"Right. Well, Chirikov will soon be clamoring for us to

bring out the picnic lunch, so I'll talk fast and make this brief. The Valliant family was storybook happy, or that is my recollection, until Mama and Papa went to visit our estate in the Highlands. They planned to be gone a month, and we had no idea anything was wrong until a messenger arrived with the shattering news. He gave it to the new Earl of Kendal, leaving James to tell the rest of us."

A barely perceptible shudder passed through Kit's lanky frame. "They were caught in a snowstorm on Rannock Moor, and all of them, the earl and countess, drivers and servants, even the horses, froze to death. They weren't discovered until a week later."

"I'm so sorry," Celia murmured into the silence that followed. "How terrible."

"Yes, especially for James. We were all devastated, of course, but he was the one saddled with responsibility for the estates, not to mention a pair of rambunctious brothers. I was five at the time, Alex nine, and James had just turned twelve. He grew up overnight, it seemed. That's what I most remember, actually—how he changed beyond recognition. Before, he was in and out of trouble with the rest of us, devising the cleverest of our pranks and taking all the blame when we got caught. Always laughing, too. He almost never laughs now, not from the heart. Have you noticed?"

She nodded, unable to speak past the lump in her throat. But he must have changed again, because she clearly remembered him smiling and laughing on his wedding day.

"He became a right proper earl," Kit went on reflectively, "starting the very moment he came into the title. He'd always been a tenacious chap, and immediately set about learning everything he needed to know, from accounting and investments to estate management and crop rotation. Alex was sent to Harrow and I was handed over to a tutor, so we rarely saw him. But never mind all that. I'll cut directly to Belinda, if you will be kind enough to fish some lemonade from that basket. My mouth is dry as sandpaper."

With shaking hands, Celia found the bucket containing a large jar of lemonade. All the ice in the bucket had long since melted, but the lemonade was still fairly cool. She filled two glasses and gave one to Kit, who smiled encouragingly.

"It's a hard story, I know," he said. "But don't be distressed, or I'll not be able to finish it."

"I'm well accustomed to hard stories," she assured him, her own sorry experiences fading to nothing in comparison. All this time she'd assumed that the wealthy, handsome, oh-so-clever Lord Kendal had enjoyed a charmed life from birth. How little we understand of others, she thought, feeling selfish and shallow of heart.

"I guessed that," Kit said softly. "One day, perhaps you will confide your own story to me." He drained his glass and held it out for a refill. "But for now, James is on the block, and Belinda is getting ready to lop off his head."

"They were in love," she said, stubbornly clinging to the illusion of how a happy marriage ought to be. They had created that illusion for her, Lord Kendal and his bride, on a long-ago Saturday morning. "I could not have mistaken that."

"*He* was in love," Kit corrected gently. "Belinda's father invited himself and his daughter to Candale, hoping to arrange a marriage, and James fell head over heels for her. Well, so did we all, I suppose. She was beautiful, high-spirited, and seemed to dote on him. So they wed, although it cost James a pretty penny in settlements, and everyone expected them to live happily ever after."

He tilted his head, frowning slightly. "In point of fact, Belinda was much like you—on the surface. She had a gift for making people feel important, for one thing, and a natural, sunny exuberance that lit up a room the moment she stepped inside. Unfortunately, she was also a—pardon the word, but it's the only one that applies—a slut."

"G-good heavens."

"Oh, she behaved herself for the first year or so. But James had a great many responsibilities and could not always dance attendance on her. She grew bored, and turned her attentions elsewhere. To Alex, I suspect, although he's never admitted to it. He came home from Cambridge for the Christmas holidays, and shortly after Twelfth Night, without explanation, he bought a commission in the army and left the country."

"Surely you are wrong. She cannot have seduced her husband's own brother, for pity's sake."

"She tried to seduce *me*," Kit said flatly. "Not until years later, though, which is why I didn't twig to what she was about in the early days. I imagine several of the footmen could have told a merry tale, or maybe not. She was careful, and possibly faithful, early on. Even Belinda realized that her excesses would not be tolerated until she provided the Earl of Kendal an heir."

Celia took a swallow of tasteless lemonade, her stomach roiling. She could sense what was coming next, and knew it would be unbearable.

"For the smartest man I've ever known," Kit said, "James was blind to what everyone else could see. When Belinda announced her pregnancy, he was in alt. And when Charley was born, he was altogether besotted with the child. Disappointed that Belinda refused to nurse the babe, I recall, and surprised when she virtually ignored both husband and son thereafter, but the proud papa made up for her lack of attention. He even rigged up a sling and carried Charley on his back when he rode out to visit the tenant farmers."

"I don't understand," Celia interrupted. "From what you are saying, he never questioned that Charley was his son. *His*. Not some other man's."

"True. Which is why we can assume that he was sleeping with Belinda when Charley was conceived. What we don't know is who else she had taken to bed, or to the hay in the barn, or to the other places where she entertained her lovers. There were plenty of lovers, we all became aware in the year after Charley was born. That was when she crept into my own bed, and scared the devil out of me, I promise you. It was all I could do to pry her loose."

Celia shook her head in disbelief. How could any woman want another man when she was loved by Lord Kendal? It was beyond her comprehension, beyond even her own vivid imagination. She wrapped her arms around her waist, afraid she was about to vomit lemonade onto the lush grass.

"Hard to credit, is it not?" Kit asked sympathetically. "I've had years to get used to all this, but I'll never understand. Belinda had a sickness of some kind, an insatiable appetite for men—a variety of men—and from then on she gave it full rein. Even James could not fail to see what she made excruciatingly obvious. It was about then he signed on with the Foreign Office and began to travel. Belinda was furious, of course. She had wanted to cut a dash in London, but he wouldn't take her along. Lord, he could scarcely bear the sight of her. He disappeared for months at a time, while she tumbled every man that would have her."

"And Charley?" How could Kendal leave him behind?

"Charley got lost in the wash, I'm afraid. I fled Candale, too, fairly sure I'd wring Belinda's neck if I stayed around. We all let Charley down, one way or another, although Kendal made the trip from London to see him fairly regularly. Until Charley's third birthday, anyway. That was when everything fell apart."

Kit swiped his sleeve over his forehead. "Here's where it gets really ugly, Celia. Are you certain you wish to hear the rest?"

At the moment she wished to kill a dead woman. "Go on."

"Well, so here it is. I came home for the celebration, which went better than I had dared to hope. But when Charley had been packed off to bed, Belinda started drinking heavily. She was in a strange mood, even for her. We were in the salon, the three of us, and it was like being in the room with a lit rocket. But she said nothing when James and I laid out the chessboard, and after a while I forgot she was there. And how much she hated being ignored," Kit added on a harsh breath.

"She must have been working herself up into a fine frenzy," he continued after a moment. "All of a sudden she stalked up to the table and swiped the chess pieces onto the floor. 'I have something to tell you,' she said. Then she went back to the sideboard and poured out three glasses of brandy. When she knocked one onto the carpet, James went over to her. I couldn't hear what he said, but she swore at him. Then she shoved a glass into his hand.

" 'It's nearly midnight,' she said, lifting her own glass. 'I think we ought to drink to Charles on his birthday. And to his father—whoever the devil he is.' "

"Dear God." Celia's nails dug into her thighs. She knew the rest without hearing it.

"At first," Kit said, his voice ominously husky, "I wasn't sure what she meant. But I remember the look in her eyes when she tossed her drink into James's face, and I remember her next words exactly.

" 'Not you,' she said. 'Maybe the stableman, maybe one of Lord Lonsdale's footmen, maybe the butcher in Kendal or the baker in Bowness. But not you, my lord husband. I came to despise you nearly from the first, so very noble and fastidious and self-righteous as you were and are. So insufferably *tedious*. I took precautions whenever you bedded me, sir. And while I cannot name the boy's real father, you may be certain that Charles is not your son.' "

"She was lying," Celia said immediately.

"I have always thought so. He wouldn't give her the glamorous life she wanted, and she set out to punish him in return by taking away what he most valued. But at the end of the day we'll never know if she was speaking the truth. And she may well have been, however much you and I wish to believe otherwise. James never questioned it."

"Then he is a fool." Celia waved a hand dismissively. "I cannot be sorry for him if he chooses to credit the word of that . . . that *bitch*!"

"A milder word than I'd have chosen," Kit said when heat flooded to her cheeks. "And to his face, I've called my brother far worse than fool. But his mind is long since closed on this matter. The Valliant men are obstinate as granite blocks, Celia, and James is the worst of us. Also the best, in every way save this one. I continue to be astonished at the way he treats Charley. Or, to be precise, at the way he refuses to deal with him at all."

Because he was so hurt, she thought. Because he had loved Belinda.

Celia could not find it in herself to make excuses for Lord Kendal, but she understood better than Kit how it felt to awaken from a dream, however misguided, into a nightmare that was all too real. She knew how it was to escape from pain by detaching herself from everything that put her in mind of it. And she had learned, from Kendal himself, the aching vulnerability of daring to love, only to be rejected.

Dear heavens. Until this very moment she'd not even mustered the courage to admit that she had fallen in love with him.

Well, there it was. Irrelevant now, to be sure, but she loved the man.

And she would get over it. What choice did she have? Nothing had changed, except that she had been forced to confront her own feelings precisely when they were of no significance.

"What can we do, Kit?" she asked with a direct gaze into his troubled blue eyes.

"Nothing I know of. If I wasn't fairly sure he could beat the stuffing out of me, I'd try to pound some sense into his thick head. But he'll soon be off again, and Charley will be alone again. I am hoping you will stand his friend and watch out for him. It's more than I've any right to ask, but there is no one else who cares for him."

"You could stay," she pointed out.

"Yes." He winced. "I *should* stay. But I won't. Feel free to despise me for it, and to be honest, I rather loathe myself every time I say good-bye to the boy and set out on one of my adventures. But that's the way I am, Celia—unable to stay put for more than a few weeks. Even Charley senses when my feet get itchy, sometimes before I do. He is far too forgiving, that one. Probably because he has been taught to expect nothing from those who are supposed to love him." With a groan, Kit stood and splayed his arms. "Here I am, trying to palm him off to a stranger. Do me a favor, Celia, and slap me good and hard."

"Better you go on feeling wretched," she ruled sternly. "I'll not give you leave to abandon Charley, nor blame you when you do. He is not your son, after all. Kendal must face up to his responsibilities. Which leads us back to where we started, of course. I'll do what I can for the child, you may be sure, but chances are his lofty lordship will put a stop to it. We are not on the best of terms."

"I know." Kit helped her to her feet. "Perhaps you can mend fences tomorrow at Charley's birthday party. I've invited every family in the neighborhood to a picnic, and James has given his promise to come."

"He'll not be pleased to see me there," she warned.

"Does that matter?"

"Not in the least. But I'll ride over when the party is in full swing and try to keep out of his way. Above all things, we must not spoil the day for Charley."

"Right." Kit pointed down the hill. "Speaking of the devil, here he comes. At least, I think that is Charley under all that dirt."

"I found a frog!" The boy charged directly up to Celia and held out his prize for her inspection. "See?"

She examined the woebegone creature and nodded approval. "A fine frog indeed. He looks to be very agile, I must say. How clever you must have been to capture him."

Charley glanced over his shoulder at General Chirikov, who was lumbering up the steep slope with a wide smile on his mud-streaked face. "Uncle Vasily caught the frog," the boy confessed. "And he said that ladies don't much care for frogs, but I was sure you'd like this one. He doesn't bite or anything. Would you like to keep him?"

Celia gazed into the boy's earnest brown eyes and recognized that he was offering her a treasure. It was all she could do to keep the tears that gathered in her own eyes from streaming down her face. Solemnly, she held out her hands and accepted the gift. "Thank you, Charley. He is quite the finest frog I've ever seen. I'd love to take him home with me. But what about his family? Won't they miss him?"

"No," Charley said very softly. "They won't even know that he's gone."

Dear God. Celia glanced over at Kit and saw her own anguish reflected in his eyes. He looked as helpless as she felt.

In his own way, Charley had just put *himself* into her hands. How could she cast him off? But she could no more take Charley with her than she could the frog, which had begun to wriggle for escape.

Seizing a deep breath, she lifted her hands to her face and planted a kiss on the damp froggy forehead. Then she brought the wide mouth to her ear and pretended to be listening.

"Mercy me," she said. "I don't speak frog language very well, but I am almost certain he is telling me he wants to go home."

Charley's eyes widened. "He can talk? Really? Can I hear him?"

Rather sure she'd backed herself into a corner, Celia looked to Kit for help.

"Frogs only speak to females," he said. "Or so I am told." He gave Celia a best-I-could-come-up-with shrug.

She returned her attention to the frog. "I can't actually hear him, Charley. It's more a matter of feeling in my heart what he is trying to say. He is very pleased to have met you, by the way, and thinks it was exceedingly kind of you to give him to me. But he's rather sweet on a young lady frog he's been courting, and wants to marry her and raise some tadpoles."

"Oh." Charley's face went red. "I didn't know that."

Nor did he understand all that business about courtship and tadpoles, Celia thought. It was certain, though, that the last thing he wanted was to hurt this frog. "I think we should take him back to the river, Charley, and set him free. I'll miss him, of course, but perhaps you and I can come back and visit someday."

"Promise?" Charley said eagerly. "Cross your heart?"

Knowing it meant a commitment to this love-starved child, she waved the frog in a vaguely crosslike gesture over her breasts. "I promise. Now show me where you found him. And let's hurry, before General Chirikov eats all our lunch by himself."

Chirikov, his mouth full of ham sandwich, waved as they set out down the hill. "Iss good to let frog go," he called.

"I like Uncle Vasily," Charley confided when they reached the Winster River, barely a stream at this time of year. "He showed me how to build a fort. But it was mostest fun when we threw rocks and broke it down."

Men! They set out so young to be warriors. With relief, since she had not the least bit of fondness for slimy creatures—even ones given to her with love—she crouched beside the muddy riverbank and opened her hands. Without a backward look, the frog sprang away and disappeared under a clump of ferns.

Trying not to be too obvious about it, she washed her hands in the muddy water and rubbed them against her skirt. Charley was gazing somewhat forlornly at the spot where the frog had vanished.

"He'll be happier where he belongs," she said reassuringly.

"But how will we find him when we come back? We don't even know his name."

Eyes burning, Celia drew the boy into a tight hug. He was so warm against her, his small hands clutching at her back, his soft hair tickling at her chin as he buried his face against her neck. I love you, Charley, she told him silently, somewhat like a frog trying to speak feelings without words.

"His name is Ribbit," she whispered. "I'm pretty sure that's what he said."

Charley lifted his head to smile at her. "Iss good!"

Chapter 17

Celia arrived at Charley's birthday picnic just when the fishing was getting under way.

Kit immediately appointed her official hook baiter, but there were few takers for her services. The children liked the wriggly worms far better than the few tiny fish they managed to pull from the lake, and after a time they set aside their poles in favor of worm races.

There were at least three dozen children of varying ages at the picnic, and half as many adults, mostly parents. Servants had been recruited from Candale to set up the canopies and tables, serve the food, and mind the horses and carriages. When he set himself to business, Celia thought, Kit knew how to get things done.

After the fishing, she joined a game of tossing coins into jars and garnered a third-place ribbon. Charley, with the focused intensity of a marksman, took first place and gallantly presented her with the winning penny. It was in her pocket now, and she knew that she would keep it always.

A light breeze ruffled her hair as she relaxed under a tree, watching Charley play Puss in the Corner with the two Wordsworth children and a pair of lively twins. Smaller than the others and unable to outrun them, Charley had been "Puss" for rather a long time.

A few boys were shying pebbles across the placid surface of Lake Windermere in a game of Dick, Duck, and Drake, while several girls rolled hoops and played at shuttlecock nearby. Kit was rounding up stray children for a three-legged race, but the adults, sedated by a lavish luncheon and the midafternoon sun, were seeking quieter entertainment. Some had set out for walks, others were trying their hand at archery, but most had settled comfortably in the shade to exchange gossip.

Celia was sitting on a blanket with Mary Wordsworth, the poet's wife, who had long since dozed off, and Dorothy Wordsworth, who kept her restless hands busy with her knitting needles. There was no telling what that tangle of green yarn was meant to be, but it was growing rapidly.

Not so rapidly, though, as Celia's barely restrained anger.

The guest Charley most wished for, the one he had watched for whenever a vehicle trundled along the track leading to the lake, was not here. Her heart had squeezed with pain to watch him hide his disappointment and welcome the latest arrivals with his frighteningly impeccable manners.

Even on the child's birthday, even though he had given his word, Kendal had chosen not to come.

She squirmed on the blanket, catching the snoozing Mary Wordsworth with the heel of her slipper and jolting her awake.

"Wh-what is it?" Mary asked in confusion.

Celia patted her hand and stood. "Forgive me, Mary. I seem to be exceptionally restive this afternoon. Perhaps a walk will help me shake off my fidgets."

She had meant to ramble alongside the lake, but the sound of laughter drew her instead to the archery field, where General Chirikov had just sent an arrow several yards wide of the target.

As she approached he slotted another arrow, sighted carefully, and let it fly. This time the misguided missile soared into the boughs of a tree, sending a startled bird off its shady perch with an irate whoop. All this to the great glee of the children, who were watching the general demonstrate his skill, or more accurately, his notable lack of it. He grinned at them after every shot.

Celia watched him launch a quiverful of arrows, and when he finally hit the target at its farthest edge, the onlookers rewarded him with vigorous applause.

"I stop now," he said, handing the bow to one of the boys. "Iss good sport. Will you shoot, Lady Greer?"

"Mercy, no. I am far too likely to slay an innocent bystander. Would you care to join me for a walk, sir? It will be much safer, I assure you."

Pronouncing himself honored, the general schooled his long stride to hers as they wandered in a southerly direction along the bank of the lake, sometimes exchanging impressions of the scenery but more often walking in companionable silence. Celia was surprised to hear nary a line of poetry the entire hour, and remarked upon it as they made their way back to the picnic area.

"Ah, I haff not reason say poems more times," Chirikov confided. "Mr. Wordsworth hass tell me many places to go, the whons where he hass writed about. So I go see them, and they iss like the poems, but not like the poems. Because there iss places, and feelinks, and words. Iss same, but different. So I understand iss better keep poems here, because feelinks iss best." He thumped at his chest directly over his heart.

Taking his meaning, she gave him a smile, although she couldn't help but think it as well that he had chosen to internalize his poetic rhapsodies.

"Next," he announced, "I vill learn to shoot weeth bow and arrow so hit eyes of bull every time."

Celia laughed. "And you will be a master of the art in no time, I am sure. But if you don't mind, I shall keep myself well distant during the early practices."

"Ah, but no worry. Tomorrow I go to Scotland for shoot with gun."

"You are leaving, then?" She felt inordinately sorry to hear it. When he had returned to Russia, it was unlikely they would ever meet again.

"I haff much luffed this England," he replied, "but now must go home. Soon, we take ship from Edinburk. I vill miss you, luffly Lady Greer, and you sweet smile and kind heart."

Tears welled in her eyes as she stood on tiptoe to plant a light kiss on his chin. "I shall miss you, too, General, and for the same reasons."

He flushed. "I iss not luffly. But I thank you."

They came within sight of the picnic, and Celia noticed right away how quiet everyone had gone. The children continued to play in small groups, but they were uncommonly subdued, and the adults sat or stood with carefully proper deportment. They might have been in a drawing room, or attending a funeral.

She looked around for Charley and saw immediately why everyone's high spirits had suddenly muted. Lord Kendal, wearing a russet coat and wide-brimmed hat, stood rigidly in front of Charley. Kit was behind the boy, one hand resting protectively on his shoulder.

They did not appear to be quarreling, from what Celia could tell at such a distance. Rather, neither Kendal nor Charley seemed to be saying anything at all. Finally, Kit made a gesture toward the canopied picnic tables and they headed in that direction.

A trifle late for luncheon, she thought sourly, the sight of Kendal fanning the coals of her anger. Not only had he arrived hours after everyone else, but apparently without the pony Kit had trusted him to supply.

For Charley's sake, Celia decided to make a quiet departure while her temper was still in check. Of late, Kendal could not be in her company without provoking a row, and her own mood was scarcely peaceable.

"I shall take my leave of you now," she told the general. "Later, will you give my apologies to Charley for not bidding him good-bye? I think he would be disappointed to learn I am leaving early, but I really must be on my way."

Chirikov looked displeased. "You haff someone be with you, Lady Greer? Iss not good for lady to ride alone."

"I've only a short way to go, sir. My butler, Mr. Carver, is waiting for me in Winster and expects me there shortly. I don't wish to worry him by arriving late."

"I take you there!" Chirikov spoke like the general he was.

Celia could not oblige. Alone, she might be able to steal off undetected, but not with this Russian behemoth in tow. "I came on horseback, sir, and you by coach. Besides, the most direct way to Winster is over the hills, and I shall be there in a trice. Good-bye, my friend. It has been a great joy to make your acquaintance."

Before he could raise further objections, she moved quickly away, choosing a circular route that avoided the tent. Kendal was now seated on a folding chair, and Charley was rummaging through one of the picnic baskets.

Reaching the spinney where Aphra was tethered, she unloosed the reins and led the mare to the path that would take them to Winster. Every minute or so she glanced back, but from all she could tell, no one had seen her depart. Soon she reached the top of a low rise and paused to look down at the picnickers.

At two of them, anyway—the tall man and the little boy alone under the blue-and-white canopy. She could barely make them out. Kendal was still seated, and Charley stood beside him, the top of his head even with his father's shoulder.

His *father*, whatever Kendal chose to think.

Were Charley not there to hear it, she would go back and make that perfectly clear.

The next hill was long and steep. She mounted it slowly. Thomas wasn't expecting her until four o'clock, and being sweet on a pert redhead in Winster, he'd not welcome an early end to his afternoon off.

She took another look, a lingering look, from the summit of the hill. At this distance, the picnic party was only a splash of color on the green grass. Just beyond, sunlight glittered from the smooth water of the lake like a scatter of diamonds on blue silk.

So long as she had to wait for half an hour before proceeding to Winster, why not wait here? Glancing around, she saw a small copse of ash trees where Aphra could be sheltered from the late-afternoon sun. When the mare was serenely nibbling grass, Celia went back to her chosen spot and sank crosslegged onto the ground.

She meant to enjoy the silence and the beauty, but within seconds unhappy thoughts began jumping about in her mind like beads of water on a hot skillet.

182

Almost certainly she had just seen Kendal for the last time before he returned to London. With Chirikov leaving tomorrow, there would be no reason for the earl to remain at Candale.

And so, it was over.

She would have no opportunity to beat sense into his head. He would go, leaving ashes in his wake. And there was nothing, *nothing* she could do.

How could he be so resolutely blind? Sometimes he put her in mind of Greer's chickens. One of the servants used to draw a line in the dirt with his finger and position a chicken with its beak pressed to the line. When he removed his hand, the chicken would hold in place indefinitely, fixed on that line and unable to see anything else.

Kendal had done something of the like. He would not look beyond the path he'd carved for himself out of the devastation of his marriage. He refused to allow for other possibilities, choosing instead a course that promised safety from emotional entanglements. The fact that it was leading him nowhere seemed not to matter.

She understood mistakes, heaven knew. She'd made a great many of them and would make a great many more. What she failed to comprehend was Kendal's persistence in repeating the *same* mistake over and over again.

There really ought to be a limit to any man's obstinacy, a point where he realized it was time to try something else. It wasn't as if he were *happy*, after all.

And still, she believed in him.

She lay back on the grass and closed her eyes, feeling the sunlight sift into her body, the breeze whisper over her bare arms. She believed in him.

She must assuredly love him, to accept what he was doing without losing all faith in the man. He would eventually come around, she was certain. But she feared it would be too late for Charley.

She knew that it was already too late for her.

It is always a good thing to love, though. Bertie was right about that. And she *had* loved. She *did* love. Loving Kendal was the most precious, the most wonderful experience of her life, and she would never permit the loss of him to tarnish what she felt.

Which wasn't to say she would not go on hurting, deeply, for a very long time. Fine resolutions about clinging to the high road were well enough in theory, but empty days and lonely nights had a way of reducing noble aspirations to simple human longings. She never walked into a room without wanting to see him there, smiling at her.

But she would survive. No, survival was an insufficient goal. Sometimes that was the best one could do, she had learned during nine years of marriage to Greer, but it was dreaming of better things that had enabled her to endure. What a fool she would be to deny her dreams now, when she needed them more than ever. Celia opened her eyes and gazed up at the clear blue sky.

She refused to yield. She trusted in heroes. She imagined miracles.

Minutes or hours later, she had no idea, she felt an eerie tingling at her spine. Sitting up, she shaded her forehead with a hand and peered down the long steep slope of the hill.

And saw Kendal. He was no more than a hundred yards away, making his way toward her with a hurried stride.

She scrambled to her feet and waited for him, unable to think beyond the fact that he was here.

But she *must* think, and have all her wits about her. She studied his face as he came closer, trying vainly to read his expression. His own gaze never lifted. He was watching the ground, fixed on it like a damnable chicken.

When he drew within a few feet of where she stood, he halted. She saw him suck in a long breath and expel it before he looked at her, his mouth compressing to a narrow line. Obviously as an afterthought, he sketched a cursory bow.

"How did you know where I was?" she asked, of all the ridiculous things.

He made a vague gesture toward her horse, a white silhouette against the green grass and trees. "Chirikov said you were on your way to Winster, and this is the most direct route. I was not certain I could catch up with you, Lady Greer, but it is imperative that we speak."

"Not about my appearance at Charley's birthday party, I trust. His wishes transcend your own, sir, and—"

"Not about that. I am here to beg a service of you, nothing more." A sheen of sweat glistened on his brow. "The other day, at Wordsworth's house, I spoke out of turn. Unforgivably. It was pure nonsense, of course. I was not myself. I rarely am, in your company, and you have suffered for it. But in this case I went beyond all bounds, and fear that my indiscretion will do harm to Paxton should you repeat what I said."

As if she would do anything to hurt Charley! She might have taken offense, were she in a position to do so. But since she had already blabbed the whole to Kit, there was no use pretending she was above reproach.

"I know what it is you wish me to conceal," she said. "And you may be sure I wouldn't dream of spreading even the most trivial snippet of gossip relating to your family. But the fact is, sir, I have spoken on that particular subject *within* the family, to your brother."

The color in his face leached away. "Damn Kit."

"He is not to blame," she said hurriedly. "It was I who raised the issue, and only because I wanted him to explain what you would not. He understood that nothing we said would go any further."

Kendal looked away from her. "Your curiosity was sated, I take it?"

"To a degree." *Hold your temper, Celia.* "Kit told me only the barest fragments, the bits that might help us figure how to be of help to Charley. He was, and is, our only concern."

"And did you find any revelations in all this exchange of confidences, Lady Greer, beyond the obvious conclusion that I have been an unfit father to a child who is not mine?"

"You cannot know that, sir."

His gaze shot to her face. "I have the word of his mother, and the evidence of what I see. He bears no resemblance to any member of the Valliant family, past or present. You could search in vain through the portrait gallery for eyes the shape and color of his. Believe me, I have done so."

"Would the picture of a distant ancestor reassure you, Lord Kendal, if you found one who sported black eyes?"

"Probably not," he conceded grimly. "In fact, my wife's eyes were dark brown, but that is nothing to the point. She had no reason to lie to me, and nothing to gain by doing so. Quite the contrary. She must have known the consequences to herself if I learned the truth."

"Indeed? Have you not wondered, then, why she told you?"

"A thousand times." He rubbed the back of his neck. "It makes little sense, but little that she said or did made sense to me. In any case, I had become aware of her . . . indiscretions, and she understood that the marriage would continue in name only. Perhaps she had learned that I'd consulted a solicitor regarding a legal separation, although I was hesitant to remove Paxton from his mother at so young an age. But if she knew I was considering it, she might have assumed I would permit her to keep the boy if—"

"If you thought he was not yours." Celia moved closer, where she could better see his face. "I am mostly ignorant of the matter, to be sure, but from Kit I got the distinct impression that Lady Kendal paid precious little attention to her child. Practically none. Have you reason to think she *wanted* to keep Charley?"

"Not for herself," he acknowledged after a moment. "More likely she simply wished to deprive me of him. In her mind, I had failed to be the tolerant, openhanded husband she'd bargained for. This was, I suppose, her way of seeking retribution."

"I daresay. But if that was her purpose, why do you assume she was speaking the truth? Would not a lie have served as well?"

He made a sweeping gesture. "Do you imagine I have not considered that? I confronted her time and again with my suspicions, but her story never changed. Yes, she might have lied to me. She had deceived me in countless other ways, beginning the day we first met, and you will not be surprised to learn she did not come to our marriage bed a virgin. Mind you, I accepted her story about a riding accident. I believed everything she told me. I was in *love* with her, God help me."

Heart pounding, Celia held in place, forbidding herself to reveal how his words affected her. "When you love, you must trust," she said quietly. "But she has been dead for many years, my lord, and I expect you ceased loving her long before that. Why do you continue to trust her?"

"Is that what I'm doing?" He lifted his gaze to the sky. "The thing is, I don't know the truth. Is the boy my son? There will never be an answer. I can *never* know."

"Just so. But what does it matter?"

"How can you ask that?" He slammed a fist into the palm of his other hand. "Of *course* it matters. What man does not wish to be sure that his children are his own?"

"Not a one, I would imagine. Women are fortunate in that regard. We cannot help but know. But your *wishes*, sir, are impossible to satisfy. For every other purpose, you have acknowledged Charley as your own. He bears your name. He will inherit your title and properties. You forbid him only the one thing he truly wants and needs. A father."

"How so, Lady Greer? Unless you, or my reprehensibly indiscreet brother, tells Paxton what I never mean for him to learn, he will have no reason to suspect I am not his father."

"Which will leave him, then, to wonder why his father does not love him." She slipped a hand into her pocket, feeling for the penny Charley had given her. "I'm not at all sure it wouldn't be kinder to tell him flat out why you rarely come home, and pay him no attention when you do."

Kendal's voice was dangerously soft. "The war has taken thousands of men from their homes, madam. I have been in service to my country."

"Hurrah for you. And what excuse will you find, I wonder, when the Vienna Congress is concluded and you have no war, nor the tying up of loose ends after a war, to keep you away? Will you request appointment as ambassador to some court or other? Pitch a tent in the House of Lords? Ship off to India?"

"My plans are none of your concern," he said coldly. "And they will have little effect on Paxton, who will soon be in residence at Harrow."

"Oh, excellent. One way or another, you can easily contrive to see him no more than once or twice a year, if that often. And I expect he will go on thinking that the sun rises and sets at your command. Already he is persuaded that you are the bestest and most important man in all England. He has told me so any number of times, with such pride that it broke my heart to see how terribly much he admires you."

She was beyond control now, she knew. And she could not care. Stalking up to him, she raised her chin and forced him by power of will to meet her eyes. She read denial on his face, in his stiff posture and icy blue gaze, and still—still she believed in him.

"There is nothing Charley would not forgive you," she said. "He thinks you are perfect. Which must mean, since you have no time for him, since you cannot care for him, that *he* must be at fault. So he tries in every way to be what he hopes will please you. What his mean-spirited governess and small-minded tutor tell him you expect of the Kendal heir."

Her hand, the one that had found the coin, was clenched into a fist. She slammed it at Kendal's chest. "They have tried to break his spirit, sir. But for all your neglect and all their efforts, he won't be broken. Charley is in pain every day of his life, but he is stronger than you or I will ever be. He refuses to let go of love. If he must, he'll find it in a puppy or a pony or a frog. He has an infinite capacity for giving and taking love wherever he can."

Kendal's face had gone white. A muscle ticked wildly at his jaw. But he held his ground, his posture rigid. "Are you quite finished, madam?"

"No. But soon, I promise you. Two things more, Lord Kendal. For one, consider this. Could Charley, whoever sired him, be any finer than he is? I know you would like to change his eyes to blue, to match your own, but in what other way would you alter him?"

"How can I answer that?" he replied harshly. "I scarcely know the boy."

"By your own choice. I met him less than a fortnight ago, but it required only a few moments to mark what a splendid child he is. Any man, any man but you, it seems, would be proud to call him son."

She had said enough, Celia knew. Too much, probably. She never knew when to stop. And she had not the slightest indication from Kendal that he really heard, let alone heeded, a single word of her tirade.

He was standing like a granite monolith, expressionless, waiting for her to be done.

In for a penny, she thought, opening her hand to show him the coin. He regarded it incuriously, but she felt the tension in his stiff body when she tossed it in the air and caught it again. For good measure, she tossed it two more times.

When she was sure she had his attention, she closed her fingers around the coin. "For a *second* thing—no, I hadn't forgot—let us play a game together."

"That seems singularly inappropriate under the circumstances."

He sounded a trifle uncomfortable, she thought. Even nervous. "Nevertheless," she said, "this is the fastest way to be rid of me, so I urge you to go along. You needn't say a word, by the way. I will toss the coin, and when it is midair, you will silently choose heads or tails. Agreed?"

His eyes narrowed. "There is some significance to the choice, I presume?"

"Certainly. This is a magical coin, sir. It holds the key to the secret you most wish to decipher. It can tell you, absolutely, whether or not Charley is your son."

"That is ridiculous! And I am in no mood for pointless games."

She tossed the coin back and forth between her hands. "Indulge me. I guarantee you will find an answer. It may not be the one you want, but what have you to lose at this point?"

"Very well, Lady Greer, proceed if you must. But do it quickly."

With a flick of her wrist, she sent the coin to a great height and they both watched it tumble down again, reflecting the sunlight as it spun around. At the last moment she snatched it midair and laid it on the back of one hand, covering it with the other.

"And so, my lord, here is the answer. Have you made your choice?"

"I have," he replied stonily.

"The coin has done so as well. Heads, Charley is your son. Tails, he is not. Heads, you will love the boy as once you did, before your wife poisoned you against him. Tails, you will go on as you have done since then."

He frowned, studying her hands intently. "I fail to take your meaning. You told me to choose before I knew what was signified by the turn of the coin."

"Well, yes. But then, you have been making choices in ignorance all these many years, have you not? When Charley's paternity was placed in doubt, you chose tails. You elected not to love him. Now we shall find out if you were right all along. Or crushingly wrong."

She held out her hands, the one still atop the other. "Shall I show you the coin, sir?"

"I—" He closed his eyes, his face pale as death. "No. I don't want to see it."

"I thought you would not. The truth about Charley, whatever it may be, is never so devastating as facing the truth about yourself. And that, you know, is the message this coin has already given you."

Stepping forward, she took one of his hands and pressed the coin against his palm, closing his stiff fingers around it. "Keep this, Lord Kendal. Charley gave it me, but it belongs to you. One day, you may recognize its value."

She left him then, before the tears in her eyes broke free. Striding swiftly to where she'd tethered Aphra, she took the reins, mounted, and headed in the direction of Winster, her heart pounding madly in her chest. Only once, when she was far enough away that he could not see the tears scalding her face, she risked a look back.

His hand was still fisted around the coin. He had not moved.

Chapter 18

Churning beneath the smooth surface of Kendal's mind, beating against his focused calm, the beasts prowled relentlessly.

Rage. Guilt. Fear. Uncertainty. Dread.

They were strong. Ferocious. They would break free, he knew. But he could hold them back for now.

The coin burned in his hand. He stopped on the crest of a hill directly above the picnic site and unclenched his fist. The penny, ordinary and worn, lay flat against his palm.

It showed heads.

But there was nothing to that. If the coin held secrets and truths, he was not prepared to decipher them. The beasts would tear him apart soon enough.

They must not have the boy, though. Paxton—Charley—asked little enough of him, which was as well, since he'd little to give. But what he could find in himself, he would scrape up and offer to his son.

There. He had said it, if only to himself. His son.

He neither believed it nor disbelieved it, but the facts regarding the child's conception, whatever they were, had no relevance now. He knew his duty.

What he didn't know was how to be a father. He had done a poor enough job when the role was cast upon him twenty years before, although Alex and Kit had managed to survive his bungling without notable scars. He would simply have to learn. And to be sure, he could scarcely do worse by Charley in the future than he'd done in the past.

Releasing a painful breath, he slipped the coin into his pocket and started down the hill.

Before he had taken more than a few steps, his gaze fixed on the ground, a shout from near the lake snapped him to a halt. Looking down, he saw people running to the shoreline.

Chirikov pulled off his boots and plowed into the water, swimming rapidly.

Kit was pushing a rowboat into the lake. Two men helped him shove off, and a third man joined him in the boat. Kit grabbed the oars and began to row.

Kendal looked beyond them, in the direction they were headed. To Belle Isle, he thought at first. He saw the pale backs of several boys who were swimming toward the island, almost upon it, and other boys crawling onto land.

Then, at a point some distance behind them, he made out a small disturbance in the water. One of the boys must be in trouble.

He broke into a run.

The crowd parted for him as he came up to the edge of the lake. He heard a voice say, "It's Paxton, milord," but somehow he had already known that.

From this far away it was impossible to tell precisely what was happening. The boat was still moving through the water. About fifty yards ahead of it Chirikov waved a hand. Kendal saw Kit point with an oar. Chirikov swam a short way to his left and dove.

He was underwater a vast time. The boat had nearly reached him when he shot up. Almost immediately, he dove a second time.

Blood thundering in his head, Kendal watched helplessly. All around him, children were crying. They were terrified, as was he, although he knew to hold still and maintain his calm. *Oh please dear God.*

When Chirikov came up again, a small figure was barely visible in his arms. Kit steered to where he was treading water and reached out his hands. The moment Kit had Charley in his arms, the other man began rowing frantically for shore.

As the boat drew closer Kendal could see his brother holding Charley facedown across his thighs, pushing at his back, trying to pump water from his lungs. *Oh God.*

It seemed to take forever. Oars dug into the lake. Kendal willed Charley to breathe. Slowly, too slowly, the boat came closer.

Unable to wait, he slogged into the water to meet them, mud sucking at his boots.

Kit, grim-faced, shook his head.

No!

Standing, balancing himself as the boat rocked, Kit put the small, limp form into Kendal's arms. Charley's still face and bare, narrow chest were pale as bone. He felt unutterably cold.

Kendal carried him back to shore, his mind clawing for some way to expel the water and put air into the child. He knew something. He had heard something, a long time ago, when he was on a ship to Naples.

Before the memory took shape, his body knew what it was. Grasping Charley's ankles, he held him upside down and shook him hard. Water dribbled from his mouth and nose, streaming down his closed eyes and forehead.

The boy's leg muscles tensed.

And then he coughed. Water spewed out, and more water.

Kendal put an arm under his chest and brought him parallel to the ground, still facedown. Water and vomit poured from his mouth. Coughing violently, Charley fought to clear his lungs.

Tipping the boy's head downward, Kendal shook him again, not so hard this time. More water came up.

The blue-white flesh was turning pink, he saw as Charley's struggles began to subside. The racking coughs grew less insistent, less frequent.

Then Kendal heard a frail, hoarse sound. "Papa?"

Turning the boy in his arms, Kendal gazed down at his wet face and bloodshot eyes. Charley looked back, dazed, his lashes clumped with water. "Papa?" he said again.

"I'm here, Charley." Bending his head, he brushed a kiss against the child's cold lips. "I'm here."

With a husky sigh, Charley closed his eyes. "Papa."

Panic surging through him, Kendal pressed his ear against

the small chest. But the heartbeat was strong, the skin beginning to warm, and Charley's breath came and went with only a slight rasp. Someone held out a blanket and helped him wrap it around the boy.

Relief was making him dizzy. Through burning eyes, he saw Chirikov clambering up the bank, his face stark with fear. When Kendal nodded at him, he dropped to his hands and knees, panting like a dog, hair and mustaches dripping lake water.

Kit ran up then, his gaze focused on Charley. Gently, he brushed a strand of wet hair from the boy's forehead. "The carriage is ready to go, Jimmie. Take him home. I'll ride for the doctor."

In the passageway outside Charley's room, Kendal and Kit paced, their wet boots making a squishing noise. Servants huddled in the shadows and on the staircase, waiting for word.

The doctor had been inside the room a damnably long time.

He'd arrived shortly after Charley was rubbed down with warm water, dried carefully, and put to bed, Kendal standing watch all the while.

The boy had spoken only once during the carriage ride. "I almost drownded, Papa."

He sounded, Kendal had thought, rather proud of his adventure. But talking made him start coughing again, and he obeyed when Kendal told him to hush. Sometimes dozing, sometimes with his dark eyes fixed on his father's face, he lay swaddled in the blanket on Kendal's lap, wrapped in his arms.

At last the door swung open and Dr. Pritchard emerged, carrying his black leather case. He was smiling.

Kendal swept down on him, backing him up against a long-case clock. "Well?"

"His lungs are clear, as clear as can be expected, his heartbeat is steady and strong, and his color is fine. After a good night's sleep, I've no doubt he will be little the worse for his swim."

"How can you be sure of that? He was underwater a long

time. He wasn't breathing when Chirikov brought him up. You didn't see how he was then."

"That is true. But I have practiced medicine in the lake country for twoscore years, my lord, and seen more than my share of drownings and near drownings. Except for a sore throat, and possibly a day or two of sniffles, Paxton will be fine."

Kendal's knees went weak with relief. At the same time he wasn't buying the story. "If you are so certain, then what the devil were you doing in there all this time?"

"Making sure," the doctor replied. "Making sure. He's more than a little overexcited right now, I'm afraid, but I don't want to give him laudanum to help him sleep."

"What do you mean, *overexcited*?"

"Well, not nearly so much as you, my lord, but he's talking more than is good for his throat. I expect he won't settle down until he sees you, so do calm yourself. While you are with him I'll give a few instructions regarding his care to Mr. Christopher. Or to the boy's nanny, if you prefer, although I place no great reliance on Miss Yallop."

Kendal had long since ordered the woman to her room and told her to keep out of the way. She was good only for wailing and wringing her hands. "You will stay the night, doctor. Kit, tell Geeson to have a bedchamber readied."

Pritchard rolled his eyes. "If I thought there were the slightest need—"

"*I* think there is. You are staying. If you wish to inform anyone where you can be found, riders will carry the messages."

"Oh, very well. I'll send word to my wife and my assistant. But I have a few orders for you, too, Lord Kendal. A few minutes, no more, with your son, and use most of them to encourage him to sleep. Someone should sit with him through the night, but not you. Understood?"

Gritting his teeth, Kendal nodded.

"Go on in, then. Don't let him talk too much. And when you come out, bring that damned puppy with you."

Stepping back, Kendal watched Pritchard separate himself from the clock and proceed down the passageway with Kit, shaking his head.

Then, heart in his throat, he went to the door and let himself into Charley's room. Only one candle was lit, placed on a sideboard where the light could not reach the boy's eyes. Kendal took it with him to the bed and set it on the night table. He had to see for himself that Charley was indeed *fine*.

Charley immediately tried to sit up. Kendal helped him, stacking pillows behind his back. In a white nightshirt, his hair still slightly damp, he looked infinitely small and frail. There was a wooden chair beside the bed and Kendal sank onto it, forearms resting on his knees.

His pulse pumped in his ears. He felt suddenly shy. Awkward. Words clogged in his throat, pushing to get out, but his thoughts were too jumbled to form a whole sentence.

"Are you mad at me, sir?" Charley asked into the silence. "Uncle Kit told me not to go in the race, but Ralph dared me, so I had to."

If he ever got his hands on Ralph—Kendal uncurled his fingers. "Nobody is angry, son. You gave us all a scare, though."

"I'm sorry, sir. I didn't mean to. It didn't look so far when I started, but then my leg hurted really bad and I couldn't kick anymore. So I stayed where I was and waved for help, like Uncle Kit taught me. Then you came out and got me."

Kendal took a deep breath. "That wasn't me, Charley. General Chirikov got there first."

"Oh. Well, I don't 'member what happened. I thought it was you, 'cause when I woke up, you were there."

Placing a hand on the boy's forehead, Kendal decided it was cool. It was hard to tell, what with the heat searing through his own body. "How do you feel now, Charley? Tell me the truth."

"Pretty tired," he admitted. "I swammed a long way. And my throat hurts a little, and my mouth tastes bad."

"That's because you drank rather a lot of Windemere Lake, I'm afraid." His fingers brushed down the boy's face, lingering on his cheek. "Dr. Pritchard says you will feel much better in the morning. He wants you to go to sleep, though. Can you do that?"

"I'll try." Charley's eyes pleaded with him. "Will you stay with me?"

"Of course. For a little while, anyway. The doctor thinks you will talk more than you should if I am here, and he's given me strict orders to wait some other place until tomorrow morning."

"That's all right, then." Charley yawned. "He told me I'm oversited. And I guess you ought to take Wellington downstairs now. He keeps wiggling."

Kendal spotted a squirming lump near Charley's feet. Reaching under the blanket, he extricated the ball of fur and held it to the boy's face for a goodnight kiss. The puppy obliged enthusiastically, lapping at Charley's nose and chin, making him giggle.

That led to a coughing spell, not a bad one but enough to scare the devil out of Kendal. Snatching the dog away, he waited until Charley was breathing easily again. "You can see him tomorrow," he said. "We'll keep him in the house until then and take good care of him."

"I don't think he's had his supper, sir."

"Then I'll make sure he does. And Charley, when we are alone together, you needn't call me 'sir.' In company, it's polite to do that, but otherwise it isn't necessary."

The boy nodded. "Does that mean you will call me Charley? I like that."

"So do I. And yes, I will." One hand wrapped around the puppy, he used the other to rearrange the pillows and settle Charley on his back. Carefully, he adjusted the sheet and blanket. "Someone will be sitting with you all night, son. Not me, because the doctor says I can't, but if you wake up and don't feel good, say so right away."

"Yes, Papa." He yawned again.

"Good. And promise me you'll sleep now."

"I promise." His eyes drifted shut. "Cross my heart."

Kendal moved the candle back to the sideboard and tiptoed to the door, opening it soundlessly.

A whispery voice floated to him from across the room. "I love you, Papa."

Tears welling in his eyes, Kendal looked back at the shadowy figure on the bed. "I love you, too, Charley. Cross my heart."

He stood there a long time, listening closely until the boy's breathing grew deep and even with sleep. Finally, worried that the wriggling puppy might start barking, he moved into the passageway.

Kit was waiting for him, a plump young housemaid at his side. Before Kendal could close the door, she slipped past him into the room.

"That's Margaret," Kit said. "Doc Pritchard told her what to watch for, and she's a good sort. Charley likes her." He moved closer, his brows raised. "What's this, Jimmie? Tears?"

"Stubble it." Kendal handed him the puppy. "The dog is to stay in the house, in case the boy wakes up and wants him. See to it. Where's Pritchard?"

"Billiard room, last I looked. Chirikov is with him."

"Good." Suddenly fired with energy, Kendal headed swiftly down the stairs.

Pritchard regarded him without pleasure as he came through the door. "Just when we were about to start a game," he grumbled.

Ignoring him, Kendal looked around for Chirikov. The general, wearing loose-fitting cossack trousers and a full-sleeved linen shirt open to his waist, was selecting a billiard stick from the rack on the wall. He turned as Kendal approached him with his hand outstretched.

"I owe you an incalculable debt, sir."

"*Nyet.*" Chirikov took his hand and pumped it vigorously. "I vill not hear thanks to me. Iss gift from Gott. All childrens iss gift from Gott."

"To be sure," Kendal replied softly. "Even so, I trust—I hope—you will apply to me if ever I can be of service."

"Hah. You already giff me Mr. Wordsworth." Chirikov leaned closer, mustaches twitching. "Tell you truth, Kental. I

199

understand nothing what he said. He talk too much, that whon. Better he write hiss poems and shut hiss mouth."

Kendal had not imagined he could laugh this particular night, but he did. Celia had been right about Vasily Chirikov. He was a rough-and-tumble fellow, but nobody's fool.

Chirikov clapped him on the back. "Maybe after Vienna meetink you come to St. Petersburk. We go for swim in Neva, where I haff swimmed many times. I swim good, hey?"

"Like a warrior, sir. And this afternoon, like an angel of God. But I'll not be traveling to the Vienna Congress after all. Pressing matters will keep me here at Candale for . . . well, for a long time."

"Iss good. Home is best place to be."

Pritchard cleared his throat. "Are we playing billiards or not, General?"

When Kendal glared at him, he shrugged. "You need to change out of those wet clothes, your lordship. Otherwise I really will have a sick patient requiring my attention. Have you satisfied yourself that young Paxton is recovering nicely?"

"No. And I think you ought to be with him."

"Females do better at times like this, you know. They have a gift for sitting quietly and focusing on a child. I repeat my injunction, Lord Kendal. Stay out of the boy's room. He's sturdy. Let his body do the work of healing, and that will happen best while he sleeps. You can play mother hen tomorrow, but only after he's had his breakfast. I've already dispatched orders to the kitchen regarding what he can eat, and I'll check on him a time or two during the night. So for God's sake, sir, stop worrying."

Kendal supposed the doctor wouldn't be playing billiards if he were the least bit concerned. Bowing to Chirikov, he returned to Charley's bedchamber and gingerly opened the door.

The maid was sitting in the near-dark room beside the bed. She looked up when he stuck his head inside the door and put a finger to her lips. Then she smiled, nodding toward Charley.

All was well, he presumed, but he wanted a closer look for

himself. After one step, though, the wet leather of his boots creaking loudly, he gave it up and backed from the room.

"Tsk, tsk," said Kit, joining him halfway down the hall. "You need to get hold of yourself, old son. You'll not do the child any good circling around him like a shark."

"And you're bloody damned cavalier, I must say. He could take a chill. Come down with a fever. Pneumonia. God knows what."

"Kids are resilient, Jimmie. And while you were in there with him I was putting Doc Pritchard through the wringer. He made a believer out of me. Keep in mind he delivered all three of us, and Charley, too. He wouldn't lie about this."

"Whatever you say." Kendal pushed open the door to his bedchamber. "Where the devil is my valet?"

Kit followed him in, grabbing the bootjack. "Most of the servants are having a meal, now that the crisis is past. Want me to ring, or can you do without him?"

"Just help me off with these boots, will you?" Kendal dropped onto a chair. "I'm officially banned from Charley's room until tomorrow morning, and damned if I can figure any reason for it. What's more, I don't know why I should take orders from Pritchard about where I can and cannot go in my own house."

"Well, for one thing, you're too overset. And stop glowering at me." Kit wrenched off a soggy boot. "And for another, Charley isn't used to you paying him so much attention. If he knows you're there, he'll try to stay awake so he doesn't miss a minute of it."

It made sense, in a painful, shameful sort of way. Charley had been exceedingly glad to see him. *Too* glad. Overexcited. Yes, the doctor was probably right about that. Kendal knew he would do as he'd been told, but he wasn't happy about it. "I'll feel a great deal better if you spend the night with him, Kit."

"I intend to." The second boot hit the floor. "And why don't you remove yourself from the house for a while? You're getting on everyone's nerves. Take a ride. Go visit someone." Kit gave him a meaningful look. "Need I mention any names?"

Kendal peeled off his coat. "Are you reading my mind, brat?"

"Like a primer, Jimmie, like a primer. It's a good idea, you know. She won't want to hear what happened secondhand, or read about it in the Kendal news rag. And if she gets the word elsewhere, it won't include the part about Charley being safe and well. Go tell her."

"It's late." Kendal removed his wet shirt and went to his dressing table, gazing into the mirror with disgust. "I need a shave. Likely she's asleep by now."

"So wake her up. Take my word for it, she won't mind. And yes, she's still at the Merry Goosegirl."

Kendal shot him a look. "Should I, Kit? I don't like leaving here, under the circumstances—"

"Do everyone a favor and go, dammit. Don't hurry back. If the boy has so much as a bad dream, I'll send for you. Now, do you want to shave and fancy yourself up, or should I tell somebody to saddle your horse?"

Now that he'd made up his mind, Kendal was in a hurry to be on his way. In the dark, it would take almost an hour to get there. He would use the time trying to work out what to say to her. "Horse. Ten minutes."

"Aye, sir." Kit snapped a salute. "You can thank me later. And Jimmie, she'll want to see Charley. Bring her home for breakfast."

Kendal spoke just before his brother reached the door. "Kit? I do thank you. And I meant to tell you earlier that I hadn't forgot about Charley's pony. It's being shipped from Ireland and was supposed to be delivered at Candale by this morning. I waited as long as I could, but there must have been some sort of delay. Finally, I went on to the picnic."

"Connemara pony?"

Kendal nodded.

"Splendid choice. Couldn't have done better myself. Well, I didn't, did I? Jimmie, old sod, I begin to suspect there may actually be some hope for you. But first, I'll see how things go with you and Celia tonight." He grinned. "One word of advice, though. Try not to behave yourself."

Chapter 19

Celia closed her book, placed it on the night table, and leaned back against the pillows with a sigh.

It must be well after midnight. The inn was quiet now, and from outside her window, she could hear the chirp of crickets and the distant *whooo* of an owl.

And so, what was she to do with herself until morning? Trying to read had proven a notable failure. She ought to be tired, and she was, but sleep was clearly out of the question.

In her own house, she would be free to wander downstairs and putter around, or take a walk in the moonlit garden. Really, she must come to a decision about a house. The agent had trolled her through several lakeside properties, all of them perfectly acceptable, but she continued to dither. Even Thomas Carver was growing impatient with her, although *he* got to spend his evenings in the taproom and take walks at night if he wanted to.

Mercy, now she was turning on poor Thomas! Such a vile mood she was in.

What she required was some means of working off her energy, perhaps a stiff wad of bread dough to knead or a heavy carpet to beat. Walloping a mallet across the back of Lord Kendal's head would nicely turn the trick.

Climbing out of bed, she straightened her nightrail and padded barefoot to the dressing table. The candlelight cast eerie shadows over her face as she sat on the spindly chair, gazing at her reflection in the mirror. Celia Greer, wealthy widow, no place to go, nothing to do.

She picked up the hairbrush.

Kendal would never let her see Charley again, that was certain. Not after what she said to him today. She wasn't the least bit sorry for it, though.

Well, perhaps the merest trifle, but if she had it all to do over again, she would. Only next time she would say it better.

As if words would have any effect on that blockhead! He must have heard them before, from Kit, and to no purpose whatever. Why would he listen to a mere female, especially one he neither liked nor respected? At the end of the day all she'd accomplished by her tirade was to deprive Charley of one of his few friends.

Too late now for second thoughts, Celia told herself, pulling the brush through her tangled curls. As usual, by acting without *first* thoughts, she had landed everyone in the soup.

The thing was, she could not bring herself to give up on him. She just *knew* that somewhere under that shell of ice was a good man, the one she had fallen in love with. But she was becoming terribly afraid that he had put himself beyond all reach. A man who could not love Charley was surely incapable of loving anyone.

A dog barked from the direction of the stable, and she heard the sound of hooves against the stone-flagged courtyard. Someone in search of a room for the night, perhaps, or a guest returning late. A few minutes later came muffled voices from downstairs and the closing of a door.

She listened intently, but the inn grew silent again. Rats. Any distraction from her gloomy reflections would have been welcome. Ah well. She went back to brushing her hair, which was practically standing on end. A storm must be on the way, she thought, glancing over at the window. She'd left it open against the humid July air, and the curtains had begun to billow as the wind picked up.

Double rats! A storm was precisely what she didn't need right now. If it kept her imprisoned in this room one single minute past dawn, she would likely take to gnawing at the furniture.

A distant rumble of thunder confirmed her fears. At about

the same time she thought she heard footsteps in the passageway. It must have been her imagination, because there was no sound of groaning hinges or the clunk of metal against wood as a door latch dropped. She was familiar with the night sounds at the Merry Goosegirl, especially those of a guest arriving, but she heard only a raspy snore from the cutlery salesman in the bedchamber next to hers.

Celia put down the brush, stretched broadly, and reckoned she could brush her teeth again. And wash her face again. She did both, using the last of her clean water, and wandered over to the open window.

A few drops of rain made plunking sounds against the windows, their casements swung wide against the walls of the inn. More drops pattered onto the wooden floor. She thought to pull the windows shut, but the wind and the electrified air felt stunningly cool against her overheated body.

Lifting her nightrail above her knees, she stood for several minutes, letting the rain dance onto her thighs and stream down her legs. A flash of lightning illuminated the distant fells and roiling clouds, followed swiftly by a sharp clap of thunder.

She knew these summer squalls, sudden, fierce, and like unfaithful lovers, quickly gone.

What was *that*?

She spun around, almost sure she had heard a thump against the door. It came again, louder this time, and then again.

Letting go her hold on the nightrail, she felt it clinging to her damp legs as she made her way across the room. "Who is it?" she asked softly when she reached the door.

Silence for a moment. Then, in a gravelly voice, "Kendal."

Oh my! Swallowing the hard lump that had jumped to her throat, she gingerly raised the latch and cracked the door. A tall shadow loomed in the dim passageway. She knew the shape of him, and even the smell of him. But what in holy heaven was he doing here in the middle of the night?

"May I come in?"

"That depends." She eyed him cautiously. "Have you come to throttle me?"

"Of course not." He curled gloved fingers around the edge

of the door and leaned closer. "The innkeeper is on the stair-case," he whispered, "and I am nearly certain he has a musket aimed in my direction. He was not pleased to admit me, I assure you. He would not even accept the considerable bribe I offered him."

"Then how did you get this far?"

"I told him we were betrothed, and had quarreled, and that I'd come to make it up. For God's sake, Celia, let me in before he blows my head off. Or send me packing if you must. But please don't do that. I must speak with you."

Backing away from the door, she watched him slip into the room, lower the latch soundlessly, and turn. His eyes widened.

At that moment she became intensely aware of wet muslin clinging to her belly and hips and thighs. She felt the lamplight from behind her outlining her body. She was all but naked. Exposed to him.

And she was *glad* of it. This was exactly how she had always wanted him to look at her, with heated, barely sheathed desire.

Or perhaps what she saw in his eyes was merely a trick of the uncertain light.

Crossing her arms around her waist, she backed up to the bed and sat before her legs dissolved under her. "Why are you here?" she asked, her voice cracking like a wishbone.

"You make me forget," he said quietly. "Looking at you makes me forget. But I have to tell you something. Many things, if you will allow me, but first of all you must know what happened this afternoon." He took a deep, shuddering breath. "Charley nearly drowned."

"Oh dear God."

He moved closer, waving his hands in a gesture of denial. "He's fine now. Truly. Forgive me for frightening you. There was no harm done, or so the doctor assures me. At worst, the boy will have a sore throat from all the water he swallowed and threw up, but devil if I believe that he will get off so lightly. I was there when he was pulled from the lake."

He swiped a hand over his forehead. "Charley was in high spirits when I left, though, and Kit is watching over him now.

Dr. Pritchard agreed, under compulsion, to stay the night at Candale, but he ordered me to leave the boy alone so that he can get some sleep. I overexcite him, it seems. In any case, I was unceremoniously cast out. So I came here."

Charley. He was calling his son Charley. Not Paxton, which was one of the devices he used to distance himself from the child, but *Charley*. Once Celia had caught her breath, she began to take note again of the man who had begun to prowl her bedchamber.

When he failed to speak, she ventured a question. "Do you want to tell me what happened?"

He appeared relieved to be given a task. "There was a swimming race for the older boys," he said. "I did not see the first of it, and by the time I got in sight of the lake, the winner had already claimed victory. The boys were swimming to Belle Isle. It's about three-quarters of a mile from where they began. You remember it?"

"Yes," she said when he waited for an answer. "I remember the island."

He stopped at the open window, propping one hand against the frame, the wind-lashed rain pelting over his boots. "No one noticed that Charley had entered the race on his own. He told me later that he'd meant to prove he could swim as well as somebody named Ralph, who had apparently been tormenting him all afternoon."

Kendal glanced at her over his shoulder. "You were right. He has spent far too much time in the company of hired staff and has no idea how to deal with other children, let alone bullies. In any case, someone finally spotted him a few hundred yards behind the last of the racers, thrashing his arms. And screaming for help, I daresay, although I was just coming over the hill that overlooks the lake and scarcely knew what was going on. I could see only a dark shape in the water and everyone else running for the shoreline."

Kendal began pacing again. "Chirikov was after him immediately. He pulled off his boots and plunged into the water like a man possessed. But by the time he swam to where we'd last seen Charley, the boy had vanished underwater. Chirikov dove, and dove again. It seemed to take forever, although I'm told only a short time passed before he came up with Charley. Kit had just got there with the rowboat, and he brought him back to shore."

He turned to face her. "Charley wasn't breathing. I can't tell you how it was when Kit put him in my arms. He was so limp, and so terribly cold. Someday I might remember where I got the idea to do what I did. In any case, it worked. All of a sudden he coughed, and then he spewed out a great deal of water. We took him home, of course, and from all indications, he has come to no harm."

"Thank God." She folded her hands to keep them from shaking.

"Yes. Thank God. It has been a long time since I prayed, but I was begging for a miracle during the eternity that Charley wasn't breathing. I swear that fifty universes could have been created before he started gasping for air. It was a near-run thing, Celia. Had Chirikov not been there—" He gave her a wry smile. "To think I've spent the last two weeks wishing him to the devil."

His smile, such as it was, combed through the last of her fears. Kendal would not be making even a slight joke if he believed that Charley's health was in the slightest question. "Thank you for telling me what happened," she said, relief making her dizzy. "If Charley is feeling better tomorrow, may I visit him?"

Kendal exhaled slowly. "You needn't ask that. You will always be welcome. He'll be very pleased to see you."

She waited, but he said nothing else. He only stood in place, regarding her with an expression she could not decipher. Why had he come here *now*, when tomorrow morning would have done just as well? If she didn't know better, she might imagine he had acted as she so often did—on impulse.

He turned to the window again and looked out into the stormy night. "There are a great many things I wish to say to you, Celia, but I cannot think where to begin. Have you the patience to hear me out? Or the slightest interest in doing so?"

His voice grew husky at the end, even uncertain. She had a

misbegotten urge to rush across the room and wrap her arms around him. But she remained seated, pleating her nightrail between her fingers, sensing that he was better left to manage on his own. "Would you care to sit down?" she asked.

He shook his head. "I would have come to see you in any case, to thank you. What you said to me yesterday afternoon was intolerable to hear, and under ordinary circumstances, being somewhat mule-headed, I'm not certain how long it would have taken me to recognize it as truth. Weeks, perhaps, or months. When you left, I knew only that I could not bear to accept any of it. No man wants to look at himself and see a monster."

At that, she could not keep silent. "Good heavens, why must men always go to such extremes? You were wrong, my lord, and other things as well, but never a *monster*. How absurd."

"It has been a day of extremes," he said after a moment. "You showed me what I had become, and I knew that sooner or later I would be forced to deal with it. I want to think that I'd have come around, and realized how infinitely precious Charley has always been. But I've little faith in my judgment of late. It's possible I'd have retreated behind the walls I had constructed to keep him out.

"But then he nearly died in my arms." Turning, Kendal gazed at her from haunted eyes. "Without question I shall make many mistakes in the future, but not the same ones I made in the past. Charley is my son. Unequivocally. The wonder is that he loves me in spite of everything. I mean to be worthy of that love, Celia. I expect him to teach me how."

"I am persuaded you will learn quickly," she told him with conviction. And with love, too. It was swelling in her own heart, however hard she tried to contain it.

"I am also taking lessons," he said roughly, "in how to apologize. I've scarcely begun, mind you, except for the part where I realize that I *need* to apologize. Most of all to Charley, but I think he would not understand. Is that wrong? Should I—"

"Absolutely not. It would only confuse him. Concentrate on being what he already thinks you are." She smiled an apology of her own. "As if I've any idea what you ought to do, my lord.

I promise that you have heard the last of my insufferably self-righteous lectures."

"Give me leave to hope that you fail to keep that promise. But I will take your advice and confess none of my sins to Charley until the day, should it ever come, that he demands justification of my neglect all these many years. I hope he never does. There is no excuse for my behavior, to be sure, but there are reasons. And better they remain hidden, if that is possible."

He referred to Belinda, she was certain. And it was equally certain that one day Charley would hear the rumors about his adulterous mother. Celia could only hope that when he did, he would be secure enough in his father's love to forgive her. It would help if Kendal had forgiven her, too. She bit her tongue to keep from telling him so.

He moved a few steps closer to the bed, the lamplight shadowing the hollows in his drawn cheeks. Each time she had seen him since coming north, he had looked increasingly weary, as if he rarely slept. Tonight he was positively exhausted, she could tell, no surprise after the ordeal he had just endured.

"I have treated you badly," he said. "Abominably. You'll not credit this, but I have never behaved in such a fashion with any woman. Not even the only woman I had reason to despise, although that may be because I took care to put distance between us. I never even lost my temper with her, but I have seemed to do nothing else with you. I am sorry for it, Celia. Deeply sorry."

"Think no more of it," she said immediately. "I provoked you."

"Oh, indeed you did." He rubbed the bridge of his nose. "Not in the ways you are thinking, though. Well, not always. I've grown particularly fond of your sharp wit, and trust you'll not blunt it on my account."

"Oh, you may be sure of that. And I accept your apology, so long as you accept mine. As you reminded me on any number of occasions, I'd no right to interfere in your personal life. Which is not to say that I've the slightest regret about doing so, at least where Charley is concerned." She paused, flushing hotly. "Mercy me, what an abysmal apology *that* was. You must enroll me in the school where you are taking lessons."

"I will never cease to be grateful that you chose to interfere," he replied simply. "I am even more grateful that you have not long since ordered me from this room. It did not occur to me that you might turn me away until I reached the door. I stood there half a lifetime, you know, scratching up the courage to knock."

"Well, I'm glad you did. At risk of a musketball, too. Do you suppose that Mr. Grigg is still lurking on the stairs?"

He looked pained. "Does that mean you wish me to take my leave now?"

It wasn't what she had meant at all. Of course she wanted him to stay. She *always* wanted him to stay. She just couldn't figure why he wished to, after saying what he'd come here to say.

Unless there was more. Her heart made little fluttery jumps in her chest.

"Celia?" He moved closer to the bed.

She licked dry lips. "Yes, my lord?"

"There is something more."

"Yes, my lord."

"Will you marry me?"

Lightning flashed. Thunder shook the walls. For a moment a brilliant light passed over his face, and in that moment she glimpsed his deepest heart.

"Yes, my lord," she said. "Yes."

He raised stunned eyes. "Yes? Just like that, *yes*? Did you misunderstand? I asked you to *marry* me."

"My hearing is perfectly sound, Lord Kendal. Were you wishing for another response than the one I gave you?"

"N-no." He scratched his head. "But I certainly *expected* one. At the least I expected to spend hours or weeks or even years changing your mind. You told me once, in no uncertain terms, that you would never again take a husband."

"I changed my mind," she said with a dismissive wave. Her doubts had vanished so quickly that she never saw them go. "But had I the least suspicion you meant to propose to me, I would certainly have advised you to lead up to it more . . . gently."

"I can do that," he said immediately. "I'll do it tomorrow, if you wish. I shall devise the most romantic proposal in history. Flowers. Musicians. Champagne. Only promise me your answer will still be yes."

"I promise." She smiled at the earnest look on his face. "But somewhere between the music and the champagne, my lord, will you get around to mentioning that you love me?"

Faster than a bolt of lightning he was beside her on the bed, gathering her into his arms, pressing urgent kisses over every inch of her face. Briefly, she was reminded of Charley's puppy. And then his lips met hers, and he whispered, "I love you," and she was lost in him.

After a long time he set her away with a shuddering groan, his hands gripping her shoulders. "I *do* love you, Celia. I suspect I fell in love with you under Lord Finlay's desk, the moment I first saw your face. And ever since, until tonight, I have been fighting it. I think you understand why, but I am sorry for being so damnably—"

She put her forefinger against his lips. "I do understand, you know. Some other time we can retrace our steps to this moment. I've a story of my own to tell, beloved, and I expect it will astonish you. For now, though, I want us to stop talking and go back to kissing."

"No." Carefully, he detached himself from her grasp and came to his feet. "That would be most unwise. I should leave now, while I still can."

"Whatever for?" Then she remembered. "You are worried about Charley."

"To be sure, although I am forbidden to see him until after he's had his breakfast. But that is not the reason. You put me beyond control, Celia. And it will be a week or more before I can send to the archbishop for a special license and have it in my hands. Three weeks if you prefer banns to be cried at the church, but I hope you'll not ask me to wait so long."

"I'm not asking you to wait at all. To the contrary." She

stood. "It's pouring rain outside, James. You cannot leave until the storm has passed."

His hot gaze swept over her body. "I'm well used to the rain."

Moving closer, she began to unbutton his coat. "All the same, I want you to stay. I insist on it. You owe me, sir. Was a time you left me alone in the bedchamber of an inn. You'll not do the same tonight. I mean us to finish what we started."

"And we shall," he said huskily. "When we are married."

"But it won't be the same, my love." Her fingers moved to the buttons of his waistcoat. "For more years than you can imagine, I have dreamed of a grand, glorious, passionate affair."

"I can safely promise you a lifetime of passion," he said, eyes widening as her hands crept over his chest.

"And I shall hold you to that promise. But it won't be the same, you see. It won't be . . . *shameless*."

"Y-yes it will. It will be everything you want."

She gripped handfuls of his shirt and pulled it from his trousers. "But I set out to take a lover, Lord Kendal. I want to have one."

"You will. Dear heavens, stop that." Her fingers had slid under his shirt and were dancing over his bare back. "I will be your lover. Soon."

"Soon isn't good enough," she murmured, raising her lips to his. "Soon isn't *now*."

With a raw sound, he wrapped his arms around her and kissed her long and deep.

"Mercy me," he said finally, breathlessly. "What am I to do with you, Lady Greer?"

She drew him inexorably to the bed. "Oh, I think you know, Lord Kendal."

He did.

Lucy in Disguise

*For Diane Hayward,
in celebration of friendship,
good times, and her excellent advice:
"Lynn, you should write a romance novel!"*

Chapter 1

Late on a moonless night, a luminous figure walked the high cliff overlooking Morecambe Bay.

Below, the tide was out. Starlight glittered on the rivulets of water left on the beach, silver ribbons across dark sand, soon obscured as clouds scudded overhead.

In the far distance, Lucy Jennet Preston saw faint golden lights.

Cocklers, perhaps, or mussel diggers. But she doubted it.

She dropped to her belly and slithered to the edge of the cliff. The lights, four of them, moved steadily inland, and she guessed them to be half-shuttered lanterns. For a time she thought they were headed directly toward her, and then she decided they were angled slightly south. It was impossible to be sure.

Ought she to stand again and hope to frighten them away? That was, after all, the whole point of being an apparition. But she held in place, watching the dim lights come ever closer, debating her next move. If they had some other destination in mind, the last thing she wanted to do was call attention to this one.

Suddenly there were more lights, six or seven brighter ones, surrounding the four she had been tracking. Lanterns snapped open—at a signal, most likely—to reveal the silhouettes of a horse and wagon, two more animals laden with wide panniers, and nearly a dozen men.

What in blazes was going on? She could see only shadowy figures illuminated by flickering red-gold light. For a minute

1

or two no one moved. Then the donkeys were led away in a northerly direction.

Three men stood near the horse and wagon, which was piled high with what she supposed to be boxes. One man reached out, and for a moment he seemed to be struggling with the horse. She heard a sharp sound, like a crack of distant thunder, and three men broke into a run. All were carrying the shuttered lanterns, and they aimed themselves south toward Jenny Brown's Point.

Meanwhile the bright lanterns went quickly in the direction in which the donkeys had been taken. One lantern lay abandoned on the sand near the wagon.

Whatever had transpired down there appeared to be over. The men were soon out of sight, but she waited and watched for a long time in case they returned for the horse and cargo they had left behind.

The horse!

By now the wagon wheels were probably sinking into the muddy sand. The few times she had wandered any distance from the shore, Lucy had found that it didn't do to stand in one place for very long. Should the stranded animal fail to pull the wagon free very soon, it was surely doomed.

Lucy scrambled to her feet, sighing. However diligently one planned, something always came along to throw a spanner in the works. She didn't even *like* horses.

Grumbling, she stripped off her costume and rolled it into a tight bundle. If she had to go out on the sands, she would do better wearing only her shirt and trousers.

How she would unhook the horse from the wagon she had no idea. With any luck, not that she ever had much of it, there would be only a few buckles to unloose. Otherwise she could only hope that the wagon had settled on a patch of hard sand, making it possible to lead the horse and wagon to safety.

She ran the short distance to Cow's Mouth Inlet, where a steep path wound down from the cliff to the beach. A flat rock jutting from the limestone headland marked the place to start.

Stashing her costume on a ledge beneath the rock, Lucy began the precipitous descent.

In the dark she had to go by feel alone, but she'd made the trip any number of times in the past few days. She always told herself it was like climbing a tree and tried not to notice when pebbles dislodged by her boots clattered down the cliffside and landed with a hollow thud.

Grasping for handholds, she lowered herself bit by bit until her feet touched the ground of the inlet. From there, the sands were invisible. She followed the narrow break in the cliff around a curve to the shoreline and aimed herself toward the lantern. At ground level, she could barely make it out.

The air was charged with electricity. It caused the hair at her nape to spring out, as it always did just before a storm. Overhead, the clouds were rolling in, sometimes releasing fat drops of rain. Only now and again could she glimpse a few stars winking in the black night, and soon they disappeared altogether.

Once her boot sank ankle-deep in a gully of soft sand, and for several terrifying moments she was not at all sure she would be able to wrench it out. But it finally popped free and from then on she moved more slowly, taking care to avoid any spot where water had pooled.

Robbie had warned her that the sands were treacherous. When the tide turned, a high wave would sweep into the bay with the speed of a galloping horse. Perhaps she ought to have paid more attention to the schedule he provided her, but until now there was no reason to venture onto the bay. Already she was much farther out than she had ever been.

As she drew closer to the fallen lantern she saw more clearly the outlines of the horse, which wore a saddle, and of the flatbed wagon. It was indeed piled with wooden boxes. An exceptionally large box had apparently fallen off and lay on the sand directly behind it.

The horse nickered and tossed its head restively. No docile wagon puller, it was an enormous beast, eyes glowing like fiery coals in the lantern light. She approached it gingerly.

"Please stay still," she said in the most soothing tone she could produce from a constricted throat. "Truly, I won't hurt you."

"I am relieved to hear it."

Lucy stopped dead in her tracks, her heart pounding. Surely not! Horses couldn't talk.

"Hullo," said the voice. "I'm back here."

She could see nothing beyond the wagon except the outline of the fallen box. "Come out then. Slowly. And hold up your hands. I have a pistol."

"You, too? Is everyone but me carrying a weapon tonight?" There was a rumble of male laughter. "I would oblige you, to be sure, but at the moment I'm unable to move. M'foot is trapped under a box."

"So you say." She advanced one cautious step in his direction. "How can I be sure?"

"I suppose you could take my word for it. Or you could come and see for yourself. Do hurry, though. Time and tide wait for no man, or so I am told, and we will both be underwater fairly soon. *I* certainly will, if you cannot help me to extricate myself. You, of course, are free to leave whenever you like."

He sounded harmless. Even amused. And he could have jumped on her long before now if he'd a mind to, or if he were able to. She picked up the lantern and moved alongside the wagon, stopping when she reached the oversize back wheel. Sure enough, a black-clad figure was stretched out behind the box. As she looked at him he sat forward, propping himself up on one elbow. His right leg was buried under the sand from the knee down, and the box was planted where his foot would likely be.

She raised the lantern for a better look at him. There wasn't much to see. His hair was covered by a knit cap and his face had been blackened. White teeth flashed at her, though, when he smiled.

"Well? Do you mean to help me or not?"

Gazing at him, she sensed disaster. Alarm prickled at her

spine. He was a large man, and powerful, if one was to judge by a set of wide shoulders and a broad chest. "Can you not kick away the box with your other foot?"

"Believe me, I've been trying. Thing is, my buried foot hit a patch of wet sand and sank in. Then the box fell off the wagon and landed right atop it. Not to mention that someone shot me along the way. My left arm is fairly useless at the moment, and I can't seem to get the leverage for a good hard push."

"Oh." She moved from behind the dubious protection of the wagon. "Who are you?"

"A smuggler, retired as of a few minutes ago. And a few minutes from now the bore tide will be upon us. Much as I hate to say this, m'dear, you really ought to head back to shore while you can."

She wanted to do exactly that, but of course she could not. After placing the lantern on the back of the wagon, she went behind the fallen box, knelt, and gave a mighty pull. It moved a fraction of an inch and dropped back again. Three more tries were equally futile. The box was heavy and it had sunk very deep.

"Try putting your foot against the top," she directed. "Shove as best you can when I give the sign." Curling her fingers around the edge of the box near the corner, she planted herself firmly and took a deep breath. "Now!"

He pushed, she pulled, and except for a sucking noise, nothing happened. They gave it several more attempts, but if anything, the box sank lower still into the quagmire.

Still kneeling, Lucy wiped sweat from her forehead with her sleeve.

"There's a knife in the scabbard on my belt," the man said quietly. "Use it to cut the horse loose and lead him to shore. His name is Jason. Take care of him, and I'll put in a good word for you at the Pearly Gates."

"Don't be stupid." She jumped onto the wagon, looking for something to stuff underneath the box. There were only more heavy boxes, nailed shut, and a battered umbrella. Taking it with her, she dropped back to the ground, opened the umbrella, and proceeded to stomp on it until all the spines had broken and it lay flat. Then she knelt and used her hands like a pair of trowels to scoop sand from the base of the wooden box. Almost as fast as she dug, the heavy wet sand settled back again.

She redoubled her efforts, frantically plowing the ground. Her nails broke down to the quick, but at last she was able to dig her fingers under the box and hold it up. It must be full of rocks, she thought, panting heavily. With her teeth, she tugged the remains of the umbrella to the very edge of the box and used her chin to push it forward, never letting go her hold on the box although her hands were aching like the very devil. She'd got the fabric of the umbrella scrunched up about two inches underneath when she absolutely had to give it up.

Not at all sure the box wouldn't crush her fingers in the process, she gave a quick mental count to three and snatched her hands away.

The edge of the box collapsed onto the umbrella, free of the boggy sand for no more than a few seconds. She crawled rapidly to the man's side and sat with her elbows on the ground and her feet planted near the top of the box. "Get ready, sir. Put your foot at the corner. When I give the word, push up and forward with all your strength."

"I'm set."

"Go!"

Groaning with effort, they shoved and shoved. The box almost came loose, but then it fell back again.

"You must leave now," he said urgently. "I mean it."

"Go!"

They pushed again until she thought her skin would burst. Slowly the box rose. This was it, she knew. Should it fall back, they would never be able to pry it up again. Together, they fought the pull of the sand, working side by side in what had to be their final effort.

And all of a sudden, as if it were lighter than a rubber ball, the box rolled over and away.

Dear Lord. For a few moments she lay flat and stared dizzily into space. Then she was up again, tunneling into the sand that imprisoned his foot. Soon his boot was exposed, and in another minute he raised his leg and made cautious circles with his ankle.

"No harm done. I'll thank you some other time, but for God's sake, get out of here." He pulled a formidable-looking knife from its sheath and passed it to her. "Cut the horse free and ride him to shore. I'll follow."

"We'll go together." She went to the harnesses and began sawing through them. "Can you get on your feet?"

He scrambled to the box that had trapped him and used it to lever himself upright. From there he tottered to the wagon wheel and clung to it.

Watching him from the corners of her eyes, she could tell he would be unable to walk more than a few yards, if that far. "Could you possibly get yourself up on the wagon, sir? From there, you'll find it easier to slide onto the saddle."

"There isn't time."

"Do it! And how can you be sure the tide is on its way in?"

"We were cutting it close as it was. Delays before we started." He heaved himself onto the back of the wagon and knelt with his shoulder propped against a box.

When the horse was free, she led him to where the man waited to climb aboard. "There is no time for niceties, sir. Unless you can mount in one try, please settle for draping yourself over the saddle."

After restoring the knife to its sheath, he did precisely that. She took up the lantern and set out for the shore.

"This is humiliating," the man grumbled.

"As if that signifies. Take care not to fall off, because we'll never get you back on." He had her so convinced that the tide would wash over them at any moment that she jumped when a drop of rainwater hit her nose. Oh, excellent, she thought. Rain was precisely what they needed right now.

The man was ominously silent. "How are you feeling, sir?"

"Merry as a grig," he assured her. "What exactly *is* a grig?" he asked after a while. "I've always wondered."

"Grigs are young eels."

"Oh. But why are they merry? How do we *know* they are merry?"

Clearly she was risking her life to save a lunatic. "I've no idea, sir. Perhaps because they don't have to deal with the likes of you." The sand was firmer there and she sensed they were on an upward slope. Raising the lantern, she was able to see the cliff looming directly ahead.

Now what was she to do?

The horse would have to stay the night in the cave, of course. The nearest way onto land for him was more than a mile away. But she dared not reveal the cave's location to the smuggler, not while there was any chance he could climb up the same way she had come down.

She was fairly sure he could not. And why bring him this far only to have him die on solid land? But to take him through the cave would put Diana at risk. Oh, damn.

With little hope, she decided to gamble he could make the ascent up the cliff. If he faltered, they would simply have to go around the other way. At least they were well beyond reach of the bore tide. She led the horse to the inlet and came to a halt beside a large boulder. "Will he stand if I let go his bridle?"

"He'll stand. Jason, old lad, behave yourself."

Lucy helped the man slip off the horse, bearing much of his weight when his feet hit the ground. She assisted him to the boulder and gestured for him to sit. "I'm going to leave you here for a short time, sir. The horse cannot go up this way, so I'll secure him a little distance down the beach, where he will be perfectly safe until I can do better for him."

"Where *is* the way up?"

"About a dozen yards behind you. It's not an easy climb. I'll be back within five minutes."

The horse was soon tethered to a rock deep inside the cave and away from the coming storm. But the man was nowhere in sight when she returned to where she'd left him. Blessedly, the rain was falling only in occasional brief sputters. Lantern in hand, she entered Cow's Mouth Inlet and discovered the man crawling on hands and knees up the path. He was nearly halfway to the top.

"If I'm going the wrong way," he called over his shoulder, "don't tell me."

"You are doing fine," she said bracingly. On her own, she'd have extinguished the lantern and left it behind, but she greatly feared he would require its light when he came to the sharp vertical climb near the top and the jutting rock directly above. "Slow a bit! Let me catch up with you." She maneuvered herself along the rocky track with the lantern handle clasped between her teeth.

He waited until she was at his heels before moving again, inches at a time. She could hear the breath rasping in his throat and almost feel in her bones what every inch of progress was costing him. He crept steadily ahead, though, without complaint.

At one point her hand fell on a wet rock. She thought nothing of it, assuming the moisture to be rainwater. But when she used the hand to wipe perspiration from her forehead, she smelled the coppery tang of blood. Nausea rose to her throat as she scrubbed her hand against her trouser leg. What if he bled himself dry there on the cliffside?

"Who are you?" he asked, pausing for a few seconds before continuing on.

She removed the lantern from her mouth. "L-Luke."

"Glad to know you, Luke. More than I can say. My name is Kit. I should advise you that I'm a trifle muzzy and am like to tumble off the edge at any moment. But I won't be any less grateful for your help as I plunge to my doom."

"Might I suggest you save your strength for the climb?" she shot back at him. "The hardest part is at the top."

He chuckled. "I should have guessed."

When he reached the last, almost perpendicular few yards of

the cliff, she tugged at his foot. "Huddle to one side, please. I shall try to go around you."

"Is that a good idea?"

"No. But you'll need me to pull you up. Take the lantern, will you?"

He did, and she slithered past him with half her body hanging over the side of the cliff. Should they both survive this ordeal, she thought, she would kill him for putting her through it. With a final burst of maniacal strength, she clambered over the jutting rock and flattened herself atop it.

"You're almost done, sir. Put down the lantern and grab hold of my hands."

"Make that one hand. I've only the one to grab with."

Knitting her fingers together, she made a sort of sling for him to hang on to as he thrust himself up and over to safety. He must have kicked the lantern on his final push. It tumbled off the cliff and fell like a shooting star, the light flaming out when it crashed against the ground below. That could have been either one of them, she realized, suddenly icy cold from scalp to toes.

He flopped onto his back, breathing heavily. "Well, that was a treat. I'll try it again about fifty years from now. Are we there yet? Or do you have another mountain for us to play on?"

If she had ever doubted it before, she was now convinced the man was daft. "It's perhaps a hundred yards from here to our destination. Can you walk if I support you, or would you prefer to crawl?"

"Walk, thank you." He lurched to his feet and seized hold of her waist.

As they teetered in the direction of the cottage, Lucy began to realize that her problems had only just begun. She could not take him immediately inside, not without warning Diana and making preparations. Somehow there must be a way to get through this debacle without ruining everything, but she had no idea what that way could be. A dark corner of her soul wished the smuggler had been shot through the heart instead of the arm. Or that he'd tumbled off the cliff.

But he was alive, drat him, a heavy weight against her now and an impossible burden to carry from here on out.

To one side, she spotted the large flat tree stump that rose from the ground a short way from the cottage. Some previous resident had smoothed the top and now it provided a nice bench to sit on, with a view of the woodlands in daylight. She detoured over to it and let go of the smuggler's waist. "You'll have to wait here a few moments, sir. Let me help you sit."

"Again?" He lowered himself onto the stump with a low groan. "We're making more stops than a London post deliverer."

"Yes. It's unfortunate. I'll be back directly." He would simply have to remain befuddled, Lucy thought as she dashed to the cottage and slipped inside.

Diana, seated at a small table beside the hearth, looked up with alarm. "What happened? Where is your witch's—"

"Never mind that. There's a man waiting outside. He's been shot." She waved a hand when Diana tried to speak again. "I can't tend to him alone, so you must be Mrs. Preston. Wear the veil and pretend to be mute."

"Is he badly hurt?"

"I don't know. He's not right in the head, and he's lost a good deal of blood. We'll need bandages, scissors, perhaps needle and thread. Any medicines you have that might be useful. Is there laudanum?"

"Yes. I'll bring everything I can think of." Taking her book, Diana went to the door that led to the cottage's only other room. "Hadn't you better fetch him inside?"

"In a moment." Lucy darted around the sparsely furnished room, grabbing up anything that might provide a clue to their identities and concealing the items in her portmanteau. Finally, taking along a sturdy walking stick, she went outside to collect the smuggler.

Chapter 2

Kit watched Luke vanish into the dark cottage, abandoning him to his tree stump.

An odd development, to be sure, but unexpected things had been happening all night. At least he was apt to be among the living come tomorrow. For a few thorny minutes there, his foot embedded in wet sand under that wretched box, he had been fairly sure he was about to cock up his toes. One set of toes, anyway.

By now, the bore tide was driving up the bay. It might already have swamped the wagon, and he would currently be making the acquaintance of the local fish had Luke not pulled him free. Only to leave him, it seemed, to pour out his life's blood on a tree stump.

With his rescuer in no apparent hurry to come back for him, he turned his thoughts from his near demise to the mystery of her identity. *Her,* for if Luke was of the male persuasion, Christopher Etheridge Valliant was the Queen of Sheba.

He certainly knew a female body when he felt one, and he'd had several opportunities to detect the swell of breasts under that heavy homespun shirt and makeshift binding. While leaning against her for support, his hand had encountered the flare of feminine hips and a sweetly rounded derriere.

He wouldn't object in the least to encountering them again. When he'd recovered his strength, perhaps she would permit him to reward her for saving his life.

The door opened again, and this time a narrow slice of light fell onto the ground. Luke strode swiftly to the tree stump, a blackthorn walking stick in her hand. "Well, come along, then," she said. "Lean on this."

One hand clutching the knobby tip, Kit lurched to his good foot and reeled precariously, struggling to regain his balance.

Luke anchored him with one arm wrapped around his waist. "Steady on. It's only a few steps more."

They tottered slowly toward the door, the sudden exertion having sucked what remained of Kit's blood to his legs. They felt like overcooked noodles, and it required iron concentration to compel them to move.

Luke towed him inside and maneuvered him to an object he could not quite make out. A large spider? he wondered dizzily as she turned him around.

"There is a chair directly behind you," she told him. "Sit."

The walking stick slipped from his hand when he tried to lower himself. Luke seized his belt with both hands and helped him settle on the chair. Then he felt a pressure against the back of his neck.

"Bend forward, sir." She pushed his head down between his knees. "Stay in this position until I tell you otherwise."

Sit. Stay. What the devil did she think he was—a bloody spaniel?

But he obeyed, and soon his head began to clear. Marginally, anyway. He became aware of a packed-dirt floor, two boots caked with wet sand, and the god-awful pain in his shoulder.

Lifting his gaze, he saw a narrow cot set in the corner, a small, rough-hewn square table beside him, and another primitive wooden chair. There was a fire at his back, he could tell, and Luke was at the hearth, pouring something liquid into a metal pot. Then he heard wood against wood as she added logs to the fire, and the crackle of sparks shooting up the chimney.

"Are you still alive?" she asked briskly.

"I believe so."

"Try to remain so a bit longer, then. When we have got things organized, we'll tend to your shoulder as best we can."

13

We? He wrenched his head from between his legs and looked around the small room. Luke was poking at the fire, but there was no sign of anyone else. He did see two doors, both closed. One would have to be the one he'd just come through, so the other probably led to a second room.

His brain felt as if it were marinating in molasses. "Where the deuce am I?"

"Not at a proper surgery where you belong, I'm afraid. The locals call this outpost Cow's Mouth Cottage, and Mrs. Preston is currently in residence here. She is gathering bandages and implements, but we've little to work with and shall be forced to improvise."

That sounded ominous. Carefully, Kit rotated his shoulder. It moved well enough, so he experimented with his arm. Everything responded as it ought, but the pain sent sweat to his forehead and from there down into his eyes, carrying with it particles of gritty charcoal dust. They filtered through his lashes and burned under his lids.

"C-could you possibly wash my face?" he asked hesitantly.

"Good heavens!" She sounded contemptuous. "We'll attend to that later. You may be sure your appearance is not of the slightest concern to anyone here."

"I'm quite serious. Grains of coal dust have set themselves to blind me."

"Oh. I beg your pardon. Yes, I shall certainly scrub you up a bit."

He heard metal again, and water being poured. Soon she set something on the table beside him and pulled off his black knit hat.

After a barely discernible pause, she plastered one hand over his eyes and set to work on his forehead with what felt like a sponge dipped in warm water. After a few dabs, she rinsed the sponge and began again.

When his lids had been cleaned, he opened his eyes and watched her work on the rest of his face. Her hair, what he could see of it, fascinated him. It was the color of pearls, a sleek,

14

silky cap tapering to her neck with an uneven fringe across her forehead.

She attended fiercely to what she was doing, never meeting his gaze, her slim pert nose slightly crinkled in concentration. Although her lips were set in a narrow line, he could tell they were naturally soft and full. Firelight was reflected in her eyes, making it impossible to determine their color. Her lashes were long but pale, best appreciated from the closeness of an embrace.

It was altogether an elegant face, perfectly sculpted, the lines clean and distinct. Her fine-grained complexion put him in mind of the most exquisite porcelain, or of fresh cream with a touch of apricot on her high cheekbones. A chap could look at this face for an infinite time, and he was in no hurry for her to finish what she was doing.

Twice she rose gracefully, emptied the fouled water outside, and returned with a refilled basin. Head swimming, Kit sagged against the chair back, allowing himself to enjoy her attentions while he could.

She had just gotten to his lips when something appeared to overset her. "*Must* you sit there grinning like the village idiot?" she demanded.

"I must," he replied amiably. "I cannot help myself. You are preposterously lovely."

Color flamed in her cheeks. "Did that box bounce off your head before landing on your foot, sir? Men are not considered to be lovely."

"Nevertheless, *you* most assuredly are."

She scrubbed at his neck with a vengeance, her lips carved in a rigid line.

"If you mean to separate my skin from the rest of me, may I suggest that sandpaper would be more efficacious?"

"Oh." She rinsed the sponge and dabbed more gently at his raw flesh. "I apologize, sir. You were talking nonsense, and I feared you were about to swoon. We must see to your wound."

"No more than a scratch, I'm fairly certain. Nothing seems

to be broken." He lifted his left arm and stroked his forefinger down her cheek. "See?"

Her eyes widened with shock. A beat later she jerked her head away. "Don't *do* that, you . . . you *dolt*."

He already regretted the move excessively but could not resist crossing swords with her. It distracted him from the pain. "Ah, moonbeam, I do love it when you talk sweet to me."

With an exasperated oath, she rose, grabbed up the basin, and stomped to the door, slamming it behind her when she returned. The basin hit the stone hearth with a resounding clang. "Keep in mind, sir, that I will soon be probing at your shoulder with something excessively sharp." She came around in front of him, hands planted on her hips. "Have you anything else objectionable to say to me?"

"Only a question, Mistress Luke. Why are you masquerading—ineptly, I might add—as a male?"

She closed her eyes. "I should have left you out there," she muttered grimly. "You would have been drowned and out of everybody's hair by now."

Before he could respond, there came a thudding sound from the back door, as if someone was kicking at it.

"That will be Mrs. Preston," Luke said in a hiss. "Be kind to her. She doesn't speak."

"*Doesn't* as in can't, or won't?"

"Oh, do shut up." She went to the door and raised the latch.

Kit watched with slightly befuddled fascination as a female clad all in black entered the room, carrying a large wooden tray heaped high with bandages, small vials and jars, and other items he couldn't identify. She wore a felt bonnet from which a heavy veil descended, thoroughly concealing her face. Without acknowledging him, she set the tray on the table.

"Bring every lamp and candle we've got," Luke instructed, "and fill the basin with hot water from the kettle." She was all business as she took up a pair of scissors and turned to Kit. "I'm going to cut your shirt away now. Are you able to remain upright and hold yourself still? Be honest. It will be easier to work if you are sitting in the chair, but you can take to the bed if you must."

Although the door and windows were closed, he'd have sworn the room was beginning to fill with fog. Kit took hold of the wooden chair seat under his right hip and held tight. "Have your way with me, Luke. I'll let you know if I'm about to slide to the floor."

Nodding, she unbuckled his belt and tossed it into a corner. "Were you shot from the front or the back?"

"Front."

She moved behind the chair. "Bend forward, please. I'll start here."

He felt the cool metal of the scissors against his back as she clipped steadily from the tail of the black woolen shirt to the neck. Then, gingerly, she lifted a flap of material from his shoulder.

"The bullet must have passed straight through," she said, relief in her voice. "I feared that I would be compelled to dig it out."

"I would not have enjoyed that." Suddenly feeling ghastly cold, he buried his head between his knees.

A cool hand pressed against his forehead, and a soft voice whispered at his ear. "Take your time," it said. "Tell me how I can help you."

He sensed confidence in her tone, and an edge to it that challenged him to rally his spirits. But he gave himself another long minute before pulling upright again. "Time for the front, I expect. Go to it."

The scissors sliced through his shirt, and when she had severed it in two, she pulled the right half down his good arm and let it drop to the ground.

That was easy enough, he was thinking just before she began to separate the fabric from the bloody mess at his left shoulder. Pain washed over him in fiery waves.

"It's stuck," she murmured, putting the scissors to work again.

17

Soon only a fragment of cloth remained directly over the wound. "This is going to hurt, I'm afraid." Slowly, strand by strand, she pulled woolen threads free of the congealed blood.

He took a deep breath, and then another. "Would you mind getting this over with in a hurry?"

"It will be better," Luke agreed. "Di—Mrs. Preston, will you put your arms around his chest and hold him in the chair?"

Two surprisingly strong, black-sheathed arms secured him in place from behind as Luke took hold of the piece of cotton and snapped it loose.

Kit heard a sharp cry of pain and hoped it hadn't come from him. A damp towel was pressed against his forehead and a slim-fingered hand rested on his neck.

"Well done, sir. I wish I could tell you it was over, but we've only just begun."

His head slowly cleared, although black spots danced in front of his eyes when he opened them again. "S-sorry to make so much trouble." Was he *whimpering*, for pity's sake?

There was a swirl of activity around him then. Luke murmured instructions to the silent Mrs. Preston, and after a few moments a length of fabric was tied around his chest, holding him against the back of the chair. Then something cold and burning was pressed against his shoulder.

"I shall tell you what we are doing. The bullet appears to have passed cleanly through a fleshy part of your shoulder, but it may have pushed bits of your shirt inside the wound. They will create problems later if not removed, so I mean to see to them as best I can. If I am forced to probe deeply, you will most definitely feel it."

She had already begun as she spoke, and he could feel it sure enough. He rather wanted to scream, and tears stung his eyes, but he held himself immobile as she worked. It was the least he could do.

Some part of his ragged mind detached itself and remained almost coherent. He decided that for his sins he probably deserved all this. He hoped the measure of pain did not reflect the seriousness of his injury. He loathed feeling so damnably helpless, and above all, he feared it.

After several years she stopped digging into his shoulder with some sort of metallic instrument of torture. He sagged against the bonds holding him to the chair, letting his head drop forward.

"We're nearly done," she said in a calm voice. "I will clean the wound now and apply a paste of Saint-John's-wort. It's all we have tonight, but we shall send for better help and medications when the storm has passed."

Kit became aware of wind whistling over the chimney and window glass rattling in the panes. Rain pelted the slate roof of the cottage. He listened with all his attention, forcing himself to ignore what Luke was doing to his shredded shoulder. Fingers, soothing fingers, stroked through his hair. Mrs. Preston, he thought, trying to help.

Disaster and miracles, both at once. He had tumbled into hell and, contrarily, fallen into the hands of angels.

He heard mumbled words from Luke, and Mrs. Preston moved away from him. Scissors cut through the band of cotton holding him upright on the chair. With effort, he kept himself erect.

"This is water," Luke said, putting a cup against his lips.

He drank greedily, welcoming the cool liquid against his parched mouth and throat. Then another vessel, a thin glass, was held to his mouth.

"This is a bit of cider laced with laudanum. It will help you sleep."

He turned his head away. "I don't want it."

"That is unfortunate. Drink it anyway."

"Dammit, I'll not be drugged." Determination scattered the tendrils of mist in his head. "I want to know what is happening."

Luke patted his good shoulder. "Nothing whatever will be happening after we get you into bed, not until the storm clears. Well, one or the other of us will watch for fever and stand ready to be of help, but the best thing for you right now is sleep. And without the laudanum—very little of it, I assure you—the pain will keep you awake."

"No, it won't," Kit assured her. "I can fall asleep within a minute, at will. I have the habit of it."

She took the glass from Mrs. Preston, who had been holding it, and poked a finger at his chest. "I saved your life tonight, sir. You owe me a favor in return. And what I want is for you to drink this down to the very last drop without further protest. Agreed?"

"What a fierce creature you are," he murmured with genuine admiration. "But I'm wet all over, you know. You won't want me soiling that bed. I shall sleep on the floor by the hearth."

"Rubbish. It will be easier for me to deal with your wound if I can reach you. And I don't care if the bedding gets wet."

"Of course not, since I'll be the one sleeping there. At the least, can we do something about these boots? The right one feels like a sausage casing."

She frowned. "I'd forgot about your foot. But it will hurt dreadfully if I try to pull off the boot."

"Then cut it off. You'll do better with the knife, I expect."

She removed it from the sheath and knelt by his right leg, frowning as she considered the best approach. Finally she slipped the blade between the fabric of his trousers and the top of the boot. "I don't believe this is going to work, sir. I am bound to cut you."

"I'll squawk if you do. Give it a try, anyway."

She gripped the hilt, angled the sharp blade against the rim of the boot, and began to saw through the fold of leather and heavy stitching. Finally she succeeded in breaking through and was able to slice quickly to the sole. Carefully, she removed the boot and used the scissors to cut away his wet, sandy stocking.

His foot and ankle were swollen, but he reckoned the injury was no more serious than a sprain. He would be limping for a few days, but he'd be able to get around.

He glanced up to see Luke holding out the glass of drugged

cider. He'd hoped she had forgot, but no such luck. "I'll make you a deal," he offered. "Permit me to remove these wet trousers and get into bed. Then I'll swallow your bloody witch's brew."

Her eyes widened.

Was she alarmed? he wondered. It wasn't as though he intended to strip directly in front of her.

Not this time, at any rate.

"Agreed," she snapped. "We'll wait in the back room. Call when you are safely under the blanket, or if you encounter any difficulties."

To his annoyance, Luke took the laudanum with her. So much for his plan to dump it somewhere and maintain he'd drunk it like a good lad. Luke wouldn't have believed him, of course, but neither would she have risked giving him a second dose. Well, she had outwitted him, so he would have to swallow his medicine like a good loser.

He unbuttoned his trousers and peeled them down his legs, using the one good arm remaining to him. It took an amazingly long time, and he was sweating profusely when they were finally heaped on the floor. Lacking the strength to pick them up, he left them where they lay and limped to the narrow cot. After a considerable struggle, he got himself settled with the blanket covering him and lowered his head to the thin, bumpy pillow. He wondered which one of them slept here, Mrs. Preston or Luke. "I'm snug in bed," he called.

When Luke came into the room, he produced a wide yawn. "I c'n scarcely keep my eyes open," he said weakly.

"Humbug." She put a hand behind his head, raised it up, and held the glass to his lips.

Casting her a scorching look, he obediently swallowed the cider. "The least you can do is tell me your real name."

"I have done all I intend to do on your behalf this night," she advised him sternly. "Now do me one single kindness, sir, and go directly to sleep."

He regarded her hazily. She was wavering in and out of his

rapidly clouding vision. "I believe that I shall call you Lucy then."

"You cannot!" She shook her head. "That is Mrs. Preston's name."

"Ah. Unfortunate." This time his yawn was real. "G'night, moonbeam. I plan to dream about you."

Chapter 3

Lucy put a finger to her lips, warning Diana to remain silent. Although Kit had begun to snore lightly, she wouldn't have put it past him to be dissembling.

Standing side by side, they watched him closely for several minutes. He never moved, and the rhythm of his breathing remained steady, but still she could not be absolutely certain.

"I think he's well asleep," she said in a booming tone. "And the poker will be heated through by now. Go ahead and secure his wrists with the rope, Mrs. Preston. We mustn't have him thrashing about while I cauterize the wound."

There was no reaction from the man on the cot.

Releasing a sigh, Lucy crossed to the fireplace. "I think we can safely speak, Diana. The laudanum appears to have sent him off, and may the devil take him up and fly away with him."

"Don't *say* such things, I beg you. What if he were to die?"

"Oh, he'll do no such thing." That would make life far too easy, Lucy thought irritably. "The blackguard will live to make us a great deal of trouble caring for him, and a great deal more trying to rid ourselves of him."

Diana removed the veiled hat and worked at the pins attaching the brown wig to her hair. "How do you conclude that he's a blackguard?"

"It's perfectly obvious. He was smuggling contraband of some sort when he got himself shot. And even if he'd chanced to be delivering a sermon at Westminster Abbey when the bullet hit him, the man is patently a scoundrel."

23

Diana had not left her position beside the cot. "He looks like a lamb."

"Pah!"

"Well, *lamb* is not the correct word, I know. But he doesn't strike me as the least bit dangerous."

"Don't be deceived by his looks. Males often appear innocent, even vulnerable, when they are asleep. I recall gazing down at Henry Turnbridge, the devil's spawn if ever there was one, all snug in his bed, with his sweet face so wonderfully peaceful that I imagined I had misjudged his capacity for evil. The very next day he set fire to the stable."

"You cannot compare a child with a grown man," Diana protested. "I fear you have been a governess too long to maintain any perspective. At the least you must grant that he is exceedingly handsome."

"And he is well aware of it, too." Lucy added water to the teakettle and hung it over the fire. "He is also aware that I am a female."

"Oh, dear."

"I'm not in the least surprised. This disguise was never meant to be seen at close range, and in all the turmoil, I didn't think to alter my voice."

Diana finished detaching the wig and shook out her heavy auburn hair. "You haven't told me what happened. Where did you come upon him?"

"Make the tea, will you? Yours always tastes so much better than mine. And to be honest, I believe I must sit for a few minutes."

While Diana set out the crockery and measured the tea leaves, Lucy gave her a carefully censored description of the events on Morecambe Bay. She omitted the long struggle to dig Kit's leg from under the box and skimmed over the arduous return to shore. Diana need not know they had escaped just ahead of the incoming tide.

"That's perfectly awful," Diana said when she was finished. "The others simply left him there? Who were they?"

"I've no idea, except that there were two separate groups of men—Kit's band of smugglers and the ones who robbed them. He was in no condition to explain what occurred before my arrival."

"His name is Kit? What else do you know about him?"

"Nothing whatever." Lucy had placed herself where she could see his face in case he showed signs of distress. Or of eavesdropping. "Nor have I the slightest notion what we are to *do* with him. If he takes a fever, I suppose we'll have to find a doctor."

"Shouldn't we do that in any case?" Diana poured hot water into the teapot. "Is there one in Silverdale?"

"Not likely. I imagine we'll have to send to Beetham, or even farther. Robbie will know. He's promised to bring a load of firewood and provisions tomorrow, although he'll not arrive until the storm has passed."

"Kit speaks well, I noticed. He cannot be a common smuggler."

Not common in any way, Lucy agreed silently. He was certainly a most *uncommon* nuisance. Because of him, her plan was unraveling, and she could not think how to weave it together again. Clearly a whole new scheme had to be devised, one that allowed for Kit and weeded him away before he could do any more damage.

She combed her fingers through her hair, a habit she had acquired soon after it was shorn. She could not seem to help making sure the rest was still there. "We must revise our scheme immediately, Diana. It's true we've no idea if our unwelcome patient will recover swiftly or take a turn for the worse, or what to do in either circumstance. But we have to begin somewhere."

Diana strained tea into the chipped ceramic mugs. "You are forever telling me that everything will work out for the best. Shall we assume that Robbie will arrive in good time, and that Kit will have slept peacefully through the night?"

Her own feigned optimism was coming back to bite her, Lucy thought sourly. But until now she had truly believed they had a reasonable chance of bringing this off. It had not been so easy a matter to persuade Diana, though. She was fragile as a butterfly's wing.

Nonetheless, she had been a rock of support this evening. Lucy considered that wonder as she watched Diana sit in the chair across from her. How lovely she was. But already, so soon, she had learned to keep the right side of her face turned away.

"You didn't answer my question, Lucy."

"I beg your pardon, but it is difficult to imagine *the best*. For now, let us consider the immediate future. I shall keep watch on him tonight, of course, but since he is in your bed, where are you to sleep? If you take my pallet by the hearth, you'll be forced to wear the wig and veil in case he wakes up."

"I'd rather not. The wig scratches and the pins give me the headache. I shall stay in the other room."

"Unthinkable. There is no heat in there."

"We'll leave the door open, then, and I'll wrap myself up in layers of clothes. Where I spend the rest of the night is the least of our problems, Lucy. What of the morning? Shall I be Mrs. Preston again, or will you?"

Lucy sipped at the strong hot tea. "And now poor Mrs. Preston is mute. What an incredibly stupid idea that was! When I thought of it, I reckoned that later I could take over the role without him recognizing the change of voices. It failed to dawn on me that whichever of us played the part thereafter would be compelled to remain silent."

"He was weak and in pain. He's had a draft of laudanum. Perhaps he won't remember that Mrs. Preston is unable to speak."

"Oh, he'll remember. Nothing escapes him, I'm sorry to say." He had even *flirted* with her, for heaven's sake, although it was only to demonstrate that he'd seen through her disguise. And, she suspected, to show her how clever he was. "I'll be Luke tomorrow, unless Robbie fails to arrive and I am forced to go into Silverdale. Kit can go on wondering why I am dressed in trousers until I come up with a plausible explanation."

Lucy rubbed the back of her neck, which ached with tension.

26

"There's another problem. I fear that Kit's smugglers were heading for our cave to stash their booty. We must relocate ourselves as soon as possible."

"But why? Didn't you say the robbers made off with—with the booty?"

"Some of it. The rest was loaded on a wagon, which must be several feet underwater by now. *Drat!* I forgot about the horse. We unhooked him from the wagon and brought him ashore. He's in the cave. There's nothing to feed him with, but I should take him some water and remove his saddle."

"I'll do it. But why are you so worried about the smugglers? They might have been going somewhere else entirely."

"Perhaps. I suppose the question is irrelevant now. Kit is here, he knows about us, and we must depart as soon as may be."

Diana looked alarmed. "For where? We have no place to go."

"Of course we do," Lucy lied smoothly. "There are thousands of places, and we have only to make a selection. But leave that to me. I shall think on it later. At the moment I cannot seem to put two coherent thoughts together in a row." She swallowed the last of her tea. "We'll be guessing from here on out, but you mustn't worry. If all else fails, we shall simply make a run for it."

Diana rose and went to fill a battered metal bucket from the oak barrel that held their supply of water. "We ought to set the barrel outside to catch the rainwater," she said over her shoulder. "It's nearly empty."

"I'll see to it." Lucy was relieved to hear a return of spirit in Diana's voice. When there was something of use for her to do, she invariably shook off her mopes and set to work. But most times she was left on her own, with nothing to distract her from her unhappy thoughts. "I'd much rather drag a barrel out into a storm, you know, than tend to a large unpredictable animal."

"Nonsense. One day I shall teach you to ride, and I promise that you'll come to love horses as much as I do. May I take the carrots we were saving for tomorrow's soup?"

"By all means. Give him anything you can find that he

will eat. And bring up the saddle pack, if it is not too heavy to carry."

When Diana had ignited a lantern and departed with the carrots, Lucy rose with a groan and went to examine the bandage on Kit's shoulder. Blood had seeped through, but not terribly much of it, and the rust-colored stain was already dry to the touch. Perhaps he would live after all, the wretch.

Not wanting to think about him right now, she began to order things for the long hours ahead. First she carried her straw pallet into the other room for Diana to sleep on and rummaged through their box of supplies for towels, which she folded into a makeshift pillow. Diana's clothes were stored in the cave, and she could use cloaks and pelisses for blankets.

There was enough firewood to see them through the night, and if the storm persisted, they could always break up the chairs for fuel.

Her brain felt mired in quicksand. She stared at the wig and bonnet for a long time before realizing they could not be left out in plain view. Gathering them up, she stowed them in her portmanteau. What else? She spotted Kit's discarded trousers on the floor and draped them over a chair by the hearth to dry. The remains of his shirt were put into the fire to burn. She ought to prepare a broth for him to drink when he awoke, but she didn't feel up to it at the moment. There would be plenty of time for that later. She'd no intention of sleeping. Should he develop a fever, she would have to do something about it. Cold compresses, she supposed. Which reminded her about the water barrel.

Rain pelted into the cottage and onto her hair and clothes when she opened the door to thrust the barrel outside. Shivering, she rushed back to the fireplace and stood facing it, spreading out her arms and legs to catch the heat. I could fall asleep right here, standing up, she thought as the warmth stole over her body. However am I to keep watch on the smuggler when I can scarcely keep my eyes open?

"What a magnificent horse!" Diana said, snapping Lucy to

attention. "Kit must have paid a small fortune for him. And he's so well mannered. He ate the carrots from my hand and stood still while I removed his saddle."

Lucy turned to see her drop the leather saddle pack on the table. She eyed it curiously. Perhaps there was some clue in there to Kit's identity, not that it mattered a great deal who he was. But information, however irrelevant it might seem at first start, had a way of becoming useful sooner or later. That was her experience, in any case, and she meant to have a look inside. But first she must send Diana, who was too well-bred to approve of riffling through a man's personal effects, off on another errand. "You had better fetch warm clothes from your luggage, I expect. And since I left my cloak outside under a rock, will you bring something for me?"

"Gladly. But it's awfully cold and dark down there. May I leave one or two of our lanterns near to the horse? He is probably frightened to be alone in such a strange place."

"He has all my sympathy," Lucy said crossly. "But we dare not light up the cave at night. You know that."

"I'd leave them well back," Diana protested, "and they cast very little light. Besides, who could possibly be out in this storm to see?"

"No lanterns," Lucy ruled. "We've enough problems as it is without drawing more attention to ourselves, however remote the chance anyone else is lurking about. Please, Diana. I'm frightfully out of temper just now. Bring up what you need for the night and get settled. It's the best thing you can do for me."

Diana fled.

Lucy knew she would feel guilty later, but she had spoken the truth. She was so on edge that she would have torn into the Archbishop of Canterbury if he materialized in front of her.

She went to the table, unbuckled the saddle pack, and sifted through its contents. There were two soft woolen shirts, of good quality but well-worn, and half a dozen cambric handkerchiefs. A pair of heavy wool stockings. A small drawstring bag filled with coins, a few banknotes, and a plain pocket watch. A razor, shaving soap, and cracked mirror all wrapped up in a piece of toweling. A copper-sheathed spyglass. Another drawstring bag, this one larger, holding pencils, a small folding knife, and pieces of charcoal. A sketchbook.

She pulled it out and flipped through the pages. Most were blank, but the first few sheets were covered with drawings. They had no particular significance that she could ascertain. He had sketched whatever caught his fancy—a yew tree, a dinghy tied up to a rustic dock, three or four faces of country folk, a clump of bracken, an ox pulling a plow.

Only one picture, of a little girl sitting on a fallen log with a doll cradled in her arms, was finished in any detail. If ever she saw that child, Lucy knew that she would recognize her immediately. Indeed, from the drawing alone, she felt as if she knew her.

She glanced over at Kit, thinking that she didn't know him at all. Oh, she stuck by everything she had already decided about him, but there was clearly more to the man than she was ready to admit. All the same, a talent for sketching was scarcely a point in his favor. Even criminals had hobbies, she supposed.

Carefully, she restored everything to its place in the saddle pack and took it into the back room. Diana was still in the cave, probably sealing her friendship with the horse. Any company was better than Lucy Preston's, what with her black mood casting shadows over every place she went.

Her real shadow, created by the fire behind her, fell over Kit as she stood with her hands clenched, staring down at him without pleasure. A lamb, indeed! A black sheep, more like, the despair of his family and a blight on decent society. He would probably hang one day, and good riddance to him.

Such a waste of a beautiful man, though. He was nothing like the pale-skinned overdressed dandies that Lady Turnbridge welcomed to her house parties, and more often than not to her bedchamber. His bronzed face and the taut musculature of his tall, lanky body gave evidence of an athletic life spent much in the out-of-doors. His hair, a sun-streaked tangle of light brown and blond, waved slightly and reached to where his collar would be if . . . if he were wearing any clothes.

His bare flesh under that thin blanket did not bear thinking of. She crossed to the hearth and jabbed at the burning logs with the poker, wondering if the fire could be any hotter than she felt. She gazed into the flames, seeing nothing and having vague, irreverent thoughts about large, unpredictable male animals.

After some time Diana came into the room and placed a bundle at her feet before departing in silence. Belatedly, Lucy murmured words of thanks that probably went unheard. Well, she would apologize in the morning for being such a bear. Anger was the only thing that fueled her now, anger at Kit and at Diana's uncle and, shamefully, at every person who had treated her unfairly when she had tried so very hard to do the right thing. Without her anger, she would probably be curled up in a bundle the size of the one Diana had brought, crying her heart out like a frightened child. And what good would *that* do?

If it took rage to keep her going, she would nurture it for however long she must. Diana would simply have to put up with her, and the smuggler deserved whatever he got.

She poured the last of the cold tea into her mug and drank it, hoping it would help to keep her awake for the rest of the night. Rain pounded against the roof and a blast of icy wind made its way down the chimney, causing the fire to sputter and shoot sparks and ashes onto the floor. She set another log on the grate and kept watch until it was blazing, aware all the while of the man who lay asleep only a short distance away.

He was such a vital presence in the room that he might as well have been standing in the middle of it, juggling lit torches.

Lucy dragged a chair closer to the hearth and straddled it with her arms folded over the top rung of the laddered back. Propping her chin on her forearm, she gazed at Kit the Demon Smuggler who had stolen what little remained of her peace.

Go away, she thought. Take the rain with you. Give us what scant chance we may yet have to escape.

Chapter 4

Kit was enjoying his decidedly erotic dream. On the sands, beneath a starry sky, he was making rapturous love with Miss Luke.

Suddenly they were both underwater.

She didn't seem to mind. Still holding him, her hands on his bare shoulders, she smiled into his eyes. But his movements slowed, and he felt himself struggling for breath. Then he began to float, rising up and looking back at her, at her soft, creamy flesh and the cap of pearls on her head. She stretched her arms to him, but try as he might, he could not reach her.

He became aware of his own body then, and a throbbing pain in his shoulder, and more pain at his ankle. He ought to do something, he supposed, but it was as if heavy coins were pressed against his eyelids. Most likely he had put them there himself, for assuredly he had no wish to wake up. He wanted only to return to his dream and reshape the ending.

But his body had its own urgency and was demanding attention. And, too, he had the eerie sensation that someone was staring at him.

Bloody laudanum. He loathed the stuff. It left a man weak and noodle-witted. Forcing himself fully awake, Kit wrenched open his eyes and looked around the cottage.

No one was there. He saw only bare stone walls, a table and two chairs, and a small fire in the hearth. He couldn't guess the time of day. Heavy black curtains hung over what he supposed to be windows, and both doors were closed. He listened, hearing only silence, and reckoned that the storm must have passed.

The odd sensation that he was being watched grew more intense. Sitting up, he scanned the room again, this time noticing the dishes, jars, and cheesecloth-wrapped packets that were set on a shelf running all along the opposite wall. Finally he glanced in the direction of the low, smoke-stained ceiling.

Two round, glossy eyes gazed steadily at him from a white heart-shaped face. The small owl, about the size of his forearm, was perched on a coat peg jutting from the wall.

"Well, hullo there," Kit said. "I don't suppose you could direct me to the nearest chamber pot?"

The owl blinked.

Kit leaned over and peered under the cot. Nothing there. "Luke?" he called. "Mrs. Preston?" No one emerged from the back room.

"It appears the ladies have deserted us, old lad." Swinging his legs over the side, he gently planted both feet on the dirt floor and examined his wrenched ankle. It was red, swollen, and somewhat painful, but it moved easily enough when he made circles with his foot. He was fairly sure he could hobble about with the help of the blackthorn cane, which was perniciously propped against the wall clear on the other side of the room.

Levering himself up, he hopped gracelessly as far as the table and braced himself against the back of a chair to catch his breath. The bouncing had jarred his shoulder, and there was no denying it hurt like the devil. He used the chair's support to cross the rest of the way and finally managed to grab hold of the walking stick.

The owl made a throaty, wheezing sound.

Kit looked up and the owl stared back, its buff-colored head turned ninety degrees in his direction to get a better look. It made the snoring noise again.

Kit suddenly realized that he was bare-arsed naked. He located his trousers, which were draped over a chair near the fire, but he wasn't about to wrestle with them now. Leaning heavily on the cane, he returned to the cot and stripped off the thin blanket, securing it around his waist.

The exertion helped clear his mind of the laudanum, which he was resolved never to touch again. Good clean pain he could deal with, but anytime he decided to get muzzy-headed, he would bloody well do so with a bottle or two of vintage wine.

By the time he crossed the room again, he'd gotten the hang of balancing on the walking stick and limping in a relatively smooth manner. Fog billowed into the room when he opened the door, and the owl swooped past his shoulder.

He could see precious little when he stepped outside—the outline of the roof when he looked back, and what might be a tree near the corner of the cottage. He aimed himself for the concealment of its trunk, although the fog would hide him well enough from anyone who might be in the vicinity.

The owl joined him and perched on a branch directly overhead, still making that throaty sound and gazing at him with keen intensity. Kit decided that he must resemble some exceptionally large form of prey.

What a stroke of luck to have stumbled into this unlikely ménage—a mute woman clad all in black, a glorious female masquerading as a boy, and a singularly demented owl. For adventure, ever his ruling passion, he had assuredly come to the right place.

Gaze focused on his bare feet, he made his way carefully back to the door and was about to step inside when he heard the sound of voices from the other side of the cottage. He crept to the corner and risked a look around.

Two figures, one slim and the other large and burly, swam in and out of the fog. Their voices were muffled, but he recognized Luke's clear alto and the gruff rasp of a Scottish accent.

"I c'n take him with me now," the man said. "Better I do."

"No. If he dies in Silverdale, the authorities will have questions. If he dies here, we can lug his body—oh, I don't know—somewhere miles away and leave it there."

"That bad off, is he?"

"In fact, I've no idea. He slept quietly and has no fever, but he lost a great deal of blood. We shall do our best for him, but once he leaves, he'll doubtless tell someone what he saw at the cottage. We must hold him here until we are gone. Bring Giles back with you, and should he rule that the man requires a doctor, we'll scarper in a hurry."

"If you say so, lass, but I mislike leaving the two of you alone with a stranger."

They moved away then, disappearing into the heavy fog. He heard the Scot ask if she wanted him to bring a pistol but couldn't make out her reply.

He limped as fast as he could into the cottage. When Luke returned he must be flat on his back, just as she'd left him. The owl swooped in as he was closing the door, took up its perch on the coat peg, and followed his every move with those bright black eyes. Kit quickly peeled off the blanket, spread it over the cot, and slid into place. He had barely lowered his head to the pillow and closed his eyes when the door swung open again.

Listening acutely, he heard Luke drop something on the table and cross to him. He felt the warmth of her body as she leaned over him and sensed her gaze probing him like a lancet.

The owl was snoring again. Excellent notion. He faked a snore of his own.

"Don't pretend you are asleep," she said sharply. "The blanket is damp and so is your hair. You've been outside."

Not easily fooled, Lady Luke. He liked her all the more for it. "So I have," he affirmed, opening his eyes. "And it wasn't easy to get myself there, I assure you. But when nature is calling, a man has little choice but to answer."

Red flags blazed on her cheeks. "Yes. I hadn't thought of that. You can walk then?"

"Only if I must. Indeed, I expected that you would eventually find me in a heap somewhere between this spot and a friendly tree. You may be certain that I'm in no hurry to try another excursion."

She tugged the blanket down his chest and examined the bandage. "Fresh blood," she said irritably. "Not much of it, but you've done yourself no good. In future, pray ask for assistance."

"I'd have done, were there anyone of use to ask. The bird was no help at all."

Her gaze shot to the coat peg. "Fidgets! However did you get in here?"

The owl shuffled on its perch, ruffling its feathers.

"I used to smuggle lizards and frogs and snakes into my room," Kit said, "but I've never known anyone to take an owl for a pet."

"He took me." Luke held out her arm and the owl immediately flew to her wrist. "And he isn't a pet. Mostly he's a nuisance. He thinks I am his mother, I expect. The nest he was in got abandoned, and I came upon it just as he was pecking his way from his egg. From then on, of course, I had to feed him— minced meat when he was a chick and whatever I could beg from the kitchen as he grew. He has rewarded me with loyalty, which I could well do without, and of late he sometimes catches a meal for himself. I keep hoping he'll fly off to live the way an owl ought to live, but he shows no inclination to do so."

"Why does he make that growly sound?"

Luke raised a pair of beautifully shaped brows. "I've never heard it. But an ostler to whom I applied for advice about food and the like told me that barn owls make odd noises when they are attempting to woo a mate." She looked at the bird. "Are you in love, Fidgets?"

The owl snorted.

"Well, I cannot applaud your taste," she said, stroking the feathered head. "But perhaps this means that you are a female."

"I certainly hope so," Kit declared. "Cannot you tell?"

"No. It isn't . . . easily apparent. And in either case, the two of you would not suit. Off with you, Fidgets."

The owl flew back to its peg and resumed staring at Kit.

Returning to the table, Lucy began to unpack a large basket. "There is fresh bread, and I made up a pot of soup this morning. Are you hungry?"

"Ravenous." It was true, he realized, hearing his stomach rumble. "Where did you come by the basket?"

"A traveling blacksmith is kind enough to deliver provisions whenever he is passing by."

"On the way to where? This cottage is scarcely on a main road. I doubt it's on *any* road."

"Then he is *very* kind to detour so far out of his way. And kinder still because he has gone to fetch his nephew, who is an apothecary, and a wagon to carry you to a physician if Giles believes that you require one."

"Will he bring along a constable?" Kit asked wryly.

She dropped an apple, which rolled into the corner. "Certainly not. What you were doing last night is none of my concern. If the authorities are searching for you, I'd as soon they find you elsewhere."

"Why is that, I wonder? Because you don't want them to find *you*?"

"Nonsense." She retrieved the apple, providing him with a delectable view of her shapely derriere when she bent to pick it up. "You, sir, are the only felon on the premises. And the sooner you are gone, the better. Mrs. Preston is deeply in mourning for her late husband and requires solitude. It would be most unworthy of you to mention our presence here to anyone."

He could not resist prodding her. "Most particularly the authorities, should they manage to nab me."

"Precisely. We will have harbored a criminal and helped him to escape. Would you punish us for this kindness by subjecting us to an inquisition? I did save your life, you may recall."

"I do, and you've nothing to fear. My word on it."

"The word of a smuggler fails to reassure me," she informed him briskly. "But should you be tempted to speak out of turn, keep in mind that I was witness to what happened last night and can testify against you in a court of law."

She had an answer for everything, he thought, abandoning his efforts to pry information from her by means of direct confrontation. This matter required subtlety, if not downright sneakiness. As she went about her work he contented himself with watching her, slim and vibrant in loose homespun brown trousers and a tan shirt worn outside the pants to conceal her shape. But whenever she passed in front of the fire, he saw the outline of her lovely backside and two small, perfectly shaped breasts.

He had always been especially partial to the company of females, but this one engaged him more than any other in his experience, which was, not to put too fine a point on it, extensive. She fascinated him, with her razor tongue and keen intelligence. She was beautiful, to be sure, and naturally he desired her, but with such ferocity that it rendered him breathless—also wildly uncomfortable in the relevant sectors of his anatomy, which he knew would be forced to wait a considerable time for satisfaction. Miss Luke would not fall easily into his embrace.

She was at the table again, slicing a chunk of bread from a crusty loaf. She tossed it onto a plate beside a mug of steaming liquid, and the aroma of chicken broth caused his belly to rumble again.

He was disappointed when she disappeared into the back room, but she soon emerged with a thin straw-filled pallet. Folding it in half, she propped it against the wall at the head of the cot and helped him to sit up. He had to wriggle backward to prop himself against the pallet, and when he did so, the blanket failed to follow him. Nor did he make the slightest effort to help it along. Well, he thought, what man would?

She blushed to a bright crimson, fixing her gaze well north of where the blanket finally settled. "Pray cover yourself, sir," she murmured, spinning away from the cot as if it had caught fire.

"Sorry." He tugged the blanket to his waist, no farther, enjoying himself immensely.

He was less pleased when she came back and tossed a towel over his chest. Then she pulled a chair to the cot and sat beside him with the plate on her lap and the mug in her hand. "If I hold the cup, can you feed yourself?"

He could, of course, but that wouldn't be nearly as much fun. "I'll try, if you wish. But I'm somewhat shaky." He held out a

38

hand and forced it to tremble. "The aftereffects of laudanum, I expect."

She regarded him suspiciously.

He gave her a look meant to appear earnest, cooperative, and helpless.

She wasn't convinced, he knew, but with a grumble she began to spoon up the soup. It was unexpectedly delicious, a hearty barley broth containing a few bits of stringy chicken, potato, and turnip. She concentrated fixedly on what she was doing, never meeting his gaze, and each time he tried to speak, she stuffed a wad of bread into his mouth.

With little left for him to do except to chew and swallow, he focused on her transparent gray eyes and wonderfully shaped lips, the finely carved cheekbones, the slope of her graceful jaw, and her long, glorious neck. Her startling complexion was pure cream whenever she wasn't blushing, and the sleek, pearly hair outlined the perfect shape of her head.

Why the devil was such a beauty as this hiding out in the back of beyond, shabbily clothed in male garb and keeping company with a veiled widow? She wasn't about to tell him, that was certain, but he suspected that she was as curious about him as he was about her. If she asked questions, though, that would give him an opening to do the same. So she pretended indifference, and he pretended helplessness, and the air between them grew overheated.

When the mug was empty she erupted from the chair, apparently forgetting about the plate on her lap because it tumbled to the floor. She left it there and went over to the owl. "Let's take a walk, Fidgets."

The owl fluttered down to her shoulder and they left the cottage.

Kit erupted in laughter. Oh, she was stubborn, that one. But he could outstubborn her and pare his toenails at the same time. Obstinacy ran in his family.

* * *

Lucy stomped a good long way before she realized that she couldn't see where she was going. Dense fog covered her body like a lover's embrace—

Oh, my. Wherever had such an image come from?

She halted, stunned by the path her wild thoughts had taken. With a sharp pull, she reined them in. Fog was fog. Fog had nothing whatever to do with lovers. And for that matter, neither did she.

Kit had gotten on her already inflamed nerves, that was all. She was snapping at dust balls these days. And really, he was the *most* annoying man on the face of the earth. He had deliberately set himself to rile her up, and she had given him the satisfaction of seeing her thoroughly riled.

"I am a complete idiot," she said.

Fidgets made a sympathetic noise.

"You will do well to stay clear of him," she advised. "Mind you, I am speaking as an idiot, and I know your kind are reputed to be wise. Nevertheless, take a lesson from my own sorry behavior, Fidgets, and direct your affections to a creature who is capable of returning them. Which like does *not*, by the way, include a certain smuggler of our acquaintance."

The owl nuzzled her scalp with its beak.

And now I am talking to a bird, she thought, wholly disgusted with herself.

But what else was there to do? A good healthy walk to dispel her churning energy was out of the question in this weather. She dared not risk the precipitous descent to the cave, where Diana was isolated with the horse and her own thoughts, and she couldn't use the stairs while Kit was awake.

Above all, she must not return to the cottage. Not yet.

So she stood in place for a long time and told Fidgets stories about the five recalcitrant boys in her charge, never mind that the owl had heard them all before.

Until now she hadn't realized how often she confided in the stubby assemblage of feathers and claws. Except for Diana, with whom she had exchanged only a few letters before the last of them begged for her help and brought her north, she had no other friends. Most times she was kept too busy to notice, of course. How came it that her loneliness, her longing for things she could never have, so forcibly struck her at a time when she had more responsibilities than ever to distract her?

Before he sent her wits begging, she had firmly intended to ask Kit for an explanation of what she had muddled into last night. She must discover if he and the other smugglers had been aiming for her cave before they were accosted on the sands. Instead she had staggered out into the fog, weak-kneed and vibrating with absurd, wholly inappropriate female vapors—she didn't know what else to call them—and now here she was. Accomplishing nothing.

Well, she *was* getting wet and cold.

That was something, she decided, and enough of an accomplishment for her to order her feet to start moving again. For several minutes she stumbled about in the fog, but eventually she ran directly into the tree stump where she had parked Kit fewer than eight hours before.

How very odd. She felt as if she had known him for a lifetime.

When the plain fact was, she didn't even know his full name.

At least she knew her way from here to the cottage. Fidgets took French leave when she arrived at the door, off on important owl business, she supposed, inconsiderately abandoning her to face Kit all by herself.

Where was an owl when a person really needed one?

Stiffening her spine, she raised the latch and entered the cottage.

Kit was sitting where she'd left him, but he hadn't been there the entire time she was gone. At the very least he'd made his way to the table and back, because he was greedily gnawing his way through the heel end of the bread loaf. The towel she had placed over his bare chest lay in a heap on the floor.

She jabbed a finger in his direction. "You are devouring Mrs. Preston's breakfast, sir."

"Where *is* Mrs. Preston?" he inquired with a full mouth.

"That's none of your business. But when she returns, she'll have nothing to eat."

His face looked contrite, but his eyes were dancing. "In that case, I am truly sorry. She has no taste, I gather, for what is contained in those jars on the shelf?"

Insufferable man! Lucy couldn't imagine why she had a sudden urge to laugh. "You must be feeling better if you can wolf an entire loaf of bread."

"To the contrary." He sank an inch or two on the folded pallet. "I was feeling frailer than a lightskirt's virtue, so I rolled off the cot and crawled to the table and forced myself to take some nourishment. You are meant to be awed by my courage and impressed by my initiative."

"How unfortunate for you, then, that I am only vexed by your effrontery." She mustered the courage to approach the chair beside his cot but lacked the resolve to seat herself. Propping one hand on the chair back for support, she focused her gaze on the wall directly above his head. "If you have no objections, sir, I wish to discuss the events of last night."

"Certainly." He popped the last nugget of bread in his mouth. "Anything to oblige. What do you wish to know?"

She decided that she trusted him least of all when he was being cooperative. "That is perfectly clear, sir. What you were doing, and where you were going, and why you were shot."

"Well, that's simple enough then. My companions and I were, shall we say, *importing* a few bottles of wine and spirits when we were rudely interrupted by a pack of thugs. Being gentlemen, and also because they were pointing guns at us, we graciously offered them our cargo." He gave her a speculative look. "You cannot have been far away, Miss Luke. Did you not see all this for yourself?"

"I was on the cliff, and it was exceedingly dark. Mostly I saw lanterns and shadows. Some of them began running in one direction and some went more slowly in the other, leading what I assume were pack animals. But I'd no idea what was transpiring, I assure you."

"Ah." He folded his uninjured arm behind his head. "So long as you are still on your feet, would it be too much trouble to fetch me something to drink?"

"Not at all." It was a relief to escape across the room, truth be told. Looking at him made it infernally difficult to pay attention to anything else. "But do proceed with your story, sir. What was your destination before the thugs appeared?"

"What's that to the point? We never got there, did we?"

"Indulge me." In fact, this was the only piece of information she required of him, but it wouldn't do to say so.

"If you must know," he said amiably, "we were headed to a spot just north of the Keer Channel. We'd have taken a more direct route, but with the tide due to turn, we elected to move closer to shore and follow the coastline."

"I see." Her hands were trembling as she filled a tankard with ale. "You understand my concern, sir. If criminals are operating in this vicinity, it will not be safe for Mrs. Preston to remain here in the cottage."

"She is in no danger from the general run of smugglers, you may be sure. Since the war embargoes ended, most are common folk who mean only to stock their cellars without paying import tariffs. The real criminals have moved on to more profitable ventures."

"Those were not *real criminals* firing bullets last night?"

"I've no idea who they were," he admitted, all trace of amusement in his voice gone. "Come sit beside me, Luke. I'll give you a plain tale, and a truthful one. You are entitled to that much, after placing your own life in danger by coming to my rescue."

Reserving judgment on how much truth she was likely to hear, she gave him the tankard and sat on the chair with her hands folded in her lap.

He took a long swallow of ale. "I pretty much abandoned the midnight trade at war's end, and was a mere dabbler before that. But I'm always ripe for a bit of excitement and chanced to meet up with three Lancashire lads in a pub house several nights ago. After a few togs of ale, they confided their plans to transport a load of goods across the sands, if only they could locate a carter willing to mark the way without betraying them to the constable. It happens I am friendly with one such, so we all joined forces."

"What precisely is a carter?"

"You are not a local then? Well, it's a dangerous business, crossing the sands. Morecambe Bay is much like a saucer, enormous but shallow. You have seen how it empties when the tide goes out. But four rivers and four smaller streams drain into the bay, and the courses of their channels are continually changing. The push and pull of the tide also creates sandbanks and areas of virtual quicksand, never at the same places from one day to the next. A carter is a guide, someone who has made it his profession to ride out when the tide has ebbed and mark a safe crossing with birch branches. Folks have been using the sands as a shortcut for centuries, and I understand the first guides were all from a family by the name of Carter." He grinned. "Well, that was a long answer to a short question. Where was I in my story before I wandered off?"

"You were drinking in a pub," she said tartly. "And plotting with smugglers."

"Nice chaps," he corrected, "and farmers by trade. This was their first venture into the business, and they'd little idea what they were about. They had gotten so far as to take delivery of the shipment but feared to use the land route to carry it from Furness to their destination. That was what caught my attention. No one patrols the roads these days, for smuggling is no longer of real concern to the authorities. Indeed, that is precisely why I lost interest in the profession—no challenge to it anymore."

"Good heavens. You broke the law because it *amused* you to do so?"

"That would be a fair assessment. But we digress. My new confederates told me they had heard of several caravans being ambushed by a band of armed hooligans. I made further inquiries among the suppliers—the fellows who transport the contraband across the Channel—and learned the attacks had begun only a few months ago. They are none too pleased, since the amateurs who have been buying their shipments are losing heart and reneging on their contracts."

"I believe, sir, that I am learning more about smuggling than I really need to know."

He laughed. "Don't forget that you were the one who insisted on this topic to begin with. I'd much rather talk about you, and where you come from, and what you are doing—"

"Never mind that!" she snapped, heat searing her cheeks. "I presume that the thugs who accosted you were the same ones who have been making trouble elsewhere. But how did they know when and where you would be crossing the sands?"

"Does it matter? I was in this for a lark, moonbeam. If thugs are robbing smugglers, someone else will have to get to the bottom of it. To be sure, I hope one day to meet up again with the rascal who shot me. There will be a reckoning then, I promise you. But otherwise, I care nothing for the hows and whys of last night's misadventure. It is done with."

She couldn't decide what she thought of his indifference to an attack during which he might well have died. In his place, she'd not have rested until she solved the mystery and saw the perpetrators hauled off to prison. Bad people should be made to pay for their crimes, or so she had always believed.

"Would you rather I were a bloodthirsty sort of fellow?" Kit inquired amiably. "I'm sorry to disappoint you. But revenge, you know, is a great waste of time. No one gains from it, the avenger least of all. And besides, why would anyone choose to dwell in the past when the future is ever so much more promising?"

"Is it?" Lucy no sooner spoke than she wished the words unsaid. They came out of their own accord, and now she could only hope that Kit did not take their meaning. She hurried to change the subject. "How came the man to shoot you, sir? Did you provoke him?"

When an entire minute passed without a reply, she dragged her gaze to his face.

It was expressionless, but he regarded her steadily from those disconcerting blue eyes. "I wondered if you ever meant to look at me again, moonbeam."

"C-certainly. Whenever there is any need to do so." She ordered her hands to stop clawing at each other. "But you have not answered my questions."

"I'll start with the first one then," he said. "Yes, it is."

He was holding her gaze so firmly that she could not tear it away, however hard she tried. She understood well enough which question he was answering, of course. "If you say so," she said lightly. "On to number two."

Kit shook his head. "Have it your way, my dear. For now. We shall speak again on the subject another day. As for why the scoundrel shot me, I can tell you only what happened. The robbers have never done violence before, so far as I know. In any case, this chap seemed to be in charge of the others. After directing them to make off with the donkeys, he took hold of Jason's bridle and tried to lead him to shore. Jason was out of temper already, mind you. He's not accustomed to being put to haul a wagon and he don't like it worth a fig. So he bit the impertinent fellow."

"Oh."

"*Oh*, indeed. That earned him a swat across the muzzle. Naturally I went after the man who had just hit my horse, but my foot hit a patch of wet sand and sank in directly as he pulled the trigger. The bullet propelled me backward, Jason jolted at the blast of gunfire, a box fell off the wagon and landed atop m'foot; everyone who was still there and able to run, ran off, and there you have it. At the conclusion Jason was still hitched to the wagon and I was trapped under the box, which was how you found us when you came to my rescue."

"A botched job all around," she said, regarding him with a distinct lack of pleasure. "No one involved in this idiotic enterprise can be pleased with the outcome. I certainly am not. And you are under a misapprehension, sir. I did not come to *your* rescue. I came out on the sands to rescue the horse."

He bent over with laughter. "B-bloody hell, woman, what won't you say? Next you'll be telling me you regret picking me up along the way."

"I've had that thought on more than one occasion," she informed him honestly. "In fact, I'm having it right now." Standing, she plucked the empty tankard from his hand and carried it to the table. "I should tell you, I suppose, that Mrs. Preston has grown inordinately fond of your horse and is taking excellent care of him. Unfortunately, it falls to me to take care of *you*."

"You drew the short straw then. But I'll be a good lad, moonbeam, and leave you in peace for a time. Fact is, there is probably more ale inside me than blood at the moment. I'm devilish near to falling asleep."

Sweeter words he could not have spoken. Lucy returned to the cot, lifted away the straw pallet, and helped him settle flat again with his head on the pillow. That required her to wrap her arms around him and lower him down, or so he insisted. He could not move without her help, he said, and she was too relieved that he meant to take a nap to argue with him.

But her palms and fingers were burning from the touch of his skin and the provocative feel of a well-muscled male back when she was done. She rounded up her straying wits. "The blacksmith and the apothecary will be here as soon as the fog lifts, sir. Until then, sleep well."

"We're expecting guests? Lucifer! I had forgot. Wouldn't want to meet 'em in the altogether, would I?" He turned angelic blue eyes to her face. "This is not what I usually say to a female, Miss Luke, but could you possibly help me get into my pants?"

"What a thing to ask!" she declared, her very bones on fire to imagine it. "Certainly not. Robbie will soon be here, and you can beg his assistance."

"Rather have yours," Kit mumbled as his lashes drifted shut.

Chapter 5

Lucy kept her fingers crossed as Giles Handa removed the bandage and examined Kit's wound through his thick round spectacles.

"Ummm," he said, poking at the swollen flesh around the bullet hole, which had already begun to seal itself.

Kit yelped when Giles bent over to check the back of his shoulder.

The apothecary took his time about it. He was an earnest young man, Lucy had discovered when first she met him at his small shop in Silverdale. Tall and gaunt, he had a self-effacing manner that belied his keen intelligence.

At long last he straightened. "The injury is healing cleanly and with remarkable speed, but it should be closely watched. Should there be signs of a high fever, or red streaks radiating from the wound, a physician must be summoned immediately. For now, I should like to clean the area thoroughly and apply basilicum ointment. I also suggest the gentleman keep his arm in a sling until the opening has fully knitted."

Kit made a face.

"Do whatever is necessary," Lucy said before he could object. "Is he well enough to return with you to Silverdale?"

"No," Kit said.

"Yes," Giles said at the same moment. "In my judgment only," he added. "The patient knows best how he feels, of course."

"Weak as a newborn kitten," the patient clarified dolefully.

"Nevertheless, it is certainly best that I go with you. My presence here is a great inconvenience to Luke and Mrs. Preston."

Indeed it is, Lucy thought, clamping her lips together. She'd wager he was feigning both the weakness and the offer to depart, which he'd rendered in a frail, resigned voice. The slight moan at the end had been a nice touch. Giles looked troubled, and even Robbie cast her a questioning glance.

"The track is rough all the way to Silverdale," Giles said hesitantly. "There is some danger that his wound will reopen."

"Oh, very well," she said, glaring at Kit. He gave her back a tremulous, grateful smile.

Giles opened his case of medicines. "Have you a length of fabric with which I can devise a sling?"

"I'll find something," Lucy replied, glad for an excuse to leave the room and Kit's mocking gaze. She rummaged through her portmanteau and found nothing suitable, unless she were to rip apart one of her two plain traveling dresses or demolish her flannel night rail. It seemed that only her shawl—her precious Norwich shawl—would do. She sighed. It was quite the nicest thing she had ever owned, and the colors, primarily deep red and rich purple, were her favorites. She draped it around her shoulders one last time before refolding it and returning to the main room.

She was wickedly gratified to see Kit wince as Giles dabbed his shoulder with ointment. But when he saw her and caught her eye, he winked incorrigibly.

Teeth clenched, she placed the shawl on the table before she used it to strangle him, which she was sorely tempted to do. "Robbie, shall we finish unloading the wagon?"

She marched out the door and headed speedily for the cliff, muttering all the while. The foggy morning had given way to a warm, cloudless afternoon, but she took no pleasure in it. The crystal-blue sky put her too much in mind of a certain gentleman's eyes.

Robbie's long stride soon brought him even with her and

they ascended the grassy slope side by side. "A bit of a lad, he is. I dinna think he's so puny as he makes himself out to be."

"He's a thumping great menace, Robbie, not to mention insufferable. But Giles is correct. Being jostled in the wagon could undo everything, and I am still hoping to avoid summoning a doctor. Some physicians feel obliged to report shootings to the authorities, I am informed."

When the grass began to thin near the top of the hill, Lucy halted. "Wait here a moment." She moved ahead cautiously, pausing again when she caught sight of Morecambe Bay. The tide was out, and miles of brown sand stretched to the horizon. Wishing she had thought to bring Kit's spyglass, she scanned for human figures, found none, and beckoned Robbie to join her at cliff's edge.

"See there?" She pointed to the wagon, still piled with boxes, clearly visible in the bright sunshine. "That's where I found him. I rather thought someone would have retrieved the other boxes by now."

"If they mean to come back, most likely they'll do so after dark. Lowest tide will be 'round about three o'clock, which means they could be on the sands anytime between one and five of the morning."

"The witch must walk, I fear. Did Giles remember to bring the ointment? After a night in the rain, my cape has been washed quite clean."

"He brought it, but that don't mean you should be usin' it." Robbie scoured his chin with an enormous hand. "Better I watch from the cliff tonight."

"You must take Giles home, Robbie, and you've already made two trips to the cottage today. There is nothing to fear, I promise you." She gazed out over the flat expanse of mud and wet sand, where sunlight danced in the rippled pools left by the ebb tide. "I mean to go into Lancaster tomorrow," she said. "Surely by now there is a letter for me at the Anchor Inn."

She spoke with more assurance than she felt. Miss Wetherwood, headmistress at the Wetherwood Academy for Young

Ladies, had been planning to retire while Lucy was a student there. Her health had worsened by the time Lucy left to take up her post as a governess in Dorset, but she was still at the academy two years later when Diana completed her studies. Perhaps she was there yet. In any case, she was their only hope.

"Lancaster is a far way to go for a letter that mightna be there, lass."

"Yes. But so long as I am in the city, I also mean to consult a solicitor."

"I dinna trust lawyers," Robbie said gruffly.

"Nor do I, although I've never actually met one, but we require legal counsel. Until now I thought it too great a risk, but as things have turned out, we have little choice. I only hope I stumble upon a solicitor who is both honest and competent, for I've no idea where to apply. And tonight I must invent a story that will draw from him the information I require without arousing his suspicions."

Robbie shuffled his feet. "I've not wanted to tell you, but there was a notice in the Carnforth newspaper two days ago. And Carnforth being not much of a town, I expect the notice has appeared from Lancaster to Kendal and beyond. A reward of five hundred pounds is offered to whoever discovers the whereabouts of Miss Diana Whitney. There was a description of her, too. A full description," he added unhappily.

Lucy's stomach coiled into a knot. "Dear heavens. Such a fortune! Everyone and his brother will be on the hunt."

Robbie opened his massive arms. "Come here, lassie."

After a moment she threw herself against his broad chest and permitted him to hold her. The blows had been coming so rapidly that she feared she could no longer withstand them on her own. She was terrified of making a wrong move, of doing the wrong thing. "What would we do without you, Robbie?" she murmured, her face pressed to his rough leather waistcoat. "How can we ever repay you?"

"Ach, never you mind about me. Miss Diana is the age my daughter would be hadna the cholera taken her. Give me one of your smiles now, lass, and let's have no more talk about payment."

Lucy couldn't remember the last time she had smiled and meant it. But she stepped back, carved her lips into what probably looked like a grimace, and blinked back the tears that had gathered in her eyes. It was purely luck, or perhaps divine providence, that she had met Robert MacNab when first she arrived in Lancashire. If it was the Lord who had put Robbie in her path, perhaps He was watching out for Diana after all.

On the other hand, it was surely the devil who had sent Kit to plague them. "I expect Giles has about finished with his patient," she said, brushing her hands against her trousers. "Shall we unload the supplies?"

"I mislike you going to Lancaster," Robbie muttered as they descended the sloping hill. "But if you willna change your mind, I'll come back in the morning with the wagon and carry you to the posthouse."

"Thank you, but it's only a few miles, and I intend to catch the coach that comes by at six of the morning. With Kit snoring away in the cottage, I doubt I'll sleep well anyway."

"You'll be Mrs. Preston?"

"Of course." She frowned as new complications rose up to assault her. "Which means that Diana will have to spend the entire day in the cave, since I cannot be back here before late afternoon. And Kit will be alone in the cottage. Drat. There's no telling what he'll get up to. Can you come by and keep watch over him?"

"Aye. I've a job to do in Beetham, but I'll take care of it first thing and come here directly after."

They reached the wagon, and Lucy gathered an armful of folded blankets, towels, and a pillow while Robbie grabbed a heavy bundle of firewood. Three trips were required before they had carried all the supplies into the cottage, where Giles was closing his medicine case and issuing quiet orders to his patient.

Kit, his arm in the sling and a saintly smile on his face, nodded as if he meant to obey them all.

Not likely, Lucy thought as she walked with Robbie and Giles back to the wagon. "Be careful tomorrow, Robbie. He'll try to quiz you, but tell him nothing. Thus far he knows only that my name is Luke, and he believes that Mrs. Preston is mute. Should he inquire where we have gone, say only that we shall return before nightfall. Giles, can he get about on his own?"

"Impossible to say, Miss Lucy. I don't know what to make of the gentleman. But I slipped a bit of laudanum in the ale I gave him to drink, so you'll not be bothered with him for the next few hours."

"Bless you!" she said sincerely. Then she saw Giles place a large leather boot in the wagon. "What is *that*?"

Giles flushed. "He asked me to get him a pair of boots, what with one of his own being cut to ribbons. I'm taking this along for sizing."

"You'll do no such thing! He'll get into less trouble bare-footed. Robbie can bring sandals for him tomorrow, but we'll hide them until he's well enough to leave."

"Very well, ma'am. I never meant to hurry the cobbler, you may be sure. And the gentleman was insistent, so I took the boot rather than quarrel with him."

She patted his hand. "I should learn tact from you, sir. Thank you."

When the wagon was on its way along the narrow track, Lucy went to the rock where she had concealed her cape the previous night. Was it such a short time ago? Twelve or thirteen hours only since she saw the lanterns on the bay? It seemed a lifetime.

She shook out her witch's garb, soaking wet from the rain-storm, and laid it out on the grass to begin drying. Once Kit was asleep, she would take the cape and wig inside and stretch them in front of the fireplace.

She gave some thought to bringing the horse up from the cave and tethering him where he could graze. This was an excellent opportunity to do so, what with the tide out and another hour or two remaining before sunset. But she simply didn't feel up to the task. She'd have to lead him nearly a mile down the beach to where the cliff gave way to a slope he could ascend, and another mile back to the cottage.

Besides, Kit might find him in the morning before Robbie arrived to stand guard. Better the horse remain where he was for now. He was in good hands, that was certain. Diana had taken her scissors to Cow's Mouth Inlet and clipped fresh grass for him to eat, and he would be company for her tomorrow in the cave.

She must be frantic to know what was happening, though. With a sigh, Lucy began the steep descent down a rocky path that any intelligent goat would balk at, marveling that Kit had managed to climb it in spite of his injuries.

A man to be reckoned with, that one. She must never underestimate what he was capable of doing, or permit herself to trust him for a single moment.

Kit woke, disoriented, sometime in the middle of the night. Except for the crackle of the dying fire, the room was eerily silent. Carefully he raised himself on one elbow and looked over at the pallet alongside the hearth.

The blankets lay flat.

He was almost certain he'd awakened earlier, and had a vague recollection of seeing Luke curled up with those blankets mounded over her. He had wanted to speak to her then, but couldn't get his mouth to move. Even now it felt full of cotton wadding.

That bloody apothecary must have put laundanum into the cup of ale. Lucifer! Next time he would be more careful, but dammit, he had *liked* Giles Handa. And for his sins, he forgot that Handa was in league with a pernicious female who seemed to like Kit Valliant best when he was unconscious.

Well, he was wide awake now. So where was *she*?

Probably she had only stepped outside for a few moments, females being subject to calls of nature, too. He lay back to await her return, resolving to try again to discover who she was and what the devil she was up to. Time was running out. She'd not been fooled by his display of weakness, he knew, although it was not wholly feigned. Almost certainly she would send him on his way tomorrow, unless he found some way to persuade her otherwise.

He lay quietly for a few minutes, watching the play of firelight on the low ceiling, considering how best to approach her. If all else failed, he would be forced to identify himself and place the considerable resources of his family at her disposal. But he hoped that would not be necessary. He much preferred to rescue her on his own, assuming she required rescuing, and his instincts told him that she did. He fancied the opportunity to prove himself a knight in shining armor, even if he hadn't so much as a pair of shoes to put on his feet at the moment.

The soft wool of the shawl that held his arm immobile tickled his neck. He sniffed at it, detecting the faint scent of lavender that he noticed whenever Luke leaned close to him. It must be hers, the shawl. He wondered if she had other female garb stashed away in that mysterious back room.

Looking over, he saw that the door was closed. Perhaps she was in there with Mrs. Preston. He listened intently for the sound of voices, hearing only the crackle of the fire and the rustle of coals and ashes dropping through the grate.

She'd been gone a devilish long time, and that was only counting the time since he woke up. No telling when she'd left the room. Losing patience, he swung his legs over the side of the cot and sat upright, pleased when there was no trace of dizziness. His head was relatively clear, the pain in his shoulder had settled to a low throb, and a check of his ankle confirmed that the swelling had gone down considerably. All in all, he felt in fine fettle and certainly well enough to go exploring.

Giles had placed the walking stick where he could easily reach it. After coming to his feet, he limped to the door that led to the back room and pressed his ear against the rough wood. Hearing nothing, he gently raised the latch and pushed, but the door remained firmly sealed. It must be barred from within.

After a mental debate, he gave up the idea of knocking for admittance and went to the black-curtained window farthest from the hearth. With one finger, he made a crack between the curtains and peered outside. The night was clear and dark, with the merest sliver of a moon suspended just above the place where woodland gave way to the sweep of grassy hill that led to the limestone cliff.

Robbie had stuffed him into his breeches, but he remained barefoot, shirtless, and had minimal use of half his supply of limbs. Good sense demanded that he wait until she came back, he acknowledged, thoroughly disgruntled. In his usual state of excellent health, he'd have tracked her down if it took the rest of the night.

Well, so long as he was up, he might as well pay a visit to the tree. A widemouthed jar had been shoved under the cot in lieu of a chamber pot, but he misliked putting it to use with two ladies in residence. Stepping outside, he paused to enjoy the cool breeze sifting through his hair and the smell of salt in the cold air. Overhead, stars winked against a black velvet sky. With a sailor's eye, he immediately picked out the North Star and traced the position of the constellations in the October sky. It was close to three of the morning, he would guess from the lie of Orion and Pegasus.

He made his way to the corner of the cottage, relieved himself, and had just buttoned his trouser flap when he caught sight of a greenish white light on the hillside. What the devil? Plastering himself against the tree trunk, he gazed past the gnarled bark at a startling apparition.

It was moving parallel with the top of the hill a considerable distance away, but then it turned and began to descend. At first the shape, somewhat triangular, seemed to be floating several inches above the ground. But as it came nearer he discerned the outline of a glowing hooded cape.

Fascinated, he saw it angle slightly away from him, heading toward the cleft in the limestone crag where Luke had brought him up from the sands last night. Or that was his guess, from the direction it had taken.

Kit put no credit in ghosts and hobgoblins. That was a flesh-and-blood creature stalking the hills, to what purpose he could not imagine, and he'd bet a pony it was Luke's lithe body under the cape.

A moment later he changed his mind. A play of wind lifted the hood from her head, and instead of Luke's boyish cap of hair, he saw long tresses flowing behind her like a bridal veil. If left to fall down her back, the hair would reach to the woman's waist.

So it wasn't Luke after all. Mrs. Preston, perhaps? The long mane of hair could well have been concealed under her hat and veil when last he saw her. The two ladies must be sisters, he decided. He'd known a good many women in his life, many of them intimately, but had never before seen hair of that unusual moonlight color. It must be peculiar to Luke's family.

The revelation, such as it was, explained nothing of any use. So what that the women were sisters? That did not account for their several disguises, especially this particularly bizarre one. As he watched, the caped figure appeared to sink into the bowels of the earth.

It occurred to him that anyone unacquainted with the mysterious goings-on at the cottage would likely take fright at what he had just seen. The figure had been walking along the cliff, he would guess, precisely to terrify anyone who might be out on the sands. Had he not known about the rugged path, the one he had climbed with such effort, he might have been spooked into giving credit to otherworldly apparitions.

What were they hiding?

He had nearly reached the front door when a whirring sound caused him to spin around. A small shape whizzed past his head, arced a turn, and swooped toward him.

"Bloody hell!" He regarded the owl with displeasure. "You scared the devil out of me."

The owl flew past and circled again.

"Want inside, do you?" Kit opened the door. "Well, come on then."

Fidgets flew into the room and dropped something small and brown at Kit's feet.

"What's this?" In the dim firelight, it was hard to tell. A small rodent of some sort, he guessed, poking it gently with the walking stick. A deceased rodent.

The owl, now perched on the coat peg, began making those familiar snoring noises. She looked, Kit thought, rather pleased with herself.

"If this is a gift," Kit advised her kindly, "you really shouldn't have. And here I didn't get you anything. Tell you what, Fidgets. It's the thought that counts. Why don't you take this luscious morsel outside and have yourself a snack?"

The owl tilted her head, regarding him from shiny eyes.

There was no help for it. Kit wasn't churlish enough to refuse the offering, so he lifted the limp creature on the tip of the walking stick and placed it on a saucer. "Yum. I'll have it for breakfast. How very thoughtful of you." He wondered if Fidgets meant to perch there watching him until he ate the thing. "But trust me, bird, I cannot fertilize your eggs, or however it is you owls make more owls. Besides, I'm a ramshackle fellow. All the ladies will tell you so. I'd only break your heart."

He set the saucer on the table, not sure how to proceed. He certainly didn't relish the thought of two round eyes fixed on him for the next several hours. "It's a lovely night," he said firmly, pointing to the open door. "A pretty young thing like you should be out kicking up your claws."

To his surprise, the owl flew out of the cottage.

Before she could change her mind, he hurried to close the door. For a moment he considered opening it long enough to toss the rodent outside, where it could make a meal for some other creature. But what if Fidgets found out what he'd done?

He must be out of his wits to worry about offending a bird's sensibilities. What next? he wondered, stirring the fire with a poker. A would-be witch stalking the headlands and a besotted owl delivering love tokens to the reluctant object of her affections.

Well, he had wanted one last adventure before coming to grips with his future. At nine-and-twenty, a man ought to have chosen a profession and made himself useful. Or so his brother pointed out rather too often. Of late, and without pleasure, Kit had begun to agree. But he enjoyed useless activities, so long as they were exciting, and every profession considered suitable for the son of an earl struck him as crushingly boring.

He had once thought of enlisting in the Royal Navy, but James wouldn't hear of it. One brother in the military would suffice, he had decreed, and Alex was by then a captain in the 44th Foot. Besides, James had reminded him, taking orders and adhering to strict discipline was not in his nature. Kit had no argument for that.

In fact, the only thing he had ever truly wanted was an enormous family—a dozen kids at the least—and a house near the water so that he could sail. Given that much, he would gladly dig ditches or quarry shale to put food on the table.

He placed two more logs on the grate. It would not come to manual labor, he knew. There was money—how much, he'd no idea—willed him by his mother and held in trust by his brother, to be released at the earl's discretion. So far James had not parted with a groat of it, preferring to keep the funds invested until Kit showed signs of settling down.

Just as well. Had James signed over the inheritance, he'd likely have squandered the whole on gifts for the ladies whose favors he enjoyed or rounds of drinks in the taprooms where he spent many of his evenings. Money streamed through his fingers like water. Kit knew better than to ask his brother to release what was rightfully his because it would be needed later, for his children.

Meantime there was the mystery of Luke and Mrs. Preston to unriddle. Surely one of them would return to the cottage before very much longer. He went to the cot, slipped between the rough blankets, and adjusted his arm in the sling. Except for a low, steady throbbing, his shoulder scarcely hurt at all. By tomorrow, he should be able to get around without difficulty, although Luke would toss him out on his ear if she knew it.

He meant to tell her, though, as soon as she came back. Show her, if necessary. It was past time they both started to give over the truth.

But no one came in through the front door, or through the door that was barred, and his eyelids began to feel like lead weights.

He tried to stay awake by reviewing what he had learned about the pearly-haired sisters. Very little, he had to admit, and every new detail left him more puzzled than before. If that had been Mrs. Preston walking on the hillside, where was Luke? And where was it Mrs. Preston was headed when she vanished? Was there something of interest at the bottom of the cliff?

After a while his thoughts began tripping over one another until they were hopelessly entangled. He wondered why Mrs. Preston wore that black veil over her face. He wondered if he was really falling in love with Luke, as he suspected, or merely indulging himself in a pleasurable fantasy. How came it that an owl had chosen him as its mate? He recalled the rodent in the saucer and wondered if he ought to get up and do something about it.

Somewhere along the way, lavender-scented and relentless, sleep washed over him like the tide in Morecambe Bay.

Chapter 6

The sound of groaning hinges prodded Kit awake. Cracking his lids the barest fraction, he saw Mrs. Preston sweep in from the back room carrying a lantern, an umbrella, and a small satchel. As before, she wore a severe black dress, long-sleeved and cut high at the neck, concealing every inch of her skin. Her hair and face were covered by the veiled hat.

She had also, he noted with interest, grown nearly two inches taller.

After placing the lantern near the hearth and the satchel and umbrella by the front door, she gathered dishes from the shelf where they were stowed and carried them over to the table. Then she froze.

Ah yes. The rodent. Kit decided that this was not a good time to pretend to be asleep. "Good morning," he said cheerfully.

The veil lifted slightly as she swung her head in his direction, offering him a glimpse of Luke's firm chin. "I expect you are wondering about the chap in the saucer," he said. "Fidgets brought it in last night. A love offering, unless I am very much mistaken, and no doubt I am expected to swallow it whole. Thus far, I've been unable to bring myself to do so."

With deliberation she set down the dishes and flatware, picked up the saucer, went to the door, and threw the rodent unceremoniously outside. She sent the saucer flying, too.

"So much for love," Kit said mournfully as she returned to the shelf and grabbed a half loaf of bread, a hunk of smoked ham, and a wedge of cheese. She flung them onto a platter with a decided *thunk*.

"Is that our breakfast?" he inquired, sitting up.

Ignoring him, she filled a battered metal tankard with ale from a large pitcher and set it with the food.

One tankard. "Are you going out, ma'am?"

She slammed a knife and fork on the table.

"May I ask where?" he persisted, solely to annoy her. She'd no intention of telling him, he was certain.

Shaking her head, she went to the door. Then she turned back and approached the cot with clear reluctance, pointing to his shoulder.

"Are you inquiring about my health?" he asked, amused. "Indeed, I am precisely at the mark where I require no further medical assistance but cannot leave here in the foreseeable future without doing severe damage to my constitution."

He was fairly certain she muttered an oath behind that heavy veil.

"I'll be gone in a week or so," he assured her with a grin. "Probably to post the banns, if Fidgets has her way with me. Shall I presume that Luke is lurking about in case I need her— er, him—while you are away?"

Tossing her hands in the air in a gesture of disgust, she flounced across the room, grabbed the umbrella and satchel, and departed in a huff.

Temper, temper, he thought, laughing aloud. But where could she be off to in such a rush? It was still pitch-dark outside, he'd observed when she opened the door.

The dirt floor was cool under his feet when he stood to test his bruised ankle. Although painful, it felt sound enough that he decided to do without the cane for the time being. He wrapped a blanket around his shoulders against the chilly predawn air, limped to the table, and tucked into his breakfast. After so many meals of bread and soup, he'd a wolf in his stomach. It was as well the ladies were not present to see him demolish every morsel without resorting to civilized manners.

There had been no sound from the other room, and he wondered if the long-haired sister was in there. When he'd finished his ale, he went to the door and listened as he had done the previous night, hearing nothing. "Hullo?" He rapped on the door. "Anyone there?"

No reply, which was as he'd expected.

"I require help, please." He put a quaver in his voice. "Quickly. I've torn open my wound and it is bleeding in a gush."

Either she didn't believe him or she didn't care. The door remained firmly closed.

Lucifer! These females were hard as standing stones. Without much hope, he tried the latch and was astonished when the door swung open to reveal a windowless cubicle no larger than a stable stall.

Feeling foolish, Kit went back to retrieve the lantern and set about examining the few items stored in the room. There was a three-legged stool, a good-size portmanteau, a wicker cage, and a long wooden box. He raised the lid and sifted through the contents, finding blankets, towels, candles, and at the very bottom, his leather saddle pack. He took it out and unclasped the buckles.

Someone had sorted through the contents, he could tell. The two shirts and half-dozen handkerchiefs were folded more neatly than he'd ever folded anything in his life. Nothing appeared to be missing, though. The searcher must have been disappointed to find so little, but on his adventures he never carried anything that might serve to identify him.

Returning the lid to the box, he seated himself atop it and considered whether it would be worth the effort to try to pull on a shirt. Unlike most females of his acquaintance, Luke seemed singularly unimpressed by the sight of his manly torso, which left him no good reason to continue leaving it bare. And even the soft thin wool of his shirt would offer protection from the cold when he went outside to explore, as he fully intended to do.

He discovered almost immediately that trying to dress himself had been a bad idea, but once started, he was determined to finish the job. A long painful time later, punctuated by searing oaths and any number of pauses to rest, he finally succeeded in stuffing both arms through the sleeves and tugging the shirt over his head.

Fresh blood—not enough to signify, he hoped—seeped through the bandage and spotted the shirt. He waited awhile to see if he'd done himself injury, still sitting on the box and looking carefully around the room in case he had missed anything.

A carpet of sorts, made of tightly woven straw and about four feet square, lay under the portmanteau. Nothing odd about that, to be sure, but his gaze kept straying back to it. There was something about its position that felt wrong. The box, cage, and stool were neatly set against the wall, but the portmanteau rested nearly dead center in the room.

Curious, he went over to it and lifted it off the carpet. His instincts were abuzz, raising the hair on his arms and driving the blood through his veins in a pounding awareness he had long since learned to trust. Setting the portmanteau on the dirt floor, he bent over and raised one corner of the straw mat, not oversurprised to see a hinged trapdoor.

One mystery solved, he thought, folding the carpet over itself to give him access. There was a slim piece of rope wrapped around one of the wooden boards, but he left it long enough to go back and wrestle his arm into the makeshift sling. The bleeding had stopped, fortunately, and the few drops of blood on his shirt were already drying to a rusty brown.

He brought the lantern closer, set it beside the trapdoor, and gingerly pulled the rope. The door lifted soundlessly on well-oiled hinges. He folded it all the way back and peered down, but even when he lifted the lantern directly over the opening, he could see no more than two or three stairs that had been hewn into the limestone. Beyond was darkness, although he scented salty air and the musty smell of rotting seaweed.

Familiar odors, they were. He had set foot in more than one seacoast cave during his desultory career as a smuggler, and several had boasted tunnels leading to concealed exits.

Kit lowered himself to the floor and swung his feet into the opening. Since his one good arm was occupied with holding the lantern, he could manage only a slow, awkward descent down the steep, moisture-slick stairs. For once, he chose to be cautious. The steps were narrow, and should he lose his footing, there was no telling how far he would fall.

At last he reached the bottom, finding himself in a small grotto. A ragged slice of pale light came through an opening directly ahead, just wide enough to slip through if he went sideways. He set down the lantern on the bottom stair, noticing that several pieces of luggage had been stowed in the darkest curve of the grotto. They were of excellent quality, much finer than the shabby portmanteau in the cottage. Jason's saddle was draped over the largest of them.

Blood pulsed in his ears. He thrived on adventure, always had, and this one was a cracker. Tiptoeing to the break in the limestone grotto, he peered out.

Another cave, perhaps thirty feet long and exceptionally high and wide until it narrowed to a smaller entrance, opened onto Morecambe Bay. Jason was tethered to one of the water-worn boulders that littered the floor of the cave, nibbling at a stack of new-cut grass. Small pink crabs scuttled over the sand and rocks, taking strict care to keep well distant from the horse.

As he stood there a fresh sea breeze lifted his hair and billowed the sleeves of his shirt. And the same breeze, stronger at the entrance of the cave, played with the long, curly auburn hair of the woman who was seated on a flat rock with her back to him, looking out into the dawn.

The other Mrs. Preston, no doubt. This time she was clad in a long-sleeved dress of hunter green. She sat motionless, her back straight, unaware that she had been discovered.

Something about her, perhaps her grave stillness, held him in place. He was reluctant to startle her or, worse, to alarm her, and an uneasy sensation tingled at his spine. He felt pain and longing resonating in his body and, most particularly, in the region of his heart. All his protective instincts went on fire. Whoever she was, she needed help.

It finally dawned on him that she did *not* possess the long, straight, pearly hair he had been expecting. This woman could not have been the specter he'd seen walking the cliffs last night, and Luke was already ruled out because her hair, while the right color, was even shorter than his own. Could there be three women instead of two hiding out in this remote cottage?

While he was considering the best way to approach her, Jason took the matter out of his hands. Kit was standing downwind, but the sea breeze had filtered through the splice in the rocks, bounced off the grotto walls behind him, and carried his odor back to the horse. Scenting a longtime friend, the bay lifted his muzzle and whickered.

The woman turned her head then, and he got the barest glimpse of a beautiful profile before she jumped to her feet. Keeping her back to him, she gestured him frantically to go away.

"It's only the gimpy lodger," he said, taking a few steps in her direction. "I was wondering where you'd gotten to."

Her gestures grew wilder.

He stopped. "You wish me to leave, I take it."

She nodded vigorously.

"My apologies, ma'am, but I'm afraid I cannot oblige you on this occasion. One of you must explain to me what is going on here, and the other young ladies are nowhere to be found."

Again she turned, showing him that splendid profile as she put a finger to her lips. Then she used it to make a negative gesture.

"Ah. I had forgot. You cannot speak."

She nodded even more forcefully and repeated her go-away sign.

"The thing is, my dear, I would bet a pony that you have a perfectly good voice. What I cannot reckon is why you are pretending otherwise. It's all some part of these mysterious goings-on, to be sure, but singularly useless when directed at me. I am not your enemy, my dear."

Suddenly she bolted forward in the direction of the sands, but she halted almost immediately, her shoulders slumping in a gesture of unmistakable resignation.

He moved slowly toward her. "I would be unable to catch you if you chose to run, you know." When he was only a few feet away, she turned slightly. He saw a tear streak down her smooth cheek. *Lucifer!* Did she imagine he would do her harm?

"I can speak," she said quietly. "But I will tell you nothing."

"Not even how I can be of service to you?"

She brushed away a second tear. "That is simple enough. Leave us, and forget that you ever met us."

"I cannot do that, butterfly. You are in some sort of trouble, and I wish to help. Actually, I insist on helping."

"How can a smuggler be of any use? The last thing we require is a hunted criminal on the premises."

"Oh, my. You begin to sound exactly like Luke, or whatever her name is."

"We don't know your name either," she pointed out.

"Christopher Etheridge," he said easily. "Call me Kit. And you are . . . ?"

"I am being sought by people who must not be allowed to find me," she said in a bleak voice.

"Then we shall see to it they do not. I *will* help you, you may rely on it, and I would die before betraying you. As Luke never fails to remind me, I owe you my life. Consider that even a smuggler may have some claim to honor."

She turned her back to him again, arms clasped around her waist as if she were holding herself together by force of will.

He remained where he was, giving her time. She was no more than eighteen or nineteen, he would guess, but he sensed enormous strength in her. At length, she came to a decision. Her spine went arrow straight, she lifted her chin, and without a word she wheeled to face him directly.

Dear God! With effort, he showed no reaction when he saw her right cheek, the one she had so carefully kept from his view until now. He looked at it, of course. He could not help himself.

Marked out in angry red ridges, the scar covered most of her cheek. It resembled a piece of mirror glass struck hard by a pebble. There was a small round scar at the center with narrow lines radiating from it that were sometimes connected by other lines, much like a spiderweb.

The injury could not have happened very long ago, a few weeks perhaps. It was healing cleanly, and he supposed that much of the redness would fade over time. But the scar would remain with her forever.

He lifted his gaze to her eyes, which were shimmering with tears as she awaited his judgment. She expected revulsion, he knew. Perhaps worse. He felt nothing of the like, but for once his glib tongue failed him. How could there be words?

He was enraged at what had been done to her. And he wanted to weep for her, but she would surely mistake his compassion for pity. In the end, not knowing what else to do, he slipped his arm from the sling, moved to her, and drew her into an embrace.

She stiffened, resisting his sympathy, but he rubbed her back with one hand and combed through her hair with the other. Her unscarred cheek was pressed against his chest. He held her for a long time, rocking her gently, and at last she went limp against his body.

Then the tears came. They soaked into his shirt as she wept soundlessly, the minutes passing one after the other while he could do nothing but hold her and wait.

"Oh, dear," she finally mumbled against his shoulder. "Forgive me. Truly, I have sworn n-never to be a watering pot when there is anyone to see me."

"Except perhaps this once," he said mildly. "Tears heal a wounded heart, or so I believe."

"You are much mistaken, sir. I have cried buckets of them, and they serve only to swell up my eyes."

He tilted her chin with his thumb and gazed at her red-rimmed hazel eyes and the long dark lashes, spiky and clumped together with salty tears. "Not this time, I promise you."

"A safe enough promise," she declared with a return of spirit, "since I cannot prove you wrong. You may be sure that I keep well away from mirrors since my . . . since the accident."

He released her, except for the one hand he put gently on her shoulder to hold the connection between them. "Will you tell me what happened, my dear?"

She sighed. "I suppose I must, since you have already found us out. But it is a long and unpleasant tale, sir. You are certain to find it tedious."

"That is most unlikely. I wish to hear every detail, or at least the ones that will direct me to how I can best be of service. But my sore ankle has begun to make its presence felt. Will that fine-looking rock seat us both, do you think?"

When he was settled on one side of the flat stone, she stepped back and regarded him thoughtfully. "The sling is tangled every which way, sir. Shall I remove it and undo the knots?"

"By all means." She required a few moments to regain her composure and order her thoughts, he understood, bending his neck so that she could lift the shawl over his head. "May I know your name?"

"Diana Evangeline Whitney," she replied, sitting beside him with the shawl in her lap. "Under the circumstances, formality would be pointless. Please call me Diana. And my friend—there is only one, by the way—is Lucinda Jennet Preston."

His heart plunged to his feet. She was married! "There really is a Mrs. Preston then," he said tightly.

"A Miss Preston," Diana corrected, working at the knot. "When it is called for, Lucy disguises herself as a widow. Unfortunately, she is compelled to use her own name when dealing with bankers and the like. But as no one knows her here in the north, it is probably safe enough."

Now it was Kit's turn to regain his composure. The brief seconds he had thought Lucy beyond his reach had all but unmanned him.

The significance of what had just happened struck him

forcibly. So there it was. So now he knew without question. He was in love with her.

Indeed, he had suspected as much. His generally reliable instincts had shouted the news when first he saw her, he realized on looking back at the scene. But at the time he'd been half-buried in the sand with blood pouring out of him, and so much had happened since to distract him that he had never decided if his strong attraction to her might be a good deal more than that.

Well, at least *one* problem had been put to rest. Love it was. Convincing her to feel likewise about him was another matter entirely, but he could not get about his wooing right away. Diana's problems, whatever they might be, were clearly more urgent. "If she is playing the part of the widow when she isn't playing Luke," he said, "then who was it masquerading as that luminescent creature I saw last night?"

"Oh, that was Lucy, too." She glanced over at him. "You have been nosing about rather energetically for a man we thought not so very long ago to be knocking at death's door."

He grinned. "Masquerades are not reserved for females, you know. But if that was Lucy on the cliff, how came she by the long hair?"

"It's a wig, of course, but—" She pressed her lips together.

"But what?"

"If you wish to know more, sir, you must ask her to explain. I am willing to tell you about myself and what Lucy has done on my behalf, but I'll not speak of matters which relate to her in a personal way. She will be more than displeased to learn I have spoken with you at all."

He had no doubt of that. "Very well. I'll not intrude, and if I forget myself, cut me off. Is it permitted to tell me why she was stalking the cliffs? Granted she was quite terrifying at first sight, and I presume she means to discourage company from dropping by. But this strikes me as a peculiar way to go about being unneighborly."

"I have never approved of the hauntings," Diana said, "although Lucy is convinced they are effective. She may well be correct. While it is no secret that a reclusive widow has taken up residence in the cottage, no one has dared to pay a friendly call. Do you reside in the area, sir?"

"These days I come and go, but I grew up within two hours' ride of here."

"Then perhaps you are familiar with the story of the Lancashire Witches." She finally succeeded in undoing the troublesome knot and stood to shake out the fringed shawl.

"Never heard of them. Westmoreland runs more to sheep than witches."

"As does Lancashire these days. But two hundred years ago, over by Pendle Hill, a number of women were tried for the practice of witchcraft. It was all nonsense, to be sure, but they were condemned and hanged nonetheless. Most every Lancashire child grows up hearing the stories. Their parents, who were told the same stories when they were children, believe that the witches still walk these hills, casting spells and doing wicked things to anyone who comes within reach."

"I see. Lucy is exploiting a local superstition to keep people away. Devilish clever of her."

"Foolhardy, in my opinion." Diana draped the shawl around his neck and moved behind him. "But she won't be stopped. Once Lucy gets something into her head, she is more stubborn than a Lancashire farmer, which is saying a great deal. Until a few weeks ago she had never set foot in Lancashire, but she soon heard the legends because there is no escaping them. And by purest coincidence, one of the poor women hanged was named Jennet Preston. That's how she got the notion, and I'm sorry to say that she found someone—the apothecary who tended to you yesterday—who could show her how to make her cloak shine in the dark. He gave her an ointment that turns the trick, and off she went to strike terror into the hearts of poor cocklers and fishermen. Truth be told, I think she rather enjoys being the Lancashire Witch."

Kit burst out laughing.

"It's not in the least amusing, sir. One of these nights, some-one who doesn't believe in supernatural creatures will accost her to prove himself right."

Still chuckling, he allowed Diana to encase his arm in the sling and adjust the length. "I'm sure you are correct," he said, trying to sound sincere. But oh, how he admired his witch for conceiving of the idea in the first place. And he wouldn't object in the least to a night of haunting in company with Lucy. It was just the sort of adventure he most relished.

"Is that comfortable?" Diana asked, holding the corners of the shawl behind his neck.

"Perfectly. Tie it off, madam. And while you are about it, tell me about Miss Preston. Does she make a habit of wearing trousers?"

"She has found it convenient from time to time, especially when she was meeting with me at my parents' "—her voice faltered—"at my uncle's estate. She masqueraded as a garden-er's assistant then. And I think she sometimes wears trousers in her usual position, but you must ask her about that."

For all his compelling wish to learn more about Lucy, he knew he must stop prodding Diana for information. He felt her hands trembling against his nape as she secured the knot. "Per-haps I will one day. But the moment has come, I believe, for you to tell me your own story."

Without responding, she returned to her place on the rock and sat with her fingers tightly laced together.

He was content to give her as much time as she required. It was early morning yet, barely an hour since dawn. The tide had moved in quickly since first he entered the cave, slowing when it reached the sloping rise that let to the cliffs. No more than twenty yards away, fluttery waves lapped at the sands. With shrill cries, a flock of sandpipers swept in and began to bustle about on whisker-thin legs.

She released a long sigh. "So much has occurred that I can scarcely think how to tell you. It began last year, when my par-ents died of the typhus. Father was the fifteenth Baron Whitney of Willow Manor, which is located to the east of Lancaster, and the title passed to his brother, who is now my guardian. I met him once or twice when I was a child, but he had not called on us this last decade or more. Father would surely have made other provision for me, had he known what manner of man his brother has become since then. My uncle was livid to discover that his inheritance is confined to the title and the entailed portion of the estate. The Whitney fortune came to me, and is being held in trust until I turn one-and-twenty. He cannot touch a penny of it."

"What sort of man is he then?" Kit asked, although to be sure, her scar fairly well told the tale.

She considered for a few moments. "A prodigiously foolish one, at bottom. When he took up residence at Willow Manor three months ago, it was primarily to escape his London creditors. I am guessing only, because he certainly does not confide in me, but it's likely that he celebrated his inheritance rather lavishly, without understanding its limitations. Now he is deeply in debt, and he has already sold a number of paintings that rightly belong to me. He daren't touch the valuable ones, of course, but he reckons that a mere female won't notice a bit of pilfering."

"You should inform your trustees, Diana. Or the solicitor who managed your father's affairs."

"Perhaps. I know little of such matters. My education was confined to the learning and accomplishments deemed suitable for a young lady who is expected only to marry well. Indeed, I have been pampered my entire life—until just recently—with no aspirations beyond a London Season and a bevy of handsome suitors from which to make my selection." Her hands twisted in her lap. "The loss of a few trivial possessions means nothing to me, sir. I loved my parents and was plunged into grief when they died. My uncle could have sold everything with my blessings, so long as he left me in peace to mourn them. But he did not."

"Have you no other relations to stay with?"

"None whatever, I'm afraid. Mama's brother and his wife went out to India, where they died some years ago, and their only son was killed in the Peninsular War. Perhaps there are distant connections somewhere, but I know nothing of them."

"My own family is much the same," he said by way of distraction when she wiped away a tear. "Nary an aunt or an uncle, no cousins, and my parents died in a snowstorm when I was a nipper. But I have two older brothers, and things are looking up because one has already produced a fine pair of sons."

She gave him a smile that caught at his heart. "I'm not altogether alone, you know. I have Lucy. But I must explain how that came about, for it is a great wonder to me. She was one of the teachers when I arrived at Miss Wetherwood's academy, terrified and shy because I had never before been among strangers. Lucy took me under her wing the first two years, and then she left the school to accept another position. Something happened to drive her away, but she will not say what it was. A few of the teachers envied her because she was popular with the students, and I expect they created difficulties for her.

"In any case, we set up a correspondence, although why she bothered with me is a mystery. I never had the slightest thing of interest to say in my letters, being totally absorbed with fashion and schoolgirl crushes on the dance master and the riding instructor. She always replied, though, even after I left school and wrote her infrequently. She had not heard of my parents' death until two months ago, when I sent a letter begging for her help. There was no one else to ask, you see. And without any questions, she came immediately."

Kit nodded, unsurprised. Lucy would do no less for a friend. However little he knew of her, practically speaking, he had already seen evidence of her courage and her loyalty, two virtues he profoundly respected. But much as he longed to hear more about the woman he intended to marry, Diana had not yet come to the heart of her own story. "What led you to call on her, my dear? The brutality of your uncle?"

"He isn't a brute, Kit. He is stupid and greedy, yes, and so excessively superstitious that he consults fortune-tellers and astrologers before making the slightest decision. I suspect that one of them advised him to marry me off to his own advantage, for nothing else could account for his insistence that I wed the man he has chosen. His name is Sir Basil Crawley, and where my uncle found him I know not, but apparently they have come to an agreement that includes a large settlement. Why Sir Basil is so determined to take me to wife is equally unclear. The arrangement was made before ever we were introduced."

"And when you were," Kit said, "you took him in dislike."

"Loathing would be the better word. I cannot explain exactly why. He is not ill-looking, although he is at least twice my age, and he was polite enough in a distant way. But I had the distinct impression that he was wholly indifferent to me. Gentlemen, the few I have met, were always drawn to my—" She waved a hand. "This is difficult. Before the injury to my face, I'm afraid that I was quite vain about my appearance. I was accustomed to being much admired and had come to expect it. But Sir Basil did not seem to *see* me, if that makes any sense."

"Perhaps he did not wish you to think he wanted to marry you only for your beauty, even if that were the truth of it. Have you considered that he might have observed you from a distance at an earlier time, been enchanted by you, and applied to your guardian for your hand?"

"I'm not an idiot, sir!"

Kit realized that he had offended her, although he was not certain why his innocuous observation made her so angry. He thought his suggestion quite reasonable, even if it proved to be inaccurate. But there was fire in her eyes when she stood to face him and fury in her voice.

"I may have wished for flattery and admiring glances from a suitor, but Sir Basil's failure to give them to me is nothing to the point. Had he composed sonnets to my beauty and gone on bended knee to profess his adoration, it would not have swayed me in the slightest. Under no circumstances would I agree to marry such a repellent man. He has eyes like a lizard's, sir, and ice where his heart should be. Had I not good reason to escape him, would I be hiding in a *cave*, for pity's sake?"

Taken aback, Kit lifted his good arm in a gesture of defense. "I did not mean to—"

"Perhaps not. But you were making excuses for him, like one man defending another in some sort of male brotherhood. You were not *listening* to me. He never admired me. He set out to buy me for purposes of his own. They must have been compelling, for when I was no longer beautiful, he persisted in his suit. Don't think it was because he could look past this disfigurement and love me for what I am. Even I do not know what that is. I used to be a spoiled child, relying on my beauty and good breeding and large fortune to carry me through life. Now I am nothing."

Heat scalded his face. She was exactly right, until the last sentence she spoke. He had leaped to Sir Basil's defense for no reason whatsoever, except that he knew men often behaved foolishly when they tumbled unexpectedly into love. His brother had been a prime example, nearly losing the woman who was now his greatest joy. And Kit was feeling none too certain about his own prospects with Lucy after the poor start they had made together, although he was fairly sure he'd be able to turn things around.

The fact remained that he was a man, which meant he thought like a man, and he definitely relied overmuch on his success at winning over most every female who caught his eye. He was too confident. He assumed he understood women when that was patently impossible. But one reason he adored them was their very complexity, and he was currently being given a hard lesson about the danger of jumping to conclusions. About being smug and patronizing, which he hadn't known he was being until Diana took him to task in no uncertain terms.

Were he not already in love with Lucy, he could very easily fall in love with Miss Diana Whitney.

"Have you nothing to say?" she demanded.

He gazed steadily into her eyes. "A litany of apologies, if

you wish to hear it. I assure you that I would mean every word from my heart. But what I most want to say is that you are splendid, Diana. I well understand why Lucy chose you as her friend."

"Don't be that way, Kit. I shall cry again if you are."

"Very well. I think I understand, but most probably I don't."

She sank back onto the rock beside him, making no objection when he wrapped his arm across her back. "I wish Lucy had been here to see this display of temper," Diana said. "She tells me I am passive and weepy and despairing, which is all true. Since writing her the letter that brought her here, which seems to have used up the last of my courage, I have left her to do everything while I float behind her like a leaf on a strong current."

He nearly assured her that that wasn't the case, but stopped just in time. What did he know of it, after all? And in his experience, Lucy took charge and snapped out orders like a field marshal. It would take a strong will to match hers under any circumstances. "You haven't told me how you were injured, butterfly," he said softly. "Have we come to that point in your story?"

"Near enough. I keep thinking of small things that added up to big ones, but there is no explaining them. And always I am guessing at my uncle's motives, not to mention Sir Basil's. He has some hold on the new Lord Whitney, that is certain. The last time he came to call, I declined his offer and made it clear I would not change my mind. Then they were closeted together for nearly half an hour before Sir Basil took his leave. I watched him go from the window of my bedchamber. A few minutes later Lord Whitney barreled into the room. He had been drinking, and he stormed around knocking things off my dressing table and the other furniture while he shouted at me."

She rested her head against Kit's shoulder. "I had to marry Sir Basil, he said, or he would be ruined. I told him I'd sooner die. Then he struck me, hard across the face. It was the first time anyone had ever raised a hand to me, and the blow took me off guard. I remember the stunned look in his eyes just before I fell. By ill fortune, my cheek landed against a fragile bit of ornamental glass, a small flat piece that failed to break when he knocked it onto the carpet. It shattered well enough when I landed directly atop it, though, and the doctor was a long time picking the splinters from my face."

They sat quietly. Kit stretched out his legs and examined his bare feet, knowing he must not push for answers to his many questions until Diana was ready to proceed.

She ought to have reported the incident to the magistrate, of course. Evidence of physical injury would be grounds for petitioning the court to remove her from her uncle's guardianship. But even if she were aware of that, which he doubted, she could not have been thinking clearly at the time. He wondered what explanation Lord Whitney had given the doctor who tended her.

"A few days later, when I learned that Sir Basil was persisting in his suit, I wrote to Lucy. My uncle had long since dismissed most of the household staff, including my maid, but the gardener smuggled the letter out and acted as a go-between when Lucy arrived. I was in the habit of walking on the grounds, so it was a simple matter to arrange meetings where we would not be seen. Each time I wore several layers of clothing under my cloak and carried a few possessions in a picnic basket for Lucy to take away with her. She was also searching for a place to hide me, and when she located this cottage, I contrived to escape."

She sighed. "There was a great deal more to it, you may be sure. The entire process required the better part of a month, and even I don't know the half of what Lucy was up to during that time. Until she met Robbie MacNab, who encountered her walking along the road and offered her a ride in his wagon, she was proceeding entirely on her own."

"And she found you an excellent refuge, I must say. But you cannot be comfortable here for any extended period of time."

"No. The cottage is too near my uncle's estate, for one thing, and I know he is looking for me. Indeed, he has posted a considerable reward for my return. Eventually someone will think to look here. We must leave as soon as may be, but we've nowhere to go and very little money to sustain us. I have no access to my inheritance, and Lucy has already spent most of her savings to bring us this far. She has written to Miss Wetherwood, the headmistress at the school where we met, and we have some hope that she will assist us. I can pay her back when I come of age, and she was always fond of me."

Kit had no great liking for this uncertain solution to their problems. He could do far better. But now was not the time to say so. "Where did Mrs. Preston run off to this morning, by the by?"

"Lancaster. Miss Wetherwood was asked to send her reply to the inn where Lucy stayed when she first arrived. We had no idea where we'd wind up, you see. Perhaps we'll have an answer today. And she has other business there, but I think she would not approve if I spoke of it."

Diana gave a short laugh. "As if she won't be furious enough when she returns to find that you have discovered the cave. And me."

"You mustn't worry, butterfly. I can handle Lucy." He managed to say that with a straight face. "Need I tell you again that you may safely trust me, or have you begun to believe it?"

She twined her fingers through his. "In fact, sir, I am convinced of it. Persuading Lucy will not be easy, but we are two against one. We must take care not to offend her, though. She has—"

"I understand completely," he said, squeezing Diana's hand. "Leave her to me. Meantime you are growing goose bumps, m'dear, and I rather expect you haven't had your breakfast. Shall we go upstairs, build ourselves a fire, and get better acquainted?"

Her eyes widened. "I nearly forgot, Kit. Robbie is coming here this morning."

"Ah. To make certain that I keep out of trouble, no doubt." He stood, still holding her hand, and drew her up.

79

"Too late for that!" she said with the first real smile he'd seen from her. "He will be vastly surprised to find us together."

Kit led her in the direction of his horse. "Jason looks to be in fine fettle, if a trifle bored." He rubbed the muzzle that pushed at his shoulder. "Don't care for being tethered in a cave, do you? I can't blame you a bit."

"I've gone out to cut grass for him with my scissors," Diana said, "and Robbie brought a sack of oats. Those must be parceled out, though. Oats are too rich for him to eat a great many at any one time without becoming ill."

"You know about horses, I take it."

"A little. I do love them. More than anything else I have left behind, I miss Sparkles. She's a pretty chestnut mare with lots of spirit. I do hope my uncle doesn't sell her off."

"If he does, we'll see you get her back." He resolved to make sure of it. Diana had little enough to cling to, after all.

When they came to the stairs that led up to the cottage, Kit sent her ahead of him and took time to study the trapdoor and what lay below it. If he had found the entrance to the cave, so could anyone else.

Something must be done about that.

Chapter 7

Lucy was unsurprised when the Lancaster-to-Lakeland coach turned up at the posthouse already chock-full of passengers. The entire day had been one disappointment after another.

A light rain had begun to fall, and she had left her umbrella at the solicitor's office. She realized that she had forgot it when she was only a short distance away, but wild horses could not have dragged her back to reclaim it.

"You'll have to ride up here," the driver told her impatiently. "Hurry it up, ma'am. We are running late as 'tis."

"I'll help you mount," the postilion said. "How far will you be going?"

"Warton." She gave him the coins she had already counted out and let herself be pushed from below and pulled from above until she was balanced precariously atop the Lakeland Flyer. Scrambling to a spot between two large portmanteaus tied to the coach with ropes, she had barely settled herself when the horses sprang forward.

Two men in rustic garb were seated at the rear, passing a bottle back and forth. One caught her eye and held the bottle in her direction. "A tot of whisky, ma'am? It'll warm your innards on this cold afternoon."

For a moment she was tempted. A little oblivion would be welcome right about now. But it was a long walk from Warton to the cottage, and the merest swallow of hard spirits invariably rendered her tipsy. She smiled at him. "Thank you, sir, but no. I appreciate your kindness."

And she did. Of late, what with Kit and the smugglers and the repellent solicitor, she was grateful for the slightest favor. Almost as unwelcome as Kit's presence in the cottage was the crumpled letter in her satchel. It had been waiting for her at the Anchor Inn that morning, a few lines of terrible news that multiplied the problems she already confronted.

The new headmistress at the Wetherwood Academy apologized for opening Miss Preston's letter, but she was unable to forward it. Miss Wetherwood had died a few months earlier, and since her fellow teachers served as her only family, they had taken it upon themselves to respond to any correspondence directed to her. Naturally they were sorry for their former student's plight. Miss Whitney's uncle had already made inquiries regarding her current location, and the headmistress promised to say nothing about Miss Preston's letter if approached with further questions. She conveyed her best wishes and her regrets that she could be of no help finding a safe place for Miss Whitney to reside.

It had been a mistake, Lucy reflected, placing all her hopes on Miss Wetherwood—God rest her soul. But who else was there? She could leave her employment, of course, and find a place far from Lancashire to hide out with Diana. For a few months they could scrape by in frugal lodgings, but then her savings would run out. More than half had already been spent to get them where they now were.

But the cottage at Cow's Mouth was no longer secure. She had purchased a copy of the Lancaster newspaper, and sure enough it carried a notice of a reward being offered for the missing heiress. That notice would continue to run, she would wager, until someone tracked Diana down and claimed the five hundred pounds.

The steady rain, little more than a drizzle, seeped through her black kerseymere dress. Beneath the felt bonnet and veil, her brown wig was already sodden.

When Diana wrote of her troubles, Lucy had thought herself capable of handling the situation. Indeed, she had felt an uncommon surge of anticipation at the prospect of a genuine adventure. Were the stakes not so high, she might have enjoyed the challenge and the chance to escape her humdrum existence for a short time. Indeed, she thought with a pang of remorse, there was a brief period in the beginning when she had actually enjoyed putting her imagination and wits to the test. She had felt positively exhilarated at her successes.

But in the end she had failed. Or was so near to failing that it made no difference.

The two men who shared the top of the coach with her had turned their backs, dangling their legs over the side and occasionally swigging from the bottle. While they were paying her no attention she raised the veil and tilted her head to the oyster-colored sky, letting the rain cool her face.

It was Diana who would pay the price for her failure. Why had she been so sure of herself? What might she have done that she failed to do?

Well, it never paid to look back, she supposed. Regrets could suck all the life and hope from a body. And it wasn't as if she could give up, call it a day, and retreat to Dorset. She had taken responsibility for Diana. She was stuck with that decision for the next two years. And she'd make the same decision if she had it to do again, so what was the point of gnashing her teeth about it?

She leaned back against a portmanteau, closed her eyes, and prayed wordlessly for divine help.

"Warton!" the driver called, jolting her from a restless half sleep.

Lucy rubbed rainwater from her lashes and peered through the heavy drizzle. Good heavens, was that Robbie standing beside the coach, his arms raised to help her alight? But why in blazes was he here? He was supposed to be at the cottage, standing watch over Kit.

"Whatever has happened?" she asked as he set her on her feet.

"The cat's from the bag," he replied laconically. "Come along, lass. The wagon's in the stable. I'll tell you the rest when we're on our way."

Knowing that he would speak when he'd a mind to and not before, she waited until he had steered the pony onto the muddy road before plucking at his sleeve. "I cannot endure this a moment longer, Robbie."

"Aye. Well, 'tis a brief tale. Your smuggler found the trapdoor this morning. Miss Whitney has told him the whole, or enough so as he knows who she is and why she's gone to ground."

And so much for the efficacy of prayer, she thought glumly. "Where is he now?"

"Still to the cottage when I left. He was building something or t'other. Sent me off to Silverdale for planks and hammer and nails. When I got back, he told me to fetch you so as you wouldn't have to walk." Robbie chuckled. "The laddie likes to snap out the orders, he does."

"And you took them like a sheep? By now he may have hauled Diana away and turned her over to the magistrate."

"If I thought he'd a mind to that, I wouldna left him alone with her."

Lucy swallowed her first several reactions and released only a sigh. What was done was done. At length she patted Robbie's hand. "There was a letter at the Anchor Inn, but the news isn't good. The lady I applied to for assistance has gone to her heavenly reward, I'm afraid, so there will be no help from that quarter."

"And from a solicitor?"

"Nothing. It was a disaster from beginning to end. The first three I approached turned me away, because I look poor, I suppose. And the fourth was a horrid little man, with greasy hair sleeked back like paint and dirty fingernails. I disliked him on sight, but he agreed to answer questions for ten minutes at no charge, and I was growing desperate."

She grabbed Robbie's arm as he made the turn onto the rough track that led to the cottage. "I made up a story, of course, to explain why I was in search of information about the rights of a legal guardian over his ward. The solicitor appeared to know little of such matters. Practically nothing, in fact. Instead of giving me answers, he kept asking more questions about my mythical younger brother. Specifically, he wanted to know where my brother lived and prodded me to bring him to the office so that he could take up his case. By then I knew he was useless, if not dangerous, and took my leave."

"Well, lassie, it's been a busy day all 'round. Now we've your smuggler to deal with. You want me to take him into Silverdale?"

"I must speak with him, of course. But when he learns about the reward, he will almost certainly try to claim the money. We dare not risk turning him loose until Diana and I are gone. Could you hold him at the cottage for perhaps twenty-four hours? That will give us time to catch a mail coach and be miles away before he finds a constable."

"Away to where?"

"It doesn't matter. The point is, we must leave here immediately."

Robbie frowned. "I can shackle him for a time, but I expect Miss Diana won't like it."

"He has charmed her, I can readily believe. He's a knack for it, and she knows nothing of the world, let alone worldly men."

"I ken she had a hard lesson from her uncle," Robbie said. "As for the smuggler, hauling a load of spirits across the sands don't make him the devil."

"Nonetheless, he is assuredly a thief, a liar, and a lecher. He cannot be trusted. The pattern is unmistakable. When we arrive, please conceal yourself until I give you a signal. He won't be suspicious if he thinks you gone and himself alone with two helpless females."

Robbie subsided into a dour silence.

She'd a fairly good idea what he was thinking, though. For all that she was eight years Diana's senior, she knew little more about men of the world.

To be sure, a number of the men in service at Turnbridge Downs had made advances when first she took up her post, but she made it pointedly clear that none would be accepted. From then on they kept their distance. Otherwise, almost the whole of her experience was confined to males under the age of eleven or twelve. Those she could handle . . . more or less.

Kit put her forcibly in mind of the spoiled, self-indulgent boys she had been governess to these past several years. He had not grown up, and his kind never did. She had observed his like when Lady Turnbridge invited her lovers, which she changed nearly as often as she changed her bonnets, to her frequent house parties. The gentlemen were all cut from the same mold—young, handsome, charming, and unrepentantly immoral.

Exactly like Kit. Well, perhaps without his intelligence and humor, but equally feckless. Kit flirted with her, and there was no mistaking that he did, but he flirted by nature with whatever female was to hand. It meant nothing. When he was gone, she would be no more in his memory than the taste of last night's dinner.

But then, men of that ilk would meet with no success were foolish females not so vulnerable to their smiles and cozening words. She ought to put him from her mind. She *must* put him from her mind.

But there he was, handsome as sin, when she entered the cottage. He was seated across the table from Diana, who was holding up a cracked mirror while he scraped a razor down his lathered cheek.

"How very cozy," Lucy said, dropping her satchel at her feet. "Have you by chance taken leave of your senses, Diana?"

"She has decided to be sensible," Kit advised, "and you are dripping water like a gutter spout. Go change into Luke, will you? No, make it the fearsome Lancashire Witch. I've a fancy to have a closer look at her."

Insufferable! "Come, Diana. I wish to speak with you privately."

Diana followed her into the back room and closed the door. "Robbie told you what happened, of course. Please don't be angry with me, Lucy. I couldn't help that he found me, and I couldn't help speaking with him, either. Nor am I sorry for it. We need his help."

"What we need is to get away from here," Lucy said in a rough whisper. "Speak softly, please. He's probably listening at the door."

"Why would he? I've told him everything. And he expects you to make a fuss about it, too. Indeed, I believe he is rather looking forward to it."

"I daresay." Lucy handed her the veiled hat and started pulling pins from the heavy wet wig. All the trouble she had taken to keep him from finding out, and he had gotten the better of her. She felt like a fool. "He appears in remarkably good health of a sudden."

Diana passed her a towel. "Kit says he is never ill, and that the best cure for a fleabite is to ignore it. This afternoon he—"

"What did he tell you about himself?" she interrupted, wanting as much information as possible before confronting him again.

"Little of significance. His name is Christopher Etheridge and he has two older brothers. Mostly he was asking me questions. When I spoke of my p-parents' death, he said that his own were killed in a snowstorm when he was a child. Otherwise, I learned almost nothing about him that I credit. He has been entertaining me with outrageous stories this last hour, but they are surely invented."

"And what did you tell him of me?" Lucy stripped off the dress and stuffed her legs into Luke's trousers.

"Only those bits that directly related to my own situation. He knows that you were teaching at Miss Wetherwood's academy when we met, and that you left to take another position. I told of writing to ask your advice, and how you have been helping me since. Of course I had to explain Luke and Mrs. Preston and the witch."

There was little else to tell, really, Lucy thought as she pulled on her shirt. The story of her inconspicuous life could be summed up in a few terse sentences. And the one time she had been summoned to do something extraordinary, she had failed to measure up. She had taken responsibility to keep Diana safe for two years, but there was no assurance she could do so for even one more day.

Diana must know it, too. She had already transferred her loyalty to a reprobate smuggler. Lucy decided not to tell her what she and Robbie planned to do. When Kit was safely under guard, she would somehow convince Diana to come away.

She wriggled her feet into Luke's boots and combed her fingers through her damp hair, aware of Diana watching her with a look of apprehension on her face. Lucy cast her a reassuring smile. "We'll come about, I promise you. And do not be overset when Kit and I wind up at daggers drawn. From the first we have disliked each other."

Diana smiled, the first genuine smile Lucy had seen since school days. "Oh, he likes you well enough. And no, he has not said so. But I can tell."

"Goose-wit." Lucy smiled back. "You know even less of men than I do."

"Perhaps that was true a year ago," Diana said softly. "I've since become acquainted with my excessively stupid uncle and the reptile he is determined to foist upon me. I know a good deal about bad men, Lucy. Kit is not one of them."

"I'm keeping an open mind," Lucy said, her hand on the door latch. "Shall we see if he can convince me he is on the side of the angels?"

Chapter 8

Kit was firmly in league with the devil, Lucy saw the very moment she opened the door.

He raised the wine bottle he was holding in a salute. "Come have a drink, Miss Luke. You look as if you need one."

"Where did you get that?" she demanded.

"There's a great lot of it out on the sands, you know. This afternoon I liberated as many bottles as I could carry."

Her heart sank. Anyone could have seen him on the bay at low tide. Had the man no sense whatever?

"Never mind scowling at me," he said. "I knew you wouldn't approve, but I'm fond of good wine and dislike seeing it go to waste. Besides, there was no one out there. I checked with my spyglass."

"As if you could spot a cockler through the fog and drizzle!"

"No more than one could spot me," he replied gently. "And if any such favored this particular area, I expect they'd long since have made off with the wine and brandy. The wagon has already sunk deep into the sand, I'm sorry to say, and the boxes will have disappeared by the next low tide." He crossed to her and pressed a cup into her hand. "Relax, Lucy. Or if you insist, Miss Preston, but I'd rather not."

"Call me what you will," she said indifferently. He would do so in any case. "Diana has told you the whole, I apprehend."

"Enough to explain how you came to be here, and why. In return, I gave her my promise to help. And yes, my dear, I'm well aware you won't permit me to do so without mounting an argument beforehand." He raised his voice. "Come on out, Diana. I require your protection."

Diana slipped through the door, clearly apprehensive.

He guided her to a chair. "It will be safer here," he advised her in a theatrical whisper. "Keep your eyes open, darling, and tell me when to duck."

Lucy glared at him. "This is not a joking matter, sir. Do you take nothing seriously?"

"In my experience, sticking a ramrod up my back never solved a problem." He poured a glass of wine for Diana. "Where is Robbie, by the way? Has he gone back to Silverdale, or is he lurking outside, waiting for the order to clamp me in irons while you scarper?"

So much for keeping one step ahead of him. "I cannot permit you to leave here until we are gone, sir. And you understand very well why that is."

"I understand you think it necessary," he said evenly. "And I mean to change your mind. Shall we invite Robbie to join us? We're going to need his help, once we've settled on a plan of action."

She put down her cup. "I'll hear you out, as if I'd any choice in the matter. But I shall not be easily convinced of your good intentions."

"Somehow I had guessed that." He fixed her with a level gaze. "Remember, Lucy, that it is Diana's future at stake. At the end of the day, she must make the decisions."

"To be sure." And now he was *lecturing* her, for heaven's sake! She stomped to the door and called to Robbie.

He emerged from the heavy drizzle, removing his hat and shaking water from the brim before entering the cottage.

"Oh, do come over to the fire," she said, instantly repentant. "I should not have left you outside in this beastly weather."

"Pay me no mind, lass." He pulled off his gloves. "I'm half m' life in the rain."

Kit handed him the bottle of wine. "This will warm you up, old sod. Finish it off while I broach another."

"Oh, lovely. Precisely what we need here." Lucy watched Robbie drop cross-legged near the fireplace and take a hearty swig from the bottle. "The pair of you foxed."

"Rest easy, Lady Temperance," Kit said. "It would take good Scotch whisky and a lot of it, too, for yon braw laddie to be feeling no pain. And as I've a long ride ahead of me tonight, three or four cupfuls will be my limit." He selected another bottle of wine. "See? You've nothing to worry about."

"Not a thing," she said, throwing up her hands. "And exactly where were you planning to ride, sir?"

"Home." He drew out the cork with the casual ease of experience. "Do you ever mean to close that door, Lucy?"

She did so with a decided slam, feeling outnumbered and overwhelmed. But not overmatched, she told herself bracingly. Should she rule that Kit was not to be trusted, Diana and Robbie would surely back her up. She had already proven herself, after all, while Kit had nothing to recommend him but a honeyed tongue and an undeniable degree of charm.

"Diana told me that you intended to speak with a solicitor today," he said. "Had he anything of use to offer?"

"To the contrary." Lucy released a heavy sigh. "I should not have approached him, knowing nothing of his competence or his character. It was a mistake."

"Seeking counsel from a stranger is generally unwise," he agreed, "but you are correct that Diana's best hope of safety lies with the courts and a legal change of guardianship. Two years is a devilish long time to hide out."

"Eighteen months," Diana amended softly, brushing her scarred cheek with her forefinger. "And I don't mind hiding, you know. I've no wish to go out in public."

"Nor will anyone compel you to do so until you are ready," he assured her. "Still, there is no reason to live in fear of discovery for so long a time. We require a lawyer, the best in the country, and I happen to know how to find him."

Lucy placed little faith in any lawyer Kit was likely to produce. This was not a matter of petty thievery or evading tariffs

91

on imported wine, after all. With effort, she refrained from pointing that out.

He was looking at Diana with a serious expression. "I owe you an apology, my dear. When I introduced myself this morning, I failed to give you the whole of my name. Forgive me, but it didn't seem relevant at the time. I had not heard your story, and because I generally take care not to entangle the family in my more unsavory pastimes, I told a half lie. The Christopher Etheridge part is true, but my surname is Valliant. Which probably means nothing to you," he added with a smile, "since you grew up in Lancashire and our estate is in Westmoreland."

"Pardon me," Lucy cut in, "but what has your name to do with anything? May we return to the point?"

"Patience, moonbeam. I'm getting there. You think me singularly useless, I know, but perhaps you will put a bit of credit in my brother, the Earl of Kendal. He served with the Foreign Office during the war and is acquainted with nearly everyone of importance. I mean to place Diana under his protection, and you may be sure that she could not be in safer hands."

"If you imagine I'll let you take her away and pass her over to a brother who may or may not exist, you are very much mistaken." She advanced on him in a fury. "This is purely nonsense. Another of your lies. You mean to return her to her guardian and pocket the reward."

"Had I such a plan in mind," he said calmly, "we would have been long gone before you returned from Lancaster."

"I know something of the Earl of Kendal," Robbie said. "My wife, God rest her, was cousin to Angus Macafee."

"The gatekeeper at Candale," Kit explained. "That's the family estate, and Angus has worked there since I was in short pants."

Struggling to compose herself, Lucy picked up her neglected cup and took a long drink. The wine felt smooth on her tongue and warm sliding down her throat.

So Kit the smuggler had turned out to be the son of an earl. Well, she could hardly be surprised. He possessed enough self-confidence for ten aristocrats, and he was certainly accustomed to taking charge and issuing orders. But his rank won him nothing from her. She'd no great liking for the spoiled sons of a privileged class, especially those who thought it a lark to box the watch or smuggle wine when they could well afford to buy it from a reputable merchant. And his sort too often assumed that any female luckless enough to cross their path, a governess, for example, was a prime target for seduction. She had stuck a long hat pin into more than one aristocratic hand that wandered where it was not welcome.

"What does it matter that your brother is an earl?" she asked stubbornly, digging her heels into what she knew was shaky ground. "Why would he help Diana? She is nothing to him. And would he not be breaking the law to conceal her from her legal guardian?"

"Bending it, perhaps. He won't mind. And the moment he is acquainted with Diana's circumstances, he will insist on taking her under his wing. I know him, Lucy. And when you meet him, you will trust him as I do."

"But I haven't met him. I've only met you. Need I go into detail about my misgivings?"

"I believe you have made yourself clear on more than one occasion," he said, grinning. "But Diana wishes me to proceed— don't you, butterfly?—so we may as well come to the sticking point. Unless you wish to prolong this row?"

She did, if only for pride's sake, but that was not reason enough. Lucy had been long in service. She knew her own unimportance, and she recognized defeat. "What will you do then?"

Kit regarded her with a look of surprise. "Well, to begin with, I mean to set out for Candale tonight and put my brother to work. He'll know better than I what must happen next, and because he is lamentably methodical, we must assume that nothing will happen quickly. Meantime Diana requires some other refuge than this. I take it that you no longer consider this cottage secure?"

"Not since you arrived," she fired back. "And if smugglers have begun operating in this vicinity, I fear one of them will learn of the cave and make use of it. We never meant to stay here for very long in any case. It is too close to Diana's home."

"She should be removed to another county, I expect, where the Lancashire magistrate has no authority. Candale, most like, but perhaps somewhere else in Westmoreland. We'll see what my brother has to say. In the interim, Lucy, while I am gone, can I trust you not to run off?"

Trust? The word never failed to set demons dancing in her head. She trusted no one, not even herself. But that was not the question, she realized when the demons had retired to the shadows again. Kit wanted to know if she kept her promises, not that she'd given him any, and she didn't know how to answer.

She would deceive him if she thought it necessary. She lied when lies were called for. Truth and trust were ideals, after all. Chimeras. Whom did she know who had kept faith with her? Diana didn't count. Diana had given her faith because she had nowhere else to turn. And by doing so, she had led Lucy to assume false identities and tell one lie after another until she could scarcely keep track of them all.

"How long is an *interim*?" she finally asked.

"Another day," Kit replied. "Two at the most, depending on what my brother advises. And since Diana will most likely be transferred elsewhere, I suggest that Robbie start taking away as many of her possessions as she can do without until she is settled again. There is a considerable amount of luggage in the cave, I couldn't help but notice."

Robbie shuffled to his feet. "If you mean to be going, I'll see to saddling the horse. And I'll carry the cases up here so the lassie can sort through them by the fire."

"Diana?" Lucy crossed to her. "Think carefully. Is this what you wish?"

Head bowed, Diana studied her folded hands. "Not if you mislike it," she said in a meek voice.

Lucy shot a look at Kit. You see how it is? she wanted to exclaim. Diana could make no decision on her own. Or she *would* not. Since writing the letter and pleading for assistance, her one positive action, she had left everything in Lucy's hands.

Kit lowered one hip on the table. "It occurs to me," he said mildly, "that she is torn between her gratitude to you and what she now considers the right course of action. And you *are* asking her to choose sides, you know."

Lucy felt heat rise up her neck. "Is that true, Diana? Do you feel obligated to agree with me against your own true opinion?"

She gave a barely perceptible nod.

Oh, damn. There was only one thing to say then, and it was the last thing Lucy wished to say while Kit was present to hear it. But he would not be dislodged, so she swallowed the frayed remnants of her pride and produced a reassuring smile. "You have mistaken me, Diana. I am quite in agreement with Mr. Valliant's plan, which far surpasses any I could devise under the circumstances. We are fortunate indeed that he has elected to take up our cause. So what do you say? Shall we seize this opportunity while it is ours?"

"Oh, yes," Diana replied immediately. "I'm so glad you think it best."

To Lucy's surprise, Kit refrained from gloating. He contented himself with a nod—of approval, she imagined—in her direction before turning to Diana. "Select only the few items you can carry with you, butterfly. Robbie will bring the rest soon enough. With luck I shall return by noon tomorrow and escort you to your next temporary home. Have you any questions before I set out?"

Diana raised trusting eyes to his face. "No, sir. But surely you will not leave while it is still raining?"

"If I wait, I'll be forced to travel in the dark." He drank the last of his wine and set the cup on the table. "Besides, the sooner I am gone, the sooner I'll be back again."

Robbie came into the room carrying three pieces of luggage. "The beastie is saddled, and I ken he's aching for a hard run."

"Well, so am I," Kit said cheerfully. "Neither of us can bear being cooped up for any amount of time. Have you a place, Robbie, to secure Miss Diana's possessions for a day or two?"

"Aye. There's storage in the rooms above the apothecary shop."

"Excellent!" Kit stood. "When I need to make contact, I'll leave word for you there."

"That's best. I'll stay close to ground, there or here. Ye'll have no trouble finding me."

"In that case, it's time for me to go. Miss Lucy, will you come along with me to the cave? I'll need directions how to proceed from there." He paused by Diana's chair and brushed a kiss on her scarred cheek. "Take courage, butterfly. All will be well."

Heart racing, Lucy went ahead of him down the stairs into the shadowy cave. A heavy mist hovered in the air, and the limestone walls streamed with condensed moisture. The horse was a dark, restless presence, digging at the ground with his hooves and sensing, she supposed, that he was soon to be free of his prison. She stayed well clear of him.

"That galled you, admitting that I was right," Kit said as he came up beside her. "Did it not?"

"I've no idea what you are referring to," she replied acerbically. "We should have asked Robbie to come down and help you mount."

He chuckled. "Confess, Lucy. It's good for the soul. You were practically chewing iron nails when you told Diana that you approved my plan."

"Oh, I did tell her so." Lucy waved a hand. "But I *admitted* nothing. You take my meaning, I am sure."

"A more bullheaded female never walked the earth," he said, ruffling her hair. "But you did the right thing, moonbeam. I'll not tease you for it."

"Thank you for patronizing me, sir. Above all things, I enjoy being treated like a nitwit."

He was standing so close to her back that she could feel the rumble in his chest when he laughed. And feel the heat of his breath against her nape, and then the hand that slipped around her waist and drew her against his body. Wings fluttered against her skin, inside her chest, everywhere that he was not touching her already. She could not account for how she felt, and it terrified her to experience such total—what? Longing? Weakness? Curiosity? She'd no idea. He snatched away every coherent thought and all but the last shreds of her will.

Unable to speak, unable to move, she simply stood where she had no right to be, in the embrace of a man who found it amusing to flirt with her. He held her lightly, his hand resting beneath her breasts, taking no other liberties. She wondered if she would permit them if he tried. She wondered if she wanted him to try.

"Diana will be perfectly fine," he said quietly. "She's a plucky little thing, and once the shock has passed, she will come about."

The sudden change of subject, the very arrogance of his words, snapped her free of his spell. She seized his hand, removed it forcibly from her waist, and turned to confront him. "How can you be so ignorant? You have no idea—none at all—what she has endured and what she will endure for years to come. Wherever she goes, people will stare at her. Some will remark on the scar, some will turn away, and always she will know what they are thinking."

"That is a most cynical view of life, I must say. The next time you are in a crowd, moonbeam, look around you. Do you flinch at the sight of a face pocked from a bout of smallpox, or take disgust when you see a man shorn of a leg or an arm? Some folks are cruel, others thoughtless, but not everyone passes instant judgment based on appearances alone."

"It's not the same thing," she protested. "Diana was meant to have a glorious London Season and marry well. It was what she was bred and educated to do. She knows nothing else. You are of her class, sir. What do you suppose would happen if she appeared at a fashionable ball? Would she even receive an invitation from a hostess who had actually seen her face?"

He looked unaccustomedly serious. "Should she attempt to make her come-out, she would not take. I cannot deny that. But London is not the world, Lucy. There are any number of men who would count themselves fortunate to win her affections."

"Because of her considerable wealth, I daresay. The gleam of golden guineas will blind them to all else. There is little doubt she can wed a fortune hunter, if she so chooses, but is there any hope of marrying for love?" Lucy was in full cry now, and could no more have held her tongue than flown to the moon. "I expect—no, I am sure—that you have enjoyed the favors of a great many women. Was any one of them less than beautiful?"

Color rose on his cheeks. "Must I answer that?"

"You have already done so." She gave him an icy glare of satisfaction.

He met her gaze steadily. "Like most men, I am attracted to beautiful females. I'll not deny it. As for my 'great many women,' you are not far off the mark. There have been more than a few. Were they all beautiful? I'm not certain if others would account them so. I am also drawn to women of wit and intelligence and courage. Women of passion. In some cases—perhaps *most* cases, although I cannot swear to it—they would not be regarded as Incomparables. But I assure you, they were beautiful to me."

The wind fell out of her sails with such a rush that she nearly toppled. And then she remembered that Kit was nothing if not silver-tongued. He could talk the bark off a tree. "Well argued, sir. So tell me this. If Diana were without a fortune, would you ever consider taking her to wife? Could you fall in love with her in spite of her scar?"

His clear blue-eyed gaze never wavered. "I expect so. Indeed, I am certain of it. She is precisely the sort of woman I most admire—gallant and honorable and loyal—Lucifer! I could list the virtues I sense in her for another hour or more. Yes, I could love her and wed her, were she the one who captured my heart. But by the time I discovered Diana skulking in this cave and came to know and admire her, I was already head over ears in love with someone else."

"Oh." Lucy felt small and foolish. Also devastated, although she could not have said why. His romantic attachments were none of her concern. "I beg your pardon, sir. I was speaking theoretically, of course. To be sure you could not wed Diana if your attentions are otherwise directed."

"And so they are. But I take your lesson to heart, moon-beam. You know better than I about Diana's state of mind, and any man who tries to guess what a woman is feeling has attics to let. Shall we cry peace?"

A prickly lump clogged her throat. It was one thing to know she could never have his love and something else altogether to know that another woman already had it. She felt as if she'd just awakened from a dream she couldn't remember. "Sh-should you not be on your way?" she asked in a murmur.

"Yes." He untethered his horse. "Is there a way out of here other than across the sands? I'm not of a mind to play another game of tag with the bore tide."

"Turn to the left," she directed, "and ride alongside the cliff. It ends about a mile down, and if you follow the track from there, you can pick up the road about two miles inland."

"I'll find it. And Lucy, stay to ground until I return. No more—what did Diana call them? Ah, yes. No more *hauntings*. Where did you come by that long wig, by the way? From a dis-tance, it looked exactly like your own hair."

"That's because it is. Did not Diana tell you that I am a governess?"

"Lucifer!" He laughed heartily. "No, she did not tell me, al-though I should have guessed it. But what has that to do with your hair?" He turned to her, his expression suddenly serious. "Never tell me your employer ordered you to cut it off?"

"She would not dare. I assure you, my employer does every-thing possible to retain my services against all but impossible odds. Before I came, no governess had survived longer than a fortnight, and I am paid exceedingly well to put up with five boys hell-bent on ridding themselves of all authority. For the most part, I have managed to keep the upper hand these last few years."

Lucy forced what she hoped sounded like nonchalance into her voice. "One night the oldest took a notion to rid me of my hair. He was ever on the lookout for my weaknesses, and must have concluded that I was vain about my appearance. So while I was asleep in my room he crept in with a pair of scissors, took hold of a sizable handful of hair, and sheared it off. I woke immediately, but not before the damage was done. There was little choice at that point but to cut off all the rest, and so I did. When I presented the remains to my employer, along with a list of demands, she gave me another rise in salary and dispatched my hair to Ede and Ravenscroft in London to have a wig made up. At the time I never imagined the use it would be put to, nor did I have occasion to wear it until I began playing the Lancashire Witch."

He was regarding her with a look she could not begin to decipher. "I see," he said, dropping the reins he'd been holding. "Stay, Jason."

Before she guessed what he was about, she was in his arms and he was kissing her. *Kissing her!* And thoroughly, too, in ways she'd never imagined that kisses could be. Time stopped, moons and planets ground to a halt, and her mind spun away, leaving the rest of her to revel in her first taste of bliss.

When he finally let her go and stepped away, she could only gaze blankly at him. Bewildered, bedazzled, she saw him swing onto his horse and look back at her with a smile on the lips she wished were still pressed to hers.

And then he was gone.

She stood for a long time, wondering what had just happened, amazed that she had let it happen. But eventually, she came back to earth. For him, it was only a routine kiss, the kind he gave to any female who raised no objections. To her shame, it had never occurred to her to object. And however soul-shaking and body-melting his kisses, she knew better than to refine too much on them.

This incident had never happened. She would not think on it ever again.

Chapter 9

The rain ceased not long after Kit rode away from the cave, and he was relatively dry by the time he arrived at Candale several hours later.

The butler greeted him with a smile that immediately collapsed into a worried frown. "Er, welcome home, Mr. Christopher. I shall have a fire built in your room immediately. Would you care for a late supper?"

"Hullo, Geeson. You are looking well. I, of course, look like hell, but I assure you that I am perfectly fine. Sorry to barge in without advance warning. I'd welcome a meal about two hours from now, after I'm done consulting with my brother. Where is he to be found?"

"Lord and Lady Kendal are in the upstairs parlor, sir."

He headed for the staircase. "Thank you, Geeson. I'll spring on them unannounced."

When Kit sauntered into the room, the earl was seated at a *secrétaire* with a pen in his hand and Celia was half-reclined on a sofa by the fireplace. "How utterly picturesque," he drawled. "A veritable portrait of domestic bliss."

"Kit!" Celia tossed her knitting aside and jumped up to embrace him. "What a lovely surprise. But what on earth has happened to you?"

He arched his brows. "Why, Celia, I cannot think what you mean."

"Oh." She fingered the fringe on his sling. "Well, then, forget that I asked."

His sister-in-law, bless her, always knew when to let him be. "Where's the infant?"

"Sleeping, I'm afraid."

"And as it required two hours to achieve this miracle," Kendal put in, "asleep he will stay. May I inquire why you are limping?"

"Am I indeed?" Kit made a show of examining his sandaled feet. "Which leg would that be?"

"Ah. I take it, then, that questions regarding the somewhat flamboyant shawl you are wearing would be unwelcome."

"Of course they would," Celia said. "Didn't he just tell us so quite plainly? We're very glad to see you, Kit, and I hope you mean to stay a long while this time. By the way, there are three letters from Charley on the dressing table in your room. He is doing exceedingly well at Harrow, despite the incident with the snake. I only wish the terms were not so long. We miss him enormously."

"I'll nip over for a visit one of these days," Kit promised. "Always a good idea to stay on good terms with the heir in case I need to borrow money." Charley was Kendal's son by his first wife, rising ten years old now, and Kit was especially pleased to hear news of a snake. There was a time the boy wouldn't say boo to a goose, let alone get up to normal schoolboy pranks.

Kendal steepled his hands under his chin. "That means, I presume, that you have dropped by to beg a loan. Or is it that the constable is hard on your heels?"

"Alas, Jimmie, you always think the worst of me. But as it happens, you are right on both counts. Well, I am by no means certain the constables have twigged they *ought* to be chasing me, so perhaps they are not. At least it is the Lancashire officials I have run afoul of this time. Westmorland has been spared my latest crime spree."

"You relieve my mind," Kendal said dryly. "How much is this going to cost me?"

"I wish I knew. What is the going rate for rescuing damsels in distress?"

"I beg your pardon?"

Satisfied that he had managed to flap his generally unflappable brother, Kit went to the sideboard and lifted the stopper from a crystal decanter. After one sniff, he put it back again. "Hog swill. You may know your brandy, old sod, but you've no respect for good wine. I need the money for the ladies, by the way. My services are free. And, I should add, unwelcome."

"They don't wish to be rescued?" Celia asked, her dark eyes wide with curiosity. "But who are they, Kit? Must you play these games? Do tell us what is going on."

"A more ungrateful pair of wenches you've never met. One of them, anyway. She would sooner see me hang than accept my help." Kit gave the bellpull a hearty tug. "She is also the woman I mean to marry."

Celia emitted a squeal of delight.

"Don't believe a word of it," Kendal advised her coolly. "Kit's love affairs have the endurance of a snowflake on a griddle."

"My *affairs*, perhaps. But when, Jimmie old lad, have you ever heard me say that I was in love?"

"Never," Kendal replied after some thought. "I grant you that. So why is this different?"

"I've no idea. How did you know you were in love with Celia?"

"I believe that you pointed it out to me."

"So I did. Good of you to admit it after all this time." He bowed. "Obviously I am able to recognize the symptoms of true love, and at the moment I've got most all of them. Oh, not the ones which had you behaving like a jackass, for I have been a perfect darling from the first. But Lucy persists in thinking me a villain, and I'll not make any progress changing her mind until the other damsel is free of her dragon uncle."

"And thereby hangs a tale." Kendal went to the sofa to sit beside his wife. "May I hope you will get to it in some comprehensible fashion before young Christopher Alexander starts howling for his next meal?"

"Sorry. I'm partial to melodrama." Kit gave himself a mental kick on the backside for even mentioning his personal interest in Lucy, which would only distract everyone from the immediate problem. Were she present, his beloved would inform him in no uncertain terms that he was being self-indulgent and more concerned with impressing—or shocking—his family than achieving his goals. Which was one of the reasons he so admired her, no doubt. It pleased him that she knew his flaws and weaknesses, of which there were a great many.

Even though she had yet to notice them, he'd been gifted with a few good qualities, too. Splendid looks, or so he had often been told by more forthcoming ladies. Charm. Energy. Humor. A quick mind. Compassion. An ability to mingle in any company, high or low. Considerable talent in the bedchamber. It was true that he'd put his gifts to waste or to no good purpose—not counting his skill as a lover—but he was yet young.

"Sir!"

The gaunt presence just inside the doorway sounded a trifle impatient, and Kit reckoned the butler had been trying to catch his attention for some time. "Sorry, Geeson. I was woolgathering." He flashed one of his sure-to-disarm smiles. "Bring up the best bottle of wine in the cellar, will you?"

With a groan, the earl signaled approval.

When Geeson had withdrawn, Kit dropped onto a chair across from Kendal and Celia. "Fact is, Jimmie, I need your help. A young woman, not the one I mean to wed, is in considerable trouble. There are lots of missing pieces to the story, you will quickly divine, but I shall tell you as much as I know."

He was well into his tale, carefully censored to omit an accounting of the events on Morecambe Bay, by the time Geeson returned with a decanted bottle of wine. Accepting a glass of claret, Kit nodded thanks and took a long, necessary drink. He had just finished describing Diana's scar and how she came by it, and his throat was painfully dry. It didn't help that tears were streaming down Celia's cheeks.

Kendal gave her his handkerchief and wrapped an arm around her shoulders. "Go on, Kit. I assume we've heard the worst, and I'm beginning to understand where you are leading."

He charged through the rest, knowing his brother would wrench order into his disorganized presentation of Diana's situation. "There is reason to believe she is no longer safe at the cottage where she has been hiding," he finished. "If I found her, others could do the same."

"You wish to bring her here then?"

"Will you have her?"

"Certainly, so long as you intend only for us to conceal her. But if you mean for me to undertake legal action against her uncle, which I expect that you do, Candale will be the first place he will look."

"So what if he does? You'd not hand her over."

"I could be forced to by legal means. Miss Whitney is subject to her guardian, however unworthy he may be. Should he elect to exercise his rights over her and pursue the matter diligently, I would have no choice but to, as you say, *hand her over*."

"Whyever not? Whitney cannot mount an army and storm the gates. Who could compel you even to admit she is here?"

Kendal released an exasperated sigh. "Kit, you have danced on the other side of the law for so long that you've forgot where the boundaries are set. I'm a civilized man, not a warlord. We'll do better to employ stealth than common deceit, let alone outright defiance."

"However much he might wish to," Celia remarked, "James will never swear to an untruth. And as you know, I have no gift whatever for deception. If Miss Whitney is here, even the most inept of magistrates would be able to read it on my face."

"There is Alex's house at Coniston Water," Kendal said thoughtfully. "We have not leased it out since the previous tenants moved away. And your own cottage in Hawkshead remains vacant, I believe."

Celia gathered up her knitting. "I have decided that I do not wish to know how you resolve this, gentlemen. I make a poor conspirator, given my lamentable habit of blurting the truth at the most inopportune times. And," she added, brushing a kiss on her husband's cheek, "men always speak more freely without a lady in the room."

Kit opened the door for her. "You're a trump, Countess. Now I won't be forced to mind my language."

"When have you ever done?" She sniffed at him and wrinkled her nose. "Mercy me, Kit. I shall have a tub brought to your room and instruct the kitchen staff to heat a lake's worth of water. Pray advise the servants when you are ready for your bath."

"Lucifer's privates!" Kit swore when she was gone. "How is it, Jimmie, that we have both fallen in love with managing females?"

"Is there any other kind?"

"None willing to put up with the likes of us, I suspect." Kit flopped onto the chair again and stretched his legs to the fire. "Sorry for any unpleasant odors wafting from my direction, by the way. The cottage where I spent the last few days didn't have provisions for bathing. Odd thing is, the ladies always smelled of fresh air and spring flowers. I've no idea how they managed it."

"And this is relevant in what way to the point at hand?"

"Right. Back to business. As you say, any property owned by the family will be a natural target for a search when our involvement becomes known. But is that inevitable? Our name cannot be kept out of it?"

"Not if I file a petition to remove Lord Whitney as the young lady's guardian and replace him with myself, which seems the next logical step. Mind you, I'm no expert on these matters. We require professional counsel before taking legal action of any kind."

"There's a chance you can be appointed her guardian? That would be the ideal solution!" Kit's enthusiasm quickly ran up against a wall. His brother had a family of his own, a large estate to manage, and scores of civic responsibilities Kit knew nothing about. What was more, the Earl of Kendal had never even met Diana Whitney. "Are you willing to take on such an obligation, Jimmie? I always assumed you would act on her behalf, but I reckoned that would involve no more than bringing her to Candale and hiring a solicitor. I never meant you should take personal charge of her."

Kendal draped his arm over the back of the sofa. "I am perfectly agreeable, so long as Celia has no objections. I cannot imagine that she will, but of course I must ask her before committing myself."

"Is that how things are done when one is married? Will I be required to ask Lucy's permission every time I want to buy a horse or . . . or brush my teeth?"

Laughing, Kendal shook his head. "I have pronounced myself willing to take on a ward I've never met and fight her case through the courts if need be, but damned if I mean to start passing out marital advice. When you are leg-shackled, Kit, you can bloody well stumble along the way the rest of us do."

"Sorry again. But the thing is, it's all tangled up together, my passion for Lucy and this mess with Diana. I can't think straight. What are we supposed to be talking about?"

"When we left off, we were discussing where to deposit Miss Whitney while I extricate her from the clutches of her uncle."

Kit adjusted his arm in the sling. "I'd figured on bringing her here, but clearly that won't do. Tell you what, Jimmie. I'm no good with the legal ins and outs, so you take charge of those. I'll put my mind to finding her a place to stay."

"Very well. But I require a good deal more information from you before I can be of service. What level of opposition are we facing?"

"Hard to tell. As I understand it, the new Lord Whitney has been living off his expectations for several years, is up to his eyebrows in debt, and stands to gain by marrying off his ward to Sir Basil Crawley. That's a considerable incentive to fight us for control."

"And what do you know of Crawley?"

"Other than the fact Diana won't have him, nothing. By her account, her uncle is a nincompoop and Crawley makes her skin crawl. He's the one pulling the strings, I have no doubt."

Kendal rubbed his chin. "I've heard his name, or read it, not too very long ago. Let me think on this a moment."

Kit used the opportunity to refill his wineglass and sort out his thoughts. It would be a wonder if his brother could make sense of the bits and pieces he had thrown at him thus far. But then again, who was better qualified? James had slithered through the courts of a dozen countries while Europe was at war, sifting solid information from the chaff of rumors and disinformation, manipulating kings and czars and ministers of state on behalf of England's foreign policy. Such as it was. He often said that England was its own worst enemy, and that he'd rather deal with Napoleon's Imperial Guard than a squabbling Parliament.

"I have it! Or I think I do." Kendal rose. "Come with me."

Kit followed his brother downstairs and into the study where he had been summoned far too many times, never willingly, to hear a lecture on proper behavior or to be punished for his latest offense. The room still made him bloody uncomfortable.

Kendal went to his desk and rummaged through the orderly stacks of paper that covered it end to end. "Yes, this is it. Have a look."

Kit took the folded card and saw his own name inscribed with those of Lord and Lady Kendal and Colonel Alexander Valliant. "He's invited us to a *ball*? Good Lord. Will you accept?"

"Under no circumstances. He has not been presented to me, and I was frankly astounded to receive this card. One only, mind you, addressed to all of us and sent by way of common post at that. I would have immediately declined, but unimportant matters are awaiting the return of my secretary, who is visiting his family in Carlisle."

"Hold off awhile longer, will you? I may decide to make an appearance."

"Is that wise?" Kendal sat behind the desk and steepled his hands. "It will draw unnecessary attention to the family before we are prepared to make our move."

"Know thine enemy, or something of the sort. Besides, I'm devilish curious to meet the fellow."

"If you must. But think on it before making a decision, will you? It won't help our case to put him on his guard."

Kit chuckled. "You never fail to underestimate me, Jimmie. I'll pop in at the ball, do a bit of reconnaissance, and pop out again, leaving Crawley none the wiser. Besides, you can hardly expect me to sit around doing nothing while you and the lawyers are huddled over your books."

"I certainly don't wish to have you hovering about and making a nuisance of yourself. But you must know it will be some time before we begin . . . er, huddling. The solicitor I have in mind to supervise the case resides in London."

"What's wrong with Carruthers? He could set to work immediately."

"To what purpose? He is well qualified to handle my affairs, but Miss Whitney's situation is quite out of the ordinary. There can be little precedent for what we mean to attempt, Kit. I have no connection to her family, nor even a long-standing acquaintance. Convincing the court to overturn her father's will, remove her from her uncle's custody, and declare her my legal ward will not be a simple matter. Indeed, I expect it to be impossible. But a battery of superb lawyers can tie this up in Chancery until Miss Whitney comes of age."

Kit mauled the back of his neck with taut fingers. "What would happen if Lord Whitney failed to contest the petition?"

"That would be altogether different." Kendal raised a brow. "Is there reason to think he will not?"

"Not a one that I know of. Just asking." Kit stood and began to pace, his mind churning with half-formed ideas. None of which he meant to reveal to his brother, of course, even when he had settled on a likely plan. "So what comes next?"

"I shall send a letter by tomorrow's post requesting that Mr. Bilbottom make the journey to Candale, and it will be well if I give him as much information as possible from the start. Tonight, I want you to write down what you have already told me, along with anything else that comes to mind. The injury done to Miss

Whitney's face is of particular importance, being evidence of her guardian's unsuitability. Pray describe it in detail."

"It happens I can do better. She allowed me to make sketches of her, although to convince her to do so, I had to half promise that no one would inspect her person directly."

"The sketches will certainly help, and I'll enclose them with your written report. But you must know that should all else fail, Miss Whitney could be summoned to testify."

"It won't come to that, I assure you."

Kendal looked displeased. "Do you mean to run wild behind my back?"

"Do you really want to know?"

"I suppose not. Just see that we are never acting at cross-purposes, and hold in mind that a young woman's future is at stake."

"I am well aware of that. Good Lord, Jimmie, I'm practically an old man. Knocking at thirty. Credit me with a particle of sense."

"One at most. But I'll spare you another of my traditional lectures, since you pay them no heed in any case." Kendal smiled. "Toddle off to your bath, ancient one. Write up your report and get some sleep. We'll meet again over breakfast."

"How the blue blazes does Celia put up with you?" Kit grumbled, slouching to the door.

"She is a woman of singular endurance, to my great good fortune. And on the subject of long-suffering females, when do I meet the one who may be required to put up with *you*?"

"Not *may*, sir. *Will,* sir. Consider, Jimmie, that if a smug, overbearing tyrant has won himself a wife like Celia, a dashing young cavalier such as myself cannot help but nab an equally remarkable bride. Mind you, if she is to have me, she must first beat out a rival for my affections."

Kendal's smile went cold. "You speak of Miss Whitney?"

"How you *do* leap to conclusions." Kit turned with his hand on the door latch. "I speak of Miss Fidgets, who happens to be an owl."

111

Well pleased with the astonished look on his brother's face, Kit made his way upstairs. The Honorable Christopher Alexander Valliant had been twelve days old when last he saw him, and two months had passed since then. Fortunately the infant was awake, to judge by the piercing screeches emanating from the room at the end of the passageway.

Celia looked up with obvious relief when he let himself into the nursery. "Come see if you can calm him down, Kit. I've been walking the room with him for an hour, but he won't stop crying."

"He's probably bored with the scenery, love. Try taking him out and about." He settled the infant in the curve of his good arm. "C'mon, rascal. I'll tell you a story about two maidens in distress and how your brave, resourceful uncle saved them from the wicked old dragon."

Celia shook her head when Christopher immediately stopped crying. "How do you *do* that?"

"Ineffable charm," he said, gazing down into a pair of wide blue eyes. "When are you going to grow some hair, young man? You put me in mind of a billiard ball. You're a beauty, though. When you've filled out some, you'll be almost as good-looking a fellow as your uncle Kit."

"I'm sorry to hear that," Celia said. "James tells me that Alex is far and away the handsomest of the Valliant brothers."

"Pay her no mind," he told the babe. "She's never seen him. I bet he'd come home, though, if he knew you were here. Has there been any word, Celia?"

"Not since the letter from Lima, and you've read that one. James replied immediately, but correspondence requires months to pass between England and South America, and Alex rarely stays in one place for very long."

"Take heed, Christopher. Everyone accuses *me* of being a here-and-thereian, but Uncle Alex is the true culprit. And I have excellent news for you tonight. By Michaelmas next, you are likely to have your very first cousin. I'm hoping she'll be a girl, though. Too many males in this family as it is."

"You are serious about this young woman you've met?" Celia asked.

"Absolutely." He glanced up. "If you've no objection, I mean to bring her here within the next few days."

"She is welcome, of course, for as long as she wishes to stay. But won't she prefer to go wherever it is you plan to put Miss Whitney?"

"I expect so. But if the lady I have in mind to ask does agree to take Diana, you may be sure I cannot send Lucy along. We are friends now, but there was a time we were a trifle more than that." Unaccountably, he felt heat rise up the back of his neck. "If you take my meaning."

"How could I not?" she said, laughing. "But will she be a suitable companion for a young girl like Miss Whitney?"

"You used not to be such a prude. Jimmie has corrupted you."

"I have corrupted him," she corrected, "and he has enjoyed every minute of it. But you must know that he can't help watching over you like a fussy hen. I know he gets on your nerves, but he practically raised you from an egg. He feels responsible for you."

"And I've not given him much to boast of since flying the nest." Kit nuzzled the infant's warm cheek, loving the milky smell of his breath and the tiny bubble that had formed at the corner of his mouth. "Your papa will be devilish surprised when I settle peaceably with my moonbeam. I'm going to hand you back to your mama now, and you are to treat her kindly. Agreed?"

The babe gurgled cheerfully, settling into Celia's arms without protest. "You will make a prodigiously fine father," she told Kit in a whisper.

"So I have always believed. And if Lucy gives me the chance, I shall also make a prodigiously fine husband."

Chapter 10

Late the next morning, Lucy took Kit's spyglass and went into the woods to look for Fidgets.

This would be their last day at Cow's Mouth cottage, assuming that all went as Kit had said it would. Diana was prepared to depart, the few possessions she meant to take with her wrapped in a woolen pelisse and tied up with string. She seemed calm, as if she had handed herself over to Kit and need no longer be concerned about her future.

With Fidgets disinclined to respond to her calls, Lucy left the trees and ascended the grassy hill to the limestone headland. The day was cool and clear, with a few clouds hanging in the sky like dandelion fluff and a fresh breeze blowing in from the ocean. She extended the spyglass and looked out over the sparkling bay. Near the shore, shallow water flowing over its long legs, a gray heron stood motionless, waiting for a meal to swim by. Leisurely, she enjoyed the view of Cartmel peninsula across the bay and the Lakeland fells rising in the distance.

At length she turned in the direction of the track that led to the cottage, amazed at how far she could see with the aid of the spyglass. All the way to the Warton road, in fact, although the road itself was invisible behind a screen of trees. She gazed over the rolling hills beyond the road and then back again, just in time to see two horsemen emerge from a break in the trees. They were moving slowly, but quite evidently had set themselves on the track to the cottage. She couldn't make out their faces, but one man was too barrel-shaped to be Kit and the other was far too small.

Wheeling, she sprinted down the hill and dashed into the cottage. "Cave!" she told a startled Diana, grabbing Mrs. Preston's dress from the hearthside where it had been left to dry. They had rehearsed what to do if a stranger suddenly appeared, so Diana went immediately to the trapdoor. Lucy closed it behind her, covered it with the thatched straw carpet, and tugged her portmanteau atop it.

A knock sounded as she was adjusting the wig. Quickly donning her bonnet, she lowered the veil, drew in a deep breath, and went to the door.

"Beggin' your pardon for the disturbance, ma'am," said a burly man with a large nose and red cheeks. "M'name is Ralph Planter, and I be constable for this parish. This here is Mr. Bartholomew Pugg come north from Bow Street, him bein' a Runner. We are come to inquire concernin' a young lady what's gone missing."

"Are you alone here?" Pugg asked, looking past her into the cottage with dark, intelligent eyes.

"Yes, certainly." She stepped aside. "Do come in, gentlemen. I would offer you refreshment, but as you see, nearly everything has been packed up for my journey."

Pugg prowled the room, examining the nearly bare shelves and the sparse furnishings. He paused to examine the spyglass, which she had dropped on the table in her rush. "This is a fine piece of work, madam."

"It belonged to my l-late husband. He died at Waterloo."

The constable regarded her solicitously. "My condolences, ma'am. Them was brave men. I lost a brother there, and another at Vittoria."

Recognizing a potential ally, she slipped her hand into her pocket and withdrew a painted miniature in a gilt frame. She had bought it at a secondhand shop in Lancaster, along with the black dress and the veiled mourning hat. The shop had been filled with items sold off by impoverished war widows, and

Lucy felt sad every time she looked at the face of the dark-haired young man, so solemn and proud as he sat for the artist.

"This is my Henry," she said, remembering to sniffle as she handed the miniature to the constable. "He sent it to me from Brussels, and it arrived a week after I had news of his death. I carry it always."

Pugg was at the window, lifting one of the heavy curtains to look outside. "An out-of-the-way place, I am thinking, for a female to be living alone."

"Oh, I have been here only a short time. Until a few weeks ago I resided with Henry's family. But they had disapproved our marriage, and resented keeping me after he was gone. Finally they decided that they had done their Christian duty by me and proceeded to toss me out."

"With nowhere to go?" Scowling, the constable gave her back the miniature. "That ain't Christian, to my way of thinkin'."

"They believed charity ought more properly to be dispensed by those of my own blood, and to be sure, I was most unhappy in their home. My sister and her husband have agreed to take in the poor relation, reckoning that I can be of help tending to their seven children." She tried to sound martyrish. "Unhappily, Henry and I had none of our own."

"That don't explain what you are doing *here*," Pugg said, turning with his hands clasped behind his narrow back.

Even through the heavy veil, she felt the force of his sharp gaze. No fool, Mr. Pugg, and singularly unimpressed with her tale of woe. But she went on with it, head bowed, for the constable's benefit. "A capricious fancy, I'm afraid, which struck me on the long journey from Devon. You see, since learning of Henry's death, I have never been alone to grieve for him. His parents are cold by nature and disliked any show of sensibility, and when I move in with my sister, there will be little chance for solitude amid so large a family. I suddenly longed to bid him farewell in my own way, near the seaside Henry and I so loved."

She made a distracted gesture. "A tedious story, I know. You must pardon me. I decided to seize a few weeks for myself before proceeding to York, so I turned west, to the coast. This cottage was available, and my savings reached to a month's rent. Does that answer your question, sir?"

He shrugged, and she could read nothing from his expression. "Seems odd for someone sez she likes the out-of-doors to keep the curtains closed. And I can't help but wonder why you are wearing that veil."

"My eyes," she said. "They can tolerate no more than a brief exposure to bright light, especially sunlight. I was born with the ailment, and it has proved a vast inconvenience, you may be sure. 'Tis a wonder Henry married me in spite of it, but he always took the greatest care to protect me. Naturally I do not wear the veil indoors when the curtains are closed, but you arrived just as I was preparing to go out for a walk." She lifted the veil and gave him a shy smile. "I am so used to having it on that I did not think to do this beforehand."

He scrutinized her cheek, and she knew that he had suspected it was Diana Whitney hiding herself under the veil. She only hoped he failed to notice that the brown wig was still damp. Pugg was an acute observer, though. Ought she to tell him she had washed her hair that morning?

No. Coming from nowhere, that would only make him more suspicious. An innocent woman is calm, she reminded herself, and curious why two officials had shown up on her doorstep. "I have told you why I took up residence in the isolated cottage, Mr. Pugg, but you've not explained why you are here."

"We are in search of a missing girl," he said shortly. "Reddish brown hair, hazel eyes, a scar on her right cheek. Seen anyone matching that description?"

"I have not, but I see almost no one save the blacksmith who brings supplies as he makes his rounds. I've been into Silverdale a time or two, but cannot recall encountering anyone with a scarred face. Is that all you wished to know?"

"Indulge me a few minutes longer," he said coolly. "If I am not mistaken, you were in Lancaster yesterday."

She gave him a look of surprise. "However did you know *that*? Good heavens. I had heard that Bow Street Runners were enormously skilled, but never imagined one might be keeping track of my inconsequential journeys. Yes, I went into Lancaster to run a few errands. How does it signify?"

"I'm not certain that it does," Pugg admitted. "A gentleman has employed me to trace Miss Diana Whitney, and yesterday a solicitor brought information regarding a veiled woman who made certain inquiries that raised his suspicions. A few routine questions at posthouses and like places directed me to you."

"Indeed? I did in fact call briefly on a solicitor and asked a few questions relating to my sister's unhappy situation. Her husband is something of a brute, and she . . . well, I shall explain the whole if you think it necessary, but I cannot see how it will help you. The solicitor struck me as something less than competent, and I confess to taking him in dislike from the first. After only a few minutes I took my leave." She wondered if Pugg could hear the blood pulsing in her ears. "Did he imagine it was the missing lady who had been in his offices, wearing a veil to conceal her scar?"

"Like as not. There is a reward for information leading to her whereabouts, and all manner of folk are turning up with claims of having seen her, most of them spurious. I followed up on this one because I'd been nosing about in the vicinity earlier in the week and heard reports of odd happenings near to this cottage."

Lucy held herself straight and forced an expression of mild interest to her face. "What sort of happenings? I have observed nothing unusual, but to be sure I generally remain indoors during daylight hours."

"It's an apparition of some sort, which appears only at night. Cocklers and mussel diggers have seen it walking along the cliff. Glows in the dark, it does."

"Some believe it's one of the Lancashire Witches," the constable put in, "come back to punish the descendants of them what hanged her."

"My word! But I must confess that I put no credit in the existence of witches."

The constable scuffed his booted toe on the dirt floor. "Most folk in these parts know the story. Down around Clitheroe, near Pendle Hill, there was some ladies charged with witchcraft and put to the gallows. This was mebbe two hunert years ago, but when I was a lad, there was tales of a witch what lived in this cottage until the landlord tried to evict her. She ran to the cliff and jumped, and he swore that he saw her fly away."

Lucy shuddered. "It's true that I'm not in the least superstitious, but by no means would I have leased this cottage if I'd known it was reputed to be haunted."

"One of the witches," Pugg said, "the leader of the coven, I believe, had the name of Preston. Same as you."

"My. That *is* an odd coincidence, sir. But I am most certainly not a witch. I do, however, occasionally take long walks at night, when I can be outside without wearing the veil. Do you suppose the cocklers saw moonlight reflecting off my clothing and let their imaginations run wild?"

Pugg rubbed at his chin with skinny fingers. "Happen they did. In my job, half the time is spent chasing rumors and following trails that lead to nowhere. But so long as we've come this far, madam, you won't object if we search the cottage?"

Her heart raced. She could think of no good reason to protest, and knew that any hesitation on her part would only increase his suspicions. So she put a smile on her face and made a sweeping gesture. "By all means, sir. There is only this room and the one through that door."

She didn't follow the men into the other room, fearing they would hear her heart thumping in her chest. There was little to see in there, so perhaps they would not remain very long. Moving to the doorway, she saw Pugg lift the portmanteau as if checking its weight. Did he imagine the missing girl was encased within it?

The constable appeared a trifle embarrassed. "Nothin' in here, sir."

"Evidently not." Pugg put down the portmanteau and examined the walls. "This bit was added on after the cottage was built. I wonder there's no window."

"Windows be taxed from time to time," the constable observed.

With horror, Lucy watched Pugg's gaze shift to the thatched carpet. Then he shrugged and started toward the door. She barely had time to exhale with relief before he abruptly went back, grabbed hold of a fraying corner, and pulled the carpet to one side.

She closed her eyes, unable to watch what was coming next.

"Eh, what's this?" The trapdoor creaked slightly as he pulled it open.

Forcing herself to look up, she saw both men bent over the square opening. Surprised that Mr. Pugg did not immediately make a move to descend the stairs, she drew closer and looked over his shoulder.

She gasped. "Dear me. I had no idea this was here." They were the only true words she had uttered since the men arrived. Instead of the shadowy cave and stone steps, there was only a wooden box about eight inches deep, the rough-hewn planks unevenly nailed together. Cobwebs matted the corners, and scattered in the sifting of dust covering the bottom were, unless she was very much mistaken, several of the shiny pellets Fidgets sometimes regurgitated. "Whatever can it be?"

Pugg lowered the trapdoor. "A hiding place for valuables, most like, dug out from the ground and lined with wood. This one's crude, but I doubt the people who constructed it had much to conceal. Any other buildings on the property, Mrs. Preston?"

"No." She followed him into the other room, the scalloped edges of the miniature she was still holding digging into her palm. "Is there anything else you wish to know, sir?"

"The location of the nearest pub house," he replied with a self-mocking laugh. "I owe Planter a pint. He told me this would be a wasted errand, and so it has proved to be. Save for the pleasure of making your acquaintance, ma'am." To her astonishment, he gave her a courtly bow.

She might have curtsied in return, but she feared her jellied knees would not lift her up again. "I am unfamiliar with the local watering places, but I expect Mr. Planter knows the best ones."

"Oh, aye," the constable said. "Sorry to have troubled you, ma'am. We'll take ourselves off now so that you can get on with your walk."

Remembering to lower her veil beforehand, she opened the door and led them outside. "I do hope you find the missing girl," she said.

"You may be sure of it." Pugg mounted his horse. "God grant you a safe journey to York, Mrs. Preston."

Lucy managed a friendly wave as they rode away and waited until the curving track took them around the woodlands and out of her sight. Careful not to appear in a hurry, she returned to the cottage and raised the trapdoor a few inches. "Diana?"

"I'm here." Her voice sounded hollow. "What is happening?"

"All's well, but stay where you are for now. I'll explain everything later."

She disliked leaving Diana alone to fret, but since the men expected her to take a walk, she had better do so. The tenacious Mr. Pugg might decide to swing past the cottage again, hoping to catch her by surprise. Taking the spyglass with her, she strolled up the long hill leading to the cliff and gazed out over the bay.

The tide had begun to retreat, and above the water she could discern the very tops of the boxes on the wagon. She'd never have spotted them if she hadn't known precisely where to look. Raising the spyglass, she pointed it in the opposite direction to the one the men had taken and slowly made a half circle. A few moments later she saw them, tiny figures rounding a small hill and, glory be, making the turn to Warton. They were soon out of sight, but caution sent her walking along the cliff for nearly a mile, checking constantly for any sign of them. If they circled back through the thick woods, she wouldn't know it until they were nearly upon her.

As she walked, disconnected thoughts tumbled over one another in her head. When first she saw the men, she'd been certain that Kit had dispatched them here. But when they did not immediately go to the trapdoor, she realized her mistake.

It had been that reptilian solicitor after all. She longed to wring his scrawny neck with her bare hands.

Kit must have nailed that box together. She had to grant he was clever, if nothing else. Well, also intelligent, witty, and leagues too handsome for his own good, she would be forced to admit if she allowed herself to think on it, which she was careful not to do.

Taking care did not always turn the trick, though. It had no effect whatsoever when she tried not to think about his kiss. That proved as impossible as not thinking about an elephant when told not to think about an elephant, after which one could think of nothing *but* elephants.

His kiss had been an elephant stomping back and forth through her thoughts ever since it happened.

Summoning all her willpower, she wrenched her concentration to Pugg. Runners were for hire, she knew, and Sir Basil Crawley must have paid him a pretty penny to come so far north. It was he who posted the reward, no doubt, since Diana's uncle hadn't two sixpence to scratch together.

Sir Basil knew about Diana's scarred face, although he'd not seen it, but it appeared he was still determined to wed her. It was a good investment on his part, Lucy supposed. Diana was a great heiress and her family had held the barony for centuries.

She wondered what it was about Sir Basil that Diana so detested. By her account he was a well-looking man, somewhat rough about the edges by the standards of old aristocratic families but impeccably dressed and well-spoken. To be sure, any man of forty probably seemed ancient to a girl half his age. In any case, Diana had found him repellent when first they met, and she undoubtedly feared him. "Even thinking about him makes him somehow present," she had once said. "I only want him *gone*."

Lucy respected Diana's feminine instincts. She only wished she had a few of her own. Pragmatism and experience had been her guides as she steered through a bramblebush life, subject to the whims and dictates of those who paid her wages and put a roof over her head.

She took another long look through the spyglass, seeing no sign of Pugg and the constable. Diana must be in agony by now, wondering what had occurred. Lucy headed down the hill, choosing the track that skirted the woodland on her way back to the cottage. Her senses were at knife edge. She expected Pugg to leap out from behind every tree she passed. But she heard only the soft sifting of the afternoon breeze through the woodlands, and birdsong, and the crunch of her boots on fallen leaves.

She ought to be making plans, she thought as the cottage came into view. But her mind felt swaddled in wool, and she could not think beyond the next footfall.

"Pssst!"

A scream jumped to her throat. Forcing it back, Lucy swung her gaze past the thick undergrowth and saw Kit leaning against the trunk of an oak, grinning at her.

She had never in her life been so happy to see anyone. And she wanted to throttle him for scaring the stuffing out of her. She threaded through the bushes to a small clearing where Kit's horse was nibbling grass.

"You arrived just in time," Kit informed her. "I'm in serious danger of being ravished."

Following his gesture, she looked up to a branch directly over his head where Fidgets was perched, staring at him with owlish concentration.

"While I've been waiting for your guests to leave and you to return, my suitor—or ought that be suitress?—has supplied a picnic lunch." He pointed to the limp figure of a vole stretched inches from his boot. "Mind you, I've always longed to be wooed. It's deuced unfair, don't you think, that men have to do all the work of seducing while females have only to flutter their lashes and flirt?"

"I never flirt," Lucy snapped. In truth, she'd no idea how to go about it. And how came they to be chattering nonsense in the midst of a crisis? "Not that you seem to care, but a constable and a Bow Street Runner were here not an hour ago, looking for Diana."

"A Runner?" Kit frowned. "Bad news, Runners. In my experience the local constabulary is a pack of well-meaning fools, but Runners are smart and relentless. They never give up until the mission is accomplished."

"You may well believe it. I told more clankers in the last hour than I've told in all the rest of my life, and I'm not sure if he credited a single one of them. They certainly did not dissuade him from searching the cottage." She shuddered to remember what had happened next. "He found the trapdoor."

"But not the cave, I take it. Feel free to praise me for divining a way to conceal it. An inspired notion, wouldn't you say?"

"I *might* say, had you not anticipated me." She gave him an exasperated look. "No wonder that poor Fidgets is enamored of you, what with you displaying like the vainest peacock in all creation. He thinks you to be some sort of oversize bird."

"*She*, please." He whistled softly, and Fidgets swooped down to perch on his shoulder. "We've been practicing this for the past hour," he told her when she gaped at him. "Come along, Lady Lucy. We have much to discuss, but Diana should be present for all the important bits."

She took the arm he offered her, keenly aware of its solid strength under the obviously expensive sleeve of a bottle-green riding coat. His left arm was still encased in the sling made from her Norwich shawl, and he limped slightly as they made their way to the cottage, but otherwise it was hard to remember that he had ever been injured.

"Tell me about the box," she said. "How is it affixed?"

"Stop that, you impertinent wench!"

Startled, she looked over to see Fidgets grooming his hair with a sharp V-shaped beak.

Kit grinned at her, rolling his eyes. "She thinks you her mother and me her mate. Would that make you my mother-in-law?"

His *mother-in-law*? Was that how he saw her? The elephant stampeded through her skull.

"I'm no carpenter, as you can tell from a close look at the box. It's propped up with sticks of wood cut to the distance between the box and the first two steps leading down to the cave, and I imagine it would collapse if given a good hard push from above. The important thing was making it simple for Diana to manage, and she practiced until she could install it in a hurry."

"It was a superb notion," she conceded. "It assuredly saved us this afternoon, sir, and I am most grateful to you."

"Hear that, Fidgets? Your mama approves of me for a change." Letting go of Lucy's arm, he opened the cottage door, but before she could enter, he leaned over to whisper in her ear, "My inamorata won't like it, I expect, but if you hope to take her with you when you leave, Fidgets ought to be confined now."

The owl was none too pleased about it, but Lucy managed to secure her in the wicker traveling cage.

"Who were those men?" Diana demanded as Kit helped her ascend from the cave.

"I'll tell you later," he replied, carrying the three-legged stool to the table. "There's no immediate urgency, sweetheart, but I'd like us to be on our way within the hour. Any questions that can wait probably should. Good work with the box, by the way."

Diana dropped onto a chair. "I was scared out of my wits."

"But you did just as you ought in spite of being afraid, which is precisely what it is to be brave. Things are well in hand now. My brother is assembling a formidable regiment of lawyers, and believes that a good case can be made for overturning your uncle's guardianship. Naturally he will do all in his power—

his *considerable* power—to bring that about, and at the end of the day, you will be perfectly safe."

"What about the first part of the day?" Lucy asked tartly. "What do we do in the meantime?"

He smiled. "I've spoken with a good friend, a widow who lives alone on a small farm not many miles from here. Her husband was killed early in the war, and since then she has made ends meet by raising pigs to sell at the local markets. The farm is isolated and a trifle rank to the nose, which helps to keep people away." He sat on the stool and took hold of Diana's hands. "You'll like her, I promise, and she welcomes both the company and the opportunity to earn a bit extra by taking in a lodger. I'll tell you more about her on the way there."

"Lodger?" Lucy had not missed his use of the singular noun. "Am I not to go with Diana?"

"One person is more easily concealed than two," he said, "and the house is small. Robbie is on his way there now with her belongings, after which he'll arrange passage for you on a coach headed south. It may not be possible, though, for you to leave until tomorrow morning. Will you mind greatly remaining alone here for the night?"

She waved a hand, unable to speak. He had taken complete charge of Diana's future and drummed Lucy Preston from the ranks as if she were no longer of the slightest use. The Earl of Kendal and his brother had stepped in with all their power and money and male arrogance, and might just as well have said, "Run along, Miss Preston. We'll handle things from here on out."

Tears sprang to her eyes, the first she could remember for many long years. She wished she had not removed the veiled hat. Kit would be even more certain he was right to dismiss her if he saw her weeping. She went to the window and lifted the curtain slightly, gazing outside with burning eyes, seeing nothing. She could not even think how to fight him. What more could she do for Diana, after all?

There was little reason not to return to Dorset and her wearisome job. And really, she had failed Diana at the end. She'd no place to take her, no money to hire a reputable barrister to plead her case in the courts, no excuse to stay. She had done her best, but it wasn't good enough. Diana would be far better off with a powerful earl to champion her cause.

Two warm hands settled on her shoulders. "What's wrong, moonbeam?"

"N-nothing. I'm glad you found somewhere Diana can be safe while the lawyers wrangle. Please thank his lordship on my behalf for his assistance. And I don't mind remaining here until Robbie comes to take me to the posthouse. My employer will be pleased to see me, I've no doubt. I told her I'd be gone a fortnight, but it's well beyond six weeks already. I simply had no idea how long it would take to steal Diana away and—"

"You're babbling, poppet. And crying, too. I suspect. Did you imagine you were to go home?" One hand lifted to stroke her cheek. "As if I'd permit you to escape so easily. You've not heard the other half of my plan, you know."

She could not help leaning into him, despising her own weakness even as she relaxed against his hard chest and savored the feel of his callused fingertip on her cheek. "W-what is the other half?" she murmured.

"Well, as to that, I cannot say. Primarily because I've not yet worked it out, but it promises to be a cracker. We shall put our heads together when you arrive at Candale."

She pulled away from him. "I cannot possibly go to an earl's estate. It's unthinkable. Just look at me."

"Mrs. Preston ought to depart the vicinity, I agree, which is why you'll first take a southbound coach. A carriage will be waiting at one of the posthouses along the way, one where the passengers are given time to have a meal. A room will be reserved for you, and a maid will be waiting there with your next disguise. Lest anyone miss you, she will transform herself into Mrs. Preston, take your place in the coach, and continue on to Liverpool for a visit with her family."

"But Mrs. Preston has to go to York! Mr. Pugg expects her

to." Lucy knew that sounded ridiculous, but she could not let go of the idea that he would verify the story she had given him.

"Should he retain the slightest interest in Mrs. Preston, which I very much doubt, he will do no more than make a few inquiries regarding her departure. If he checks at any of the coach stops, people will recall seeing her, and she must necessarily go south before transferring to a coach heading across the Pennines. He'll not attempt to trace her very far, I assure you, and we are taking excessive precautions as it is."

She supposed so. But he had not met Mr. Pugg, nor experienced the terror she'd felt when he probed her with his sharp, assessing gaze. All the same, she might as well go along with Kit's plan since she had none of her own to propose. "I—perhaps this is an improper question, but I must ask why it is Diana must stay on a stranger's pig farm instead of—"

"If you imagine she is unwelcome at Candale, that is far from the case. But when it becomes known that the earl has taken up her cause, Mr. Pugg and his like will come looking for her there. It's remotely possible that Lord Whitney could secure a warrant to search the estate and the several other properties in the area owned by our family. Better she be stowed safely elsewhere, I am persuaded. Only Robbie and I will know where she is, so that the rest of you can in all honesty deny any knowledge of her location."

"But I *wish* to know. And I am an exceedingly good liar."

"Such an accomplishment!" he chided, grinning. "So am I, as it happens. But the truth is easier to keep track of, and this one time I am heeding Kendal's advice. He is a master of deception—used to be a diplomat, y'know—and he instructed me to tell him absolutely nothing he did not need to know. The same applies to everyone else, including you. Don't quarrel with me on this subject, Lucy. It is for the best."

She slipped around him and went to where Diana was sitting quietly, waiting while other people made decisions on her behalf. In her place, Lucy knew that she'd be furiously demanding to express her own opinions on the subject of her future.

"Are you in agreement, Diana? Will you mind staying with someone you have never met?"

"No. It is precisely what I most wish, a quiet place where I can come to terms with myself. There has been no time for that before now. But I'm glad you are not returning to Dorset just yet, and that you'll be close by." She lifted her gaze to Kit. "Might she send me letters, telling me how things are proceeding?"

"Why not? I'll deliver them when I visit, or she can send them through Robbie. We don't mean to abandon you there, butterfly. This is a temporary arrangement only. I think we should be on our way now, since I mean to take a roundabout way to the farm. Are you ready to go?"

"Nearly." She stood. "Let me fetch my cloak and gloves. They're in Lucy's portmanteau."

"Dig out the witch's cape and wig, will you? I want to take them with me."

"Whatever for?" Lucy asked as Diana went into the other room.

"They may prove useful. I'm not altogether sure how, but as I told you, I'm still thinking about my next plan. Meantime we need to complete the one in progress. Are you clear on what you are to do?"

"I am to wait here for Robbie, who will take me to the coach, probably tomorrow morning. At some point I'll leave the coach and change into clothing provided me by a servant. How am I to know which posthouse is the right one?"

"The driver and the maid will be watching for you. Don't worry about the details, Lucy. Robbie and I are seeing to them. You have only to relax and do your part. By tomorrow evening at the latest, you will be joining the family for supper at Candale."

He could hardly have said anything more likely to rock her on her heels. As it was, she put a trembling hand on the table for support. "Is that necessary? The last thing I wish is to encroach on your family. I would much prefer to remain somewhere out of the way."

"The countess would not hear of it," he said in an amused voice.

Diana returned, wearing her cloak and gloves, Lucy's black cape folded neatly in her arms. "The wig is wrapped inside," she said, handing the bundle to Kit before turning to embrace Lucy. "Thank you so very much for all you have done. I can never repay you as you deserve, but I shall always pray for your happiness. And please don't be concerned for me. I have never seen a pig, you know, but I expect I'll come to like them."

Eyes burning, Lucy could only hug her tightly. She had loved few people in her life, and none who failed to betray her trust. Even Miss Wetherwood had dismissed her from the academy after heeding the lies of another teacher. Although she later discovered the truth, apologized, and offered Lucy her former job with a rise in salary, Lucy had declined. She corresponded with the headmistress during the next few years, but their relationship was never the same.

It was difficult to admit to herself that she loved Diana, and impossible to say so aloud, but she knew that she did. She hoped that Diana, with the fine-tuned instincts Lucy so admired, was aware of it, too.

"Ahem," Kit said from the door. "Not to interrupt, but you'll be seeing each other again sooner than you expect. Detach yourself, Diana, and come along."

Lucy followed them to where the horse was tethered, feeling an unexpected shot of jealousy when Kit helped Diana to mount and swung himself onto the saddle behind her, wrapping one arm around her waist. And all with one arm in a sling, Lucy thought with some amazement.

"Last chance, moonbeam. Any questions?"

Probably a score of them, but she couldn't think of one. "No. I suppose not."

"I'll see you tomorrow then. Give Fidgets my love." With the slightest nudge of his knee, he turned the horse and guided it deeper onto the narrow track.

Lucy suddenly thought of a question. "What disguise?" she called after him. "What sort of costume are you sending me?" She heard him laugh as he disappeared around a curve.

Chapter 11

In other circumstances, Lucy might have enjoyed the luxury of Lord Kendal's elegant crested carriage as it made its way along the turnpike road. Beside her in the wicker cage, Fidgets had long since gone to sleep, leaving her alone with her tumultuous thoughts.

So far, all had transpired exactly as Kit said it would. At a posthouse south of Lancaster, a pretty young girl led her to a room where a change of clothing was laid out for her on the bed. Then the former Mary Fife, now Mrs. Preston for the rest of her own journey, went downstairs to join the other passengers as they reboarded the Lancaster-to-Liverpool Comet. Lucy was to wait, Mary told her, until a footman came to get her.

Alone in the bedchamber, she took the time to examine her appearance in the cheval mirror. In the rush, she'd paid no attention to what she was putting on, but when she had a moment to look, she scarcely recognized herself. The lavender carriage dress had been made over to fit her, she could tell, but she'd never worn a lovelier gown. It was embroidered at the hem and around the neck with violets, and there was a pelisse of darker purple to match.

When had she become so vain? She had never been so before. But she could not help turning her head this way and that, delighting in the French bonnet of tulle and watered silk with lush satin ribbons that framed her face to advantage. Only her black half boots, the ones she had to wear because the lavender kidskin shoes sent along with the dress were far too small, spoiled the image of the otherwise proper lady gazing back at her.

After a few minutes a footman had appeared to lead her to the coach. And now here she was, within a few miles of Candale, shaking like a custard.

It wasn't as if she were unaccustomed to fancy houses and aristocratic families. At Turnbridge Manor, she was sometimes permitted to dine at table when there were no guests of importance, so she knew how to make polite conversation with those above her rank. Primarily, of course, she knew how it felt to be ignored.

Her parents had been too busy deliberately ignoring each other to pay her any mind at all. When she turned nine they had stashed her at Miss Wetherwood's academy and separated, her mother to go off with a man who had a bushy mustache, which was all Lucy knew of him, and her father to bring his mistress to live with him at the small family estate. He ceased to pay tuition for her schooling when she was six-and-ten, and from then on she was left to her own resources.

Neither ever answered the letters she wrote so earnestly for the first few years, until she finally awakened to the fact that they cared nothing for her. So she stopped caring about them, and had not since let herself care overmuch for anyone else.

Thinking on her parents never failed to put her in the dismals, so Lucy unfolded Kit's note and read it for the dozenth time.

The man was addled, really he was. She had now been cast in the role of Miss Lucinda Jennet, since using the name of Preston might call untoward attention from itinerant Bow Street Runners. She was newly come north to meet the family of her betrothed, the Honorable Christopher Valliant, who had met her on his travels and fallen irremediably in love. She was advised to create a suitable background for herself, unless she wished to adopt the one he had thought up. They would discuss it when she arrived, to make sure they got their stories straight.

The next time she saw the reprehensible Kit Valliant, she

would set *him* straight. Fiancée indeed! Under no circumstances would she agree to this infamous deception. What he had told his family she could not bear to imagine, but they would hear only the truth from her. Except the part about her abbreviated name, which suited her well enough. Lucinda Jennet she would be, for the short time she remained where she did not belong.

The coach drew up before a tall set of wrought-iron portals, and a kilted Scotsman hurried from the gatehouse to swing them open. He must be the one related to Robbie's late wife, she thought, smiling when he gave her a friendly wave of welcome.

But her spirits plummeted again when the enormous three-story house came into view a few minutes later. On a low grassy hill, a large square building was set between two wings, forming a block letter *H*, the effect more imposing than graceful. But it was a beautiful house nonetheless, with tall shade trees planted just where they ought to be and an ornamental lake curving around the west wing as if in an embrace. Pale afternoon sunlight glittered off the mullioned windows and turned the massive gray stone walls to silver.

A marble-pillared portico sheltered the wide entrance doors, which swung open just as Lucy was alighting from the coach. A breathtakingly lovely woman with curly golden hair stepped out, a warm smile curving her lips. The countess, Lucy thought, feeling painfully anxious at the prospect of meeting her. She could not bring her feet to move any closer.

Lady Kendal came to her, skirts billowing as she rushed to the coach with her arms open. "Miss Jennet. I am delighted to meet you. Welcome to our home."

Lucy managed an awkward curtsy. "Thank you, ma'am. I shall try not to be any bother."

"Nonsense! We adore bother. Come along and meet Kendal, and then I'll show you to your room and give you a chance to catch your breath. Kit isn't here, I'm afraid. We had no idea what time you would arrive, and he's gone off on one of his errands. It doesn't do to ask him where or what, but he will be back in time for dinner."

Rather sure she'd been caught up in a whirlwind, Lucy accompanied the chattering countess through the marble-tiled entrance hall and down a long passageway.

"Now, I should advise you, if Kit has not already done so, that the earl is not nearly so starched up as he first appears. He spent a great many years in the courts of Europe and acquired a bit too much cosmopolitan polish, but it is beginning to wear off. Don't let him intimidate you, Miss Jennet. It is the last thing he would wish."

Thoroughly intimidated already, Lucy was ushered into an impressive study lined with bookshelves and glass-topped cases. She couldn't see what they contained, her attention riveted by the gentleman seated behind a large mahogany desk. He rose when the ladies entered the room and inclined his head in response to her curtsy.

Her first thought was that Lord Kendal looked nothing like his brother, although they were both tall, slim, and broad-shouldered. But the earl had light brown, close-cropped hair, graceful, long-fingered hands, and a decided air of elegance about him. She thought him handsome, in a quiet way, like sculpted glass. Only his blue eyes put her in mind of Kit, and only for a moment. Kendal's eyes were cool and watchful, not dancing with high spirits and good humor.

His voice was dark velvet when he spoke. "You are most welcome to Candale, Miss Jennet. May I offer you a glass of sherry?"

"Oh, don't be silly," the countess said, taking hold of Lucy's trembling arm. "She has had a long journey hard on the heels of a mighty adventure. I shall sweep her away now, and you will have to wait until dinner to become better acquainted. Come along, my dear, and tell me what you would like to have with your tea as we make our way upstairs. Cook baked apple tarts this morning, and I can testify that they are delicious because I've already devoured three of them."

Lucy stole a glance over her shoulder as Lady Kendal pulled her from the room. The earl was smiling.

"You must pardon me for rabbiting on," the countess said a few minutes later as they sat drinking tea in a beautifully appointed suite of rooms while servants filled a copper bathtub with steaming water. "We receive so little company these days, Miss Jennet, and I've not had another female to coze with since months before Christopher was born. He is ten weeks old now, with a temper he must have gotten from me and a demanding nature inherited from his father. I am trying not to spoil him, but it is difficult to do otherwise. Kit tells me you have been governess to five young boys, so you must know how it is."

"I've little experience with infants," Lucy said, the first words she'd had a chance to say for quite some time. And just as well, since her tongue seemed to be swollen in her mouth. She was overwhelmed by these charming aristocrats and their lavish hospitality. "May I see your son? Only if that would be acceptable, of course."

"Whyever would it *not*? You must run tame at Candale, Miss Jennet. Go where you will and do whatever you like. We do not stand on ceremony here." The countess patted her hand. "I daresay you will feel more comfortable when Kit returns. And now I must leave you to your bath before it grows cold. Have yourself a good nap and use the bellpull if you require anything at all. We keep country hours, so dinner will be at seven."

Moth wings beat inside Lucy's stomach. "Must I join you, Lady Kendal? I've nothing to wear, and—"

"Mercy me! Did I not tell you? More than half the gowns in my wardrobe no longer fit since I began eating like a horse. Nursing a babe makes me voracious, and of course my breasts are swollen like ascent balloons. When Kit told us you were to pay a visit and explained the circumstances, I put a seamstress to work altering a few of my dresses to your size. It's a hurried bit of patchwork, I'm sorry to say, but there are several gowns hanging in that armoire, and the chest of drawers contains whatever else I could think of—night rails, robes, handkerchiefs, and the like. If you require anything I forgot, you have only to ask."

"Th-thank you. I am most grateful."

"Piffle! You can have no idea how pleased I am to have you here." She rose, plucking an almond biscuit from the tea tray. "Young Betsy Slate aspires to be a lady's maid, so I hope you don't mind if she practices on you. She'll come to your room an hour before dinner to help you dress and show you the way to the parlor for a glass of wine before we sit at table. Kit insists on wine before dinner, and we accommodate him whenever he comes home."

Lucy stood, dazed and uncertain what to say or do. The next she knew, she was swept up in a warm embrace.

"May I call you Lucy?" the countess asked when she stepped away. "And will you call me Celia?"

Melting under her smile, Lucy could only nod. She would never be able to address the countess by her Christian name, she was certain, but now was not the time to say so. Lady Kendal blew her a kiss as she left the room, and Lucy stood for a long time staring at the closed door, wondering how on earth she could endure another hour in this house. Every minute she stayed here would make her want more, and it would never do to become accustomed to such luxury.

As they departed the dining room Kit drew Celia aside, leaving his brother to escort Lucy to the drawing room for coffee. Her hand stiff on the earl's arm, Lucy cast him a sulfurous look over her shoulder, the first sign of spirit he'd seen from her all evening.

"What the devil's the matter with her?" Kit asked when Kendal and Lucy were out of earshot. "She pushed food around on her plate all evening and hardly spoke ten words altogether. Have you been beastly to her?"

"Oh, indeed. We imprisoned her in the wine cellar the entire afternoon." Celia gave a delicate shrug. "She is a trifle uncomfortable among strangers, I daresay, although from your description, I had not expected her to be shy."

"Well, she isn't, and I'm not a stranger. I don't think she

looked at me above twice, though. It must be the neckcloth. I knew I shouldn't have worn it." He sliced Celia a grin. "Dire measures are called for, I'm afraid, if I am to get my Lucy back. Methinks a good row will turn the trick."

"Mercy, Kit. You don't mean to pick a fight with the poor girl?"

"That would be ungallant, m'dear, and I am a prince among men. I merely plan to invite her to a ball."

"Oh, dear."

"Precisely. Do me a service, will you, and extricate your husband from the drawing room before the fireworks begin." He took her arm. "*Now* would be an excellent time."

Kit watched with appreciation as Celia tactfully maneuvered Kendal from the room within a few minutes. Lucy tried to follow them, but he intercepted her before she could reach the door. "I take lots of sugar in my coffee," he said, steering her to a chair beside the low table.

Lips set in a rigid line, she dutifully filled a cup with coffee, chipped off a sizable hunk of sugar to sweeten it, and held it out. All without once looking in his direction.

He took a sip. "Perfection. Thank you. Now, do you intend to tell me why you are blue-deviled, or must I drag it from you?"

"You know very well why!"

Well, that didn't take long, Kit thought. There was much to be said for loving a woman with a flashpan temper.

"Men never know *why*, moonbeam. And why is it you females always force us to guess what we've done wrong?"

"Because you ought to know, that's why." She threw up her hands. "You are hopeless, the lot of you. But I shall explain in words even you can understand. *I do not belong here.*"

"If you think that, you are the only one who does."

"I haven't finished. *I am not your fiancée.*"

"A mere bagatelle. Sometimes the facts take a while to catch up with the truth."

"What in blazes does *that* mean? No, don't tell me. I am sure I do not want to hear any more of your moonshine."

She was looking at him now, her gray eyes shooting sparks and sending heat all up and down his body. That's my girl, he thought, readying himself for the next assault.

"Lord and Lady Kendal have been prodigiously kind, and I feel horrid to repay them only with deceit. Masquerades are defensible when there is no other choice, sir, but this one serves no purpose at all."

"Ah, there you are wrong. It is a significant part of my plan, the one I am working on. Not all the pieces are in place, but it's coming together, and meantime we are laying the groundwork. Consider this. When constables and lawyers and Runners start prowling around, how else to explain your presence at Candale?"

"No explanation would be required if I weren't here. And I wish to leave. Tomorrow."

Kit drank the rest of his coffee while he considered how to proceed. Telling her that he understood her feelings—which he did—would probably result in the coffee service being thrown piece by piece at his head. She was in no mood to be soothed, that was clear. For now, he had better concentrate on bending her to his will, which he had learned was best accomplished by confronting her with a challenge.

"You are not a prisoner here, Lucy, but you are very much needed. You are the one Diana trusts. If you abandon her, she will lose all faith in the rest of us."

"I— Do you think so?"

"You must finish what you began, moonbeam. We can none of us consider our own wishes until Diana is free of her uncle and the man who is pulling his strings. Am I right?"

"Aren't you always?" she grumbled, twisting a silver spoon in her hands. "But how am I of any use? What am I to *do*?"

"I'm delighted that you asked." He set his cup and saucer on the tray, using the time to seize a deep breath. "As it happens, Sir Basil Crawley has invited us to a ball."

"What?" She regarded him in disbelief. "How could he? He doesn't know that I exist."

"Well, technically, it's Kendal he hopes to snag. But Kendal

139

won't go, and Celia cannot because she is nursing her son, which leaves it up to us. My name was on the invitation, too, and I would hardly attend a ball without my fiancée, would I?"

He expected her to object ferociously to the whole idea, but she sat back in her chair, brow wrinkled as she considered the possibilities. Or he hoped she was considering. There was no way to tell from her expression.

"I would certainly like to meet the blackguard," she said thoughtfully. "But what is to be gained from making his acquaintance, short of satisfying our curiosity about him?"

In his opinion, that was quite enough reason by itself. But he was a creature of the process, preferring the journey to the destination, while she required definite goals. What a perfect team they were going to make. "I mean to befriend him, if the opportunity arises. No, *befriend* is not the proper word. *Insinuate myself*, perhaps. Someone needs to take his measure, you must admit, and what better chance will we ever have?"

"There are other difficulties to consider. I have nothing to wear, I have not danced since lessons at school, and I may kill him on sight."

Kit burst into laughter. Only Lucy would say such a thing. And mean it, too. "The ball is Friday night, so we have four days to rig you out in style and practice our dancing. As for your homicidal instincts, I am inclined to share them. But we'll keep each other in check."

"You've already sent an acceptance, haven't you?"

Flames darted up his cheeks. "Maybe."

She shook her head. "I may be towed to the gallows for murdering you long before I get my hands on Sir Basil."

At least the fire was in her again. She was Lucy once more, not the pale, nervous creature he'd sat to dinner with two hours earlier. "And no one would blame you for it. I am a great trial to all who know and love me." He grinned. "Have I groveled sufficiently, or must I go on?"

"Oh, I think you must, but at a later time. Let me sleep on this, Kit. I know it's a perfectly stupid idea, attending the ball, but I confess that I am tempted. At least I'd be *doing* something instead of wafting around this enormous house, getting in everyone's way and feeling indebted to strangers, however kind they may be."

He held out his hand. "Come with me, moonbeam. I want to show you something."

The nursery was lit only by a single candle when he led her inside. The young maid keeping watch from a chair near the cradle stood, curtsied, and withdrew to the passageway, closing the door gently behind her.

Holding back, Kit watched Lucy approach the cradle on tiptoe, clearly fascinated and a trifle reluctant. She stopped about two feet away, bending forward to look down at the sleeping infant.

"He's so very *small*," she whispered.

"And so very fierce," he said, moving to stand beside her. "He rules this house and everyone in it. The rest of us can only stand in awe of him. He is a miracle, Lucy. All children are miracles. The world is their inheritance, and we are no more than caretakers. One day he will stand, gazing down on his own son or daughter, and think the same thing as we are thinking now. This is what matters . . . love and family and children. This is what we are born for, and why we live."

She gazed up at him, candlelight dancing over her smooth, flawless cheeks. "I think I don't understand you at all, Kit."

"That's why I brought you here. If ever you wish to know me, past the smuggling and the willfulness and the constant irritation I provide you, remember what I just said." He took her arm and led her to the door. "For now, I mean to sit with the Terror of Candale for a time. I shall see you tomorrow, Lucy, when I've returned from visiting Diana."

Chapter 12

Lucy stood precariously on a footstool while the assistant seamstress draped her with yet another swath of glittering material.

"Tiens!" The mantua-maker shook her head. "With hair of such a color, she is most difficult to clothe. And I regret to say she has not enough bosom for the pattern she has chosen."

"Then I shall select another pattern," Lucy said irritably. She could scarcely grow larger breasts in three days. "Any of them will do, Madame Broussard. It matters little how I look."

"I cannot agree. My reputation must be considered, mademoiselle." She turned to the countess, who was observing the proceedings from a sofa. "Will you leave this in my hands, Lady Kendal? In the shops, I shall discover a fabric to suit both the young lady and the gown I have in mind for her."

"What think you, Lucinda? Shall we give Madame Broussard carte blanche?"

"By all means." Lucy jumped down from the stool. "If it means an end to this poking and prodding and measuring, she may outfit me in a burlap sack."

"Bon." The mantua-maker beckoned to her assistant, who began to gather up the lengths of material strewn over the furniture. "On Thursday, the gown will be ready for fitting."

Remembering her manners, Lucy smiled. "Thank you, madame. I am certain to like it enormously."

"Certainement. You are a beauty, mademoiselle, and I shall create a gown to bedazzle all the gentlemen." Two hawkish

eyes examined Lucy one last time. "Have you any pearls to wear?"

"Yes," said Lady Kendal before Lucy could reply. She stood. "A tray of refreshments will be sent up for you, madame. Lucinda, will you join me in the nursery?"

Lucy suspected that she was in for a well-deserved chiding. "I was terribly rude, wasn't I?" she said on their way upstairs. "But this all seems so . . . frivolous."

"Under the circumstances, I am certain that it does. You may be sure, however, that madame took no offense. She is herself rather plainspoken."

"That is no excuse for my reprehensible conduct. Everyone has been so kind, and all I do is snap and snarl."

Lady Kendal paused outside the nursery door. "You are on edge with worry about your friend, which is perfectly understandable. And somewhat nervous about the ball, yes? But the dance lesson went exceedingly well this morning, Monsieur d'Alacoque informs me, and before Friday you will feel quite confident taking the floor with Kit. He is a splendid dancer."

That was *not* what she needed to hear. "We are going to this ball only to scrutinize Sir Basil Crawley. It will not be necessary to dance."

"That would be a shame, but you must do as you wish. Take care that Kit does not stampede you. The Valliant men, at least the two I have met, are fond of having their own way."

And generally got it, Lucy thought sourly. "I would not mind so much if Kit would cease introducing me as his fiancée. How will it reflect on your family when nothing comes of our supposed engagement?"

"That doesn't signify in the least. We are quite accustomed to Kit's scandals, you know. And compared with a jailing, a mere jilting is of no consequence whatsoever." Lady Kendal smiled. "To be sure, we shall be sorry if you decide not to wed him after all."

"There can be no question of marriage! Did he not make it clear that this betrothal is only another of his games?"

Celia looked evasive. "He said something to that effect, I suppose. You have probably discovered that it is sometimes difficult to tell when he is being serious. May I give you a word of advice?"

"Oh, yes," Lucy replied hastily. "Please do."

"When I was in difficulty, Kit was a rock. You may trust him."

Lucy waited, but that brief pronouncement was the total of Lady Kendal's counsel. And it wasn't very helpful. Lucy was not inclined to trust *anyone*, let alone a highborn scoundrel like Kit Valliant. "Thank you, ma'am. I shall hold in mind what you have said."

"Fustian! You are thinking that my situation cannot compare with your own, but you are quite mistaken. My mother was the daughter of an impoverished baronet and my father . . . well, the less said of him, the better. I was so eager to escape him that I married an elderly man who bred chickens." She shuddered. "But this is a long story, and as I can hear my son squalling for his luncheon, I shall save my tale for another time. Just know that I was not born into Lord Kendal's world, and I well understand how it is to feel an outsider." She opened the nursery door. "You won't mind if I leave you now? While nursing Christopher, I can think of nothing but him."

Unable to speak through the knot of envy in her throat, Lucy waved a hand and turned away. Her breasts, the ones Madame Broussard had dismissed so cavalierly, began to ache as she imagined how it would be to hold a babe in her arms and feel its tiny mouth suckling at her nipple.

The fantasy possessed her all the way to the stable, where she fled for refuge from the imposing house and any possibility of encountering Lord Kendal. He had been kindness itself since her arrival, but he intimidated her nonetheless. She was far more comfortable in the company of Fidgets, who had settled into the stable as if she owned it.

My only child, she thought. *An owl!* Well, one must make do with what one has. And at the moment she desperately craved a bit of affection, whatever the source.

As she stepped inside, a redheaded lad of about nine years looked up from the saddle he was polishing. "C'n I help you, milady?"

"I came to visit Fidgets, if she is anywhere about."

"Right over there." He pointed to a ladder propped against the wall. Fidgets was perched on a middle rung, regarding her sleepily. A moment later the shiny eyes closed.

So much for birdly love. Sighing, Lucy sat on a bale of straw beside the stableboy. With young boys, at least, she always felt at ease. "Will you mind if I keep you company for a little while?"

His freckled face lit up. "I likes company. Mr. Reese sez to tend to the saddles, though, so I gots to keep workin'."

"Do go on. I am Miss Jennet, by the way."

"Oh, I knows that. You is the one what will marry Mr. Christopher. I be Timothy Slate, but everybody calls me Timmy."

Good heavens, even the servants thought her betrothed to Kit! Servants gossiped with the townsfolk, as well she knew, so perhaps this was a necessary lie. But she was growing sick at heart at the deception. There had been too many lies, too many disguises. Sometimes she wondered who she really was, and how she would find herself again when this latest masquerade was concluded.

"Your owl is an uncommon fine 'un," Timmy said. "I've not seen any so friendlylike as 'e is. Most is skeered of people."

"*He?* Are you sure of that? I had thought Fidgets to be female."

"Oh, 'e's a boy all right. The boys be a mite smaller than the girls and they gots whiter feathers in the front."

Lucy stifled a laugh. "Are you absolutely certain?"

"Oh, aye. I knows lots about owls. They looks to be smart, but they mostly be stupid. The same way as some people. Hard to tell about folks just from lookin'."

Profound wisdom from a stableboy. "Well, don't tell anyone

else about Fidgets's gender," she advised him. "It will shatter a number of illusions if you do."

"If you say so," Timmy agreed cheerfully. "What's a 'lusion?"

"Well, it's rather like a dream, or a wish. Something a person wants to think is true even if it isn't." Rather like imagining Kit in love with her.

"They be good then," Timmy piped. "I got lots of 'lusions. Nothin' much else to do when I is workin' but to dream 'bout doin' somethin' else."

"What do you dream of?" she asked curiously. For all her tedious existence, the one she would soon return to, Timmy's prospects were even less promising.

"Mostly I 'magines meself a jockey, me bein' small and good with 'orses. But sometimes I thinks about sailin' boats on the lakes, or mebbe even the ocean. One day I means to do one or t'other."

"I am certain that you will, Timmy." She stood, catching the rough heel of her half boot on the hem of her skirt. She had been measured for new shoes, but they would not be delivered before tomorrow. Meantime she clomped about Candale in her weather-beaten boots, wearing Lady Kendal's made-over dresses, wishing she could be Luke again. Or even Mrs. Preston, cloaked head to toe in black. Anything but a patched-together frump!

Fidgets made a low noise in his throat, and she turned to see him poised for flight. A second later he swooped past her. She heard the sound of hoofbeats then, and guessed that Kit had returned.

Shading her eyes against the afternoon sun, she went outside and saw him rein in, Fidgets perched atop his hat. A misbegotten pair if ever there was one, she thought. Almost as unlikely as the Honorable Christopher Valliant mated with Lucinda Jennet Preston, governess.

Dismounting, Kit opened the saddle pack and removed a parcel tied with string. "I brought Fidgets a present," he said.

"The least I could do, considering the number of voles she's dropped at my feet."

"What of Diana?" she demanded impatiently. "How is she?"

"You may read the news for yourself." He withdrew several folded sheets of paper from his coat pocket. "She sent a letter."

Lucy seized it and quickly scanned the pages, inscribed with a pencil in Diana's elegant handwriting. Then she read it again, more slowly, while Kit was in the stable with Timmy, seeing to the horse.

Fidgets had relocated to his shoulder when Kit returned, examining his beaver hat with a frown. "Look at this," he said, holding it in front of her. "Cost me a pretty penny, this bonnet."

She saw several small holes in the crown where eight talons had knifed in. "Better the hat than your head," she said unsympathetically. "Consider it the price of love."

He gave Fidgets a stern look. "Just for that, milady, I may not give you your present after all."

The owl made a low moaning sound.

"The letter tells me Diana is happy and well, but of course she would say that. You spoke with her, Kit. How is she truly getting on?"

"Far better than I expected. Country life appears to suit her. When I arrived she was mucking out a sty and singing naughty songs to the piglets. Later she introduced me to geese and ducks and cows and goats, each one by name." He regarded her with a pensive expression. "It is well, I believe, that she has work to occupy her time and new experiences to keep her from reflecting overmuch on the old ones."

She nodded. That had often been her thought at the cottage, where Diana had little to do but mope. "Was she making a pretense, do you think, so that we'd not be concerned about her?"

"She would likely have done so, were it called for. But Nell—er, her hostess—confirmed my own impressions. They have already become fast friends and were planning to cook up a batch of jam this afternoon. I am promised several jars for the Candale pantry on my next visit."

Her heart considerably lighter at such an encouraging report, Lucy smiled. "Well then, I shall worry about her only every other minute. And, Kit, I *am* sorry about your hat."

"As you said, the price of love." He tossed it onto a fence post and offered her his arm. "Will you walk with me for a few minutes? There is something I wish to discuss with you."

Her heart sank again. From the glint in his sky-blue eyes, he was up to something she was not going to like. But what could be worse than his last appalling idea—their appearance at Sir Basil Crawley's ball—or the one before it that cast her as his fiancée? Fingers crossed that he had only minor devilry in mind this time, she allowed him to escort her to the hill that rose up behind the paddocks.

As they began the climb a cool breeze tugged at her bonnet and lifted his hair, burnished to gold by the midafternoon sunshine. The hill was mostly bare, sprinkled with scarlet-berried rowans and birches cloaked with gold-brown autumn leaves.

Fidgets picked his way down Kit's other arm and began to peck at the string tied around the parcel in his hand. "Such a greedy wench you are," Kit chided.

"What did you bring hi—her?"

"Chicken feet. Celia won't allow poultry on the premises, so I was forced to import them from the farm."

She eyed the parcel dubiously. "Are owls partial to chicken feet?"

"Devil if I know, but they're a far sight easier to come by than voles. Shall we find out?"

When they reached the top of the hill, Kit placed Fidgets on a tree branch and moved about twenty yards away. The owl immediately flew to his shoulder. "No, no, my dear." He returned Fidgets to the branch. "Be a good girl and stay where I put you."

A few moments later Fidgets was on his shoulder again. Patiently, he repeated the exercise several times, with similar results.

"Whatever are you doing?" Lucy asked as he carried the owl back to the tree once again.

"Trying to get a stubborn female to obey me, which I daresay no man has succeeded in doing since the dawn of time." He stroked Fidgets's head. "Stay, beloved. Please. Do it for *me*."

This time Fidgets remained in place when Kit walked away. Keeping his back to the owl, he opened the parcel and withdrew a gray-pink chicken foot. Then he turned and held it out. "Come, Fidgets. Come and get it!"

The owl tilted its head, regarding him curiously, but stayed where it was.

"You're confusing the poor thing, Kit. First you tell her to stay, and then you insist that she come."

"Precisely. There really is a point to this, moonbeam. All will be made clear. I simply want to discover if Fidgets can be persuaded to come to me when I give her the signal, and apparently a chicken foot fails to turn the trick. It seems I'll be put to hunting down a mousie to tempt her."

"Will that not signify that Fidgets has trained *you*?" she observed tartly.

He chuckled. "I'm doing something wrong here, obviously. What draws an owl to prey? Odor? A rustling sound in the undergrowth?"

"Either would do, I suppose. Owls generally hunt at night, which is about all I know of the matter. They can see creatures moving in the dark, don't you imagine, the way cats do?"

"Lucy, you are positively brilliant. That's it, of course. Watch this!" He waved the chicken foot back and forth in an arcing motion.

With a shrill cry, Fidgets swooped from the branch, plucked the chicken foot from his hand, and settled on the ground to gobble it up.

"Well done," Kit said, "but that beak came a bit too close to m'fingers. I'd as soon not lose any one of them on our next try."

Lucy watched him tie the string that had secured the parcel around a chicken foot and move some distance away. Then he swung the string round and round over his head. In a flash,

Fidgets was onto the target with extended claws, ripping chicken foot and string from Kit's hand and carrying it to the tree branch.

Kit followed, drawing his knife from the sheath to detach the string before Fidgets swallowed it. "That's the secret," he called to Lucy over his shoulder. "She flies to whatever moves, so long as it resembles a meal. By tomorrow, with practice, I'll have her coming and going whenever I wish."

Bully for you, Lucy thought, toes curling inside her half boots. He could not rest until he had seized control of everything and everyone. Even a befuddled, infatuated owl must be trained to obey him.

He placed another chicken foot on the branch for Fidgets, retied the parcel, and approached Lucy with a wide grin on his face. "Let me guess. You are wondering what this is all about."

"Male supremacy, I would presume. A demonstration of how clever you are."

"I am sometimes clever," he said unrepentantly. "But the man who thinks himself supreme is a fool."

"Just so."

"Lucifer! A man could shave with the edge of your tongue. Cry peace, will you, long enough for me to explain?"

Contrition burned in her throat. "I beg your pardon, sir. I have no right to speak to you in such a way. It is—I mean—oh, I don't know what I mean! In future, I shall think twice and then again before—"

"Don't you dare," he said softly. "I mean it, Lucy. Speak your mind with me at all times. Have you ever known me to take offense?"

"N-no. But I always assumed that was because you didn't give a twig what I had to say. Like not taking offense when a dog barks or a frog croaks."

"Ah. I see." He put down the parcel and placed his hands on her shoulders. "I've not made myself clear. Believe me, I do give a twig, Lucy mine, for every word you say and for every expression on your face and for every gesture you make. I give whole forests for each one of your rare, beautiful smiles."

Breathless, she gazed into his clear blue eyes. It would be so easy to lose herself in him.

"Come," he said, releasing her shoulders. "Beyond that cluster of birches is a splendid view of the fells."

When they reached a promontory shaded by a large oak, they stood in silence for several minutes, gazing over the sheep-studded dale to the rugged crags beyond. In the far distance, the fells looked to be made of twilight-blue smoke.

"I have been thinking," he said, "what else can be done for Diana. She is in good hands, of course, but Whitney still holds the trump card. So long as he owns the legal right to demand she be returned to his custody, he can make matters exceedingly difficult. He'll not get hold of her, you may be sure. No one within a hundred miles will defy the Earl of Kendal on this matter. But should Whitney petition the Chancery Court, and I expect he will, things could get slippery."

"How? I know nothing about the courts. Tell me exactly."

He gave her a lopsided smile. "My acquaintance with the law is primarily from the opposite side, Lucy. You must ask Kendal to explain the finer points. I do know that Chancery moves at the speed of a glacier and that there's little chance Lord Eldon will render a final judgment before Diana comes of age, at which point the ruling becomes moot. But she may well be called to give depositions, and there is a remote possibility she'll be summoned to London for questioning."

"We mustn't let that happen," Lucy said instantly. "It would be a frightful experience."

"The more so because she originally said that the injury to her face was the result of a fall, without explaining it was Whitney caused the fall by striking her."

"But she only lied because she fears him. Anyone who sees her face will understand why."

Kit ran his fingers through his hair. "I should never have gone down this track. It has alarmed you and led me away from my point. Diana will not be returned to her guardian under any circumstances, and Kendal will stand her protector so far as the law permits. But should Whitney dig in his heels, she is certain to be subjected to a great deal of unpleasantness before the case is finally resolved in her favor. I wish to spare her that."

"By all means!"

"*Any* and all means," he said. "Keep to that thought while you hear me out. Our problem is simple enough—we must convince Whitney to sign over custody of Diana to my brother without taking the matter to court. We know Basil Crawley has been pulling his strings, but we're not altogether certain why."

"He wants to marry Diana. You already know that. She inherited a considerable fortune."

"But he is, by all accounts, a wealthy man. Possibly a greedy one, which would explain his persistence, but he may have an altogether different motive. Perhaps Kendal's investigation into his business affairs will disclose what it is, although we'll have no answers anytime soon."

"So how can they signify?" She scowled at him. "You are dancing around the point, sir."

"Yes. Sorry. I'll come at it directly, if you promise not to object until I've finished explaining how we shall bring Whitney to heel."

"There is a way to do that?"

"Of course." He grinned widely. "I have a plan."

Oh, dear, she thought, sealing her lips and gesturing him to proceed.

With boyish enthusiasm, he launched into a plot so outrageous that she could not believe her own ears. With growing dismay, which soon ratcheted up to stunned disbelief and went from there to absolute horror, she listened to the most improbable scenario ever devised by a supposedly sane man. By the end, she was practically sputtering.

"So," he said, looking excessively pleased with himself. "What do you think?"

What she thought was easily summarized. "You are deranged."

"That aside, you have to admit it's a devilish ingenious scheme."

"It's sheer lunacy. Who could believe such a thing?"

"No one with a crumb of sense, to be sure, but we are dealing with Lord Whitney. And if you pause to consider, Lucy, playing at witchcraft was your idea in the first place."

She threw up her hands. "That was to keep anyone from venturing too close to the cottage where we were hiding. And yes, mostly to scare Lord Whitney away. When Diana told me he was superstitious, it put me in mind of my name, Jennet Preston, and the Lancashire Witches. But what I did was nothing whatever like what you have proposed."

"Nonetheless, I am convinced it will work. This morning I spoke at length with Diana about her uncle. Did you know that he keeps a pair of scissors under the doormat to prevent witches from entering his house? Don't ask me how scissors could stop a witch, were there any such thing, but he is sure they will. He picks up every bit of metal he sees on the ground—nails, pins, discarded tin cups—lest a witch craft it into a weapon to use against him. Diana says he has filled a trunk with the metal odds and ends he has accumulated. He is forever touching wood and tossing salt over his shoulder and muttering imprecations meant to keep devils at bay."

"Lots of people are more or less superstitious," she cut in. "Their habits are generally harmless."

"But few people are quite so stupid as Lord Whitney. What's more, he feels guilty for what he did to his niece. I must take her word on that, but she said that he has wept and apologized profusely on more than one occasion."

"Crocodile tears. He hoped to use her beauty to his own advantage, and now he has destroyed it."

"I'm not so sure that he is insincere, Lucy. And he's lost nothing, because Crawley still wishes to wed her despite her appearance. Keep in mind our primary goal. If Whitney is spooked into signing a few legal documents, Diana will not be dragged through the courts. Isn't that worth taking a long shot? And consider this. Superstition, stupidity, and guilt make a potent brew. We have only to light a spark and Lord Whitney will go up in flames."

Lucy gave him a penetrating look. "*You* are the one consumed by this farce, sir. You are so caught up in the theatrics of your scheme and the childish notion of running wild on All Hallows' Eve that the end result is inconsequential. May I hope you told Diana nothing of your absurd plan?"

"You may be sure I did not. She has enough on her plate as it is. And I expected you to react in precisely this fashion, Lucy, so don't imagine I'll be talked out of having a go. After leaving the farm, I rode over to Silverdale and spoke with Robbie and Giles Handa. They've agreed to join up, and Giles has all sorts of ideas I'd never have thought of. Apothecaries can do wondrous things with saltpeter and sulfur and charcoal. You will be amazed."

Her heart plunged to the vicinity of her toes. She'd have sworn that stolid, sensible Robbie would have no part of this circus. And serious-minded Giles Handa? But of course, she recalled in some wonder, they had believed in her when she asked their help, asking no questions, trusting her instantly.

She had never brought herself to return their trust. At every moment she expected them to betray her, especially when she learned of the reward posted for Diana's return. But they had remained loyal and generous, with little hope of repayment for all they had done on behalf of two strangers. Tears welled in her eyes to think of it. She turned away so that Kit would not see them.

She felt him move behind her then, sensed the warmth of his body against her back and the brush of his breath against her hair, and nearly fled from the startling intimacy of his closeness. But she couldn't find the strength to move. To her horror, she didn't even try very hard. Nor did Kit touch her, although he sifted through her skin and flesh in a way that made her almost believe in spirits and demonic possession.

"Will you enlist with us, moonbeam?" he asked softly. "You'll be sorry if you don't. I mean to bring Timmy into the plot, and Fidgets, too. Just imagine how it will feel to be left behind, wondering what we are up to and fretting because you aren't there to see it."

It was plain as a pikestaff that she had no choice in the matter. Kit would proceed with or without her, and someone in possession of a full deck of wits had to go along to keep an eye on him. "Oh, very well," she said, turning to face him. "What part will I be playing this time?"

"Why, the witch, of course. And so will I. A copy of your wig is being made for me to wear, and I shall have a lovely new cloak, too. Fidgets will play the Demon Owl from Hades, and I'll think up a ghoulish role for Timmy." He grinned. "Wait until you see the creepy setting I've selected for our drama. I'll take you there tomorrow."

"Thank you." She shook her head in profound disgust. "I can hardly wait."

Chapter 13

"We're almost there," Kit said, reaching for the silver-knobbed walking stick he'd borrowed, along with the crested coach and liveried footmen, from his brother. "Chin up, moonbeam. It won't be as bad as you are imagining. In fact, I expect we'll have ourselves a fine time tonight."

Lucy ceased pleating her skirts between stiff fingers long enough to glare at him.

"None of that when we are inside," he warned. "Remember, you adore me."

"Yes, and I am a twittering imbecile to boot. Fear not, sir. I know my part. But keep to your promise that we won't stay overlong."

"I have already done so, merely by arranging for our late arrival. Be glad of it. We'll not have to walk the gauntlet of a receiving line."

The carriage turned onto a circular drive and drew up in front of the entrance porch. Kit had been a guest at the house on two or three occasions when it still belonged to the Witherspoon family, as it had done for several generations of Witherspoons. But a series of bad harvests quickly plunged them into debt. The mortgages were called, the house was sold at auction, and Sir Basil Crawley had snagged himself a bargain.

A footman let down the steps and Kit jumped out, turning to assist Lucy to the ground. Music floated down from the ballroom, light poured from every window, and a regiment of servants waited in the entrance hall to accept their cloaks and Kit's hat and cane.

"Welcome to Crawley Hall," the butler said archly, gesturing to the sweeping staircase. "Follow me, if you please. Whom shall I announce?"

"Not a soul," Kit responded blithely, taking Lucy's arm. "We prefer to enter quietly, seeing as how we are so late. M'fiancée took a devilish time primping herself out, didn't you, m'dear? But I must say it was worth it."

And so it was, a thousandfold. Her ball dress was not one he'd have chosen for this occasion and the role she was to play, but it suited her to perfection. She might have been clothed in pure moonlight, so pale was the gauzy silk that draped gracefully and unadorned over her slender figure. An invisible thread studded with pearls had been woven through her hair, and three strands of pearls formed a high collar around her long, graceful neck. She wore kidskin gloves that reached above her elbows, pearly satin slippers, and carried a delicate ivory fan.

Were he not already in love with her, he'd have tumbled head over heels at first sight of the elegant beauty who descended the staircase at Candale only a few hours before. She had been more than a little impressed with him as well, although she took care to give no sign of it. But when she thought he wasn't looking, she had cast admiring glances at the fine figure he cut in formal evening wear. It was almost worth enduring the constriction of a high starched collar and elaborately crafted neckcloth to see her regard him with unprecedented approval.

She clutched at his arm as they slipped into the ballroom and took shelter in a quiet corner behind a potted orange tree. The company was thin, Kit saw immediately, no more than sixty or seventy people in a room meant to hold twice that number. A lively country dance was under way.

No expense had been spared in decorating the ballroom, which had been undeniably shabby when last he saw it. Crimson brocade wallpaper and large gilt-framed mirrors adorned the walls, flamboyant chandeliers hung from the ceiling, and the new and intricate parquet floor was waxed to a high sheen. Beside a burbling indoor fountain, the orchestra was ensconced on a satin-draped stage. The overall effect was showy, lavish, and of decidedly inferior taste.

He turned his attention to the others guests, recognizing several wealthy landowners and a few notable parvenus. Not one of Westmoreland's aristocratic families was represented, although they must have received invitations. If Crawley was so bold as to send a card to the Earl of Kendal, he'd not have overlooked peers of lesser distinction.

"I do believe," Kit remarked to Lucy, "that I quite outrank everyone here. And considering how frightfully low on the order of precedence we younger sons of earls are to be found, that is something of an accomplishment."

"How pleased you must be. But is that of any significance?"

Trust her to come directly to the point. "It is to our advantage, I believe. No one with a speck of good breeding will approach us, which I am sure you are delighted to hear. But more consequential is the pronounced smell of ambition in the air. I surmise that Sir Basil has a fancy to climb the social ladder, and a wife of impeccable birth and breeding would give him a great boost up."

"Yes, indeed." Her brow furrowed. "That would explain a good deal, wouldn't it? I wish we knew more about his origins. Diana said only that he used to live in Manchester and that he was granted a knighthood on recommendation of the prince regent."

"Then we may assume he purchased it, at least indirectly. Prinny is in debt up to his several chins. When my brother has sniffed out how Sir Basil came by his money, I'll be very much surprised if he acquired it honestly."

"Where do you suppose he is? I see no one matching the description Diana provided me."

"Nor do I. Not precisely a cordial host, our dear Sir Basil. But perhaps he is disappointed at the turnout and considers the few guests that did show up to be unworthy of his attention."

"Which would make him nearly as toplofty as the highest-ranking gentleman in the room," she observed with a sly smile. "We came here only to meet him, Kit. There can be no reason to stay if he's already toddled off to bed."

"Nice try, moonbeam, but we'll keep our anchor in the water a bit longer. The cotillion is forming, I see. Would you care to dance?"

Her cheeks drained of color. "No, please. I am quite sure I've already forgot the steps."

"Then we shall make a grand circuit, arm in arm. You will gaze insipidly at me while I look down my nose at everyone else." He threaded her arm through his, feeling her tension, keenly attuned to her mood and to the warmth of her body and the faint fragrance of lavender that hovered about her. Ordering his unruly body to behave itself, he led her in procession along the edge of the dance floor, smiling coolly at the people he knew without approaching them and ostentatiously ignoring the others.

Lucy despised the role she was playing this night, he knew, but he was even less at ease. In other circumstances, he'd have greeted old acquaintances instead of shunning them, danced with the prettiest girls and with the wallflowers, too, and flirted with all the dowagers. He was unused to walking high in the instep, as he was doing now, and found it devilish unpleasant.

They were making the turn that would lead them in front of the orchestra's stage when he glanced toward the ballroom door and saw five men enter. One, a large stocky man with spiky black hair, he recognized immediately. It was the man who had shot him.

"What's wrong?" Lucy asked softly, following the question with a fatuous giggle.

Good girl! "Don't be obvious about it, but steal a look at the men who just came into the room. Could any one of them be Crawley?"

"Yes," she whispered after a moment. "He's the tall man with the beaked nose. But we must leave here immediately. Bartholomew Pugg is with him."

Kit seized a flute of champagne from a passing servant and turned to Lucy, shielding her with his body. "Who the devil is Bartholomew Pugg?"

"The Bow Street Runner. The one who came to the cottage. The one who is coming this way right now."

"Damn." Feigning a laugh, he held the glass to her lips. She sipped obediently, pretending to look into his eyes while she watched the Runner. A tiny shrug of her left shoulder told Kit when Pugg was close to them, and on which side. With a move designed to appear casual, he drifted a turn, keeping himself between Lucy and the spot where the Runner had halted. He felt the man's sharp gaze pronging into his back.

"What are we to do?" Lucy mouthed silently.

"Nothing. Go on as you are. Touch my cheek and act besotted."

Her fingers lifted to his face and curled around his jaw. For a moment he nearly forgot the Runner, and why they were there, and everything else on the planet.

She still had hold of her wits, it seemed. "He is bound to know me," she murmured into his neckcloth. "I was Mrs. Preston then, but although he saw my face only in the dim light from the fireplace, he's the sort who could pick me out in a crowd of thousands."

Kit, reckoning he could find her in a crowd of millions, took her certainty to heart. "We'll do best to get it over with then. I am going to steer us in his direction. Take the glass, Lucy, and follow your instincts."

The orchestra's music cooperated, by luck swinging into a bouncy rhythm that practically begged people to dance. Kit swept Lucy into his arms and improvised a jig, aiming himself at the Runner. Seconds later they collided. Lucy sloshed champagne over Pugg before dropping the glass, which shattered on the floor. He staggered backward, champagne streaming down his ill-fitted coat.

Kit regarded what happened next with considerable awe.

Lucy brushed at the Runner's coat with both hands. "Oh my heavens!" she exclaimed in a tone nearly an octave higher than her usual husky alto. "How terribly clumsy of me. I have ruined your coat."

" 'Tis nothing, ma'am." Pugg held up a pair of gnarled hands. "I assure you."

"Kittikins says I've no head for champagne, but I do love it so. The bubbles go up through my nostrils and make me quite giddy. Do I know you, sir?"

Her knees bent, and Pugg grabbed her elbow to hold her upright. For what seemed to Kit an infinite time, he studied her face. Then he turned his gaze to Kit for a long moment before looking back at Lucy. "If we had met, I would recall the time and place," he said in a flat voice. "Perhaps I do. Too soon to tell."

As a servant arrived to sweep up the glass, Pugg released her and gave a short bow. "My apologies, madam, for stepping into your path."

"It was my fault entirely," Kit said, taking Lucy's arm. "Come, beloved. We are in the way of the dancers."

"How could you *fling* me at him in such a way?" she demanded when they had seated themselves on one of the padded benches that lined the wall.

"It was effective, was it not? Now we are certain that he failed to recognize you. He has left the room without speaking to Crawley, which he would surely have done if his suspicions were aroused."

"But they are. He *did* recognize me. I saw it in his eyes. I cannot guess why he said it was too soon to tell when he already knew, unless he meant to throw us off our guard."

"Look happy as we converse," Kit reminded her, relaxing his shoulders against the wall and stretching out his legs. "Perhaps he meant precisely what he said—too soon to *tell*. Pugg is a Runner, not one of Crawley's minions, and he needn't report everything he learns."

She smiled at him blissfully, but her voice could have scorched paint from a wall. "He will be snooping about Candale and watching our every move, you may be sure of it. There can be no more visits to Diana, Kit, and your unholy drama will have to be called off."

"We'll see. Meantime, Crawley is looking in our direction." He took her hand and began to play with her fingers. "I suspect he has no great regard for females, so when he comes over to greet us, confirm his opinion by being exceptionally goose-witted. I'm hoping to draw him into a private conversa—"

"You'll not leave me here alone, Kit. I won't have it!"

He looked up and saw fear trembling behind the fire in her eyes. Lucy had just faced down a Bow Street Runner, but the prospect of spending a few minutes among strangers in a ball-room was unbearable to her. Well, so be it. "We are insepa-rable, don't you know? I'll not abandon you, but in turn you must convince him that it is perfectly safe to speak freely in your company."

"Because I have the intelligence of a doorstop. Yes, I do understand."

"Take no insult, moonbeam. He will think much the same of me, if all goes well. Ah, here he comes. This would be a good time to fondle any part of me that takes your fancy."

She chose his knee. And she was making such good work of it when Crawley made his bow that Kit could only gaze blankly at the man he'd taken so much trouble to meet.

"You are most welcome to my home," Crawley intoned in a stiff voice. "I beg your pardon for failing to greet you when you arrived."

Kit detached Lucy's hand from his knee and stood. "You would be Sir Basil then? Pleased to make your acquaintance. I am Christopher Valliant, and the beauty is m'fiancée, Miss Lucinda Jennet. C'mon, puss, up you go! Make a proper curtsy to our host."

She rose, staggering a trifle, and managed a dip before grasp-ing Kit's arm to regain her balance. "I can't think why I am so clumsy of a sudden, sir." She fluttered her lashes. "What did you say your name was?"

"Sir Basil Crawley," he replied, looking pained. "A pleasure to meet you, Miss Jennet."

"She's had a bit too much champagne," Kit confided in a whisper. "Goes right to her head, it does, but she *will* keep tippling. Don't much care for the stuff m'self."

"Might I offer you something more to your taste then? Although I have been in residence here for only a few weeks, I made it a point of urgency to establish a prime cellar, and there is quite a passable vintage decanted in my study. Will you join me, sir? My cousin, Mrs. Milque, will be pleased to introduce Miss Jennet to some of the other guests while we become better acquainted."

Lucy grasped Kit's arm and clung like a limpet. "But I don't *want* to meet these tiresome people," she whined.

Slicing Crawley a man-to-man look, Kit shrugged. "Another time, perhaps. She has already plowed into a gentleman and spilled her drink over him. No telling what she'll get up to next, especially if she thinks I've deserted her. She don't like letting me out of her sight. Isn't that right, puss?"

She hiccuped.

"Bring her along then," Crawley said in a resigned tone. "I quite understand her reluctance to mingle in this company. Take no insult, but Westmoreland society is not at all what I had hoped it to be."

With Lucy teetering alongside him, still clutching his arm, Kit followed Crawley from the ballroom into the passageway. He wondered what had become of the man who had put a bullet in his shoulder. With all that had happened since first he saw him, Kit had lost track of his location. Just as well. If they came face-to-face, he might have been tempted to do something rash. The confrontation with Pugg had been enough of a rumpus for one night, he supposed, and beating his onetime assailant to a pulp would attract far too much attention of the wrong kind.

Reluctantly, Kit consigned his personal grievance to the distant future. At the very least, he had learned this night that Crawley was more than a persistent suitor for Diana's hand. He was in league with the ruffians who had been terrorizing peaceful smugglers in order to stock his wine cellar, and at least one of those thugs had no scruples about killing.

Crawley ushered his guests into a dim room overcrowded with furniture. A large desk was covered with ledgers and stacks of paper, all neatly ordered, showing him to be a man of precise habits. After directing Lucy and Kit to a sofa near the fireplace, he went to an array of crystal decanters on the mahogany sideboard. "I regret that the earl was unable to join us this evening," he said, filling two glasses with wine and reaching for a third.

"None for my puss," Kit advised him. Lucy had rested her head on his shoulder and turned a vacant gaze to the ceiling, her expression so stupefied that it was all he could do to keep from laughing. "As for Kendal, he can't be pried from the house these days. Not since that squalling brat took up residence, although why he wanted another when he's got an heir stashed away at Harrow escapes me. But there it is. He has become quite a bore."

"The countess is his second wife, I understand. No doubt she wanted children of her own."

"Most like. And he is well under her thumb already, I can tell you. It's all very well to be in love with one's wife, but quite another thing to hand over the reins. When Lucinda and I are leg-shackled, I mean to call the shots." He wrapped an arm around her limp body. "There is much to be said for choosing a bride in possession of a large fortune and very few wits."

Crawley handed him a glass of wine. "Will you reside in Westmoreland after you are wed?"

"It is undecided. She fancies a London town house, and for that matter, so do I. But her money will soon run out if I spend it as we both wish, and then where would we be? Her family wants us to settle in Devon, of course, so that they can keep an eye on me." He forced an aggrieved look to his face. "They're in trade, you know. Don't pass that around. M'brother is none too happy about it, but without sixpence to scratch with, it's not as if I could marry within my own class."

"You have an aversion to trade?"

"Always did, until I met my pussycat." Kit glanced at the head resting on his shoulder. "Lord, I think she's gone to sleep. Can't say I'm sorry for it. When she's awake, she chatters like a magpie."

"A considerable distance from here, Devonshire. Are there no eligible young ladies closer to hand?"

"Any number of them, although few have claim to beauty and fortune. One or t'other, but not both."

"Indeed, it is a rare combination." Crawley sipped at his wine. "Did you perchance pay court to a Miss Diana Whitney? I am informed that she is a considerable heiress and exceedingly well favored."

"Never heard of her. No Whitneys in Westmoreland, I'm fairly sure, or none of any consequence. Is she out?"

"The family estate is a little way south of Lancaster, I believe, and her debut was postponed due to the tragic death of her parents."

"There you are then. Stands to reason I'd not have come upon her. And now, of course, I have my Devonshire puss. Couldn't cry off even if I wanted to, not since her father towed me out of the River Tick. Only to throw me into parson's mousetrap, to be sure, but I go willingly. She's a lusty armful when she ain't rattling on."

Crawley rubbed his long nose with a stubby-fingered hand. "We must all marry to advantage one way or another. I find myself in an equally difficult predicament, with a fortune derived from trade and a wish to better myself socially."

"Then you should buy yourself a wife from the aristocracy in the same way my turtledove's family is buying me." Kit held out his glass for a refill. "This is superb, I must say. French?"

"Of course." Crawley settled on a chair across from him.

"Have you considered investing your wife's dowry in a profitable venture? I don't mean to intrude in your private affairs, sir, but it happens I know of several ways to multiply your investments if you are willing to take a few minor risks. Please stop me if you prefer I not continue."

"By all means, do go on. What have you in mind?"

"Naturally, I can offer no particulars until you have the money in hand. Circumstances and opportunities come and go, and what I would recommend today will be unavailable tomorrow. But when you are in a position to act quickly, I shall be honored to be of assistance."

"In exchange for what?" Kit asked bluntly. "A percentage of the initial investment, perhaps, or a slice of the profits?"

"Dear me, no. What little I could amass in such a fashion is scarcely worth my time. But I apprehend that you are a man of the world, sir, with a grasp of—shall we say?—tit for tat. I propose to inform you of business opportunities, the same ones I select for my own speculations, in exchange for a few introductions."

"Well, that's simple enough. But I should warn you that my reputation hereabouts is not altogether without blemish. Fact is, some of the high sticklers won't have me in their drawing rooms, and once I'm leg-shackled to a cit, my credit will sink even lower."

"My word." Crawley's thin lips curved ever so slightly. "One could imagine you to have no interest in our proposed arrangement."

"Oh, but I do. Just wanted you to know how the wind is blowing." Deciding that he'd endured quite enough of Sir Basil for one evening, Kit nudged Lucy with his elbow. "If you are still of a mind to proceed, we'll speak again when the puss's dowry is burning a hole in m'pocket."

"I hope that will be soon. In the meantime, may I trust that you—"

Lucy shot upright with a squeal. Turning a wide-eyed gaze to Crawley, she shook her head as if to clear it. "Who in blazes are *you*?"

Kit wrapped his arm around her. "Wake up, pussycat. You must have been having a bad dream."

She slumped into his embrace. "Oh, there you are, Kittikins. What happened to the ball? Why aren't we dancing?"

"Why not indeed?" He glanced at Crawley and rolled his eyes.

"Rather have s'more champagne. I'm *thirsty*."

"I shall be pleased to escort you to the ballroom," Crawley said, coming to his feet. "Mr. Valliant, you'll not object if I have several bottles of this excellent wine delivered to your carriage as a token of my esteem? And, if I may be so bold, as a seal on the bargain we have struck?"

"Delighted, I'm sure," Kit replied, stifling a laugh. The blackguard was oiling him up with the selfsame wine he'd stolen from him not ten nights before.

When they arrived at the ballroom, it was apparent that a number of guests had already taken their leave. Several couples were rather lackadaisically engaged in a contredanse, and others hovered around the tables where a supper had been laid out.

"You will pardon me if I do not join you," Crawley said with a bow. "I have pressing matters of business to attend to. Honored to make your acquaintance, Miss Jennet. Good night, Mr. Valliant. Do enjoy yourselves for the rest of the evening."

"Thank heavens!" she said when he was finally gone. "What a horrid man. All the time you were speaking with him, I was longing to claw my fingernails down his face."

"Far less than he deserves," Kit agreed, drawing her away from the open doors into a shadowy alcove. "And all the time I was speaking to him, this is what I was longing to do." Before she could object, he wrapped one hand around her waist and the other around her neck and brought his lips to hers.

He meant only to give her a brief embrace, one that revealed nothing of the passion that burned in him, one she might accept without becoming enraged. But to his astonishment she melted against him, her soft breasts pressing against his chest as she put her hands on his shoulders and allowed him to deepen the kiss.

They were both breathing heavily when he finally lifted his head and looked into her stunned eyes. She rallied quickly, though. Too quickly.

"I didn't mean to do that." Stepping back, she straightened her skirts and stiffened her spine. "It was the champagne. Spirits really do render me witless. Pray forget it ever happened."

"As if I could, moonbeam," he said gently. "But I'll not kiss you again unless you ask me to."

"See that you don't! May we leave now, please?"

"Not quite yet. For one thing, we must allow time for the wine Crawley promised me to be stowed in the carriage. And for another, you have expressed a wish to dance. He will expect us to do so." Kit seized her hand. "Come along, puss. I hear the first notes of a waltz."

Her gaze was plastered on his neckcloth as they joined the other couples, only four of them, on the dance floor. But she moved in tune with him, never missing a step, graceful as a willow in a summer breeze, for all her efforts to hold herself stiffly away from him.

"Never again," she said between her teeth, "are you to call me 'puss.' "

"Agreed . . . until the next time I hear 'Kittikins.' "

She unbent long enough to cast him a saucy grin. "It suits you. But truly, Kit, what was the point of coming here? We learned that Sir Basil is a swine, but we already knew that from Diana's report. Or did you not believe her? You have made a deal with him that you've no intention of honoring, which accomplished nothing whatsoever. A Bow Street Runner is now on to our masquerade and will be lurking in the shadows, expecting us to lead him to his quarry. I told you from the first that this was a terrible idea, but you would not listen. You *never* listen."

"Of course I do. Make no mistake, Lucy. I have the highest regard for your intelligence and judgment."

"Which is why you invariably ignore whatever I say and charge ahead, towing everyone else in your wake."

He took a deep breath. Her words had hit home, or near to, and they hurt. But he'd nothing to hide from her. If they spent the rest of their lives together, which was his firm intention, she was bound to uncover every last one of his flaws. "I demand my own way, Lucy, because I am willful, self-indulgent, impulsive, and—until I met you—without purpose."

Her eyes widened. And her mouth opened to speak, but nothing came out.

For once, Kit reflected bleakly, he had managed to silence her. And startle her, too, with a confession he hadn't wanted to make yet. This was scarcely the time and place to bare his soul. With some effort, he relocated the original subject. "You may well be correct that it was a mistake to have come here," he said. "Nevertheless, I have learned a good deal more than you imagine, and I believe that the information will prove of use."

"What could you have discovered that I failed to note? I have been with you the entire time."

Since he'd already resolved not to tell her about recognizing the man who shot him, there was no clear answer to her question. Nor was he thinking at all clearly, what with her so supple in his arms and so infinitely lovely. A magical creature woven of moonlight and pearls, his Lucy—when she wasn't flaying him alive with her tongue. "We have all the long journey back to Candale to discuss the events of this night, Lucy, or to have a row if you prefer. But for now, I cannot be sorry for any circumstance that permits me to hold you in my arms. The waltz will soon come to an end, moonbeam. Until it does, will you simply dance with me?"

Perhaps it was only that he wanted to think so, but it felt as if she drew closer to him. The tension in her body seemed to dissolve. And the waltz played on, far longer than he dared to hope, attuned to his deepest wishes. Imperceptibly the meter slowed. The tone of the violins grew deep and sonorous, vibrating to the passion banked inside him.

She was gazing somewhere beyond his shoulder, or into herself, her eyes dreamy and unfocused.

He nearly always knew what she was thinking before she told him, and she generally left him in no doubt whatever by speaking her mind. But at this moment, bewildered by the expression on her face and the unfathomable mystery in the curve of her lips, the wistful lift of her brows, and the faraway look in her eyes, he felt powerless.

Kit rested his cheek against hers for a moment. "Tell me what you are thinking about, moonbeam."

Her murmured reply was nearly inaudible.

He thought . . . but no. That wasn't it. She could not possibly have said "elephants."

Chapter 14

In the chill October night, Lucy was glad of her heavy cloak and the oilcloth tarp lining the pit, which was a little larger than a grave but not so deep. She was perched on a small footstool with a swath of black serge draped over her cape to conceal its green-white glow.

Time passed slowly in a peat pit. From her position, she could see nothing but the black sky directly overhead, blazing with stars and the gibbous moon. Wind stirred bracken and dry autumn grasses, and in the copses of hazels and oaks, rooks and wood pigeons beat their wings.

The conspirators had been in position for nearly an hour. Timmy was stationed on a hill overlooking the road, ready to give the signal when Robbie and Lord Whitney came into view. Lucy placed no great faith that they would appear at all.

In her opinion, this entire scheme was sheer lunacy. It had held together thus far only because Kit swept away all objections and plowed directly ahead, relying on everyone else to follow. Which they had done, to be sure.

Giles Handa was stationed in a thick spinney with any number of props and implements spread out on a blanket, including a large thin sheet of metal and a drum. Timmy had practiced until he could deliver a spine-chilling howl, which was meant to sound like a wolf baying at the moon. Since none of the conspirators had actually heard a wolf, there was no way to be certain of its accuracy, but during their practice session it had echoed quite effectively off the surrounding hills.

High atop the burned-out ruin of Arnside watchtower, which he had reached with the use of a grappling hook and rope, Kit was crouched behind the battlement with his own supply of props and devices, including an iron bedwarmer filled with hot coals. From her position about a hundred yards away, she could detect no sign of him. The derelict pele tower, with its broken walls, collapsed masonry, and gaping window openings, was a hoary presence looming near the top of a long sloping hill. The first time Kit brought her here she had looked inside, but there remained only the corbels meant to support the burned-away floor and a spiral staircase ending in midair.

As the minutes dragged by and the moon climbed higher, Lucy grew more and more convinced they ought to pack it in. Lord Whitney would surely refuse to set out for a remote destination in the middle of the night. Especially *this* night, All Hallows' Eve.

Kit's confidence had never wavered. He'd rehearsed Robbie for hours, preparing him to deal with every question and objection Whitney might raise. To avoid being recognized when the escapade was over, the Scotsman had even dyed his luxuriant copper-colored beard, padded one shoulder to give him the look of a hunchback, and inserted pebbles in his shoes to remind himself to shuffle.

If Lord Whitney was at home when Robbie arrived, and if he admitted the disreputable creature past the gate, he'd have heard a plain-enough tale. "Old Fergus," an itinerant ne'er-do-well who sought out deserted crofts and barns to sleep in, had come upon a young woman with a scarred face on the previous night. He saw her through the window of an isolated cottage, moved on to seek shelter elsewhere, and thought nothing more of the incident until he spotted a notice about the reward posted in a shop window.

Now they waited to learn if Lord Whitney had fallen for Robbie's story. Kit had advised her to be patient, for it was a long journey to this spot from Willow Manor, and the last several miles had to be navigated on a rough track through marshy land.

A soft whistle, nearly imperceptible, sounded from beyond a fringe of trees to her right. She listened closely. Next came two shorts and a long, the signal that Robbie was approaching in company with another man. Lucy's heart began to pound.

Dropping to her knees, she rigged a makeshift ladder by placing the footstool atop a small wooden box at the spot where she would emerge from the pit. Kit had demonstrated for her one afternoon, and it had truly appeared that he was ascending from the underworld. Clad in the luminescent cape, her long wig glistening in the moonlight, she would be a ghoulish specter indeed.

She had little idea what was supposed to happen before her cue to rise up, and not much better a notion what would transpire afterward. Kit had told her to follow her instincts, because everything depended on Lord Whitney's reaction to what he saw and heard. She arranged the black serge loosely around her so that she could quickly throw it off and picked up a length of twine knotted around the tiny corpse of a white mouse.

They would come from her right, she knew, pass behind her, and from there follow the curved track that wound up the hill. It would take them directly between where she waited and the shadowy watchtower. Soon she heard the slow beat of hooves against the boggy ground and the creak of wagon wheels. Voices floated to her, the words indistinguishable until the men were only a short distance away.

"I don't like this," said one of them in a nervous, high-pitched tone. It had to be Lord Whitney. "This cannot be the way."

"She's well hid, and that's a fact." Robbie spoke in a rough growl. "I recollect the tower, m'lord. Come by it t'other night, I did."

"We don't even know that she's still there," Whitney grumbled.

"Can't say. Happen she moved on. The cottage be mebbe a mile from here. You be wantin' to go back?"

"No, no. We'll have a look. Cannot this nag move any faster?"

"Not while 'e's goin' uphill."

As the wagon lurched past her hiding place, flickering orange light slid over the pit. Lucy huddled lower until the pit was in darkness again, tracking the wagon by sound. It was making the arc that would take it up the hill.

Soon now. She felt perspiration on her forehead and ordered her hands to stop trembling.

A roar of thunder shattered the night. It seemed to be coming from all directions, bouncing off the hills and echoing back again. Then she heard a loud crack. A bright ball of light soared across the sky.

Lifting her head over the edge of the pit, Lucy saw the wagon at a stop about fifty yards in front of her. Two lanterns hung from the side panels, making a small pool of ruddy light. Robbie had gone to take the frightened horse's bridle, and a pudgy man was crouched beneath the wagon, apparently trying to make himself invisible. He jumped noticeably when the thunder sounded again.

There came an unearthly wail from the pele tower, and another fireball sailed overhead.

For a few moments the night went still. Then she saw, atop the battlements, an explosion of light and a cloud of white smoke. In the midst of the smoke appeared a glowing figure, arms upraised. It was clad in a luminous cape. Long white-gold hair streamed out like a banner in the wind. Flames danced at the witch's fingertips.

"Crambe est vinum daemonium!" it bellowed. *"Ergo bibamus!"*

With a shrill cry, Whitney scrambled from under the wagon and broke into a run.

"Halt or die!" Sparks shot from the battlement, cascading down the stone wall like a waterfall of fire.

Whitney stopped immediately and swung around, head uplifted, to face the tower.

"You have offended!" The apparition jabbed a finger in his

direction and sparks flew from the tip. "Hear me now, insect. I pronounce your doom."

"Wh-who are you?"

"Retribution. Malediction. *Damnation!*"

That was her first cue. Lucy raised her arm and swung the mouse over her head. What with all the fire and smoke and thunder, she rather thought Fidgets would have long since flown to cover in the trees. But he swooped from a tower window with an earsplitting screech, passing within inches of Whitney's head on his way to supper. Whitney screamed as the owl flashed by.

Keeping hold of the twine, Lucy drew Fidgets into the pit and whispered an apology as she pulled off the black serge and used it to hide the mouse. "You can have this later," she promised. He cast her a doleful look and began pecking at the serge.

When she looked out again, she saw another flash from the tower and another cloud of smoke. When it cleared, the figure on the battlement had vanished. That marked her second cue.

"Aaaieee!" she cried, getting into the spirit of things. Her hands were coated with phosphorescent ointment, and she waved them overhead as she mounted the footstool and ascended from the pit. "Aaaieeee!"

Whitney spun around.

"A thousand curses fall on your head," she proclaimed, half chanting the words. "May open sores spring up on your putrid flesh. Arise, ye boils and carbuncles. Devour him alive from his skin down to the very marrow of his bones. He has offended all the powers of heaven and hell."

"Nooo! Please!" He backed away, staggering like a drunken sot until his heel caught on a rock and sent him to the ground. He landed on his buttocks with a cry of pain.

Lucy only wished Diana were there to see this. She advanced a few steps, careful not to get too far from the pit, her shimmering forefinger pointed at his head as another roll of thunder echoed off the hills. "Because you have sold your soul for money, I condemn you to the gutters without a penny to buy a crumb of bread. Because you have brought pain, I judge you to feel pain a hundredfold. Because you have destroyed beauty, I rule a film shall coat your eyes with blindness so that you never more know the rising of the sun."

From behind the tower came the mournful howl of a wolf.

When Whitney turned to look, two fires suddenly blazed from the battlement. For a moment Lucy was as astonished as Whitney must have been. Between the fires came another flash and a puff of smoke, and then the witch appeared again.

Hurriedly, Lucy scampered back to her pit and drew the concealing serge over her cape. "Get ready, Fidgets," she whispered, coaxing him onto her wrist. "We've practiced this. Look up there."

He kept looking down at the mouse she'd exposed until she planted her foot atop it. "Up, Fidgets. Watch the tower."

She did not see the motion that drew him away, but when he left her wrist she peeked out in time to see Whitney flatten himself on the ground as the owl whizzed by. Distracted by the motion, Fidgets circled him once before heading on to the battlement. Kit must have put something tasty on his shoulder. Fidgets landed there, white breast feathers glowing in the firelight as he gobbled up his snack.

Her own part done now, Lucy watched from the pit as Kit began the coup de grâce.

"Kneel, wretch!"

Whimpering, the wretch obeyed.

"You have heard your fate, pernicious one. On any other night but this, it would be firmly sealed. But tonight is Allhallows, when graves open and the spirits of the good and the evil stalk the earth."

The wolf howled again.

"On this night, voices cry out to the Powers who rule us all. Petitions may be granted. Have you aught to say in your defense before I pronounce the words that damn you forever?"

"H-how can I defend what I do not know? What is my crime?"

"Dare you mock the Lord of Darkness?" With another flash of light the figure was again wreathed in smoke, but this time it did not disappear. "Diana, my sister in spirit since time began, bears the mark of your brutality. She can no longer fulfill her destiny. And still you seek her, and scheme to sell her to a creature more loathsome than yourself. Do you deny this, worm?"

"But I never meant to hurt her. It was an accident."

"The scarring of her face? I know that. We all know."

Thunder again, and more howling.

Kit was in full cry now, Lucy thought with grudging admiration as he held out his arms, sending the flames to his left and right flaring higher. She'd no idea how he was doing it, but the effect was stunning.

"Wh-what can I do?" Whitney mewled. "Tell me what to do."

"Repent!" Kit's voice sliced through the cold air.

She couldn't help herself. "Repent!" she echoed from the concealment of the pit.

"Repennnnnt," came a voice from the copse.

"Repent!" Timmy piped from behind the tower, following up with a wolf call.

"I *do*," Whitney squealed. "I repent. Give me penance. I'll do anything you ask."

"We ask nothing. We *command*! Free our sister."

"But how can I free her? I can't even *find* her."

"Fool! We have her in our keeping. The Dark Angel holds watch with a sword of fire, and you could sooner catch the wind than seize her from our protection. Come near to her and you will surely perish."

"I'll not come near her. I promise. Tell her she is free of me."

"You lie!"

"You lie!" Lucy called.

"Lie lie lie!" came from the copse.

Timmy howled.

Whitney huddled in a pudgy lump. "On my mother's grave, I swear to free her."

"Do we believe him, sisters?"

"Nooo."

"Nooo."

177

"Nooo."

Kit turned his face to the owl, as if consulting with his familiar. Then he flung his hands up, and one of them must have tossed a chicken leg over his shoulder because Fidgets swooped away and disappeared behind the tower. "We demand proof," ruled the witch in sepulchral tones.

Whitney lifted his arms in supplication. "But how can I prove what I say? What must I do?"

"A way will be given you. Watch and listen. You will know it when it comes. We have been merciful this night, dog. But heed my warning. Fail to keep your promise, and the wrath of heaven and hell will be visited on you a thousandfold."

"Oh, I will. I mean, I won't. That is, I'll do as you say. Bless you. Thank you for your mercy. I—"

"Enough! Go home. Meditate on your sins." Kit pointed a finger at Robbie. "You bear guilt for your part in this abomination. Take this mound of dung to where you found him and hie yourself across the waters. If you be in England at next quarter moon, we shall come for you."

"I'm g-gone, Your Majesty." Robbie practically threw Lord Whitney onto the back of the wagon and jumped to the driver's bench. "And I ain't comin' back."

Kit sent another shower of sparks off the tower. "Hear me, Sister Timothea. Dissolve now into pure spirit and follow them on the night wind. And you others, daughters of Lucifer, brides of Asmodeus and Astaroth, come with meee. . . ."

In a flash of light and a puff of smoke, he disappeared.

Lucy ducked back into the shelter of the pit as Robbie turned the wagon and guided it swiftly down the slope. *My heavens.* Lord Whitney had fallen into Kit's trap like a witless rabbit. No rational man could possibly credit that demons and witches bothered with the affairs of puny mortals, after all. Surely they had better things to do.

She removed her wig and luminous cloak and wrapped them tightly in the black serge. The chill wind knifed through her shirt. Speedily she drew on the greatcoat Kit had provided her.

She always felt more secure wearing male garb, especially when it was much too large for her body. It became armor of a sort, protecting her from Kit's heated glances and her own undeniable weakness. Her female clothes were waiting at the inn where the witches and wolves had gathered earlier that evening. Kit had planned well, she had to admit. Whenever she imagined a potential difficulty, he had already arranged a solution. There was a room for her at the Downy Duck if she chose to stay the night, and a coach and driver to return her to Candale whenever she wished to go home.

Home? What a thought! Lucy Jennet Preston had never had a home—only places to be at the sufferance of those who allowed her to be there.

She picked up the length of twine and swung the mouse overhead, hoping that Fidgets hadn't gone off on an adventure of his own. He appeared within moments, though, and she snatched the mouse from his talons. Circling, the owl returned and landed near the edge of the pit, regarding her with round accusing eyes.

She held out her right hand. "Come, Fidgets."

He waddled forward and halted just beyond her reach.

"Yes, I'm a wretched tease. But we require Kit's knife to cut through the twine, which I am persuaded would not agree with you."

With a snort, he hopped onto her wrist and allowed her to put him in the wicker cage. Owls were ever so much easier to reason with than little boys—or grown men who behaved like little boys.

Timmy came bounding up the hill, waving his arms. "They be far gone now, sir."

Lucy gathered her bundle, the mouse, and the cage, set them on the ground, and climbed from the steamy, acrid pit. The last few hours had given her a new respect for peat cutters.

When she reached the tower, Giles was crouched inside the door opening, using a tinderbox to light a pair of lanterns.

"Catch, Timmy!" Kit tossed down his cape and the wig, which landed at Lucy's feet.

She'd not seen it close up before now. "What is this made of? It looks like horsehair."

"Mane and tail," Kit said, fixing the prongs of the grappling hook and dropping a thick rope over the side of the tower. "Only place the wigmaker could find hair the like of yours."

How quickly he doused her secret vanity. Turning away, she went to stand in front of the tower door, cutting off the night wind that was making it difficult for Giles to ignite the lanterns. She hadn't liked watching Kit make the dangerous ascent and could not bear to watch him come down. She heard his boots striking stone as he lowered himself, using the tower wall to slow his descent, and finally the dull sound as they hit the ground.

Safe! Her heart returned to its usual spot in her chest.

Two arms wrapped around her from behind. "You were unutterably splendid, Sister Lucy. Altogether magnificent! When you rose up from that pit, shining in the moonlight like a cold fire, I swear my hair stood on end."

With his warm body pressed against hers, it was impossible to think clearly. "Fidgets wants the mouse," she said.

"And well she deserves it!" Releasing her, he took the cage from her hand and addressed the owl. "A remarkable performance, madam. Flawless. So where is this mouse you covet?"

"Here." Lucy handed him the length of twine. "It needs to be cut free."

While Kit gave Fidgets his reward, she went to Timmy and helped him wrap the horsehair wig in the cape. He was thrumming with excited energy, very much like Kit, and probably disappointed that the adventure was done. "You were a prodigiously fine wolf," she told him. "And how fast you scampered from place to place. I never knew which direction you would howl from next."

"It were so much fun, miss! I got to shoot the flare gun. Did you see?"

"Yes indeed. It quite startled me, I assure you. So did the thunder."

"Mr. Handa made it, with a big piece of steel or somethin'. Next time I wants to make the thunder."

"So you shall," Kit said, joining them and bowing to Timmy. Solemnly, he shook the boy's skinny hand. "Thank you, young man. No one could have done better than you did this night."

"That man wuz cryin' all the time I followed the wagon, sir. He thunk we all be devils."

"Good. Let's hope he keeps thinking that long enough to sign custody of Miss Whitney over to Lord Kendal." Kit turned to Giles, who emerged from the tower with both lanterns lit. "I thank you, too, sir. For all that you've elected to be an apothecary, you have the soul of a pirate."

"I have always thought so," Giles replied calmly. "It was a pleasure to indulge a few of my secret fantasies, although I should not wish to do so on a regular basis. I have the will, but not the imagination."

"Give me leave to doubt that, sir. You surprised me constantly." Kit made a sweeping gesture. "I pronounce us all brilliant, our melodrama a triumph, and rule that we toast our success over wine—lemonade for you, Timmy—at the Downy Duck. Come, sisters, and let us be off."

"But what about the footstool?" Lucy protested.

Three pairs of startled eyes swung in her direction.

"Oh, you know what I mean!" she told Kit sternly. "We cannot leave all this evidence of our trickery behind. And what of the rope and grappling hook? How in heaven's name are you to get it down from the tower?"

"I've no idea," Kit replied with a shrug. "But I'll figure a way when Timmy and I return to gather up the *evidence*. Not that I think for a moment that Lord Whitney would dare set foot here again. You needn't worry, Lucy. When I'm done, there will be no trace of our presence for anyone to find."

She believed him. How could she not? His outrageous plan had come off exactly as he predicted, although she had balked at every step along the way. But he had swept her up with his enthusiasm and confidence, and she'd obeyed his instructions even as she argued with him because she could not help herself. When she was with him, she found herself believing in the impossible.

And that, she reminded herself, could only lead her to disaster. Turning her back on him, she went to retrieve Fidgets's cage.

Kit took up a position beside her as they followed Timmy and Giles along the path that crossed Beetham Fell. Their destination was a trifle less than three miles away. Far too long to be in his company, she thought, knowing her own weakness and the powerful lure of Kit Valliant. "However did you produce such a display of smoke and fire," she asked with false brightness, "from nothing more than a bedwarmer and a few hot coals?"

"Oh, I'd considerably more to work with than that," he informed her with a cocky grin. "In the last few days I made several trips up and down the tower with supplies. Giles helped enormously. Apothecaries make excellent coconspirators, I have discovered. They know how to do such marvelous things. He prepared torches that would blaze up with the slightest application of a glowing coal and showed me how to cascade sparks down the side of the tower. The smoke and flash of light were produced by tossing a wad of gunpowder onto the coals. That was my idea. I used to throw gunpowder onto campfires when I was a boy."

Which you still are, she thought, keeping her gaze focused on the path because she dared not look at him. A handsome boy with the body of a man who delights in playing pranks and flirting with susceptible females. Few of them resisted him, she was certain. She was less certain that she could do so, what with him being all but irresistible, but she meant to try with all her might. Her already unsatisfactory life would be pure misery if she had to live it with a broken heart.

"You were impressive, I must admit." Lucy knew she sounded like a starchy governess, but at the end of the day, that was precisely what she was. "I thought you a trifle overtheatrical at times, but I suppose you could not help yourself."

"No indeed. I was quite caught up in the moment, and Whitney was such delicious prey. He groveled divinely, don't you think? How was my voice? High enough? Did I sound like a female?"

"Not like a *human* female. Timmy produced a better impression of a wolf than you did of a woman. What you said was clever, though," she added grudgingly. "Except for the Latin bit, which made no sense at all."

He took Fidgets's cage from her hand. "I was never any dab hand at Latin. Couldn't see the point of learning it. Practically nobody speaks it these days but tutors and popish clerics, have you noticed? But a few words were drummed into my head at school and I thought I'd try them out. What did I say?"

"Something to the effect that cabbage was the wine of the devil and we should all drink up."

"Cabbage?" He winced. "Well, let's hope Whitney is no more a scholar than I. In any case, I am quite convinced that I belong on the stage. We younger sons require employment, you know. What do you think, moonbeam? Should I tread the boards? Would you come to the greenroom after the play and offer me carte blanche?"

"Certainly not! And Lord Kendal would never permit you to take up such a profession. Have your wits gone begging?"

Chuckling, he wrapped an arm around her waist.

She'd have pulled away from him, but on the narrow path, there was no away to pull to. Hawthorn bushes hedged them in on both sides, Giles and Timmy were directly ahead with the lanterns, and she could not go running back to the tower. "You are impertinent, sir. It is unfair of you to take liberties when I am unable to evade them."

"I do know how to choose my moments," he said unrepentantly. "But you needn't fear that your reputation is being compromised. Giles and Timmy know of our betrothal."

"Oh, infamous! I promised myself I'd remain in charity with you until we reached the inn, but already I am railing at you like a fishwife. Why do you deliberately set yourself to raise my temper? If you release me, we can have a civilized conversation or walk in silence, which I would greatly prefer."

"But I'm quite partial to your temper, Lucy. It gives me hope."

She looked up at him. "I don't understand."

His smile was singularly sweet. "There's a saying I once heard. Perhaps you've heard it, too. 'When the heart's afire, sparks fly from the mouth.' "

Her heart *was* afire. She could not deny it. The blaze consumed her from the inside out. But whatever he imagined, the source was fury. Not love. Never love. She refused to give him the satisfaction of thinking he'd won her over the way he did all the other women he'd flirted with, or more, before discarding them.

"I'm angry, yes," she told him plainly. "Nearly all the time. But that's because you came swanning in and took over everything—me, Diana, our plans, *everything*. You allow me no choices. You expect me always to do your will."

His fingertips pressed at her waist, and even through the heavy greatcoat she felt them burning against her as if they were touching her bare flesh.

"I know how it is, moonbeam," he said gently. "I've been a burr in your side. But stay the course a little longer. We are going somewhere wonderful, you and I."

Chapter 15

Taking a folded newspaper with him, Kit entered the formal parlor, selected an out-of-the-way chair, and settled back to observe the proceedings.

His brother, somewhat to his surprise, had demonstrated a flair for the dramatic while arranging for this afternoon's spectacle. The lord-lieutenant and the justice of the peace had arrived and were accepting glasses of sherry from a footman. Near the fireplace, the half-dozen solicitors who had been in residence at Candale this week were deep in conversation.

Kit couldn't resist a friendly wave at the pair of constables standing off by themselves, looking singularly ill at ease. At one time or another each had held him in custody. He supposed they had been invited to swell the line of infantry meant to throw Lord Whitney on the defensive immediately he stepped into the room. The heavy artillery—among them two viscounts, three barons, and the Earl of Lonsdale—were waiting with the Earl of Kendal in the upstairs salon until time for their grand entrance.

When last he saw them, Lucy and Celia were in the nursery, fuming. Kendal had ruled that no females were to be present at this settlement conference, and both took great exception to his order. "Men conduct business with other men," he had said firmly. "Like it or not, that is the way the world turns."

Kit was inclined to agree with him, although he understood Lucy's indignation. She had well earned the right to see the end of what she had begun. At least they all hoped that today's events would mark the conclusion, but all remained in doubt until Lord Whitney affixed his signature to the documents.

Kendal's battalion of solicitors had descended on Lord Whitney the very morning after his encounter with the Lancaster witches. By all accounts he had been pale, panic-stricken, and willing to sign anything short of his death warrant. Because his servants could attest to his disordered state of mind in the event of a later appeal, the solicitors wisely left a mountain of papers for him to examine, advising him to engage a solicitor to act on his behalf.

No one could be certain what he would do at this meeting. It was possible he'd declare his intention to pursue the matter in the courts, especially if he still retained the financial backing of Sir Basil Crawley. If not, there was little question that he would attempt to renegotiate, in his favor, the terms Kendal's attorneys had offered him. Which would mean a long, tedious afternoon, Kit thought, opening the newspaper and pretending to be absorbed in what he was reading. The pompous lord-lieutenant had begun to sidle in his direction, apparently bent on striking up a conversation.

"Sir Basil Crawley and . . . er, Mr. Bartholomew Pugg," the butler announced from the doorway in a soft voice that shouted his opinion of their worthiness to be there.

No one else paid the slightest attention to their arrival, but Kit immediately went on full alert. Crawley had brought along his pet Runner, which could not be a good sign. He lifted the newspaper so that it covered most of his face and watched as Crawley accepted a glass of wine from the footman. Pugg declined, and then both men headed in his direction.

"Mr. Valliant, it is my pleasure to see you again," Crawley said with a bow as Pugg separated himself far enough for discretion and close enough to hear what was said.

Kit lowered his newspaper but did not rise, a mild insult that Crawley noted with a flash of anger in his steel-gray eyes. But he never lost his polite smile, and Kit gave him points for self-control. "Lud, half the population of north England must have been invited to this party," he said, lounging back on the chair with his legs crossed. "I don't suppose you know what is happening here?"

Crawley looked puzzled.

"No? Well, that makes us a pair. M'brother is up to something, I daresay, but damned if I can make any sense of it. Some sort of legal kafuffle, I suppose, what with a clutch of lawyers infesting the place."

"You are not involved in this matter?" Crawley asked, recovering his stiff poise.

"Lord no. My beloved Lucinda—you met her t'other night—is having one of her moods, and I'm far safer here than elsewhere in the house. The woman can peel the hide from a fellow with her tongue." He shuddered theatrically. "So why have you come? If it's to pay a call on the earl, allow me to advise you this is not the best of times."

"So I apprehend. But as it happens, I have some minor stake in this afternoon's proceedings."

"Well, don't tell me about it." Kit waved a negligent hand. "I mean to drink Kendal's wine, read my paper here in the corner, and maybe have m'self a snooze. But who is that odd chap came in with you? He looks disposed to pilfer the silver."

Crawley gave him a cold smile. "I doubt he will. He's a Bow Street Runner."

"Indeed?" Kit raised the quizzing glass he'd borrowed from Kendal for this occasion and examined Pugg from head to toe. "Never saw one before now. Can't say I'm very much impressed, though he looks smarter than the two constables lurking across the way. What's he doing here?"

"I could ask the same about the constables," Crawley said, dancing to his own evasive tune.

"Lord Whitney," the butler intoned, "and his associates." Geeson stepped aside to admit the guest of dishonor, who was followed by two men wearing badly fitting coats, baggy breeches, and furtive expressions.

"M'brother is keeping sorry company these days," Kit said,

clicking his tongue. "Who is the one looks like a bloated codfish?"

"A fool," Crawley said tersely. "Perhaps a madman. He claims to see witches and demons, and fears that a giant bird will rise up from hell to peck out his eyes. Pray excuse me, but unfortunately I have need to speak with him."

"By all means." Kit turned his attention to Lord Whitney, taking note of his blotched, pasty skin, his bulbous red nose, and the belly sagging over the waistband of his breeches. He had been no great beauty when Kit saw him cowering on the ground at Arnside Tower, but in the three days since, he appeared to have gone entirely to seed.

Were Diana's fate not at stake, Kit might have enjoyed this circus. He would certainly have liked to eavesdrop on what Crawley was saying to Lord Whitney, but the Runner had stationed himself where he could observe everyone in the room. He was sure to notice if Kit showed even a mild interest in Crawley's business.

Unaccustomed to sitting back and allowing someone else to order events, Kit found it devilish hard to maintain his careless pose. He'd passed the reins to Kendal, which was without question the correct thing to do, but that failed to stanch his frustration. Lucy must have felt much the same when Kit Valliant swept onto the scene and immediately took charge.

With a considerable degree of ceremony, Geeson stepped into the parlor and read off a long series of names and titles. One by one, virtually everyone of rank in the county of Westmoreland made a dignified entrance. Lord Kendal was the last to appear, and Kit covered an inordinate desire to laugh by coming to his feet.

The earl, impeccably clad in a pewter coat, darker breeches, and dove-colored stockings, entered his parlor as if it were the court at Versailles. A hush descended and all eyes were focused on him as, supremely aloof, he paused and slowly swung his gaze around the room. When it fell on Lord Whitney, the baron's face turned an alarming shade of purple.

Paying him no special notice, Kendal continued to briefly examine each man in turn until he came to the tall, hook-nosed Sir Basil. With a slight frown, his head slightly tilted, he studied him as he might a bug pinned to a blotter.

Kit decided he could not bear to miss the fireworks. He sauntered across the room, plucking a full glass of wine from a footman as he passed by, and greeted his brother with an elaborate bow. "I thought you'd never get here, my lord earl. Precisely whom are we burying this afternoon?"

Kendal turned his icy gaze in his direction. "This is none of your concern, Christopher. Unless you can identify the two . . . er, gentlemen standing with Lord Whitney. I cannot think what they are doing in my home. Are they perchance friends of yours?"

Crawley moved forward and bowed. "I have a slight acquaintance with your brother, Lord Kendal, but he is in no way responsible for my presence here. Will you do me the honor of allowing him to introduce me?"

"If I must." With a small sigh, Kendal sliced a meaningful look at Lord Lonsdale, who immediately turned to one of his fellows and struck up a conversation. Others took the cue and moved away, leaving the three men to speak privately.

No one, Kit thought admiringly, exercised power with such exquisite finesse as his brother. Careful not to meet his eyes for fear of laughing, he presented Sir Basil Crawley. "Lucinda and I attended a ball at his home near Flookburgh," he added. "Remember? You were invited, too."

"Was I? Then my secretary must have sent my regrets."

Kendal said nothing more, merely gazing with resigned boredom at a place beyond Crawley's shoulder. Kit recognized his brother's strategy, having been its victim on many nasty occasions, and knew that Crawley would soon jump in to fill the uncomfortable silence.

He made the leap within moments. "I hope you will pardon me for the intrusion, Lord Kendal, but it happens that I have considerable interest in whatever decisions are made concerning Miss Diana Whitney."

"Indeed? I cannot imagine why. Your name has not appeared on any of the documents relating to her case."

"My interest is personal, sir. Perhaps Lord Whitney failed to mention it, but I have offered for the young lady's hand in marriage."

Kendal raised a brow. "And how did she reply?"

"Unfavorably, I regret to say. But that is entirely my doing, for I approached her at an inappropriate time." Crawley contrived to look bereft and repentant, although neither sentiment reached his eyes. "She was yet grieving for her parents, snatched from her so cruelly, but I was unaware that they had perished only a few months earlier. I am newly come north from Manchester, you see, and had no acquaintance among the local gentry until I chanced to meet Lord Whitney. He introduced me to his niece, and—well, how shall I say this? It will sound altogether foolish from a man of my years, but I was irreparably smitten when first I clapped eyes on her. My impressions of her worth were confirmed as I came to value, even more than her beauty, the charm, intelligence, and grace that stole my heart and sealed my fate."

Horse manure! Kit thought, longing to plant him a facer.

Kendal looked profoundly uninterested.

Tiny beads of sweat had formed on Crawley's brow. "The thing is, I rushed my fences. Instead of allowing her time to recover from her loss, I immediately paid my addresses. Quite naturally, she refused my offer."

"Then I continue to wonder why you are here. Does not her rejection of your suit mark an end to your involvement with Miss Whitney and her affairs?"

"Had I courted her when and how I should have done, you would be correct. But I am persuaded that, given time, she will come to see me in a new light." He lifted his arms in a helpless gesture. "Would you have me forsake all hope?"

"Perish the thought," Kendal murmured.

Crawley drew himself up. "Mock me if you will, sir, but my

intentions are both sincere and honorable. And in my defense, I was more precipitate than I might otherwise have been due to her particular circumstances. Lord Whitney is something of a loose screw, and I feared for Miss Whitney's well-being. Alas, my judgment of her guardian's nature was proven correct when she fled him in terror."

Kit growled low in his throat. How his brother could listen to this hogwash without the slightest reaction was beyond his comprehension.

But Kendal had the situation well in hand. "Your concern for Miss Whitney's welfare was well taken, but no longer necessary. You will be pleased to hear that she will shortly be removed from her uncle's guardianship and given over to my protection." He produced a chilly smile. "As for your wish to marry the young lady, I see no reason to object if she expresses a desire to accept you. Naturally you will wait a decent interval, a year at the very least, before approaching her again."

Left with no other choice, Crawley inclined his head. "As you say, Lord Kendal. But before taking my leave, I should like very much to pay my regards to Miss Whitney and assure myself that she is content with the arrangements you have made for her. Have I your permission to speak with her for a few moments?"

"I would naturally grant it, were she here, but Miss Whitney is not in residence at Candale. When the opportunity arises, I shall make certain to convey your good wishes. And now, if you will excuse me, a number of gentlemen are awaiting my attention. Christopher, be so kind as to show Sir Basil out."

Well done, Kit applauded silently before turning his attention to Crawley. He was staring at Kendal's back, color high in his cheeks. His usually blank eyes had gone on fire.

"We have both been dismissed, it seems," Kit said lightly. "Just as well, considering the company in this room. Dull dogs, the lot of 'em. Shall we take ourselves off before my brother has us thrown out on our ears?"

Beckoning to Pugg, Crawley stalked to the door, sneering at the butler who held it open for him to pass.

There was more trouble ahead from that source, Kit was certain. Crawley was the sort of man who nursed a grudge and plotted vengeance. He would make no move anytime soon, fully aware that his adversaries were on their guard, but the Valliant family had not heard the last of him.

While a footman went to see his carriage brought around, Crawley drew the Runner aside and clutched his elbow as he spoke in an urgent whisper.

Knowing better than to intrude, Kit took shade under the portico with his shoulders propped against a marble pillar and sipped at his wine, gazing off into the distance. He pretended to be startled when Crawley approached him again.

"I shall bid you farewell now, Mr. Valliant, and expect that we'll not meet again until after the turn of the year. I have business to put before Parliament regarding a turnpike road between Ulverston and Carnforth, along with proposals for the extension of several canals in this area. Likely these matters will keep me in London for a considerable time."

"I'm sorry to hear it, but perhaps we will meet sooner than you imagine. Lucinda is nagging me to take her to London for the Season. And by then I'll have her dowry in m'pocket," he added, "in case you have ideas how I ought to invest it."

"I haven't forgot," Crawley said, his eyes opaque. "You may be sure I'll stay in touch. Might I ask you one last question, as we are business associates of a kind?"

"Fire away." Kit grinned at him. "I always cooperate with anyone who can help me get rich."

"Is it true that Miss Whitney is not in residence anywhere on Lord Kendal's estate?"

"Well, if she is, I ain't seen her. And I'll tell you something else. Jimmie was born with a javelin up his spine. You know the sort—honor and duty and all that rot. If he said she's not here, she's not here."

"I did wonder. The earl appeared to take me in dislike, and I thought he might be fobbing me off."

"Oh, he takes most everyone in dislike. He don't like *me* above half, and I'm a darling. Think no more of it."

With a stiff bow, Crawley went to the carriage that had just pulled up.

Kit watched with amusement as the man who had shot him opened the paneled doors and let down the steps for Sir Basil. Unfinished business, he thought, but it would have to wait for a suitable opportunity. He couldn't very well call out a *flunky*.

"A moment of your time, sir?"

Turning, Kit saw the Runner approach him from the other direction, leading a saddled horse. "By all means." He produced his sunniest smile. "Mr. Pugg, is it?"

"Pugg will do. Sir Basil has informed you that he is on his way to London?"

"So he did, although I cannot imagine why his whereabouts should interest me. You are in his employ, I believe?"

"At one time, but no longer. I can tell you, sir, that it's a sad day when a Runner elects to leave a job unfinished. But so I have done. Sir Basil will learn that I am off the case when I choose to tell him, which will not be in the near future. Meantime he won't be hiring anybody else, if you take my drift."

"As a matter of fact, I've haven't the foggiest clue what you are blathering about."

Pugg grinned, revealing a set of spiky teeth. "If you say so. My regards to the young ladies, sir."

"Which young ladies would those be?" Kit inquired blandly.

Pugg mounted his horse with considerable grace. "Oh, the one what sometimes call herself Mrs. Preston when she ain't dancing with you at a ball, and the one what are at the pig farm." He lifted his hat and bowed from the saddle. "If ever you be in need of a Runner, sir, you c'n find me at Bow Street."

Well, well, Kit thought as Pugg nudged his horse to a canter and sped away. Who would have guessed it? The Runner had found them out and jumped over to their side.

In a reflective mood, Kit rested his shoulders against the pillar once again and turned the glass of wine in his hand, watching the deep red liquid swirl around. One day he would seek out the honorable Mr. Pugg, invite him to a pub house, and ply him with enough ale to loosen his tongue. If he ever lost guard of it, to be sure. There was a good chance Kit would never discover exactly what Pugg had learned and how he'd come by his information, but he wanted to buy the man a drink anyway.

Ought he to tell the others about this? he wondered. Not Diana, certainly. She should never know how close they had come to disaster. His brother, yes, and Celia, no. As for Lucy, he would have to think on it. From here on out he wanted no more secrets between them, but a few matters might do better to wait until his ring was on her finger.

Meantime he was supposed to be witnessing the events going on in the parlor so that he could give her a full report. Quickly finishing off his wine, Kit returned to the house, steeling himself to endure an hour or two of lawyerly gibberish.

Chapter 16

"I cannot bear this another moment!" Lucy looked again at the clock on the mantelpiece in Lady Kendal's private parlor. The hands appeared to have frozen in place. "Why is it taking so long?"

"One must allow for posturing and long speeches, I expect. You must have observed at table this week that Mr. Bilbottom admires the sound of his own voice. The other solicitors will attempt to match him, if only to justify their fees, but there can be no doubt of the outcome. Kendal has everything well in hand."

Lucy was not so sure, although she couldn't very well say so to his wife. Lady Kendal had not been fighting this battle for nearly two months, on the brink of losing it a hundred times or more. She wouldn't understand how it felt to be excluded from the final confrontation when no one had a greater right to be there.

The countess scowled at whatever it was she had been knitting and began to unravel the yarn. "I simply cannot get the hang of this, Lucy. Whatever I knit grows into a shapeless, unrecognizable *thing.*"

"Why do you keep at it then?" Lucy asked indifferently.

"Oh, I don't know. Because I want to see my babies wearing mittens and caps I have made for them with my own hands, I suppose. At least I am able to provide them with blankets, although the blankets all started out to be something else entirely." She glanced up with a smile. "Why not go for a walk while the weather is so fine? It will spare the carpet you are wearing down with your pacing, and if you stay in sight of the house, you will see the carriages come around when the gentlemen are ready to depart."

Realizing that she was making a nuisance of herself, Lucy curtsied and headed for the door. "I shall go to the hill behind the stable," she said. "Please send for me if anything happens that I ought to know about."

She stopped by her bedchamber for gloves and a bonnet before taking the back way out of the house. Carriages, some bearing crests, were lined up in the stable yard, and several of the drivers and postilions were hunkered over a game of dice. Timmy waved at her from atop one of the coaches, where a kindly driver was apparently showing him how to hold the reins.

Life goes on, she thought. How few people in the world knew what was transpiring in Lord Kendal's parlor this afternoon. And when Diana's fate was settled, primarily by men who had never even met her, how few would care what became of her.

No one at all, save Diana, would care what became of Lucy Preston. She would return quietly to Dorset and take up her position at Turnbridge Manor, if Lady Turnbridge had not already hired someone to replace her. Eventually, whatever befell her when the boys were grown and she was turned off, she would dwindle into an old lady who had once experienced a splendid, terrifying adventure.

When she reached her destination, she immediately regretted returning to this spot. Instead of contemplating Diana's situation and her own future, she kept imagining Kit as he had been a few afternoons ago, with a parcel of chicken feet in his hand and Fidgets perched on his shoulder. Which led to thoughts of Kit wearing a horsetail wig and cascading a fall of sparks down the pele tower on All Hallows' Eve. From there she went all the way back to the first time she saw him, trapped in the sands of Morecambe Bay, and began to relive, in vivid detail, each moment they had spent together since then.

There was a stir at the back of the house, and she shaded

her eyes with her hand to better see what was happening. From such a distance, she could make out only that a carriage was in motion, and then another. The gentlemen were leaving. It was over!

Lifting her skirts, she pelted down the hill, her thoughts two steps ahead of the rest of her. What had happened? What if Lord Whitney had refused to set Diana free? From the nursery window she had seen Sir Basil Crawley's arrival and knew that he'd come to make trouble. Had he succeeded? Oh, dear God!

She reached the steepest portion of the hill, where she ought to be watching her step, but by now she was accelerating rapidly. Her feet, with a will of their own, pounded at an alarming rate, and it was all she could do to remain upright. Then a figure loomed directly ahead of her and she lost control. Arms spinning like windmills, she flailed for balance, felt her shoes slip on the grass and out from under her, and next she knew, she was hitting the ground on her backside with a loud *oomph*.

When she regained her breath and her wits, she lifted herself up on her elbows and found herself at eye level with a long pair of broadfine-clad legs. They were Kit's legs, of course. She would have known them anywhere. And it was no more than her usual bad luck to have fallen like a hailstone at his feet.

He dropped to one knee beside her, his brow etched with concern. "Have you hurt yourself, moonbeam?"

"Only in the vicinity of my pride," she said in a strangled voice. "Never mind that. What about Diana?"

"The Earl of Kendal has got himself a ward, signed and sealed. Delivery will have to wait until tomorrow morning, but I'll go first thing and fetch her to Candale."

"But she knows the meeting was to be today," Lucy protested. "You cannot permit her to worry all of tonight about the outcome. You must go immediately and tell her that the news is good!"

"A footman is already on his way with the message I dispatched after Lord Whitney signed the documents. There was another half hour of nattering about hows and whens and wherewithals before the assembly broke up, and then I came after you." He sat beside her, drew up his legs, and folded his arms across his knees. "For all practical purposes, Kendal is her legal guardian until she comes of age. You may as well know—although Diana need not—that Whitney could petition the lord chancellor for reinstatement should he change his mind. But there is no reason to believe that he will."

"Sir Basil Crawley is a reason. You know very well that Lord Whitney was his creature when this nightmare began, and I've no doubt he can bend Whitney to his will yet again."

"Nor do I. But Crawley is on his way to London and will not return until spring, if then. Meantime Kendal will continue to investigate his background and business practices. Should he attempt to make trouble in the future, we shall be better prepared to deal with him. I believe Diana is perfectly safe, but you can be sure we'll not lower our guard until she has reached her majority. Well, not even then. She is part of our family now, you know."

Amid her relief and gratitude, Lucy felt a shot of monstrous envy. But Diana truly *needed* the support of others. Lucinda Jennet Preston had gotten on very well by herself until now and would continue to do so until she'd stuck her spoon in the wall. "What about the . . . the wherewithals?" she asked, plucking spears of grass from the ground one after another.

"Trifles, actually. Kendal has arranged for an immediate evaluation of the contents of Willow Manor, since they belong to Diana by her father's will. Until she has a home of her own to take them to, Lord Whitney will be accountable for every last teaspoon. Whitney has also agreed to vacate the premises for a month, during which time Diana can retrieve her clothing and whatever else she wishes to take with her."

"This all sounds too good to be true, sir. Did not Whitney bargain for anything on his own behalf?"

Kit rested his chin atop his folded arms. "In fact, Whitney's solicitors protested every jot and tittle, whatever a tittle is. And all the while Whitney poured wine down his throat, scarcely attending to what was going on. Not until the question of Diana's injury came up did he assert himself, and then he refused absolutely to accept responsibility. His lawyers produced signed testimonies from a dozen people who heard Diana say it was an accident, and we know well enough that she did. If ever the truth is to be known for the public record, she will have to face down her uncle in a court of law and retract her previous statements."

"She will never do that."

"I know. We would prefer, of course, that Whitney had admitted to striking her, but this will only become an issue if the case is ever dragged into Chancery Court. Should that happen, we shall deal with it. Any other questions before I turn the subject?"

What happens to *me*? she thought instantly. But she already knew the answer. "No more questions, sir." She rose and brushed down her skirts. "I wish to go to Diana now. Her whole life is in the balance and you sent a *footman* to give her the news? That was badly done. She should be brought here straightaway."

Kit was on his feet before she could move past him. "Tomorrow will be soon enough, love. She is reticent about being seen, and at Candale she will be facing a great many strangers. Allow her a little time to prepare herself."

"Yes. I hadn't considered that."

He tilted her chin with his forefinger. "She will do well enough, Lucy. You must cease worrying about her now and begin considering your own future."

Elephants charged through her head. She gazed at him mutely, wishing she were Mrs. Preston again, veiled and not expected to speak. How could she, when he was looking at her the way he was just now, his blue eyes glowing with an inner fire and a smile of uncommon sweetness curving his lips?

"Marry me," he said softly. "Will you, moonbeam? I meant to lead up to this gracefully, but I cannot wait a moment longer. I even prepared a speech, but I can't remember it now. I'll give it to you later, with all the words of love and fidelity you could possibly want, and I'll mean every one of them. Just please, please, Lucy, say that you will marry me."

"No!" she blurted before she said something appallingly stupid, like *yes*. Before she said what she wanted to say, which was also *yes*.

He must have been expecting a refusal, because his confident smile never wavered. If anything, he looked mildly amused. "You don't mean that, beloved. You know that you don't. Tell me why you said it anyway."

She turned her back because it was impossible to face him when she had to tell lies. His eyes, or so she imagined, could see past all her defenses, into her very soul, and even she didn't know what was buried down there. She could not bear the thought that he knew her better than she knew herself.

Above all things, she must be rid of him before either one of them made a terrible, unalterable mistake. "You do me too great an honor, sir," she said in a voice so calm that she was amazed to hear it. "When you have taken time to reflect, you will realize that I am a wholly unsuitable wife for one of your position."

"Balderdash. You were more on the mark when you thought me a ragtag smuggler and far beneath your notice. The accident of my birth into the Valliant clan is nothing to the point, and I've certainly done no credit to the family name. What has my *position* to do with love? Think of Celia. She came from nowhere to marry an earl, and you won't find two happier people in England. Just ask her—"

"What, sir? I am not she, and you are not your brother. *They* fell in love. You and I have done nothing but quarrel since first we met."

"*You* have quarreled, Lucy. I have been a model of patience."

That was so true that it infuriated her to hear him say it. She had been a shrew, no question about it, but how dare he point it out in such a way? Surely a lover, a true lover, would not recount her flaws in the middle of a proposal!

"You have been caught up in an adventure, sir, and think to

prolong it with a wedding. But there is nothing in the least romantical about what we have done, you and I, during this last fortnight. We were merely coconspirators. When you come to your senses, you will accept that the adventure ended when we rescued the fair maiden."

He came around in front of her and seized both her hands in a firm grip. "Whatever are you nattering about now, moonbeam? I am in full possession of my senses. Asking you to be my wife is the most sensible thing I have ever done. It's my heart that has gone missing. I lost it to you early on, perhaps the moment I first saw you, and it will be in your keeping forever. I'm asking only that you take the rest of me, too." He grinned. "Some parts of me, I promise, you'll be glad to have."

Were he not holding on to her, she would surely have dissolved into a buttery puddle. She wanted so much to believe him. To trust him. But Kit Valliant was a charmer of fits and starts and whims who lived only in the present moment. He would change the very next second, and the next, giving all of himself to whatever new adventure and new woman had crossed his path.

And if it happened that she was wrong about him, she was certainly right about herself. No one had ever loved her before. How could *he*?

Not that she was ashamed of what she was. Lucinda Jennet Preston was getting on very well, thank you, and she had actually been of genuine value in one person's life. Not everyone could boast so much, certainly not the likes of Lord Whitney or Sir Basil Crawley, to list the first examples that sprang to her mind. No indeed, she did not underrate herself, nor did she feel sorry for herself. She was simply wise enough to know that golden men did not fall in love with dagger-tongued governesses.

She pulled her hands free and squared her shoulders. "Whatever you believe at this moment, sir, we are not at all suited. It won't be terribly long before you come to agree. When I have returned home—"

"That is out of the question. Your home is with me."

"No, Kit, it is not. You know nothing about me and nothing of my plans." She forced her traitorous body to stand straight and still. "My home will soon be with the man I intend to marry."

Ashen-faced, he gazed at her with a stunned expression.

"I am betrothed to the curate of a church not far from the estate where I am employed. We might already be wed, had not Diana's letter called me north." Lucy picked out her words with care. "So you see, there was never any possibility of my developing a *tendre* for you. I have all this time been promised to another man. And naturally, I must go to him as soon as may be."

She had meant to say more, but her courage had all run out. Not daring to look at Kit, she made a quick curtsy and fled down the hill.

Chapter 17

The next morning, Kit went to the pig farm to collect Diana and escort her to Candale.

Lucy had declined to accompany him, which was not unexpected as she'd spoken scarcely a dozen words to him since refusing his marriage proposal. He had watched her push food around her plate at supper and escape to her room shortly thereafter, pleading a headache. He had not seen her since.

Nor was she waiting with James and Celia in the entrance hall when he led Diana into the house, and he wondered if perhaps she was truly ill.

Celia came forward, arms outstretched. "Welcome, Miss Whitney. We are so pleased that you will be staying with us."

Diana curtsied prettily. "Thank you, Lady Kendal. The house is very lovely."

"Indeed it is not!" Celia protested with a laugh. "Candale was too long in the hands of men, who are more apt to decorate the stables for their horses than replace worn carpets in the drawing room. I am making little progress undoing so very many years of neglect and hope you will be kind enough to assist me."

It was exactly the right thing to say, Kit thought. Diana visibly relaxed, the notion that she could be useful instead of a burden drawing color to her pale cheeks.

"Come meet your new guardian," Celia said, taking her arm. "You must not let him intimidate you, even when he scowls. He's not nearly so formidable as he likes to appear."

"Take no notice of anything she says about me," the earl advised, smiling warmly. "We are both delighted to have you stay with us, and you may be sure that I stand as your guardian for legal purposes only. You needn't fear that I'll interfere with your wishes or attempt to manage your life. Think of Candale as your home, and feel free to ask for anything that will make you more comfortable."

"I am so very grateful to you, Lord Kendal." Diana clutched at her skirts. "I cannot think how I shall ever repay your kindness and generosity."

"Mercy me!" Celia declared. "*Repay?* That word has no meaning here. But you must be wanting to see your room, Diana. May I call you Diana? Go on about your business, gentlemen. We ladies are off to have a cup of tea and a good gossip."

Kendal arched a brow as his wife towed a bewildered Diana up the stairs. "There is much to be said for managing females," he observed dryly. "This one will see that my new ward settles in before nightfall. Join me for a glass of sherry, Kit?"

Vague alarms sounding in his head, Kit followed his brother to the study and held his peace until he'd downed one helping of wine and poured himself another. "Where is Lucy?" he asked, trying to sound casual and failing miserably. "Is she ill?"

Kendal went to the chair behind his desk. "In fact, Kit, she's gone."

A cannonball thudded into his stomach. "Where?"

"She wouldn't say, beyond that it was a journey of several days. Directly after you left this morning, she came downstairs with her portmanteau in hand and a determined look in her eyes. Celia and I tried to hold her here, of course, but she would not be stopped."

"Lucifer! She has a five-hour start on me. How is she traveling?"

"Post chaise. She intended to use the public coaches, but there I drew the line. William Reese is driving for her and will arrange accommodations along the way. She'll be perfectly safe under his protection. Oh, and she insisted on leaving me her written voucher to repay every penny of the costs, including Reese's salary. A headstrong young woman, your Miss Jennet."

"You don't know the first part of it." Knees melting under him, Kit dropped onto the sofa. "And her surname is actually Preston, by the way. Never mind why we told you otherwise. It's a long story."

Kendal steepled his hands. "Do you care to tell me what happened? It's perfectly obvious that she departed in a hurry to avoid seeing you again. Have you quarreled?"

"No more than usual. What set her off was my proposal of marriage, which she speedily rejected. That led to the quarrel, and now she's scarpered. Tell you what, Jimmie. I rarely know what to expect of her, but never once have I conceived of her running away. She stands her ground or she advances, but she never retreats."

"Going where she chooses to be is not an act of cowardice, Christopher. It is a decision. When a lady declines an offer of marriage, it must be accepted with good grace. You cannot compel her to be your wife."

"Don't bet on it. Nothing has changed since yesterday, save that now I must go and fetch her back." He took a drink of wine. "The moonbeam is proving devilish hard to snare."

"And that, I suspect, only whets your appetite for the hunt. Consider her feelings in this matter. Has it crossed your mind that she simply does not love you?"

"I thought of nothing else the whole of last night. It was the worst night of my life. Did you know, Jimmie, that thoughts have claws and fangs? That they can shred a man from the inside out? It was quite the revelation to me."

"I have felt them," Kendal said quietly. "Too often to count. You have been fortunate to have escaped those fangs and claws for so long a time."

"Last night was enough for any man, I assure you. But I wrestled the demons down." He grinned. "Good practice for the next match with my formidable Lucy. I need the use of your curricle, m'lord. And the bays."

Kendal groaned. "Not the *bays*."

"The bays," Kit said firmly, coming to his feet. "And a bit of the ready. Make it a large bit. I've no idea how long this is going to take."

"Dare I point out that you don't even know where to go?"

"Diana knows where she lives. I'll wring the information from her." At the door, he turned back. Kendal wore an expression of weary disapproval, which Kit had seen far too many times over the years. He'd given his brother more than enough reason for concern, God only knew, but this time he was aimed directly on target. "In case you are wondering, Jimmie, I do care about Lucy's feelings. Profoundly. And in this instance, I know better than she does what they are. The moonbeam loves me, that's certain, but she's got it in her head that she can't have me. I mean to convince her that she can't get rid of me."

Kendal shook his head. "Coxcomb."

Laughing, Kit took the stairs two at a time and came upon Celia as she was leaving Diana's room. She put a finger to her lips and drew him down the passageway to a small parlor.

"You are in remarkably good spirits, Kit. I rather expected you to be downcast at the news."

"Being downcast accomplishes nothing, in my experience. I'm going after her, of course, but I need to speak with Diana. Unless you chance to know where Lucy is headed."

"Not precisely. She once mentioned that her employer's estate was in Dorset, if that is of any use. Do please take a chair, Kit, before you knock something over."

"Sorry. I can't stay still. Chafing to be off, actually. Why did you wish to speak with me?"

"To prevent you from speaking with Diana, and you needn't glower. I'm on your side, you know. Don't forget that I pursued your brother quite shamelessly, with no regard to the rules of proper conduct, and I mean to help you as best I can. That does not include placing Diana in a difficult situation, however. She is unable to bear the weight of any more troubles, even if they are not her own."

"How so?" He was genuinely puzzled. "Everything has worked out far better than we had any reason to expect. I'd have thought she would be happy."

"Men! Sometimes I despair of the lot of you. Never mind that she is but ten-and-nine, has endured a terrible ordeal, has been brought to live among strangers, and will wear that scar for the rest of her life. She will be happy one day, please God, but not anytime soon."

Kit rubbed his head. "Lucy told me something of the like. And you are both right, of course. But why cannot I ask her one perfectly simple question?"

"Where Lucy has gone to? I asked that question myself, and I assure you that if she would not tell me, she'll not tell you. Lucy left her a good-bye letter, and apparently it contained a plea to keep her destination strictly secret. Think on it, Kit. Ought we to ask Diana to choose between loyalty to her friend and the sense of obligation she doubtless feels to us?"

He had heard words much like those some weeks ago, but at the time they had come from his own mouth. He'd been advising Lucy not to put Diana in a position similar to the one he'd been about to create by demanding an answer she could not in good conscience provide. "No, Celia. I'll not ask it of her. Forget I ever thought of doing so. But dammit, what am I to do? Call at every house in Dorset in hopes of finding Lucy there?"

"If you must. But I expect you can catch her along the way." She went to the escritoire and drew out paper, pen, and ink. "William Reese has made the journey south a hundred times or more. He knows the best places to change horses, have a decent meal, and spend the night. On the occasions James and I have traveled with him, he invariably stopped at the same posthouses."

"You're a trump, Celia!" He paused to ruffle her curls on the way to the door. "Write them down while I pack. And instruct a footman to put out a ladder and unlock the attic, will you? I mean to rummage through a few trunks."

"Mercy me. Whatever for?"

"Oh, there are all sorts of things up there. My ancestors were hoarders of the first order. Never threw anything away. You should have a look sometime."

Lucy made it through her first day on the road without a tear, but it took every ounce of her failing strength to hold them back until William Reese escorted her to her room at the comfortable posthouse where she was to spend the night.

Then her tears fell in torrents.

But by morning, which dawned cold and clear, she was dry-eyed again and even more firmly resolved to continue on. There had been times, a great many of them during her sleepless night, when she was tempted to turn back and accept whatever Kit could offer her, for however long it lasted. She had even come to the point of being willing to accept the pain when he tired of her and wandered off to another adventure and another woman. Surely a brief, shooting-star love was better than no love at all.

But reason prevailed. She had maneuvered through a life mostly crammed with closed doors by being practical about the few opportunities that opened to her. Beyond doubt her only hope for a secure future lay with Jonathan Stiles.

He no more loved her than she loved him, to be sure, but their circumstances did not permit either of them to be overly particular. A cleric in hopes of securing a parish of his own required a wife, and a governess longing for a home and children required a husband.

Jonathan was kindly, unimaginative, and steadfastly devoted to his duties. He rather feared her, she'd often thought. She was too plainspoken and assertive. He invariably stammered in her presence and rarely looked her directly in the eyes. It must have required an act of courage for him to approach her with an offer of marriage.

In the year that had passed since then, he had not dared to

press her for an answer. Now and again, when they met after services or at a charity event, he referred obliquely to the pending matter of their betrothal. But she always suspected he meant only to remind her that he stood ready to honor the proposal he had made. He certainly showed no great enthusiasm, and he was clearly in no rush to meet her at the altar.

She had done him a disservice, she thought guiltily, by withholding a response. He might have cast about for a more suitable bride had he not felt obligated to her. But he would have her answer shortly, and she would do her very best to make him a good wife.

She was picturing herself taking the vows, wondering how many lies she would be telling when she did so and trying in vain to remember what her future groom looked like, when the carriage suddenly veered to the right and shuddered to a halt.

"Stand and deliver!"

Dear heavens. She leaned forward and looked out the window.

Astride a gargantuan white horse, a spectacular creature brandished a sword in one hand and a pistol in the other. Sprung from a century or two ago, he was clad in midnight-blue brocade, with deep flared cuffs on his sleeves and bucket-topped boots that reached to his knees. Lace billowed at his throat and wrists. Atop a flamboyant black periwig sat a tall-crowned hat festooned with ostrich feathers.

Oh, for pity's sake! Lucy flung open the carriage door, jumped to the ground, stalked directly up to the would-be highwayman, and planted her hands on her hips. "What in all creation do you think you are doing?"

"Why, I'm pillaging and plundering, of course." He boomed his lines as if playing a part in another of his overwrought melodramas. "Surrender your valuables, wench, and be quick about it."

"Don't be ridiculous! And put away that gun before you shoot somebody."

"You quite disarm me, m'dear." He slipped the pistol into his saddle pack. "It isn't loaded, by the way."

"I should think not. The sword, too."

With a dramatic sigh, he slid it into the scabbard at his waist and swung down from the saddle. "Madam, you leave a gentleman of the road no choice but to pluck your treasures with his bare hands."

"Someone has plucked your wits, sir. Of all the fits and starts you have taken, this is the most addlepated yet. Now you get right back on that horse, Kit Valliant, and take yourself away this very instant!"

He laughed. "Is this how you address the unfortunate young fellows in your charge, my terrifying little governess? No wonder they went after your hair with a pair of shears."

Her cheeks burned from that telling blow, but she quickly rallied. "This is *precisely* how I deal with feckless, refractory little boys. And wherever did you come by that foul wig? I just saw a moth fly out of it."

"Lucifer!" He ripped it off and flung it to the ground. "Devilish uncomfortable things, wigs. Good thing I wasn't prowling about when they were all the crack. I rather fancy the lace, though." He waved his belaced wrists in the air. "What do you think? Shall I take up the fashion?"

She was seized with a pernicious desire to laugh. "Kit, do go away and allow me to proceed with my journey. Everything that needed to be said between us has already been said."

"I quite agree." He moved toward her. "Let us proceed directly to the kissing."

She backed up hastily, raising both hands to hold him away. "Don't you dare."

"Come now, sweetheart. We rogues have a reputation to maintain. Just one little kiss, for the road?"

"I am a betrothed woman, sir. And an honorable one. I'll not betray—" She couldn't think of his name! "My betrothed man," she added belatedly.

"Ah. I'm glad you mentioned him. I'd nearly forgot my main purpose for accosting you this fine afternoon. Wanting to kiss you never fails to send my wits scattering to the winds." He made a flourishing gesture. "Oh, look! There they go again."

The laugh rose in her throat, nearly choking her as she fought to hold it in. He truly was the most *impossible* man. "P-purpose," she reminded him.

"Wait." He raised a forefinger to his temple. "Yes. It's coming back to me now. I galloped all the way here to save a hapless cleric from a lifetime of misery."

Suppressed laughter transformed itself to fury. "That is a reprehensible thing to say! I shall make him an excellent wife."

"I'm certain you mean to try. But you will be unhappy, and perforce he will be unhappy. Stands to reason."

"Why should I not be happy? How little you understand, sir. I have wished above all things to have a home of my own to live in, and children of my own to care for."

"And marrying your curate is a means to that end, I presume? One might as well put an advertisement in the newspapers. 'Ferocious young woman requires compliant male to sire children. Must be in possession of a house.' "

"Oh, do stop it!"

" 'He mustn't mind that she is in love with another man, or that her thoughts will be with said other man on her wedding night and every night thereafter.' "

That was so true that she could find no words to throw back at him. And because it was true, she accepted that she could not, *must* not, marry Joshua. Jeremy? The *curate*.

The ground under her feet dissolved. She felt suspended in air. Any moment now she would plunge into a deep dark pit.

Two strong arms wrapped themselves around her. "You have disappointed me, moonbeam. I had not thought it possible you would run away. What became of the daring girl who set aside all else to help a friend? What happened to my brave Lucy, who risked her life to save a smuggler on the sands of Morecambe Bay?"

She drew a steadying breath. "I don't know who she is, Kit.

Someone who is not me. And I don't know who I am either. I don't seem to know anything at all."

"You know that you love me," he said simply.

Her mouth opened to deny it, but this was the one lie that she would never tell. She rested her head against his shoulder and said nothing.

"The trouble is, has *always* been, that you have made up your mind I'll hurt you." His fingers slipped through her hair. "You are afraid to give yourself into my keeping, and take me into yours, because you assume I'll not hold to my vows. Is that a fair thing to say?"

She mumbled a *yes* into the fall of lace at his throat. She could imagine no greater pain than allowing herself to trust him, only to have him betray her.

"Some people believe," he said, "that if you save a life, you become responsible for that life. My life belongs to you, moonbeam. I trust you to care for it the way I mean to care for you. Will you put faith in me, beloved? You may as well, because you'll not rid yourself of me. I'll hound you from here to Dorset and from there to the ends of the earth. Spare us both the chase, I beg you, and say you'll marry me."

Lucy raised her head, looked into his glorious blue eyes, and felt all her doubts and fears go up in flames. Just like that, she thought deliriously. Off they went like ashes in the wind.

"Mmm," he said, bringing his lips to hers. "I heard that *yes* you didn't say."

A long time later, after a great many elephants had thundered by, she gulped a deep breath and produced a firm, heartfelt "Yes."

She saw him close his eyes then, and saw a tear escape one corner to streak down his cheek. He hadn't been so sure of her as he'd made himself out to be, she realized, deeply touched. She held his happiness in her hands as surely as he held hers.

Tears blinded her own eyes for a moment. But when she was able to see him clearly again, a smile that was purely Kit's—

cocksure and dancing with good humor—wreathed his handsome face.

"Brace yourself, Lucy," he said in a mournful tone. "We have one more difficult task ahead of us, and we must confront it together."

Alarm seized her for the barest moment before skittering away. She knew to trust him now. "And what is that, sir?"

He contrived to look serious. "There is another female nearly as besotted with me as you are, I'm afraid. Have you forgot her, moonbeam? Just how are we to break the news of our betrothal, our *real* betrothal, to Miss Fidgets?"

"Trust me, Kit," she said, standing on tiptoe for a kiss. "He won't mind in the least."

About the Author

Lynn Kerstan's Regency and historical romance novels have won a score of awards, including the Golden Quill, the Award of Excellence, and the coveted RITA. A former college teacher, professional bridge player, folksinger, and dedicated traveler, she lives in California, where she plots her stories while walking on the beach or riding the waves on her boogie board. Visit www.lynnkerstan.com for more about the author, her books, and the times and places in which her stories are set.

Lynn Kerstan

Love, intrigue, and
unforgettable adventure...

Dangerous Deceptions
0-451-21248-7

The Golden Leopard
0-451-41057-2

Heart of the Tiger
0-451-41085-8

The Silver Lion
0-451-41116-1